THE RETURN OF
NAGASH

The Empire is beset as never before. In the north, the hordes of Chaos ravage Kislev. The only thing keeping them at bay is the Auric Bastion, a mighty edifice of stone, magic and faith created by Balthasar Gelt, Supreme Patriarch of the Colleges of Magic. To the west, Bretonnia has fallen into civil war and anarchy. And at the heart of Emperor Karl Franz's realm lurks a great darkness. In the haunted land of Sylvania, the vampire Mannfred von Carstein is set upon a great and terrible purpose. For now, he is trapped, kept at bay by the Wall of Faith like the one to the north. But as von Carstein gathers allies, artefacts and prisoners of holy blood, those with the wit to perceive it can see the shadow of something monstrous gathering over Sylvania. Nagash, first of the necromancers, is returning...

WARHAMMER®
THE END TIMES

THE RETURN OF
NAGASH

JOSH REYNOLDS

BLACK LIBRARY

To Lindsey and Graeme for making this, among other things, readable.

A BLACK LIBRARY PUBLICATION

First published in 2014.
This edition published in 2015 by
Black Library,
Games Workshop Ltd.,
Willow Road,
Nottingham, NG7 2WS, UK.

10 9 8 7 6 5 4 3 2

Cover by Paul Dainton.
Internal illustrations by Paul Dainton and Nuala Kinrade
Map artwork by John Michelbach.

A CIP record for this book is available from the British Library.

UK ISBN: 978 1 84970 938 5
US ISBN: 978 1 84970 943 9

See Black Library on the internet at
blacklibrary.com

Find out more about Games Workshop
and the world of Warhammer at
games-workshop.com

Printed and bound by CPI Group (UK) Ltd, Croydon, CR0 4YY

The world is dying, but it has been so since
the coming of the Chaos Gods.

For years beyond reckoning, the Ruinous Powers have
coveted the mortal realm. They have made many attempts to
seize it, their anointed champions leading vast hordes into
the lands of men, elves and dwarfs. Each time, they have
been defeated.

Until now.

In the north, Archaon, a former templar of the warrior-god
Sigmar, has been crowned the Everchosen of Chaos.

He stands poised to march south and bring ruin to the
lands he once fought to protect. Behind him amass all the
forces of the Dark Gods, mortal and daemonic, and they
will bring with them a storm such as has never been seen.
Already, the lands of men are falling into ruin. Archaon's
vanguard run riot across Kislev, the once-proud country
of Bretonnia has fallen into anarchy and the southern lands
have been consumed by a tide of verminous ratmen.

The men of the Empire, the elves of Ulthuan and the dwarfs
of the Worlds Edge Mountains fortify their cities and prepare for the inevitable onslaught. They will fight bravely and
to the last. But in their hearts, all know that their efforts
will be futile. The victory of Chaos is inevitable.

These are the End Times.

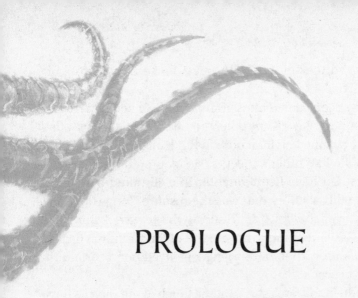

PROLOGUE

Late summer 2522

The world was dead.

It simply didn't know it yet.

That was the bare truth of it, and it pleased the one who considered it to no little end. Oh, there were things to be done yet, debts to be paid and webs to be spun or broken, but the weight of the inevitable had settled across the way and weft of the world. Time was running out, and the beast was all but bled white.

Long fingers – scholar's fingers – stroked the murky surface of the blood that filled the ancient bronze bowl before him. The bowl was covered in the harsh, jagged script of a long-dead empire. It had once belonged to another scholar, who had come from a still-older empire even than the one that had produced the bowl. That scholar was dust now, like both of the empires in question: all three erased from the tapestry of history by hubris and treachery in equal measure. There were lessons there, for the man who had the wit to attend them, a voice that may or may not have been his own murmured in the back of his head.

He shrugged the voice off, the way a horse might shrug off a stinging fly.

The scryer considered himself susceptible to neither arrogance nor foolishness. Were it any other moment, he might have admitted that it was the height of both to think oneself beyond either. As it was, he had other concerns. He ignored the soft susurrus of what might have been laughter that slithered beneath his thoughts with a surety that was the result of long experience, and bent over the bowl, murmuring the required words with the necessary intonation. The empire of Strigos might be dead, and Mourkain with it, but its language lived on in certain rituals and sorcerous rites.

The blood in the bowl stirred at the touch of the scryer's fingertips, its surface undulating like the back of a cat seeking affection. Its opacity faded, and an image began to form, as though it were a shadow flickering across a stretched canvas. The images were of every time and no time, of things that had been, things that would be and of things that never were. The scryer desired to know of the calamitous events that afflicted the world, events whose reverberations were felt even in his tiny corner of the world. The world was dead, but with a voyeur's eagerness, he wanted to see the killing blows.

The first image to be drawn from the depths of the bowl was of a twin-tailed comet, which blazed across the crawling canopy of the heavens, fracturing the weak barrier between the world of man and that which waited outside as it streaked along its pre-destined course. In its wake – madness.

A storm of Chaos swept across the world, spreading outwards from the poles to roll across the lands of men and other than men one by one. Daemons were born and died in moments, or tore their way through the membrane of the world to sow terror for days or weeks on end. There was no rhyme or reason to any of what followed; it was merely the crazed whims of the Dark Gods at work. The scryer watched it all with a cool, calculating eye, like a gamesman sizing up the opening move of an oft-played opponent.

In the cold, dark reaches of Naggaroth, the sound of drums set the ice shelves to shivering and caused avalanches in the lower valleys. A horde of northmen poured across the Ironfrost Glacier, and in their vanguard swooped down the elegant, crimson shape of Khorne's best beloved. They smashed aside the great watch-towers, and the mighty hosts sent against them only stoked the fires of their fury. As Valkia exhorted her followers towards the obsidian walls of Naggarond itself, the scryer stirred the bowl's contents, eager to see more.

The image shifted, and then expanded into great walls of pale stone, which thrust up from the green nest of the jungles of distant Lustria; here, scaly shapes warred with nightmares made flesh in the heart of the ruins of Xahutec. Elsewhere, the jungle was afire, and once great temple cities had been cast into ruin, as a continent heaved and burned.

Lustria's death pyre flared up so brightly that the scryer winced and looked away. When he looked back at the bowl, the scene had changed. Red lightning lit the sky and strange mists spread down the slopes of the Annulii Mountains, bringing with them the raw power of Chaos unfettered. The land and its inhabitants became warped into new and terrible forms, all save the elves. The walls of reality wore thin and tore, and daemons flooded into Ulthuan. The forests of Chrace burned as the rivers of Cothique and Ellyrion became thick with virulent noxiousness, while in the heartland of the elven realms, the great cities of Tor Dynal and Elisia fell to the assaults of Chaos, rampaging daemons overwhelming their embattled defenders. As daemons scrambled in a capering, cackling riot towards a battle line of Sapherian Sword Masters, and elven magi drew upon every iota of power at their command to throw back their enemy, the image shattered like a reflection in a droplet of water, reforming into another scene of warfare.

Across the glades and valleys of Bretonnia, disgraced knights and covetous nobles flocked to the serpent banners of Mallobaude, illegitimate son of Louen Leoncouer, and would-be king of that divided land. The scryer watched as the nation over the mountains descended into fiery civil war, and his eyes widened in surprise as he saw Mallobaude throw down his father at Quenelles with the aid of a skeletal figure clad in robes of crimson and black. A skull blazing with malignant power, with teeth as black as the night sky, tipped back and uttered a cackle of victory as Leoncouer was smashed to the ground, seemingly dead at his offspring's hand. Arkhan the Black was in Bretonnia, and that fact alone tempted the scryer to try to see more. But the image was already dissolving and he let the temptation pass. There would be time later for such investigations.

A new picture rippled into view. In the deep, ice-cut valleys and towering heights of the mountain range known as the Vaults, the dwarf hold known to the scryer as Copper Mountain tottered beneath the assault of a tempest of blood-starved daemons. The legion that assailed the stunted inhabitants of the hold was so vast that the hold's defences were all but useless. But as the dwarfs prepared to sell their lives in the name of defiance, if not victory, the daemonic storm dissipated as suddenly as it had gathered, leaving only blue skies and a battered shieldwall of astonished dwarfs in its wake. As the dwarfs began to collect their dead, the scene dissolved and a new one took its place at the scryer's barest gesture.

The scryer chuckled mirthlessly as the next image wavered into being. Another mountain hold, but not one that belonged to the dwarfs. Not any more, at least. In the deep halls and opulently decorated black chambers of the Silver Pinnacle, the self-proclaimed queen of the world, Neferata, mother and mistress of the Lahmian bloodline, led her warriors, both dead and undead, in defence of her citadel. A horde of daemons, backed by hell-forged artillery, attacked from above and below, laying siege to the main gates of Neferata's chosen eyrie, as well as surging up from its lower depths. But these daemons vanished as abruptly as those who had attacked Copper Mountain. The scryer frowned in annoyance. It would have been far better for his own designs for the mistress of the Silver Pinnacle to have fallen to the daemon-storm. He gestured again, almost petulantly.

What came next returned the smile to his face. The great city on the mount, Middenheim, reeled beneath the tender ministrations of the Maggot King and the Festival of Disease. Pox-scarred victims staggered through the streets, begging for mercy from Shallya and Ulric. The open sores that afflicted them wept a noisome pus and their bodies were thrown on the pyres that marked every square, still crying out uselessly to the gods. How Jerek would have cringed to see that, the scryer thought, as he laughed softly. The image wavered and changed.

His laughter continued as beneath the shadowed branches in the depths of Athel Loren, the great edifices known as the Vaults of Winter shattered, and a horde of cackling, daemonic filth was vomited forth into the sacred glades of Summerstrand. Ancient trees, including the Oak of Ages, cracked and split, expelling floods of maggots and flies, and the forest floor became coated in the stuff of decay. Desolate glades became rallying points for monstrous herds of beastmen, who poured into the depths of the forest, braying and squealing. Amused, the scryer waved a hand, dispelling the image.

His amusement faded as the blood rippled, revealing a scarred face, topped by a massive red crest of grease-stiffened hair. An axe flashed and a beastman reeled back, goatish features twisted in fear and agony. It fell, and the axe followed it, separating its malformed head from its thick neck. The wielder of the axe, a dwarf, kicked the head aside as he trudged on through the fire-blackened streets of a northern city, fallen to madness and ruin. The dwarf, one-eyed and mad, was familiar to the scryer from a past encounter of dubious memory. Snow swirled about the dwarf as he battled through the city, his rune axe encrusted with gore drawn from the bodies of beastmen, trolls, northern marauders and renegades, all of whom lay in heaps and piles in his wake. The scryer saw no sign of the doom-seeker's human companion, and wondered idly if the man had died. The thought pleased him to no end.

The image billowed and spread as the dwarf trudged on, and the scryer was rewarded by the sight of the River Aver becoming as blood, a scarlet host of howling daemons bursting from its tainted waters en masse to sweep across Averland, burning and butchering every living thing in their path. As with the other daemonic incursions, the bloody host evaporated moments before they reached the walls of Averheim.

Averheim grew faint and bled into the dark bowers of the Drakwald. Trees were uprooted and hurled aside as a veritable fang of stone, taller than the tallest structure ever conceived by man, tore through the corrupted soil and speared towards the sky. The crown of the newborn monolith was wreathed in eldritch lightning. Similar malformed extrusions rose above the tree line of Arden Forest and the glacial fields of far Naggaroth, as well as in the Great Forest and the embattled glades of Athel Loren. Some wept flame, others sweated foulness, but all pulsed with a darkling energy. Beastmen gathered about them to conduct raucous rites, the worst of which caused even a man as hardened to cruelty as the scryer to grimace in repulsion. With a hiss of disgust, he dashed his fingers into the blood, banishing the activities of the beasts from sight and eliciting another image.

Nuln erupted into violence as crowds of baying fanatics and self-flagellating doomsayers filled the streets. The mansions of the wealthy were ransacked and unlucky nobles were hung or torn apart by the screaming crowd. Even the Countess von Liebwitz was dragged from her boudoir, amidst a storm of accusations ranging from adultery to sorcery. The scryer stabbed the swirling blood, dissolving the Countess's screeching visage and replacing it with the snowy hinterlands of Kislev.

As with Naggaroth, Kislev shuddered beneath the tread of masses of northmen, all moving south. All lands west of Bolgasgrad were awash with daemons and barbarians. Along the River Lynik, the Ice Queen led her remaining warriors in a series of running battles with the invaders. As the Tsarina led her Ungol horsemen against the howling hordes, the scryer stirred the bowl, trying to ignore the murmur of the voice that pressed insistently against his awareness, demanding to be heard.

He was in Bretonnia again, as a figure clad in green armour hurled aside his helm, revealing the features of Gilles Le Breton, lost founder and king of that realm, now found and ready to reclaim his throne. The scryer laughed and wondered what Mallobaude and Arkhan would have to say about that.

He focused on the rippling blood, banishing images of the reborn king, and saw the armies of Ostermark, Talabecland and Hochland clash with a ragged host marching under the banner of the sorcerous monstrosity known as Vilitch the Curseling in the fields and siege ditches before the battlements of Castle von Rauken. Aldebrand Ludenhof, Elector Count of Hochland, mounted the ramparts of the besieged castle and put a long rifle bullet into one of the Curseling's skulls, forcing the creature to retreat and scattering its host.

The scryer waved a hand. The images were coming faster now, some of them appearing and vanishing before he could properly observe them. His skull ached with the frequency and intensity of the scenes playing out in the bowl.

The hordes of the Northern Wastes did not merely assault the south and west. They went east as well, hurling themselves at the Great Bastion in their thousands. Khazags, Kul and Kurgan mustered daemon engines, and dozens of warlords and chieftains led their warriors against the defences of the Bastion. The smoke of the resulting destruction could be seen as far south as the Border Princes. The image wavered and faded before the scryer could see whether the Bastion had fallen.

In the desiccated deserts of the south, the unbound dead of a long-gone empire readied themselves for invasion, and the chariots of the tomb kings rolled westward, towards the caliphates of Araby. The dwarfs sealed their holds or mobilised for war as the foundations of the world shuddered and long-dormant volcanoes rumbled, belching smoke. In the Badlands, the numberless hordes of greenskins gathered and surged towards the civilised lands as one, as if in response to some unspoken signal. The ogre tribes too were on the march, bulbous bellies rumbling. In the roots of the world, the clans of the skaven scurried upwards, attacking the unprepared nations of Estalia and Tilea in such unprecedented numbers that even the scryer was slightly dumbfounded. City after city fell, and the tattered clan banners of the Under-Empire rose over the lands that had once belonged to men.

Perturbed, he swept out a hand, stirring the blood without touching it. A familiar sight, this one, and his lips peeled back from his teeth in a triumphant snarl. An old man, clad in the robes and armour of the Grand Theogonist of the Empire, wrestled against a dark shape, cloaked in shadow. The shape twisted, becoming first a man – aquiline, noble and yet feral, with eyes like crimson pits and a mouthful of fangs – then swelling to a giant, clad in armour such as no man had ever worn, wreathed in eerie green flame. The giant's features were fleshless, and its head was a skull bound in black iron and bronze. Skeletal jaws opened wide, bone stretching and billowing impossibly as the giant thrust the struggling shape of the old man between its jaws and swallowed him whole.

The scryer dismissed the image quickly, before the eyes of that giant could turn towards him. Something chuckled and spoke, just out of earshot. He ignored it, and concentrated on the next image as it began to form in the swirling blood. The bowl began to shake slightly, as if it were being rocked by the weight of the pictures rising up out of it.

The scryer hissed in recognition as the world's northern pole, where the membrane between worlds was nonexistent, came into view. Daemons beyond measure were assembled there, divided into four mighty hosts of damnation such as had once sought to envelop the world in aeons past. The scryer cursed loudly and virulently, his composure momentarily shaken. What he was seeing was the merest spear-point of an invasion force, a host of such magnitude that only the raw unreality of the Chaos Wastes could contain the sheer number of daemons gathered. From amid the numberless hordes came four exalted daemons – those creatures highest in the esteem of the Dark Gods.

One by one, each of the four sank down to one knee before a figure that was tiny by comparison. The latter was clad in heavy armour, and cloaked in thick furs, its features hidden beneath a horned helm. The helm turned, and eyes that blazed with a radiance at once malignant and divine met those of the scryer, across the vast stretch of time and space that separated them. The blood in the bowl began to bubble and smoke. A will more than equal to his own beat down suddenly against the scryer like a hammer-blow. A voice like seven thunders reverberated through his skull and said, '*Rejoice, for the hour of my glory fast approaches.*'

The bowl shattered. What was left of the blood slopped across the scryer's hands and splattered on the stone floor. Snuffling, grey-skinned, hairless shapes, wearing the filthy remnants of what had once been fine clothing, crawled across the floor, splotched tongues licking at the spilled blood with eager whimpers. The degenerate creatures were all that remained of the once proud family that had, in better times, called Castle Sternieste its home. Now, they wore the miscellany of ancestral finery, smeared with grime and foulness, as they capered and gibbered in debased mockeries of courtly dances for their master's amusement, or raided the tombs of their ancestors for sustenance.

Mannfred von Carstein sucked the blood from his fingers as

he considered the remains of the bowl speculatively. He glanced up at the body whose blood he'd carefully drained to fill it; the corpse was clad in the robes of an acolyte of one of the great Colleges of Magic – the Light College, Mannfred knew, by their colour. He'd opened the boy's throat with his own fingers and strung him up by his feet from one of the ancient timbers above, so that the dregs of his life would drain into the bowl. There were few ingredients more effective for such sorceries than the blood of a magic user. The ghouls looked up at him expectantly, whining with eagerness. He gestured and, as one, they gave a ribald howl and began leaping and tearing at the body, like hounds at the feet of a man on the gallows. With a sniff, Mannfred pulled his cloak tight about himself and left the chamber, and its contents, to his ghoulish courtiers.

Well, wasn't that informative? The world writhes, caught in a storm partially of your making, and where are you? The voice he'd heard as he watched the images in the bowl, the voice he'd heard for more centuries than he cared to contemplate, spoke with mild disdain. Mannfred shook his head, trying to ignore it. A shadow passed across his vision, and something that might have been a face, or perhaps a skull, swam to the surface of his mind and then vanished before he could focus on it. *Where are you, then? You should be out there, taking advantage of the situation. But you can't, can you?*

'Shut up,' Mannfred growled.

Konrad talked to himself as well. As his habits went, that was probably the least objectionable, but still… We know how he ended up, don't we?

Mannfred didn't reply this time. The voice was right, of course. It was always right, curse it. Laughter echoed through his head and he bit back a snarl. He wasn't going mad. He knew this, because madness was for the foolish or the weak of mind, and he was anything but either. After all, could a madman have accomplished what he had, and in so short a time?

For centuries he had yearned to free Sylvania, which was his by both right of blood and conquest, from the yoke of the Empire. And, after the work of many lifetimes, he had accomplished just that. The air now reeked of dark enchantments and an unholy miasma had settled over everything within the province's borders. He strode out onto the parapet and looked out towards the border with Stirland, where a massive escarpment of bone now towered over Sylvania's boundaries. The wall encircled his domain, making it over into a sprawling fortress-state. The wall that would protect his land from the doom that waited to envelop the world was the result of generations of preparation. It had required the blood of nine very special individuals – individuals who even now enjoyed his hospitality – to create, and getting them all in one place had been an undertaking of decades. He'd done it, however, and once he'd had them, Sylvania was his and his alone.

So speaks the tiger in his cage, the voice whispered, mockingly. Again, it was correct. His wall, mighty as it was, was not the only one ringing his fiefdom. 'Gelt,' he muttered. The name of the Arch-Alchemist and current Supreme Patriarch of the Colleges of Magic had become one of Mannfred's favoured curses in the months since the caging of Sylvania. While Mannfred had battled an invasion force led by Volkmar the Grim, the Grand Theogonist, and enacted his own stratagem, Gelt had been working furiously to enact a ritual the equal of Mannfred's own. Or so Mannfred's spies had assured him.

Mannfred frowned. Even from here, he could feel the spiritual weight of the holy objects that caged his land. In the months preceding his notice of secession from the broken corpse that was Karl Franz's empire, he'd sent the teeming ghoul-packs that congregated about Castle Sternieste to strip every Sylvanian temple, shrine and burial ground of what holy symbols yet remained in the province. He'd ordered the symbols buried deep in unhallowed graves and cursed ground, so that their pestiferous sanctity would not trouble his newborn paradise.

Or such had been his intent. Instead, Gelt had somehow managed to turn those buried symbols into a wall of pure faith. Any undead, be they vampire, ghost or lowly zombie, that tried to cross it was instantly obliterated, as several of his vampire servants had discovered to their cost. Mannfred was forced to admit that the resulting explosions had been quite impressive. He couldn't help but admire the raw power of Gelt's wall. It was a devious thing, too, and only worked in one direction. The undead could enter Sylvania, but they could not leave. It was the perfect trap. Mannfred fully intended to congratulate Gelt on his cunning, just before he killed him.

In the months since he'd destroyed Volkmar's army, Mannfred had pored over every book, tome, grimoire and papyrus scroll in his possession, seeking some way of countering Gelt's working. Nothing he'd tried had worked. The wall of faith was somehow more subtle and far stronger than he'd expected a human mind to conceive of, and his continued failure gnawed at him. He had wanted to isolate Sylvania, true – but on his own terms. To be penned like a wild beast was an affront that could not be borne.

But Gelt's sorcerous cage wasn't the only problem. Dark portals had opened in certain, long-hidden places within Sylvania, vomiting forth daemons by the score, and the distraction of putting paid to these incursions had eaten into his studies. After the last such invasion, Mannfred had resolved to find out what was going on in the rest of the world. The young acolyte of the Light College whom he'd used to fill his scrying bowl had been taken prisoner, along with a dozen others, including militiamen, knights and a few wayward priests, during Volkmar's attempt to purge Sylvania.

Finding out that Sylvania wasn't the only place afflicted by sudden daemonic sorties hadn't quelled his growing misgivings. In fact, it had only heightened the pressure he felt to shatter Gelt's wall and free Sylvania. The world was tottering on the lip of the grave and, amusing as it was to watch, Mannfred didn't intend to go over with it. There were still things that needed doing. There were tools that he still required, and he had to be able to cross his own borders to get them.

Tools for what, boy? the voice asked. No, not 'the voice'. It was pointless to deny it. It was Vlad's voice. Mannfred leaned over the parapet, bracing himself on the stone, his eyes closed. Even now, even centuries after the fact, the shadow of the great and terrible Vlad von Carstein hung over Mannfred and all of his works. Vlad's name was still whispered in the dark places and burying grounds, by the living and the dead alike. He had etched his name into the flesh of the world, and the scar remained livid even after all this time. It galled Mannfred to no end, and even the joy he'd once taken from his part in his primogenitor's downfall had faded, lost to the gnawing anger he felt still.

He'd hated Vlad, and loved him; respected him and been contemptuous of him. And he'd tried to save him, though he'd engineered his obliteration. Now, for his sins, he was haunted by Vlad's voice. It had started the moment he had begun his great work, as if Vlad were watching over his shoulder, and only grown stronger in the months that followed. He'd been able to ignore it at first, to dismiss the shadows that crept at the corner of his eye and the constant murmur of a voice just out of earshot. But now, when he least needed the distraction, there it was. There *he* was.

Do you still think that the design of the web you weave is yours, my son? Vlad hissed. Mannfred could see his sire's face on the periphery of his vision, so much like his own. *Can you feel it, boy? The weight of destiny sits on you – but not yours.* As if to lend weight to the thought, Mannfred caught sight of his shadow; only it wasn't his – it was something larger, and a thousand times more terrible than any vampire, lord of Sylvania or otherwise. Something that flickered with witch-fire and seemed to stretch out a long arm towards him, seeking to devour him. *You speak of tools, but what are you, eh?* Vlad purred. *Who is that who rides you through the gates of the world?*

'Quiet,' Mannfred snarled. The stone of the parapet crumbled in his grip. 'Go back to whatever privy hole your remains were thrown in, old man.' Without waiting for the inevitable reply, Mannfred drew his cloak about him and turned to go, not quite fleeing the voices and shadows that taunted him, but moving swiftly all the same.

He made his way through the half-ruined corridors to the great open chamber that crouched at the top of the southernmost tower of the castle. Once, it had been a meeting room for the Order of Drakenhof, a brotherhood of Templars devoted to eradicating the evil that they believed had corrupted Sylvania. Vlad had taken great pleasure in hunting them over the course of long centuries, Mannfred recalled. Every few hundred years, the knights of the order stirred in their graves, reforming and returning to their old haunts. The definition of insanity, Mannfred had heard, was doing the same thing over and over again and expecting a different result. If that was the case, then the Drakenhof Templars had been quite mad.

While Vlad had been content to play with them, as a cat plays with mice, Mannfred had little patience for such drawn-out displays of cruelty. They served no purpose, and to have such a thorn work its way into his side every few decades was an annoyance he felt no need to suffer through. When he had returned to Sylvania in the wake of Konrad's disastrous reign, he had immediately sought out every hold, fortress and komturei of the order and wiped them out root and branch. He had wiped out entire families, butchering the oldest members to the youngest, and leaving their bodies dangling from gibbets about the border of Sylvania as a warning to others. He had made a point – unlike Vlad or Konrad, Mannfred would not tolerate dissent. He would not tolerate enemies on his soil, worthy or otherwise. After the last knight had gasped out his final breath in a muddy ditch south of Kleiberstorf, he had reformed the order and turned it over to those of his creatures that found pleasure in parodying the traditions of knighthood.

Where once men had met to discuss the cleansing of Sylvania, Mannfred now stored the tools of his eventual, inevitable triumph, both living and otherwise. A ghoul clad in the remains of a militiaman's armour and livery crouched near the entrance to the chamber, leaning against a gisarme that had seen better years. The ghoul jerked in fright as Mannfred approached and yowled as he gestured sharply. It scrambled towards the heavy wooden door to open it for him. As it heaved upon it and turned, something hurtled out of the chamber beyond and caught the ghoul in the back of the head with a sickening crunch.

The ghoul flopped down, its rusty armour rattling as it hit the floor. The chunk of stone had been thrown hard enough to shatter the cannibal's skull and Mannfred flipped a bit of brain matter off the toe of his boot, his mouth twisting in a moue of annoyance. 'Are you finished?' he asked loudly. 'I can come back later, if you'd prefer.'

There was only silence from within the chamber. Mannfred sighed and stepped through the aperture. The room beyond was circular and large. It stank of rain, fire, blood and ghouls, as most of the castle did these days. But unlike the rest of the castle, the stones of this chamber thrummed with a heady power that was just this side of intoxicating for Mannfred. It was the one place that he was free from Vlad's voice and the lurking shadows that dogged his steps.

The room was lit by a profusion of candles, made from human fat and thrust into the nooks and crannies of the walls and floor. The latter was intercut by gilded grooves, which formed a rough outline of Sylvania, and a semicircle of heavy stone lecterns, each carved in the shape of a daemon's claw, lined the northernmost border of the province. Giant grimoires, bound in chains, sat on several of the lecterns, their pages rustling with a sound like the whispers of ghosts.

At the heart of the chamber sat a plinth, upon which was a cushion of human skin and hair. And resting on the cushion was the iron shape of the Crown of Sorcery. To Mannfred's eyes, it pulsed like a dark beacon, and he felt the old, familiar urge to place it on his head stir within the swamps of his soul like some great saurian. The crown radiated a malevolent pressure upon him, even now, and even as quiescent as it was. There was an air of contentment about it at the moment, and for that he was grateful. He knew well what monstrous intelligence waited within the crown's oddly angled shape, and he had no desire to pit his will against that hideous sentience. Not now, not until he'd taken the proper precautions. He'd worn it, briefly, on his return from Vargravia, and that had been enough to assure him that it was more dangerous than it looked.

He was so caught up in his study of the crown that he didn't turn as another rock surged towards his head. He caught the missile without looking and crushed it. He held up his hand and let the crumbled remains dribble through his fingers. 'Stop it,' he said. He looked at the walls behind the barrier of lecterns, where his nine prisoners hung shackled. Except that there were only seven of them. Two were missing.

Mannfred heard a scrape of metal on stone and whirled. A man clad in once-golden but now grime-caked and dented armour, decorated with proud reliefs of the war goddess Myrmidia, lunged for him, whirling a chain. Snarling Tilean oaths, the Templar of the Order of the Blazing Sun swung his makeshift weapon at Mannfred's face. The vampire jerked back instinctively, and was almost smashed from his feet by the descending weight of a heavy stone lectern in the shape of a daemon's claw, wielded by a brute clad in furs and a battered breastplate bearing a rampant wolf – the sigil of Ulric.

Mannfred backhanded the Ulrican off his feet with one hand and snagged the loop of the Myrmidian's chain with the other. He jerked the knight towards him and wrapped the links of the chain about his neck. He kicked the knight's legs out from under him and then planted his foot between the man's shoulder blades. Wrapping the chains about his wrist, he hauled upwards, strangling the man.

The Ulrican gave a bellicose roar and staggered towards him. Burly arms snapped tight around Mannfred's chest. He threw his head back and was rewarded by a crunch of bone, and a howl of pain. Mannfred drove his foot into the back of the knight's head, driving him face-first into the stone floor and rendering him unconscious. Then he turned to deal with the Ulrican.

The big man staggered forwards, blood streaming from his shattered nose. His eyes blazed with a berserk rage and he roared as he hurled himself at Mannfred. Mannfred caught him by the throat and hoisted him into the air. The man pounded uselessly on the vampire's arm, as Mannfred slowly choked him comatose. He let the limp body fall to the floor and turned to face the other seven inhabitants of the chamber. 'Well, that was fun. Anyone else?'

Seven pairs of eyes glared at him. If looks could kill, Mannfred knew that he would have been only so much ash on the wind. He met their gazes, until all but one had looked away. Satisfied, he smirked and looked up at the shattered dome of the tower above, where fire-blackened support timbers crossed over one another like the threads of a spider's web. He could see the dark sky and stars above, through the gaps in the roof. He whistled piercingly, and massive, hunched forms began to clamber into view from among the nest of wood and stone.

There were two of the beasts, and both were hideous amalgamations of ape, wolf and bat. Mannfred had heard it said that the vargheist was the true face of the vampire, shorn of all pretence of humanity. These two were collectively known as the Swartzhafen Devils, which was as good a name as such beasts deserved. One of the creatures clutched something red and wet in its talons and gnawed on it idly as it watched him. He had given the beasts orders not to interfere with any escape attempts on the part of the captives.

Mannfred claimed the body of the ghoul and dragged it into the room by an ankle. The vargheists were suddenly alert, their eyes glittering with hunger. He rolled the body into the centre of the outline of Sylvania and stepped back. The vargheists fell upon the dead cannibal with ravenous cries. The captives looked away in disgust or fear. Mannfred smiled and set about rebinding the two men. That they'd escaped at all was impressive, but it wasn't the first time they'd tried it, and it wouldn't be the last. He wanted them to try and fail, and try again, until their courage and will had been worn down to a despairing nub.

Then, and only then, would they be fit for his purpose.

His eyes flickered to the lone nonhuman among his captives. The elven princess did not meet his gaze, though he did not think it was out of fear, but rather disdain. A flicker of annoyance swept through him, but he restrained the urge to discipline her. Instead, he moved towards the prize of the lot, at least in his eyes.

'Bad dreams, old man?' Mannfred said, looking down at Volkmar, Grand Theogonist of the Empire. He sank down to his haunches beside the old man. 'You should thank me, you know. All of you,' he said, looking about the cell. 'The world as you knew it is giving way to something new. And something wholly unpleasant. Outside of Sylvania's borders, madness and entropy reign. Only here does order prevail. But don't worry, soon enough, with your help, I shall sweep the world clean, and all will be as it was. I shall make it a paradise.'

'A paradise,' Volkmar rasped. The old man met Mannfred's red gaze without hesitation. Battered and beaten as he was, he was not yet broken, Mannfred knew. 'Is that what you call it?' Volkmar shifted his weight, causing his manacles to rattle. The old man looked as if he wanted nothing more than to lunge barehanded at his captor. A wound on his head, a gift from one of the vargheists, was leaking blood and pus, and the old man's face was stained with both. Mannfred could smell the sickness creeping into the Grand Theogonist, weakening him even further, despite the holy power that was keeping him on his feet.

'I didn't say for whom it would be such, now, did I?' Mannfred said. He rose smoothly and pulled his cloak about him. He looked down at Volkmar with a cruel smile. 'Don't worry, old man... When I consummate my new world, neither you nor your friends will be here to see it.'

PART ONE

Alliance
Autumn 2522–Spring 2523

ONE

 Stirland-Sylvania border

The world was dying.

It had been dying for a very long time, according to some. But Erikan Crowfiend, in his long trek from the battlefield of Couronne, had come to the conclusion that it was finally on its last legs. There was smoke from a million funeral pyres on the wind, not just in Bretonnia but in the Empire as well, and the stink of poison and rot was laid over everything. In the villages and way-places, men and women whispered stories of two-headed calves that mewled like infants, of birds that sang strange dirges as they circled in the air, and of things creeping through the dark streets that had once kept to the forests and hills.

Beasts and greenskins ran riot, carving red trails through the outskirts of civilisation as nightmare shapes swam down from the idiot stars to raven and roar through the heart of man's world. Great cities reeled from these sudden, unpredictable assaults, and the great gates of Altdorf, Middenheim and Nuln were barred and bolstered, almost as if it were intended that they never be opened again.

JOSH REYNOLDS

Erikan had seen it all, albeit at a remove. He had been forced to fight more than once since crossing the Grey Mountains, and not just with beasts or orcs. Men as well, and worse than men. Then, Erikan wasn't exactly a man himself. He hadn't been for some time.

Erikan Crowfiend's heart had stopped beating almost a century ago to the day, and he had not once missed its rhythm. He moved only by night, for the sun blistered him worse than any fire. His breath reeked of the butcher's block and he could hear a woman's pulse from leagues away. He could shatter stone and bone as easily as a child might tear apart a dried leaf. He never grew tired, suffered from illness or felt fear. And under different circumstances, he would have been happy to indulge his baser instincts as the land drowned in madness. He was a monster after all, and it was a season for monsters, from what little he'd seen.

But he was no longer the captain of his own destiny, and hadn't been since the night a pale woman had taken him in her arms and made him something both greater and lesser than the necromancer's apprentice he had been. So he moved ever eastwards, following a darkling pull that urged him on, across beast-held mountains and over burning fields, and through forests where the trees whimpered like beaten dogs and clawed at him with twisted branches.

Above him, a swarm of bats crossed the surface of the moon, heading the gods alone knew where. Erikan suspected that they were going the same place he was. The thought provided no comfort. The call had come, and he, like the bats, had no choice but to obey.

'Erikan?' a wheezing, slurred voice asked, interrupting his reverie.

'Yes, Obald,' Erikan said, with a sigh.

'It could just be the alcohol talking, or it could be the constant seepage from these inexpertly, if affectionately, placed poultices of yours making me light-headed, but I do believe that I'm dying,' said Obald Bone, the Bone-Father of Brionne. He took another swig from the mostly empty bottle of wine he held in one bandaged claw. The necromancer was a wizened thing, all leather and bone, wrapped in mouldering furs and travel leathers that, to Erikan's knowledge, had never been washed. Obald lay in a travois made from the stretched hide and bones of dead men, constructed by equal parts sorcery and brute strength. He blinked and forced himself up onto one elbow. 'Where are we?'

'Just about to cross the border into Sylvania, Obald,' Erikan said. He was hauling the travois behind him on foot, its straps of dried flesh and stiffened gut lashed about his battered and grime-encrusted cuirass. Their horse had come down with a bad case of being digested by something large and hungry that even Erikan had been hard-pressed to see off. He didn't know what it was, but he hadn't felt like sticking around to find out. Monsters once confined to the edges of the map were now wandering freely, and setting upon any who came within reach, edible or not. 'And you're not dying.'

'I hate to be contrary, but I am a master of the necromantic arts, and I think I know a little something about death, imminent, personal or otherwise,' Obald slurred. His travois was cushioned with empty bottles, and he reeked of gangrene and alcohol. He'd been getting steadily worse since Erikan had extracted the arrow that had taken him in the belly in the last moments of the battle for Couronne, just before the Green Knight had struck off Mallobaude's head.

For the first few weeks, Obald had seemed fine, if in pain, but the wound wasn't healing, and they weren't the sort whom the priestesses of Shallya normally welcomed. Obald had survived worse in his time, but it was as if he, like the world, were winding down.

Obald sank back down onto the travois, dislodging several bottles. 'Did I ever tell you that I'm from Brionne, Erikan? Good pig country that.'

'Yes,' Erikan said.

'I was a pig farmer, like my father and his father before him. Pigs, Erikan – you can't go wrong with a pig farm.' Obald reached out and swatted weakly at the sword sheathed on Erikan's hip. 'Blasted Templar blade. Why do you still carry that thing?'

'I'm a Templar. Templars carry Templar blades, Obald,' Erikan said.

'You're not a Templar, you're my apprentice. It's not even a proper sword. Hasn't even got a curse on it,' Obald grumbled.

'But it's sharp and long, and good at cutting things,' Erikan replied. He hadn't been Obald's apprentice since he'd been given the blood-kiss and inducted into the aristocracy of the night. He smiled at the thought. In truth, there was very little aristocratic about hiding in unmarked graves and devouring unlucky peasants.

'Where's my barrow-blade? I want you to have my barrow-blade,' Obald said muzzily.

'Your barrow-blade is still in the body of that fellow whose horse we stole,' Erikan said. The flight from Couronne had been as bloody as the battle itself. When the Serpent had fallen, his forces, both the living and the dead, had collapsed in an utter rout. Obald had had an arrow in the belly by then, and Erikan had been forced to hack them a path to freedom as the dead crumbled around them.

'Ha! Yes,' Obald cackled wetly. 'The look on his poxy, inbred face was priceless – thought that armour would save him, didn't he? Oh no, my lad. A dead man's sword will cut anything, even fancy armour.' He rocked back and forth in the travois, until his laughter became strangled coughing.

'So you taught me,' Erikan said.

'I did, didn't I?' Obald hiccupped. 'You were my best student, Erikan. It's a shame that you had to go and get mauled by that von Carstein witch.'

'She's not a witch, Obald.'

'Trollop then,' Obald snapped. 'She's a tart, Erikan.' He belched. 'I could do with a tart about now. One of those fancy ones from Nuln.'

'Are we still talking about women?' Erikan asked.

'They put jam – real jam – right in the pastry. Not sawdust and beef dripping, like the ones in Altdorf,' Obald said, gesticulating for emphasis.

'Right, yes,' Erikan said. He shook his head. 'I'm sure we can find you a tart in Sylvania, Obald.'

'No no, just leave me here to die, Erikan. I'll be fine,' Obald said. 'For a man who wears as many bones as I do, I am oddly comfortable with notions of mortality.' He upended the bottle he held, splashing much of its contents on his face and ratty beard. 'Bones, bone, Bone-Father. I can't believe you let me call myself that. Bone-Father... What does that even mean? The other necromancers were probably laughing at me.'

He was silent for a moment, and Erikan half hoped he'd fallen asleep. Then, Obald grunted and said, 'We showed them what for though, didn't we, Erikan? Those blasted nobles and their treacherous Lady.' Obald and a handful of other necromancers had flocked to Mallobaude's serpent banner after the dukes of Carcassonne, Lyonesse and Artois had declared for King Louen's bastard offspring, and they'd raised legions of the dead to march beside the Serpent's army of disgraced knights. But Obald and his fellows had been a sideshow compared to the real power behind Mallobaude's illegitimate throne – the ancient liche known as Arkhan the Black.

Why Arkhan had chosen to aid Mallobaude, Erikan couldn't say. He had his reasons, just as Obald and Erikan did, the latter supposed. And with the liche on their side, Bretonnia was brought to its knees. At the Battle of Quenelles, Erikan had had the pleasure of seeing the Serpent cast his father's broken body into the mud. The southern provinces had fallen one by one after King Louen's death, until the Serpent had cast his gaze north, to Couronne.

It had all gone wrong then. Mallobaude had lost his head, Arkhan had vanished, and...

'We lost,' Erikan said.

Obald gave a raspy chuckle. 'We always lose, Erikan. That's the way of it. There are no winners, save for death and the Dark Gods. I taught you that too.'

Erikan hissed in annoyance. 'You taught me a lot, old man. And you'll live to teach me more, if you stop straining yourself.'

'No, I don't think so,' Obald coughed. 'You can smell it on me. I know you can, boy. I'm done for. A longbow is a great equaliser on the battlefield. I've only survived this long out of nastiness. But I'm tired now, and I'm all out of spite.' He coughed again, and Erikan caught the whiff of fresh blood. Obald doubled over in the travois, hacking and choking. Erikan stopped and tore himself loose from the travois. He sank down beside his old mentor and laid a hand on his quivering back.

Obald had always looked old, but now he looked weak and decrepit. Erikan knew that the old man was right. The arrow that had felled him had done too much damage to his insides. That he had survived the journey over the Grey Mountains and into the provinces of the Empire was due more to stubbornness than anything else. By the time they'd reached Stirland, he'd been unable to ride, and barely able to sit upright. He was dying, and there was nothing Erikan could do.

No, that wasn't true. There was one thing. He lifted his wrist to his lips. He opened his mouth, exposing long, curved fangs and readied himself to plunge them into his wrist.

He paused when he saw that Obald was watching him. Blood and spittle clung like pearlescent webs to the old man's beard. He smiled, revealing a mouthful of rotting teeth. Obald patted him on the cheek. 'No need to bloody yourself, Erikan. My old carcass wouldn't survive it, anyway.'

Erikan lowered his arm. Obald lay back on the travois. 'You were a good friend, Erikan. For a ravenous, untrustworthy nocturnal fiend, I mean,' the necromancer wheezed. 'But as the rain enters the soil, and the river enters the sea, so do all things come to their final end.'

'Strigany proverbs,' Erikan muttered. 'Now I know that you're dying.' He sat back on his heels and watched the last link to his mortal life struggle for breath. 'You don't have to, you know. You're just being stubborn and spiteful.'

'I've been stubborn and spiteful my whole sorry life, boy,' Obald croaked. 'I've fought and raged and run for more years than you. I saw Kemmler's rise and fall, I saw Mousillon in all of its pox-ridden glory and I visited the secret ruins of Morgheim, where the Strigoi dance and howl.' The old man's eyes went vacant. 'I fought and fought and fought, and now I think maybe I am done fighting.' His trembling, wrinkled fingers found Erikan's wrist. 'That's the smart choice, I think, given what's coming.' His glazed eyes sought out Erikan's face. 'Always get out before the rush, that's my advice.' His voice was barely a whisper. Erikan leaned close.

'I miss my pigs,' Obald said. Then, with a soft grunt, his face went slack, and whatever dark force had inhabited him fled into the crawling sky above. Erikan stared down at him. He'd been hoping that the old man would make it to Sylvania. After leaving Couronne, they'd learned that the other survivors were going there, drawn by some bleak impetus to travel across the mountains. There were stories of walls of bone and an independent state of the dead, ruled by the aristocracy of the night. They'd even heard a rumour that Arkhan's forces were heading that way.

It was the beginning of something, Erikan thought. Obald had mocked the idea, in between coughing fits, but Erikan could feel it in the black, sour hollow of his bones. There was smoke on the air and blood in the water, and the wind carried the promise of death. It was everything he'd dreamed of, since his parents had gone screaming to the flames, the taste of corpses still on their tongues. He'd seen a spark of it when Obald had rescued him then, flaying his captors with dark magics. In those black flames, which had stripped meat from bone as easily as a butcher's knife, Erikan had seen the ruination of all things. The end of all pain and hunger and strife.

And now, that dream was coming true: the world was dying, and Erikan Crowfiend intended to be in at the end. But, he'd been hoping that Obald would be by his side. Didn't the old man deserve that much, at least? Instead, he was just another corpse.

At least he was free, while Erikan was still a captive of the world.

Erikan carelessly pried the old man's fingers off his wrist and stood. He dropped his hand to the pommel of his blade and said, casually, 'He's dead.'

'I know,' a woman's voice replied. 'He should have died years ago. He would have, if you hadn't been wasting your time keeping his wrinkled old cadaver from getting the chop.'

'He raised me. He took me in, when anyone else would have burned me with the rest of my kin, for the crime of survival,' Erikan said. His hand tightened on the hilt of his blade and he drew it smoothly as he whirled to face the newcomer. 'He helped me become the man I am today.'

In the sickly light of the moon, her pale flesh seemed to glow with an eerie radiance. She wore baroque black armour edged in gold over red silk. The hue of the silk matched her fiery tresses, which had been piled atop her head in a style three centuries out of fashion. Eyes like agates met his own as she reached out and gently pushed aside his sword. 'I rather thought that I had some part in that as well, Erikan.'

He lowered his sword. 'Why are you here, Elize?'

'For the same reason as you, I imagine.'

Erikan stabbed his blade down into the loamy earth and set his palms on the crosspiece. 'Sylvania,' he said, simply.

Elize von Carstein inclined her head. A crimson tress slipped free of the mass atop her head and dangled in her face, until she blew it aside. He felt a rush of desire but forced it down. Those days were done and buried. 'I felt the summons.' She looked up at the moon. 'The black bell of Sternieste is tolling and the Templars of the Order of Drakenhof are called to war.'

Erikan looked down at the pommel of his blade, and the red bat, rampant, that was carved there. It was the symbol of the von Carsteins, and of the Drakenhof Templars. He covered it with his hand. 'And who are we going to war with?'

Elize smiled sadly and said, 'Everyone. Come, I have an extra horse.'

'Did you bring it for me?'

Elize didn't answer. Erikan followed her. He left Obald's body where it lay, to whatever fate awaited it. The old man's cankerous spirit was gone. His body was just so much cooling meat now, and Erikan had long since lost his taste for such rancid leavings.

'Are we all gathering, then?' Erikan asked, as he followed her through the trees, towards a quiet copse where two black horses waited, red-eyed and impatiently pawing at the earth. Deathless, breathless and remorseless, the horses from the stables of Castle Drakenhof were unmatched by any steed in the known world, save possibly for the stallions of far Ulthuan. He took the bridle of the one she indicated and stroked it, murmuring wordlessly. He'd always had a way with beasts, even after he'd been reborn. He'd kept company with the great shaggy wolves that Obald had pulled from their forest graves, leading them on moonlit hunts. The day Obald had taught him how to call up the beasts himself was the closest he had ever come to true happiness, he thought.

'All who still persist, and keep to their oath,' Elize said. 'I arrived with several of the others. We decided to journey together.'

'Why?' Erikan asked.

'Why wouldn't we?' Elize asked, after a moment, as she climbed into her saddle. 'Is it not meet that the inner circle do so? I saw your trail, and decided to see if you were interested in joining us. You are one of us, after all.'

'I don't recall you asking me whether I wished to be,' he said, softly. Elize kicked her horse into motion and galloped away.

Erikan hesitated, and then climbed up into his own saddle and set off after her. As he rode, he couldn't help but muse that it had always been thus. Elize called and he came. He watched her ride, her slim form bent low over her mount's neck, her armour glinting dully in the moonlight. She was beautiful and terrible and inexorable, like death given a woman's shape. There were worse ways to spend eternity, he supposed.

She led him into the high barrows and scrub trees that populated the hills and valleys west of the border with Stirland. Ruins of all sorts dotted the area, the legacy of centuries of warfare. Shattered windmills and slumping manses towered over the gutted remains of border forts and isolated farmsteads. Some were more recent than others, but all had suffered the same fate. This was the no-man's-land between the provinces of the living and the dead, and nothing of the former survived here for long.

As they left the trees and the fog that had clung to them, he hauled back on the reins of his horse, startled by the sight of the distant edifice of bone, which rose high up into the sky, towering over the area. It was far larger than the rumours he'd heard had intimated. It was less fortress rampart than newborn mountain range. Only the largest of giants would have had a chance of clambering over it. 'Nagash's *teeth,*' he hissed. 'I'd heard he'd done it, but I never expected it to be true.' The sense of finality he'd had before, of endings and final days, came back stronger than ever. Sylvania had always seemed unchanging. A gangrenous wound that never healed, but never grew any worse. But now, now it was finally ready to kill. He wanted to laugh and howl at the same time, but he restrained himself.

'Yes,' Elize said, over her shoulder. 'Mannfred has seceded from the Empire. Our time for hiding in the shadows is done.' The way she said it made him wonder if she were entirely happy about it. Most of their kind were conservative by nature. Immortality brought with it a fear of change, and a need to force the world to remain in place. Erikan had never felt that way. When you were born in squalor and raised amid corpses, a bit of change was not unwelcome.

Erikan urged his horse on. 'No wonder the bells have been sounded. If he's done all of this, he's going to need as many of us as he can get.' The thought wasn't a comforting one. Vampires could, by and large, get along, if there was a reason. But the inevitable infighting and challenges for status that would result were going to be tedious, if not downright lethal.

Elize didn't reply. They rode on through the night, galloping hard, the endurance of their steeds never faltering. More than once, Erikan saw distant campfires and smelt the blood of men. The armies of the Empire were on the move, but he could not tell in which direction they were going. Were they laying siege to Sylvania? Or were the rumours of another invasion from the north true? Was that why Mannfred had chosen now of all times to make such a bold statement of intent?

All of these thoughts rattled in his head as Elize led him towards one of the ruins close to the bone bastion. It was far from any of the campfires that dotted the darkness and had been a watch tower once, he thought. Now it was just crumbled stone, blackened by fire and covered in weeds and moss. He saw that three men waited inside, as he climbed down from his horse and led it to join the others where they were tied to a gibbet. Elize led Erikan into the ruin, and he nodded politely to the others as he ducked through the shattered archway. There was no light, save that of the moon, for they needed none.

'What is *he* doing here?' one of the men growled, one hand on the hilt of the heavy sword belted to his waist. Erikan kept his own hands well away from his blade.

'The same as you, Anark,' Erikan said, as Elize went to the other vampire's side, and put her hand over his, as if to keep him from drawing his blade. Anark von Carstein was a big man, bigger than Erikan, built for war and clad in dark armour composed of serrated plates and swooping, sharp curves. The armour had seen its share of battle, to judge by the dents and scratches that marked it. Anark had been fighting in the Border Princes, the last Erikan had heard, leading an army of the dead on behalf of one petty warlord or another.

Elize leaned into Anark and whispered into his ear. He calmed visibly. She had always had a way with the other vampire, Erikan recalled. Then, much like Erikan himself, Anark was a protégé of the Doyenne of the Red Abbey, and had even been allowed to take the name of von Carstein, something Erikan would likely never achieve. Nor, in truth, did he wish to. He had his own name, and he was content with it. That, he thought, was why she had cooled to him, in the end. She had offered him her name, and he had refused. And so she had found another blood-son, lover and champion. And Erikan had left.

He looked away from them, and met the red gaze of the other von Carstein present. 'Markos,' Erikan said, nodding. Markos was hawk-faced and his hair had been greased back, making him resemble nothing so much as a stoat. Where Anark was a simple enough brute, Markos was more cunning. He had a gift for sorcery that few could match, and a tongue like an adder's bite.

'Crowfiend, I never thought to see you again,' Markos said. 'You know Count Nyktolos, I trust?' He gestured to the other vampire, who, like Anark and Markos, was clad in a heavy suit of armour. Nyktolos wore a monocle, after the fashion of the Altdorf aristocracy, and his grin stretched from ear to ear, in an unpleasant fashion. Unlike Anark and Markos, his flesh was the colour of a bruised plum, flush with a recent feeding, or perhaps simply mottled by grave-rot. It happened to some of them, if the blood-kiss wasn't delivered properly.

'Count,' Erikan said, bowing shallowly. He'd heard of the other vampire. He'd been a count of Vargravia once, before Konrad had stormed through, in the bad old days. Nyktolos smiled, revealing a mouthful of needle fangs, more than any self-respecting vampire needed, in Erikan's opinion. If he was Konrad's get, that and his odd hue were probably the least of his problems.

'He's polite. I like him already,' Nyktolos croaked.

'Don't get too attached,' Anark said. 'He won't be staying long. Erikan doesn't have the stomach for war. A real war, I mean. Not one of those little skirmishes they have west of the Grey Mountains.'

Erikan met Anark's flat, red gaze calmly. The other vampire was trying to bait him, as he always did. Just why Anark hated him so much, Erikan couldn't really fathom. He was no threat to Anark. He tried to meet Elize's eyes, but her attentions remained on her paramour. No, he thought, no matter how much he might wish otherwise, he posed no danger to Anark, in any regard. 'I hope you weren't waiting for me,' he said to Markos, ignoring Anark.

'No, we were waiting for– Ah! Speak of the devil, and he shall appear,' Markos said, looking up. The air was filled with the rush of great wings, and a noisome odour flooded the ruin as something heavy struck its top. Rocks tumbled down, dislodged by the new arrival as he crawled down to join them, clinging to the ancient stones like a lizard. 'You're late, Alberacht,' Markos called out.

The hairy body of the newcomer remained splayed across the stones above them for a moment, and then dropped down. Erikan stepped back as Alberacht Nictus rose to his full height. The creature, known in some quarters as the Reaper of Drakenhof, extended a hooked claw and caught Erikan gently by the back of his head. He didn't resist as the monstrous vampire pulled him close. 'Hello, boy,' Alberacht rumbled. His face was human enough, if horribly stretched over a bumpy, malformed skull, but his bloated body was a hideous amalgamation of bat, ape and wolf. He wore little armour, and carried no weapon. Having seen him at work, Erikan knew he needed none. His long claws and powerful muscles made him as dangerous as any charging knight.

'Master Nictus,' Erikan said, not meeting the vampire's bestial gaze. Alberacht was unpredictable, even for a vampire. He looked less human every time Erikan saw him. Sometimes he wondered if that was the fate that awaited him, down the long corridor of centuries. Some vampires remained as they were, frozen forever in their last moment. But others became drunk on slaughter and lost their hold on what little humanity remained to them.

'Master, he says,' Alberacht growled. His face twisted into a parody of a smile. 'Such respect for this old warrior. You see how he respects me?' The smile faded. 'Why do the rest of you fail to follow suit?' He turned his baleful gaze on the others. Bloody spittle oozed from his jowls as he champed his long fangs. 'Am I not Grand Master of our order? Must I break you on discipline's altar?' The others backed off as Alberacht released Erikan and turned towards them. He half spread his leathery wings and his eyes glowed with a manic light. He stank of violence and madness, and Erikan drew well away. Alberacht was fully capable of killing any of them in his rage.

'Not for centuries, old one,' Elize said smoothly. 'You remember, don't you? You gave up your post and your burdens to Tomas.' She reached out and stroked Alberacht's hairy hide, the way one might seek to calm an agitated stallion. Erikan tensed. If Alberacht made to harm her, he would have to be quick. He saw Anark gripping his own blade, and the other vampire nodded tersely when he caught Erikan's eye. Neither of them wanted to see Elize come to harm, however much they disliked one another.

'Tomas?' Alberacht grunted. He folded his wings. 'Yes, Tomas. A good boy, for a von Carstein.' He shook himself, like a sleeper awakening from a nightmare, and stroked Elize's head, as a weary grandfather might stroke his grandchild. 'I heard the bells.'

'We all did, old beast,' Markos said. 'We are being called to Sternieste.'

'Then why do we stand here?' Alberacht asked. 'The border is just there, mere steps from where we stand.'

'Well, the giant bloody wall of bone for one,' Count Nyktolos said, shifting his weight. 'We'll have to leave the horses.'

'No, we won't,' Elize said. She looked at Markos and asked, 'Cousin?'

'Oh, it's up to me, is it? Since when did you take charge?' Markos asked. The flat gazes of Anark and Alberacht met his and he threw up his hands in a gesture of surrender. 'Right, yes, fine. I'll get us in the old-fashioned way. Subtlety, thy name is Elize. Form an orderly queue, gentles all, and Erikan as well, of course. Let's go home.'

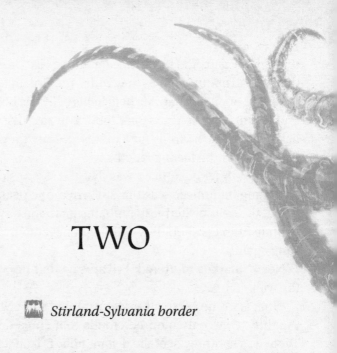

TWO

🏔 *Stirland-Sylvania border*

Dawn was cresting the tops of the hills by the time they reached the foot of the bastion. As the red, watery light washed across the ridges of pale bone, Erikan sought some sign of an entrance, but he saw none as they galloped along its base. 'How are we getting in there? There's no gate,' he shouted to Markos. The other vampire glanced at him over his shoulder and grinned.

'Who needs a gate?' Markos laughed. He jerked his reins, causing his horse to rear, and flung out a hand. Dark fire coruscated about his spread fingers for a moment as he roared out a few harsh syllables. A bolt of energy erupted from his palm and slammed into the bone bastion, cracking and splintering it. 'Master Nictus, if you please!'

There was a shriek from above as Alberacht hurtled down, swooping towards the point of impact. The gigantic vampire slammed into the wall and tore through it with a thunderous crash. Markos kicked his horse into motion before the dust had cleared, and Erikan and the others rode hard after him. The wall began to repair itself with a horrible rustling sound as they rode through the gap. And there was something else – a weirdling light that spread about them as they rode, and Erikan felt as if something had opened a burning hole in his belly. He heard Elize gasp and Count Nyktolos curse out loud, and saw that they were all lit by witch-fire, but only for a moment. Then they were clear of the wall, and the feeling faded.

The first thing he noticed was that the sky was dark. The second thing he noticed was the dull, rhythmic pealing of distant bells. 'The bells of Sternieste,' Alberacht crooned, swiping shards of bone from his shoulders. 'I thought never to hear their lovely song again.'

'Nor I,' Markos muttered. Erikan saw that he was looking at the wall.

'What is it?' he asked. Thunder rumbled somewhere amongst the thick charcoal-coloured clouds that choked the dark sky. There was lightning over the distant hills. Erikan felt invigorated and captivated, all at the same time.

'Did you feel something? As we passed over the border?' Markos asked.

'I did. You?'

'Aye,' Markos grunted. His eyes narrowed to slits for a moment. Then, with a growl, he shook himself. 'We should go. If the bells are sounding, then Mannfred will be at Sternieste. And so will Tomas and the others.'

They rode on, more slowly now. Sylvania was much as Erikan remembered it, from his last, brief visit. He had been at Elize's side then, learning the ways of their kind, and she had brought him to Sternieste for a gathering of the Drakenhof Order. Elize had spoken for him, and Alberacht had welcomed him into the order with terrifying heartiness. The old monster had been a good Grand Master, as far as it went. Erikan glanced up at Nictus as he swooped overhead, and felt a pang of what might have been sadness.

They made their way to the castle by the old paths, known to their kind. They passed isolated villages and outposts that sought to throw back the omnipresent darkness with torches mounted on posts and lanterns chained to the walls. There was still life of sorts in Sylvania, though how long that would be the case Erikan didn't care to guess. Most vampires needed little in the way of nourishment, but then, most had the self-control of a fox in a chicken coop. Many of those little villages would not last out the week, he knew.

They rode through the camps of Strigany nomads and sent ghoul-packs scrambling from their path as their deathless steeds sped along the dark track. Loping wolves and shrieking bats kept pace with them from time to time, as did other, worse things. Erikan had heard that when Mannfred had returned to the damned province and first set about the taming of Sylvania, he had thrown open the vaults of Castle Drakenhof and let loose every foul thing that Vlad had ever interred. All were heading east, towards Castle Sternieste. It was as if every dark soul were being drawn to that distant manse, like metal splinters to a lodestone.

It looked like a grasping talon, its trio of crooked towers jutting ferociously towards the moon above. Even from a distance, the crumbling citadel was magnificent. It was a feat of engineering that had, in its day, claimed a third of the lives employed in its construction, and their tattered souls still clung to the rain-slick stones. It crouched in the open, seemingly in defiance of those who might march against it, and Erikan could guess why Mannfred had chosen it – Sternieste was impressive, as citadels went, but it was also situated perfectly along the main artery of Sylvania. Any invaders who took the traditional routes would have to take Sternieste, before they could do anything else. Sternieste, more so than Fort Oberstyre or Castle Drakenhof, was the keystone of the province.

There was also the fact that Castle Sternieste rose high over a field of rolling hillocks. Each of the latter was a cairn of stupendous size and depth, from a bygone age. It might contain a hundred corpses or merely one, but whatever the number of its inhabitants, each dome of soil and withered, yellow grass pulsed with dark energy. And each and every one of them had been broken into. As they rode through the sea of graves, Erikan could feel the ancient dead stirring, disturbed by the passing presence of the vampires.

They passed the burgeoning earthworks being erected by an army of the recently dead. Zombie knights in shattered armour laboured beside equally dead handgunners and militiamen in the mud and dirt, raising bulwarks and setting heavy stakes. Sternieste's master was readying his lands for siege.

Anark had taken the lead, and he led them towards the gaping main gate of the castle. The portcullis had been raised and the gates unbarred and flung open. There were no visible guards, but then, did a citadel of the dead really need them?

As they clattered into the wide, open courtyard, a flock of crows hurtled skywards, disturbed from feasting on the bodies inside the gibbet cages that decorated the inner walls. Heaps of rotting bodies lay everywhere in the courtyard, strewn about like discarded weapons and covered in shrouds of more squabbling carrion birds.

'Lovely,' Markos said, as he slipped out of his saddle. 'It's like paradise, except not.'

'Quiet,' Elize murmured. She tapped the side of her head. 'Can't you feel it, cousin? Can't you feel him? He's watching us.'

'Who?' Erikan asked, though he knew the answer as well as any of them. He could feel the presence of another mind scrabbling in the shadow of his own, prying at his thoughts and probing his feelings.

'Who else? Welcome to Sylvania, my brethren,' a voice called out as the doors of the outer keep opened with a squeal of long-rusted hinges. The heavy, bloated bodies of two gigantic ghouls, each the size of three of its lesser brethren, burdened with chains and rusty cow bells, moved into view as they shoved the doors open. Each of the creatures was shackled to a door, and they squalled and bellowed as a group of armoured figures stepped between them and moved to meet the newcomers.

'Well, look what the dire wolf dragged in, finally. Elize, Markos and... some others. Wonderful, and you're all late, by the way. I expected you days ago,' Tomas von Carstein said as he drew close. The current Grand Master of the Drakenhof Templars looked much the same as he had when Erikan had last seen him. He'd been handsome enough as a living man, but centuries of undeath had crafted him over into a thing of cold, perfect beauty. The warriors who accompanied him were cut from much the same stripe – blood knights, Templars of the Drakenhof Order, who'd fought on thousands of battlefields. Each of them was a capable warrior, more than a match for any living man or beast. Erikan knew one or two of them, and these he nodded to politely. They returned the gesture warily – as Elize's get, he'd been inducted into the inner circle of the order almost immediately, and Tomas was among those who'd been somewhat incensed by what he saw as her profligate ways.

'Welcome to Castle Sternieste, where the seeds of our damnation have been sown,' Tomas continued, extending his arms in a mocking gesture of welcome.

'Very poetic, cousin. But I, for one, have been damned for a very long time,' Markos said. Tomas laughed harshly.

'This is a different sort of damnation, I'm afraid.' He frowned. 'We're trapped.'

'What do you mean? Explain yourself,' Anark demanded. Tomas made a face.

'Must I? You felt it, didn't you? That grotesque frisson as you crossed the border?' He looked at Anark. 'We are trapped here, in Sylvania. We cannot cross the borders, thanks to the sorceries of our enemies – rather, say, Mannfred's enemies.'

'Lord Mannfred, you mean,' Elize corrected.

'Yes, yes,' Tomas said, waving a hand dismissively. 'Lord

Mannfred, in his infinite wisdom, decided to openly secede our fair homeland from the Empire. They responded in kind.' He laughed. 'They locked the door behind us after we left, it seems.' His laughter grew, becoming a harsh cackle. He shook his head and looked at them. 'Still, I am glad to see you. At least I'll be in good company for the next millennia.'

'Are we the only ones to arrive?' Alberacht rumbled. 'Where are the others? Where is the rest of the inner circle? Where is my old friend Vyktros von Krieger? Where are the Brothers Howl and the Warden of Corpse Run?'

'Maybe some of us were smart enough to run the other way,' Markos muttered.

Tomas laughed harshly. 'Vyktros is dead, killed trying to breach the damnable sorceries that have us trapped. As for the others, I don't know. What I do know is that Mannfred wished to see us – you – as soon as you arrived. And he's been getting impatient.' He smiled. 'It is to be as it was in the old days, it seems, with us at his right hand. Exactly what it is that we'll be doing, seeing as we are confined to this charming garden of earthly pleasures, is entirely up for debate. Come,' Tomas said. He turned and stalked across the bridge. Erikan and the others shared a look, and then followed their Grand Master through the dark gates of Castle Sternieste.

The castle was a hornet's nest of activity. Skeletons clad in the armour and colours of the Drakenhof Guard marched to and fro, in a mockery of the drills they'd performed in life. Bats of various sizes clung to the ceilings and walls, filling the air with their soft chittering. Ghouls loped across the desiccated grounds, the leaders of the various packs fighting to assert dominance. The dead of ten centuries had been wakened and readied for war, and they stood, waiting silently for the order to march.

There were vampires in evidence as well, more of them than Erikan had ever seen in one place. Von Carsteins as well as others – Lahmians, in courtly finery, and red-armoured Blood

Dragons, as well as gargoyle-like Strigoi. For the first time in centuries, Castle Sternieste rang with the sound of voices and skulduggery. They clustered in the knaves and open chambers, sipping blood from delicate goblets, or fed on the unlucky men and women rounded up at Mannfred's orders from what few nearby villages had not been abandoned and dragged to Sternieste to serve as a larder for the growing mob of predators. They spoke quietly in small groups or pointedly ignored one another. They duelled in the gardens and plotted in the antechambers.

None of them attempted to hinder Tomas and his companions. Everyone knew who the Drakenhof Templars were, and gave them room – even the scions of Blood Keep, who eyed them the way a wolf might eye a rival from another pack. No one was tempted to try their luck at gainsaying him just yet. It wouldn't be long, though. Erikan could smell resentment on the air. Vampires, by their very nature, seethed with the urge to dominate and they chafed at being under another's dominion.

Tomas led them through the castle, up curling stone stairwells and through damp corridors where cold air, and things worse than air, slipped in through broken walls. Ghostly knights galloped silently through the corridors, and wailing hags swept upwards, all drawn in the same direction as the vampiric Templars. It was there, in the bell tower of Sternieste, that the great black bells tolled, calling the dead to their master's side. The sound of the bells was as the creak of a coffin lid and the thud of a mausoleum door; it was the crunch of bone and the wet slap of torn flesh; it was the sound all dead things knew, deep in the marrow of their bones.

Tomas's warriors peeled off as they approached the narrow stairwell that led up to the bell tower. The meeting was obviously only for the inner circle. Erikan felt a twinge of doubt as they ascended, and the others seemed to share his concern, save for Anark and Elize, who chatted gaily to Tomas as they went. Markos caught Erikan's eye and made a face. Something was going on. Erikan wondered if Mannfred had truly summoned them, or this was some ploy on Tomas's part. *Or Elize's,* a small, treacherous voice murmured in the depths of his mind. Those who took the von Carstein name tended towards ambition. To assume the name was a symbol of your devotion to the ideals of Vlad von Carstein, of a vampire-state, of an empire of the dead, ruled by the masters of the night. Only the ambitious or the insane announced their intentions so openly.

When they climbed out into the bell tower, the air throbbed with the graveyard churn of the bells, and the soft cacophony of the gathered spectral hosts that surrounded the top of the tower. Hundreds, if not thousands of spirits floated above the tower, pulled to and chained by the dull clangour. The bell-ringers were ghouls, and they gave vent to bone-rattling howls and shrieks as they hauled on the ropes.

And beyond them, his back to the newcomers, his eyes fixed on the innumerable spirits dancing on the night wind, stood Mannfred von Carstein. He had one foot set on the parapet, and he leaned on his raised knee as he gazed upwards. He did not turn as they arrived, and only glanced at them when Tomas drew his sword partially from its sheath and slammed it down.

'Count Mannfred, you have called and we, your most loyal servants, have come. The inner circle of the Drakenhof Order is ready to ride forth at your command and at your discretion,' Tomas said.

'I'm sure you are,' Mannfred said. His eyes flickered over each of them in turn, and Erikan couldn't help but feel nervous. He'd only ever served the creature before him at a remove. To see him in the flesh was something else again. Mannfred was tall, taller even than Anark, taller than any normal man, if not gigantic. He seemed swollen with power, and his gilt-edged, black armour was of the finest quality, despite its archaic appearance. A heavy cloak made from the hairy pelt of a gigantic wolf hung down from his shoulders, and a long-bladed sword with an ornate basket hilt was sheathed on his hip. His scalp had been shorn clean of hair, and his face was aquiline and aristocratic, with a fine-boned grace to his features. 'While I am glad that you have come, I expected more of you, cousins and gentles all.'

'These are the greatest warriors of the order, my lord,' Tomas said. 'The blood of the von Carsteins runs thick in the veins of the inner circle. Will you do us the honour of explaining your purpose in summoning us?'

'I should think it would be obvious, cousin,' Mannfred said. He reached out a hand as the ghost of a wailing child drifted close, as if to comfort the spectre. Instead, he crooked his fingers and swept them through its features, causing the ghost to momentarily stretch and distort. 'I am readying myself for the war to come. To wage war, I require warriors. Hence, your presence. Or must I explain further?'

'No, no, most wise and fierce lord,' Tomas said, looking at the others meaningfully. 'But one must wonder why we have been summoned into a land that we cannot then leave.'

Mannfred gave no sign that Tomas's words had struck a nerve, but somehow Erikan knew that they had. The lord of Sylvania examined Tomas for a moment. Erikan saw his eyes slide towards those of Elize, who inclined her head slightly. His hand found the hilt of his blade. Something was definitely going on. He was sure of it now. There was an undercurrent here he didn't like. 'What are you implying, cousin?' Mannfred asked.

Tomas cocked his head. 'Surely you can feel it, my lord. It is the talk of your court, and of the guests who shelter beneath the bowers of your generosity. The borders are protected against our kind. We can enter, but not leave. And as mighty as your walls are, and as great as your army might be, we find ourselves wondering why you gave us no warning?' He looked around him, at Erikan and the others, seeking support. Anark began to nod dully, but Elize's hand on his arm stopped him. Erikan traded glances with Markos. The latter smiled thinly and gave a slight shake of his head.

'If I had, dear cousin, would you have come?' Mannfred asked, turning away.

Tomas tapped the pommel of his blade with a finger, and gave Mannfred a speculative look. 'So what you're saying is that you've knowingly trapped us here, in this reeking sty you call a fiefdom. Wonderful, truly. Vlad's cunning was as nothing compared to your own ineffable wisdom.' He turned to look at the others again. 'Yes, your brilliance is as bright as the light of the Witch Moon in full glow, my Lord Mannfred. I, and the rest of the inner circle of the Drakenhof Templars, stand in awe of your puissance and forethought in calling us all back and trapping us here, in this overlarge tomb of yours.' Tomas clapped politely. 'Well done, sirrah. What will be your next trick, pray tell? Perhaps you'd like to juggle a few blessed relics, or maybe go for a stroll in the noonday sun?'

'Are you finished?' Mannfred asked.

'No,' Tomas said, all trace of jocularity gone from his voice. 'Not even a little bit. I – we – came in good faith, and at your request, Lord Mannfred. And you have betrayed even that shred of consideration and for what – so that we might share your captivity?'

'So that you might help me break the chains that bind Sylvania, dear cousin,' Mannfred purred. 'And you did not do me a favour, Tomas. You owe me your allegiance. I am the true and lawful lord of Sylvania, and your order is pledged to my service, wherever and whenever I so require.'

'Not quite.' Tomas smiled thinly. 'We do serve the Count of Sylvania, but that doesn't necessarily mean you, *cousin.*'

Erikan blinked. Even for a vampire, Tomas was fast. The gap between thought and deed for him was but the barest of moments. His blade was in his hand and arcing towards Mannfred's shaved pate as he finished speaking, and the other had started to turn.

Mannfred was not so quick. But then, he didn't have to be. Tomas's blade smashed down into Mannfred's waiting palm, halted mere inches from the crown of his head. Mannfred examined the blade for a moment, and then tore it from Tomas's grip with a casual twitch of his wrist. Still holding the sword by the blade, he looked at Tomas. 'In a way, Tomas, you are correct. However, in another, altogether more important way, you are decidedly incorrect.' Without a flicker of warning, Mannfred caught Tomas a ringing blow across the side of his head with the hilt of his sword.

Tomas was sent flying by the force of the blow. Mannfred tossed the now-broken sword over the parapet and strode towards the fallen Grand Master. Erikan and the others drew back. Tomas had made his play without consulting them, and the consequences would be on his head alone. He'd likely hoped they'd join him, when they learned of the trap. Then, he had never been very smart, Erikan reflected as Mannfred reached down and grabbed a handful of Tomas's hair. Mannfred hauled the other vampire to his feet effortlessly. 'This, Tomas, is why I called you back. This weakness, this bravado, this mistaken impression that you, that *any of you,* are my equal.' He pulled Tomas close. 'I have no equal, cousin. I am Mannfred von Carstein, first, last and only. And I cannot abide weakness.' He flung Tomas against the wall hard enough to rattle the latter's armour. 'I have begun something. And I would have my servants at my disposal, rather than traipsing off, pursuing their own petty goals when they should be pursuing mine.'

Tomas clawed at the wall and dragged himself upright. He glared at Mannfred. 'The only weak one here is you. I remember you, Mannfred, cousin, scrabbling at Vlad's heels, hiding from Konrad – you were a rat then, and you're a rat now, cowering in your nest.'

Mannfred was silent for a moment. His face betrayed no expression. Then, he made a single, sharp gesture. The air and shadows around Tomas seemed to congeal, becoming sharp and solid. For a moment, Erikan was reminded of the jaws of a wolf closing about a field mouse. The darkness obscured Tomas, and there came a strange squeal as though metal were scraping against metal, and then a horrid grinding sound that made Erikan's fangs ache in his gums.

Tomas began to scream. Blood spattered the stones, and torn and bent bits of armour clattered to the ground. To Erikan, it sounded as if the Grand Master were being flayed alive. Whatever was happening, Mannfred watched it with glittering eyes and with a slight, savage smile creasing his aquiline features.

When it was done, there was little left of Tomas – just something red and raw that lay in the detritus of its former glory, mewling shrilly. Mannfred looked down at the squirming ruin and said, 'Anark, see to your predecessor. I have other, more important matters to attend.'

Anark started. His nostrils flared, but he gave no other sign that his sudden rise to prominence had surprised him. His lips peeled back from his fangs as he drew his sword and advanced on the remains of his former comrade.

Mannfred stepped back and turned to Elize. He stroked her cheek in such a way that Erikan thought it lucky for one of them that Anark was occupied with his butchery. Mannfred leaned towards her and murmured, 'And so I have kept my promise, cousin.' Erikan glanced at the others surreptitiously, but he seemed to have been the only one to hear the exchange. Mannfred drew his cloak about him and left them on the parapet. Erikan waited for the sound of his boots to fade and then said, 'Well, that was unexpected.'

'But not unwelcome,' Elize said. She drifted towards Anark, and rubbed a spot of blood from his cheek. 'Tomas was a fool, and we all know it. His end has been a century in coming, and I, for one, am glad that we do not have to put up with him longer than was absolutely necessary. If we are trapped here, then Mannfred is our best chance of escape. And besides, Tomas had no concept of honour or loyalty. Anark will make a better Grand Master, I think.'

Anark grinned and ran his hand along his blade, stripping Tomas's blood from it. 'Unless someone objects?' He looked at Erikan as he spoke. 'Well, Crowfiend?'

Erikan didn't rise to the bait. 'I wasn't under the assumption that we had been given a vote.' He inclined his head. 'Long live the new Grand Master.' The others followed suit, murmuring their congratulations.

Alberacht even looked as if he meant it.

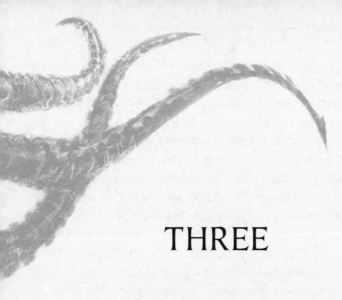

THREE

 Castle Sternieste, Sylvania

Mannfred strode through the damp, cool corridors of Sternieste, trying to rein in the anger that had threatened to overwhelm him for days now. The hunched shapes of his servants scurried out of his path as he walked, but he gave them little notice.

Gelt's barrier of faith still resisted every attempt to shatter it. He had wrung his library dry of magics, and had made not the slightest bit of difference. Soon enough, once the northern invasion had been thrown back, as they always, inevitably were, Karl Franz would turn his attentions back to the festering boil on the backside of his pitiful empire and lance it once and for all. There was nowhere to run, nowhere to go. It might take centuries, or millions of lives, but Mannfred had studied the Emperor for a decade, and he knew that there was no more ruthless a man in the world, save himself. Karl Franz would happily sacrifice Ostland and Stirland, if it meant scouring Sylvania from the map.

Mannfred wanted to scream, to rant and rave, to succumb to the red thirst and rampage through some village somewhere. Everything he had worked for, everything he had conquered death for, was coming apart in his hands before he'd even begun, leaving him still in Vlad's shadow. Tomas had scored a palpable hit with that painful truth, before Mannfred had dealt with him. That the blow was not physical made it no less painful, nor any less lingering. Most of his followers knew better than to question him, either out of fear or because they lacked the wit to see the trap for what it was. In a way, the preponderance of the latter was his own fault. He had eliminated most, if not all, of his rivals amongst the aristocracy of the night. Vlad had bestowed the gift of immortality as a reward, without much thought as to the consequences, and Konrad had been even more profligate, turning dockside doxies, common mercenaries and, in one unfortunate incident that was best forgotten, a resident of the Moot.

Mannfred had dealt with all of them, hunting them down one by one over the centuries since his resurrection from the swamps of Hel Fenn. Any vampire of the von Carstein bloodline who would not serve him, or was of no use to him, he destroyed, even as he had destroyed Tomas. Most of Vlad's get had been swept off the board at the outset. Tomas and the other members of the inner circle of the Drakenhof Templars were among the last of them, and with Tomas's death, Mannfred thought that they were sufficiently cowed. Elize was more pragmatic than the others, and could be counted on to keep them under control. At least in so far as monsters like Nictus, or weasels like Markos, could be controlled.

He reached up and ran both hands over his shorn scalp. He wondered if, when all was said and done, he would finally be free of Vlad's ghost. When he had finally broken the world's spine and supped on its life's blood, would that nagging, mocking shade depart.

No. No, I think not, Vlad's voice whispered. Mannfred neither paused, nor responded. The voice was only in his head. It was only a trick of long, wasted centuries, some self-defeating urge that he could ignore. *Am I though? Or am I really here with you still, my best beloved son?* the voice murmured. Mannfred ground his teeth.

'No, you are not,' he hissed.

The voice faded, leaving only the echo of a ghostly chuckle to mark its passing. Mannfred hated that chuckle. It had always been Vlad's signal that he was missing something that the latter thought obvious. And perhaps he was. But he had weighty matters on his mind at the moment. Most notably that his demesnes were already subject to invasion, albeit not a large one, and not one initiated by the Empire. But it was still enough to give Mannfred pause. His nascent realm had already suffered attack once, by a horde of daemons. Those had been easy enough to see off, but this new threat was proving to be more persistent. He'd sent out wolves and bats to shadow the intruder's approach, but every time the beasts came closer to the newcomer, Mannfred's control over them had slipped away. That could only mean that the invader was another master of the Corpse Geometries, and one unlike the other wretched creatures that had thus far made it across the border.

Whoever it was had made no attempt to either openly challenge or offer fealty to the lord of Sylvania. Mannfred had at first suspected that it was the self-styled Lichemaster, Heinrich Kemmler, who'd been his ally for an all-too-brief moment, before he'd chafed beneath the goad and taken his leave of Mannfred's court, his hulking undead bodyguard Krell following behind him. Mannfred had kept tabs on the necromancer, and the last he'd heard the lunatic sorcerer had raised an army of the dead to lay siege to Castle Reikguard, for reasons fathomable only to him.

But the intruder's aura, the taste of his power, was different from Kemmler's. It was older, for one thing, with its roots sunk deep in disciplines that had existed for millennia. And it was greater, possibly even a match for Mannfred's own. There were few creatures who could wield such power so negligently – that wretched creature Zacharias the Ever-Living for one, or that perfumed dolt Dietrich von Dohl, the so-called Crimson Lord of Sylvania. And this newcomer was neither.

Which left only one possibility.

Mannfred forced down the anger as it threatened to surge again. If the intruder was who he suspected, he would need all of his faculties to deal with him in the manner he deserved. But before he marshalled his energies for such a conflict, he would need to be certain. Time was at a premium, and he could not afford to waste his carefully husbanded strength battling shadows. That said, the thought of such a conflict did not displease Mannfred. Indeed, after the weeks of frustration he had endured, such a confrontation was an almost welcome diversion. To be free at last to strive and destroy would be a great relief to him.

The loud, raucous communal croak of a number of carrion birds let him know he'd reached his destination, and he quickly assumed a mask of genteel calm. It wouldn't do to show any weakness, emotional or otherwise, to a creature like the Crowfiend. He'd asked Elize's creature to meet him in the castle's high garden. There were things Mannfred needed to ask him, to lend weight to or dismiss those theories now burgeoning in his mind.

A brace of skeletons, clad in bronze cuirasses and holding bronze-headed, long-hafted axes, guarded the entrance to the open-air, walled garden. He stepped past them, and as he entered the garden, a flock of black-feathered birds leapt skywards, screaming in indignation. He watched them swoop and wheel for a moment. Vlad had always felt a ghastly affection for the beasts. Mannfred had never understood how a creature as powerful as Vlad could waste his attentions feeding sweetmeats to such vermin, when there were more important matters to be attended to.

The Crowfiend sat on one of the cracked, discoloured marble benches that encircled the garden's single, crooked tree. The fat-trunked monstrosity was long dead, but somehow it still grew, drawing gods alone knew what sort of nourishment from the castle into whose mortar it had sunk its roots. Erikan stood as Mannfred approached. Mannfred gestured for him to sit. He gazed at the other vampire for a moment.

The Crowfiend had a face that radiated feral placidity. There was no obvious guile in him. Cunning, yes, and cleverness, but no guile. He was not a subtle creature, but neither was he stupid. There was something familiar there as well – a raw need that Mannfred recognised in himself. A hunger that was greater than any bloodthirst or flesh-greed. Mannfred drew close to the other vampire and caught his chin in an iron grip. He pulled Erikan's face up. 'I can see the ghoul-taint in your face, boy. Elize tells me that your kin were corpse-eaters, though not so debased as those that prowl these halls.'

'They were, my lord,' Erikan said.

'They were burned, I am given to understand.'

'Yes,' Erikan said, and he displayed no more emotion than if he'd been speaking of a rat he'd killed. Mannfred wondered if such lack of feeling was a mask. Vampires, contrary to folk belief and superstition, did not lose the ability to feel emotion. Indeed, undeath often enhanced such things. Sometimes every emotion was redoubled and magnified, stretched almost into caricature. Love became lust, passion became obsession, and hatred... Ah, hatred became something so venomous as to make even daemons flinch. And sometimes, they became as dust, only a fading memory of emotion, a brief, dull flicker of fires burned low.

'If I were to say to you that the world is soon to die, what would you say?'

'I'd say that I'd like to see that, my lord,' Erikan said.

Mannfred blinked. He meant it, too. He let him go. 'Is existence so burdensome to you?'

Erikan shrugged. 'No. I merely meant that if the world is to burn, I might as well help stoke the fires,' he said.

'You believe it is time for a change, then?'

Erikan looked away. 'Change doesn't frighten me, my lord.'

'No, perhaps it doesn't, at that. Perhaps that is why Elize chose you – she has always had a streak of perversity in her, my lovely cousin. She was a sister of Shallya once, you know. She was at Isabella's side, when she passed over from the wasting illness, and Vlad wrenched her back from Morr's clutches. Poor, gentle Elize was Isabella's first meal upon awakening. And she served as the countess's handmaiden until her untimely end.'

Erikan said nothing. Mannfred smiled thinly. 'Very loyal is Elize. Loyal, trustworthy, her ambition kept on the tightest of leashes. Why did she toss you aside, I wonder?' The other vampire cocked his head, but did not reply. For a moment, Mannfred was reminded of a carrion bird. He gestured airily. 'I don't suppose it matters. She brought you over, and that is more a gift than most get in this fallen world.' He turned away and strode to the tree. 'You came from Couronne, I'm given to understand,' Mannfred said. He gazed up at the tree. Idly he jabbed a talon into the spongy surface of the trunk. Black ichors oozed out of the cut. He glanced back at Erikan and sucked the sour sap off his finger.

Erikan nodded slowly. 'I did.'

'The Serpent fell, then,' Mannfred said.

Erikan nodded again. 'We were defeated.'

'And what of Arkhan the Black?'

Erikan jolted, as if struck. 'What about him, my lord?'

'What happened to him in the aftermath?'

'I don't know, my lord,' Erikan said. 'I and– I was with Mallobaude's bodyguard.' His face twisted slightly. He shook himself. 'Some say Arkhan was never there at Couronne to begin with. That he had used Mallobaude as a diversion for some other scheme. Others say that the Green Knight struck off his head as he had Mallobaude's.'

Mannfred grunted. 'No such luck,' he muttered. He looked back at Erikan. 'But he was there – in Bretonnia – of this you're certain?'

'I saw him, though only at a distance, my lord. It was him. He rode in a chariot of bone, which bore banners of crackling witch-fire and was pulled by skeletal steeds surmounted by the skulls of men, which screamed out in agony as they galloped.'

Mannfred nodded. 'That sounds just ostentatious enough to be truthful,' he murmured. The liche had long since lost any subtlety he had possessed in life. Arkhan had none of a vampire's inbuilt sense of discretion. He was almost... theatrical.

What had the liche been after, he wondered? He was about to inquire further as to Arkhan's activities when movement drew his eye, and he glanced up. A pale face stared down at him from among the crooked, arthritic branches of the tree, its features twisted in a mocking smile as flickering shadows gathered at the corner of his vision. Was it Vlad's face? Or someone else's... The features were at once Vlad's and those of a youth from some other land, handsome and terrible and noble and bestial all at once. The thin-lipped mouth moved, but no sound came out. Nonetheless, Mannfred heard it as clear as if it had whispered in his ear. 'La Maisontaal Abbey,' he muttered. He blinked and shook himself. The face was gone, as were the shadows, leaving behind only a dark echo of a man's sonorous chuckle. He felt like a child being guided towards a treat. Irritated, he gouged the trunk of the tree again, leaving five suppurating wounds in its soft bark.

Of course it was La Maisontaal. Of course! Why else would the liche have bothered with a backwater like Bretonnia? Mannfred stared at the sap seeping from the tree. But why come here, now? Unless... He grunted. Arkhan's goals were as unsubtle as the liche himself. He had ever been Nagash's tool. He had no more free will than the dead who served him.

He was coming for those items that Mannfred now possessed, and had spent no little effort in acquiring. His lips peeled back from his fangs as he contemplated the audacity of the creature – to come here, to Sylvania, to take what was Mannfred's by right of blood and conquest? No, no, that would not do.

'Once a thief, always a thief,' he snarled. He turned, his cloak flaring about him like the stretched wing of a gigantic bat. Erikan started, and tried to stand as Mannfred swooped upon him. He grabbed the other vampire gently by the throat with both hands, forcing him to remain still. 'Thank you, boy, for your candour. It is much appreciated,' Mannfred purred. 'Tell your mistress and her oaf of a progeny Anark to ready the defences of this citadel. I expect the Drakenhof Templars to defend what is mine with their lives, if it comes to it.'

He released Erikan and strode towards the doorway, cloak swirling. Erikan rose to his feet and asked, 'And what of you, Lord Mannfred? What should I say you are doing?'

'I, dear boy, am going to confront the invader in person. I would take measure of my enemy before crushing his skull to powder beneath my boot-heel.'

💀 *Vargravia, Sylvania*

If he had been capable of it, Arkhan the Black would have been in a foul mood. As it was, he merely felt a low throb of dissatisfaction as he led his rotting, stumbling forces through the blighted foothills of Vargravia. It had been a matter of mere moments to use his magics to rip a hole in the immense bone wall that carved off Sylvania from the rest of the world, but the blackened and shattered bone had repaired itself with an impressive speed. More than half of his army had been left on the other side of the gap, but there was nothing for it. He could always raise more to replace them. If there was one thing that Sylvania didn't lack, it was corpses.

And it would be easier now, as well. There was something in the air, here; or, rather, there was something missing. He looked up, scanning the dark sky overhead. It had been daylight when he'd crossed the border, only moments before. But the skies of Sylvania were as black as pitch, and charnel winds caused the trees to rustle in a way that, had he still possessed hackles, would have caused them to bristle. He could taste death on the wind the way another might smell the smoke of not-so-distant fire.

But despite all of that, they were going too slowly. It had taken him longer than he'd hoped to reach Sylvania. The power of Chaos was growing, and Arkhan could feel the world quiver, like a man afflicted with ague. The winds of magic blew erratically, and things from outside the walls of reality were clambering over the threshold in ever-increasing numbers. More than once, he'd been forced to defend himself from cackling nightmares from the outer void, drawn to the scent of sorcery that permeated him. Beasts gathered in the hills and forests, making them traps for the unwary, and the land heaved with conflict in a way it never had before. It was as if the world were tearing itself apart in a frenzy.

Perhaps that was why his master had begun to speak to him once more. Ever since he had been resurrected from his first death by Nagash's magics, an echo of the latter's voice had occupied his head. A comforting murmur that had never truly faded or weakened, even when Nagash himself had ceased to be. For years he had refused to acknowledge it for what it was, and had lied to himself, boasting of autonomy to the soulless husks that did his bidding. An easy thing to do when the voice grew dim, retreating to a barely heard buzz of mental static. But, over the course of recent decades, it had begun to grow in volume again. It had whispered to him in his black tower, compelling him to rise and strive once more, though there seemed to be no reason to do so.

His first inkling that it was not merely a stirring in the dregs of his imagination was when the armies of Mannfred von Carstein had marched on the ruins of Lahmia. Such arrogance was well within the remit of every vampire he'd ever met, but the sheer scale of the undertaking was a thing unmatched in his experience. Von Carstein had wanted something from the ruins of

Lahmia. Whether he'd found it or not, Arkhan did not know. Von Carstein had fled before the might of Lybaras and its High Queen. But something had compelled the vampire to strike at Lahmia, and then later, Nagashizzar.

When Queen Khalida had made to return the favour a few centuries later, Arkhan had travelled with her to Sylvania, in pursuit of one of Mannfred's get. Mannfred himself was long dead by that point, sunk into the mire of Hel Fenn, but the dark spirit that had compelled him to attack the Lands of the Dead was obviously present in those creatures of his creation. They came again and again, looking for something. In this case, it had been one of Nagash's lesser staves of power – not Alakanash, the Great Staff, but a weaker version of it.

And like all tools forged by the Great Necromancer, it had had a whisper of his consciousness in it. Nagash had ever imparted something of himself, something of his vast and terrible soul, in everything of his making. Arkhan had taken the staff for his own, and though he'd held it aloft, the voice he'd long thought banished from his mind returned. It had howled in his mind, the chains of an ancient subjugation had rattled and he had begun his quest.

Upon Nagash's destruction by the brute hillman now venerated by the people of the Empire, those artefacts of his design had been scattered to the four winds by plot and chance. The will that pressed upon Arkhan's own had whispered to him his new task – to find these missing treasures. He was to seek out and gather the nine Books of Nagash, the mighty Crown of Sorcery, the Black Armour of Morikhane and the Great Staff, Alakanash, all of which had vanished into the weft and way of history. And there was the Fellblade of foul memory, and certain other things that must be brought together. Lastly, he required the withered Claw of Nagash, struck from the Great Necromancer's arm by the edge of the Fellblade, and lost for millennia.

Once all of these had been gathered, Arkhan could begin the

last great working. Then, and only then, could the Great Necromancer return to the world, which was his by right of birth and fate. And it was Arkhan's task to help Nagash do so, even if it meant his obliteration in the doing of it. Such thoughts had rebounded against the walls of his skull for centuries, growing stronger and stronger, until it had reached a crescendo of such power that Arkhan was hard pressed to tell his thoughts from those of his master.

Two of the Books of Nagash were in his possession even now, strapped to the backs of his servants. And he knew where Alakanash and the Black Armour were. But someone had beaten him to the other items, or so the voice in his skull whispered again and again. And that someone, he had been assured, was Mannfred von Carstein, resurrected from the grave even as Arkhan himself had been.

That the information had come from the sore-encrusted lips of one as untrustworthy as Heinrich Kemmler, the self-proclaimed Lichemaster, did not make Arkhan doubt its veracity overmuch. Kemmler had returned to the Grey Mountains after some time in the Empire, retreating to lick his wounds after nearly losing his head to the bite of a dwarf axe at Castle Reikguard. Mallobaude had sought him out, despite Arkhan's objections. The Lichemaster could not be trusted in such matters. His mind was disordered and he chafed at subordination.

Nonetheless, he had been intrigued to learn of Kemmler's brief alliance with von Carstein, as well as the vampire's acquisition of an elven princess of some standing. Kemmler had seen several of the items in question during this affair, and he, being no fool whatever his other proclivities, knew that there was some black plan brewing in the vampire's crooked brain.

What that plan was, Kemmler hadn't been able to say, and Arkhan felt disinclined to guess. The Books of Nagash were tomes of great power, and the Crown was a relic beyond all others. Any one of them would have served Mannfred adequately in whatever petty dreams fed his ambition. But to gather them all? That was a mystery indeed.

From somewhere far behind him, there was a great crackle of blossoming bone. He turned to watch as the yellowing shell of the wall repaired itself at last. A number of his slower followers were caught and pulverised, their rotting carcasses disintegrating as spears and branches of bone tore through them. Arkhan leaned on his staff, one fleshless palm resting on the pommel of the great tomb-blade that sat in its once-ornate and now much-reduced sheath on his hip.

'*Well, that's interesting,*' Arkhan rasped. It had required great magic to create that wall, and maintain it. Mannfred had been busy. He reached up and scratched the maggoty chin of the zombie cat laying across his shoulders. He'd found the animal in Quenelles and, on some dark, unexplainable whim, resurrected it. In life, it had been a scar-faced tomcat, big and lanky and foul-tempered. Now, it was still as big and even worse-tempered, albeit sloughing off its hair and skin at an alarming rate, even for a zombie. Arkhan suspected that the animal was doing it to be contrary. The cat gurgled in a parody of pleasure and Arkhan clicked his teeth at it. '*Isn't that interesting?*'

Mannfred had sealed off Sylvania efficiently enough, but Arkhan did not think he was responsible for the sour ring of faith that now enclosed the province as effectively as a dungeon door locked and barred by a gaoler. No, that particular working stank of Chamon, the yellow wind of magic – dense and metallic. That meant the involvement of men, for only they employed such basic sorceries for such complex tasks. Arkhan had little familiarity with the barbaric lands of the Empire, though he'd warred on them more than once. That they had sorcerers capable of such a wreaking was moderately surprising. That Mannfred had aggravated them into doing so, was not.

'I still can't believe that you brought that cat with you.' Arkhan turned at the harsh croak, and examined the angular, patchwork face of the man who stomped towards him. Ogiers was – or had been – a nobleman of Bretonnia. Now he was a horse-less vagabond, whose once-minor interest in necromancy had suddenly become his only means of protection, in the wake of Mallobaude's failed rebellion. He was also a giant of a man, who towered over the bodies of his former men-at-arms.

'*And I can't believe that something so inconsequential weighs so heavily on your mind,*' Arkhan said. '*And you do have a mind, Ogiers. That's why I pulled you from under the hooves of your kinsmen's horses. What of the others? Did we leave anyone on the other side?*'

'Some. No one consequential. That jackanapes Malfleur and that giggling maniac from Ostland. Fidduci made it through, as did Kruk,' Ogiers said with a shrug. Arkhan stroked his cat and considered the man before him. Ogiers's beard, once so finely groomed, had become a rat's nest, and his face was splotched with barely healed cuts and bruises. Big as he was, he slumped with exhaustion. He'd discarded most of his armour during the retreat over the Grey Mountains, but he'd kept what he could – more, Arkhan suspected, for sentimental reasons than anything else. The other necromancers likely looked just as tired. He'd pressed them hard since they'd reached the borderlands, keeping them moving without stopping. He forgot sometimes, how heavy flesh could be. It was like an anchor around you, bone and spirit.

He considered leaving them, while he forged ahead, but knew that would only be inviting trouble. They were frightened of him, but fear only went so far. He needed to keep them where he could see them.

Mallobaude's rebellion had stirred a hornet's nest of necro-mantic potential. In the months before his first, tentative missives had reached Arkhan in his desert exile, Mallobaude had sought to gather a colloquium of sorcerers and hedge-wizards to coun-ter the witches of the lake and wood who bolstered the tottering throne of his homeland. Dozens of necromancers and dark sorcerers had responded, trickling over the Grey Mountains in ones and twos, seeking the Serpent's favour. When Arkhan had arrived at last, he'd been forced to initiate a cull of the gathered magic-users. Most were merely fraudsters or crooked creatures with only a bit of lore and a cantrip or two – hardly useful in a war. These he butchered and added to the swelling ranks of dead, where they'd be more useful.

Others he'd sent off to the fringes of the uprising, to distract and demoralise the enemy. The rest he'd gathered about him as his aides. He'd rescued the best of these in the final hours of the rebellion, gathering them to him and whisking them away from harm. Many hands made quick work, and he had much to do. The angles of the Corpse Geometries were bunching and skewing as the world shuddered beneath the weight of some newborn doom. The world had teetered on the edge of oblivion for centuries and it appeared that something had, at last, decided to simply tip it over.

The thought was neither particularly pleasant nor especially unpleasant to Arkhan, who had long ago shed such mortal worries. Death was rest, and life a burden. He had experienced both often enough to prefer the former, but the latter could never entirely be shed, thanks to the grip Nagash held on his soul. '*We will keep moving. Let the dead fall. This land is full of corpses, and we no longer have need of these. They merely serve to slow us down.*' He swept out a hand, and the shambling legions at their back twitched and collapsed as one with a collective sigh, all save the two enormous corpses that bore the heavy, iron-bound Books of Nagash in their arms. The two zombies had, in life, been ogre mercenaries from across the Mountains of Mourn. They and a mob of their kin had been drawn to Bretonnia by the war, and slain in the final battle at Couronne. Arkhan had seen no sense in wasting such brawny potential, and had resurrected them to serve as his pack-bearers.

'This is the first time we've stopped in days. We are not all liches, lord,' Ogiers said, looking about him at his fallen warriors. Arkhan had dispatched them with the rest. If Ogiers disapproved, he was wise enough to say nothing. 'Some of us still require food, sleep... A moment of rest.'

Arkhan said nothing. Behind Ogiers, Fidduci and Kruk made their way towards them over the field of fallen corpses. Franco Fidduci was a black-toothed Tilean scholar with a penchant for the grotesque, and Kruk was a twisted midget who rode upon the broad back of the risen husk of his cousin, clinging to the wight like a jongleur's pet ape.

'What happened? All my sweet ones fell over,' Kruk piped.

'Our master has seen fit to dispense with their services,' Ogiers said.

'But my pretty ones,' Kruk whined.

'If you're referring to those Strigany dancing girls of yours, they were getting a bit mouldy,' Fidduci said. 'Best to find some new ones, eh?' He looked at Arkhan. 'Which we will, yes? This is not a land for four innocent travellers, oh most godly and grisly of lords,' he said cautiously.

'*Frightened, are you?*' Arkhan rasped.

'Not all of us have escaped death's clutches as often as you,' Ogiers said. He looked around. 'Maybe we should take our leave of you. We will only slow you down, lord, and you disposed of our army, thus rendering our contribution as your generals moot.'

The cat examined the gathered necromancers with milky eyes. Its tail twitched and its yellowed and cracked fangs were visible through its mangled jowls. Arkhan stroked it idly, and said, '*No, you will not leave my side. Without me, you would be dead. Actually dead, as opposed to the more pleasing and familiar variety. We all serve someone, Ogiers. It is your good fortune to serve me.*'

'And who do you serve, oh most puissant and intimidating Arkhan?' Fidduci asked, fiddling with his spectacles.

'*Pray to whatever gods will have you that you never meet him,*

Franco,' Arkhan rasped. *'Now come, we are a day from... What was it called, Kruk?'*

'Valsborg Bridge, my lovely master,' Kruk said. The diminutive necromancer hunched forward in his harness and pounded on his mount's shoulders. 'Come, come!' The wight turned and began to lope in a northerly direction.

Arkhan gestured with his staff. *'You heard him. Come, come,'* he intoned. Fidduci and Ogiers shared a look and then began to trudge after Kruk. Arkhan followed them sedately. As he walked, he considered his reasons for coming to Sylvania.

Bretonnia had been, if examined honestly, an unmitigated disaster. He had intended to use the civil war as a distraction in order to crack open the abbey at La Maisontaal and secure the ancient artefact ensconced within its stone walls, but Mallobaude had failed him. He'd been forced to retreat, gathering what resources he could. He intended to return, but he required more power to tip the balance in his favour. And time was growing short. The Long Night fast approached, and the world was crumbling at the edges.

There was no easy way to tell how long it took them to reach the bridge, even if Arkhan had cared about marking the passage of time. More than once, he and the others were required to fend off roving bands of ghouls or slobbering undead monstrosities. Bats swooped from the sky and wolves lunged from the hardscrabble trees, and Arkhan was forced to usurp their master's control to protect his followers. Ghosts haunted every crossroads and barrow-hill, and banshees wailed amidst the bent trees and extinct villages that they passed on the road to Valsborg Bridge. It was Mannfred's hand and will behind these obstacles, Arkhan knew. The vampire was trying to slow him down, to occupy his attentions while he mustered his meagre defences.

The bridge was nothing special. A simple span of stone across a narrow cleft, constructed in the days of Otto von Drak, before the Vampire Wars. A thin sludge of water gurgled below it. Arkhan suspected that it had been a raging river in its day, but the arteries of running water that crossed Sylvania were fast drying up thanks to Mannfred's sorcery. Storm clouds choked the skies above, and thunder rumbled in the distance.

His companions had collapsed by the roadside, exhausted by the gruelling pace. Even Kruk hung limp in his harness, stunted limbs dangling. Arkhan looked up at the churning sky, and then back at the bridge. Then he turned to his pack-bearers and motioned for them to drop to their haunches. They sank down, jaws sagging, blind, opaque eyes rolling in their sockets. They would not move, unless he commanded it, and they would not let anyone take the books they carried without a fight. He hefted his staff and stroked the cat, which made a sound that might have been a growl.

Someone – something – was coming. He could feel it, like a black wave rolling towards the shoreline, gathering strength as it came. Arkhan glanced down at his followers. '*Wait here,*' he said. '*Do not interfere.*'

'Interfere with what?' Ogiers demanded as he clambered to his feet. 'Where are you going?'

'*To parley with the master of this sad realm,*' Arkhan said as he strode towards the bridge. '*If you value your insignificant lives, I'd draw as little attention to yourself as possible.*' He walked across the bridge, ignoring Ogiers's shouts, and stopped at the halfway point. Then he set his staff, and waited. He did not have to wait long. The sound of hooves gouging the ground reached him several minutes later, and then a steed of bone and black magic, bearing a rider clad in flamboyant armour, burst into view, trailing smoke and cold flame. At the sight of it, the cat curled about his shoulders went stiff, and it hissed.

The rider hauled on his reins, causing the skeleton horse to rear. Its hooves slammed down on the stone of the bridge, and it went as still as death. Its rider rose high in his saddle and said, 'It has been some time since I last saw you, liche.'

'*I have counted the years, vampire.*' Arkhan scratched his cat's chin. '*Have you come to surrender?*'

Mannfred von Carstein threw his head back and unleashed a snarl of laughter. Overhead, the sky trembled in sympathy. 'Surrender? To a fleshless vagabond? It is you who should prostrate yourself before me.'

'*I have not come to bend knee, but to reclaim that which is mine by right.*'

Mannfred's sneer faded into a scowl. 'And what might that be?'

Arkhan held up his hand, fingers extended. As he spoke, he bent his fingers one by one. '*A crown, a severed hand, and seven books of blood-inked flesh.*' He cocked his head. '*You know of what I speak.*'

Mannfred grimaced. 'And why should I yield these artefacts to you?'

'*Nagash must rise,*' Arkhan said, simply.

'And so he shall. The matter is in good hands, I assure you,' Mannfred said. 'Go back to the desert, liche. I will call for you, if I should require your help.'

'*I am here now,*' Arkhan intoned, spreading his arms. '*And you seem to be in need of help. Or have you discovered a way of freeing your land from the chains that bind it and trap you?*'

'That is no business of yours,' Mannfred snarled.

'*That is up for discussion, I think,*' Arkhan said. He held out a hand. '*Nagash must rise, leech. Nagash will rise, even if I must destroy this blighted land to accomplish it. That is my curse and my pleasure. But he has always held some affection for your kind. If you serve him, perhaps he will let you keep your little castle.*' Arkhan cocked his head. '*It is a very pretty castle, I am given to understand.*'

Mannfred was silent, but Arkhan could feel the winds of death stirring as the vampire gathered his will. The air seemed to congeal and then fracture as Mannfred flung out his hand. A bolt of writhing shadow erupted from his palm and speared towards

Arkhan. The liche made no attempt to move aside. Instead, he waited. A freezing, tearing darkness erupted around him in a squirming cloud as the bolt struck home. If he had still possessed flesh, it would have been flayed from his bones. As it was, it merely tore his cloak and cowl. The cat on his shoulder yowled, and Arkhan gestured negligently, dispersing the cold tendrils of shadow.

Arkhan laughed hollowly. '*Is that it?*'

'Not even remotely,' Mannfred snarled.

More spells followed the first, and Arkhan deflected them all and returned them with interest. Incantations he had not uttered in centuries passed through his fleshless jaws as he pitted his sorceries against those of the lord of Sylvania... and found them wanting. Arkhan felt a flicker of surprise. Mannfred was more powerful than he'd thought. In his skull, his master's chuckle echoed. Was this a test then, to separate the wheat from the chaff?

Dark sorceries and eldritch flames met above the bridge between them for long hours, crashing together like the duelling waves of a storm-tossed sea. Cold fire bit at writhing shadows, and black lightning struck bastions of hardened air, as the muddy turf of the riverbanks began to heave and rupture, releasing the tormented dead. Bodies long buried staggered and slumped into the guttering river, splashing towards one another. More skeletons, clad in roots and mud, crawled onto the bridge and groped for Arkhan as he batted aside Mannfred's spells. The cat warbled and leapt from his shoulder to crash into a skeleton, knocking it backwards.

He ignored the others as they clawed at him. There were few forces that could move him once he had set himself. The biting, clawing dead were no more a threat to him than leaves cast in his face by a strong breeze. Nonetheless, they were a distraction; likely that was Mannfred's intent. It was certainly Arkhan's, as he directed his corpse-puppets to attack Mannfred.

The vampire smashed the dead aside with careless blows and hurled spells faster than Arkhan could follow, hammering him with sorcerous blows that would have obliterated a lesser opponent. The stone beneath his feet bubbled and cracked. It had survived a weathering of centuries, and now it was crumbling beneath the onslaught. Arkhan was beginning to wonder if he was going to suffer the same fate. He could feel his defences beginning to buckle beneath the unyielding onslaught. Mannfred's power seemed inexhaustible; vampires were reservoirs of dark magic, but even they had their limits – limits that Mannfred seemed to have shed. Where was he drawing his power from? Some artefact or... Arkhan laughed, suddenly. Of course.

Mannfred had sealed off Sylvania, blocking the sun and the rivers and the borders. Such a working would require some source of mystical power. Mannfred was drawing on those same magics now, and it gave him a distinct advantage. But, such a resource, while advantageous, was not infinite.

Certain now that he had his foeman's measure, Arkhan redoubled his efforts. If he could force Mannfred's hand, he might be able to simply outlast him. Sorcerous talons and bone-stripping winds lashed at him, but he held firm, his hands clasped around his staff. Overhead, the clouds swirled and contracted. Fire washed over him, and a thousand, thudding fists, which struck at him from every side. Wailing ghosts and serpentine shadows sought to drag him down, but Arkhan refused to fall. He sent no more spells hurtling towards his foe, instead bolstering the dead who fought at his behest.

Mannfred was howling with laughter, and Arkhan could feel the weight of the mighty magics that thrummed around the vampire, waiting to be unleashed. As Mannfred gathered them to him, the words to a powerful incantation dropping from his writhing lips, Arkhan readied himself.

Nevertheless, the first shaft of sunlight was as much a surprise to him as it was to Mannfred. It burst from the clouds high above and struck the bridge between them. The latter's skeleton mount reared and hurled him from his saddle. Arkhan staggered as the pressure of his enemy's magic faded. The expression on Mannfred's face as he clambered to his feet was almost comical. The vampire looked up, eyes wide and hastily released the murderous energies he had been preparing to hurl at Arkhan back into the aether. The clouds roiled and the sunlight was once more choked off by the darkness.

'*Well, that was an amusing diversion,*' Arkhan rasped. He started across the bridge. '*Are you prepared to listen to reason now?*'

Mannfred shrieked like a beast of prey, and drew his blade. Without pause, the vampire leapt at him. Arkhan drew his tomb-blade and blocked Mannfred's diving blow in a single movement. The two blades, each infused with the darkest of magics, gave out a communal cry of steel on steel as they connected, and cold fire blazed at the juncture of their meeting. Mannfred dropped to the bridge in a crouch before springing instantly to his feet. He sprinted towards Arkhan, his sword looping out. This too Arkhan parried, and they weaved back and forth over the bridge, the screams of their swords echoing for miles in either direction. Overhead, the sky growled in agitation, and the noisome wind swept down with a howl.

Below them, in the mud and stagnant water, the dead fought on, straining against one another in a parody of the duel their masters fought above them. Arkhan could feel Mannfred's will pressing against his own. He'd foregone magic, save that little bit required to control the dead. Their battle was as much for mastery of the warring corpses below as it was against each other. The vampire came at him again, teeth bared in a silent, feral snarl. His form flickered and wavered as he moved, like a scrap of gossamer caught in a wind storm. A living man would have found it impossible to follow the vampire's movements, but Arkhan had long since traded in his mortal eyes for something greater.

He matched Mannfred blow for blow. It felt... good, to engage in swordplay once more. It had been centuries since his blade had been drawn for anything other than emphasis or as an implement of ritual. The ancient tomb-blade shivered in his hand as it connected again with Mannfred's. The embers of old skills flared to life in the depths of Arkhan's mind, and he recalled those first few desperate battles, where a gambler's skill in back-alley brawls was put to the test by warriors whose names still lingered in legend. It was good to be reminded of that time, of when he had still been a man, rather than a tool forged by the will of another.

Arkhan wondered if Mannfred knew what that was like. He thought so. The vampire's magics had that taste, and his voice was like the echo of another's, though he knew it not. Arkhan could almost see a familiar shape superimposed over his opponent, a vast, black, brooding shadow that seemed to roil with amusement as they fought.

I see you, Arkhan thought. This was a test and a pleasure for the thing that held the chains of their souls. Arkhan's master had ever been a sadist and prone to cruel whimsy. This battle had been a farce, a shadow-play from the beginning. There was a power in that knowledge. A power in knowing exactly how little of it you yourself possessed. It allowed you to focus, to look past the ephemeral, and to marshal within yourself what little will your master allowed.

Arkhan the Black was a slave, but a slave who knew every link of the chain that bound him by heart. Mannfred had yet to realise that he had even been beaten. Their blades clashed again and again until, at last, Arkhan beat the vampire's sword aside and swiftly stepped back, his now-sodden and torn robes slapping wetly against his bare bones.

'*We are finished here, vampire.*'

Mannfred's eyes burned with rage, and for a moment, Arkhan thought he might continue the fight. Then, with a hiss, Mannfred

inclined his head and sheathed his sword with a grandiose flourish. 'We are, liche. A truce?'

Arkhan would have smiled, had he still had lips. '*Of course.
A truce.*'

FOUR

 Heldenhame Keep, Talabecland

'The problem isn't getting in. It's just a wall, and walls can be breached, scaled and blown down,' Hans Leitdorf, Grand Master of the Knights of Sigmar's Blood said, glaring at the distant edifice, which towered along the border of Sylvania. That it was visible from such a distance was as much due to its sheer enormity as to the height of the parapet he and his guests stood atop. 'It's what's waiting on the other side. They've had months to erect defences, set traps and build an army out of every scrap of bone and sinew in Sylvania. And that's not even taking into account the things slipping over the border every night to bolster the cursed von Carstein's ranks. Strigany nomads, strange horsemen, beasts and renegades of every dark stripe.' He knocked back a slug from the goblet he held in one hand. Leitdorf was old but, like some old men, had only grown harder and tougher with age. He was broad and sturdily built, with a barrel chest and a face that had seen the wrong end of a club more than once. He wore a heavy fur coat of the sort Ungol horsemen were fond of, and had his sword belt cinched around his narrow waist. 'We've tried to stop them, but we're too few. I don't have enough men to do more than put up a token effort. And when I ask for more men from the elector and Karl Franz, I get, well, you.' He looked at his guest.

Captain Wendel Volker gave no sign that Leitdorf's insult had struck home. The fourth son of a largely undistinguished Talabecland family tree, he hadn't expected a man like Leitdorf to be happy with his arrival. His uniform was still coated in trail-grime, and he shivered beneath his thin officer's cloak. It was cold up on the parapet, and it had been a wet trip. Volker was young, with a duellist's build and a boy's enthusiasm. The latter was swiftly being sapped by the circumstances of his current posting, but, as his father had said on multiple occasions, one mustn't complain.

'Oh he's not so bad, is our young Wendel. He guarded me ably enough on the road from Talabheim,' the third man on the parapet rumbled, as he stroked his spade-shaped red beard with thick, beringed fingers. He was a big man, like Leitdorf, though his size had more to do with ample food supply than anything else, Volker thought. There was muscle there, too, but it was well padded. Despite that, he was the most dangerous of the three men on the parapet. Or, possibly, in the entire keep. 'Able, aristocratic, attentive, slightly alcoholic... All virtues as far as I'm concerned,' the third man went on, winking cheerfully at Volker.

'You hardly needed an escort,' Leitdorf said. 'The Patriarch of the Bright College is an army unto himself. There are few who would challenge Thyrus Gormann.'

'I know of one,' Gormann grunted, tugging on his beard. He waved a hand and, for a moment, a trail of flickering flame marked the motion of his fingers. 'Still, neither here nor there, all in the past, all friends now, hey?' He scratched his nose and peered at the distant wall of bone that separated Sylvania from Imperial justice. 'That is one fine, big wall the little flea has erected for himself, I must admit.'

'The little flea,' Volker knew, was Mannfred von Carstein. Even thinking the name caused him to shudder. Still, on the whole, it was better than going north with the rest of the lads. He'd take the dead over daemons any day. Nonetheless, he couldn't repress a second shudder when he looked at the distant wall. He caught Leitdorf looking at him and stiffened his spine. As terrifying as Mannfred von Carstein was, he was over there, and Leitdorf, unfortunately, was right here. Leitdorf snorted and turned back to Gormann.

'Volkmar isn't coming back,' he said.

'Did you think he would?' Gormann asked. 'No, he'd have torn those walls down if he'd been able. It was a fool's errand, and he knew it.'

'He had to try,' Leitdorf said softly.

'No, he bloody didn't.' Gormann shook his shaggy head. 'He let his anger blind him, and now we have to muddle through without him. Stubborn old fool.'

'Friend pot, have you met cousin kettle?' Leitdorf asked.

Gormann looked at the knight and frowned, but only for a moment. He guffawed and shook his head. 'I always forget that you have a sense of humour buried under that scowl, Hans.'

Volker watched as the two men – two of the most powerful, if not influential, in the Empire – continued to discuss the unpleasantness just across the border and decided, for the fifth time in as many minutes, to keep his opinions to himself, just as his mother had counselled. 'Keep quiet, head down, ears perked, nose to the trail,' she'd said. A hunting metaphor, of course. Big one for hunting was mumsy, big one for the blood sports and the trophies and such.

Blood had always made Volker queasy. He licked his lips and looked longingly at the jug of mulled wine that Leitdorf clutched loosely in one hand. Occasionally, the Grand Master would refill his goblet, or Gormann's. Volker had not been offered so much as a taste. Another snub, of course. A sign of his new commander's displeasure. Mustn't complain, he thought.

As the wizard and the warrior conversed, Volker kept himself occupied by examining his new post from the view the parapet afforded. He'd heard stories of Heldenhame as a boy, but to see it in the flesh, as it were, was something else again.

At its inception, Heldenhame had been little more than a modest bastion, composed of a stone tower and a wooden palisade. Now, however, a century later, Heldenhame Keep was the grandest fortress in Talabecland. The old stone tower had been torn down and replaced by a castle that was many times larger, and the wooden palisade had been discarded in favour of heavy stone walls. Within the walls and spreading outwards from the castle was a bustling city, filled with noise and commerce. It was a grand sight, for all that it still bore the marks of the greenskin tide that had sought to overwhelm it the year previous.

The western wall was still under repair from that incident. Volker watched the distant dots of workmen reinforcing and repairing the still-crippled span. It was the only weak point in the fortress's defences, but such repairs couldn't be rushed. Volker knew that much from his studies. As he examined the wall, he saw what looked to be a tavern near it. His thirst returned and he licked his lips. 'Worried about the western span, captain?' Leitdorf asked, suddenly. Volker, shaken from his reverie, looked around guiltily.

'Ah, no, sir, Grand Master,' he said hastily, trying to recall what sort of salute one gave the commander of a knightly order. Leitdorf gazed at him disdainfully.

'You should be,' he grunted. 'You'll be stationed there. You're dismissed, Volker. I trust you can find your quarters and introduce yourself to the garrison without me holding your hand?'

'Ah, yes, I believe so, sir. Grand Master,' Volker said. Leitdorf turned, and Volker, relieved and dying for a drink, scurried away.

Karak Kadrin, Worlds Edge Mountains

Ungrim Ironfist, king of Karak Kadrin, ran his thick, scarred fingers across the map of beaten bronze and gilded edges that lay before him on the stone table. The map was a thing of painstaking artifice and careful craftsmanship, and it was as lovely in its way as any silken tapestry or a portrait done by a master's hand.

Ironfist, in contrast, was a thing of slabs and edges and could, in no way, shape or form be called lovely. Even for a dwarf, the Slayer King was built on the heavy side, his thick bones weighed down by layers of hard-earned muscle, and his face like a granite shelf carved sharply and suddenly by an avalanche. His beard and hair were dyed a startling red and, as ever, he wore a heavy cloak of dragon-scale over his broad shoulders.

His craggy features settled into a taciturn expression as he stared at the map. It wasn't alone on the table. There were others stacked in a neat pile near to hand, and opposite them a number of metal tubes, containing statements and reports culled from every watch-post and lookout tower for a hundred miles in every direction. Ironfist had read them all and more than once. So often, in fact, that he knew what each one said by heart.

More reports were added by the day, as rangers and merchants brought word to the Slayer Keep from the furthest edges of the dwarf empire. These too Ironfist committed to memory. None of what he learned was comforting.

There was a strange murk upon the dust-winds that rolled west from the Dark Lands over the eastern mountains, and the sky over that foul land was rent by sickly trails of green, as if the moon were weeping poisonous tears upon the blighted sores that covered the skin of the world. Plagues such as the world had not seen in a thousand years were loose in the lands of men, and worse things than plagues, too. Devils and beasts ran riot in the Empire, and traders returning from Tilea, Estalia and Araby brought word that it was just as bad in those lands. The vile rat-things had burst from their tunnels in unprecedented numbers, and subsumed whole city-states and provinces in the same way they had the holds of his people so long ago.

The Badlands were full to bursting of greenskins; the clangour of the battles fought between the orc tribes carried for miles in all directions, and as soon as one ended, another began. Soon, as was inevitable, they would flood into the mountains and the lands beyond, hunting for new enemies. But this time they would do so in unprecedented numbers: in their millions, rather than their thousands.

However, that was as nothing compared to word from the north, where strange lights writhed across the horizon and arcane storms raged across the lands. Daemon packs hunted the high places and barbarians gathered in the valleys as long-dormant volcanoes belched smoke and the earth shook as if beneath the tread of phantom armies.

Ironfist had, in all his centuries, never witnessed such a multitude of troubles, all occurring at once. Bad times came and went, like storms. They washed across the mountains and faded away with the seasons. But this was like several storms, rising and boiling together all at once, as if to wipe away the world. He shook his head, trying to clear his thoughts of the miasma of foreboding that clung to them.

Ironfist tapped a point on the map. 'What word from the Sylvanian border? Are the rumours true?' he asked the dwarf sitting across from him. Snorri Thungrimsson had served at his king's right hand for more years than could be easily counted. He was old now, and the fat braids of beard that were tucked into the wide leather belt about his midsection were as white as the morning frost on the high mountain peaks. But he still served as his king's hearthwarden and senior advisor. It was Thungrimsson who collected and organised the diverse streams of information that came into the hold from messengers, scouts and spies, and readied it for Ironfist's study.

'You mean about the, ah, bones?' Thungrimsson asked, gesturing. He grimaced in distaste as he asked it.

'No, I mean about this year's turnip festival in Talabheim. Yes, the bones,' Ironfist said.

'They're true enough. The whole land is surrounded by battlements of bone. It's sealed off tighter than King Thorgrim's vaults.' Thungrimsson traced the border of Sylvania on the map. 'The rangers can't find a way through, not that they tried very hard.'

Ironfist sat back in his chair with a sigh. He tugged on his beard and let his gaze drift across the high alcoves of the library, where the watery light of hooded lanterns illuminated stone shelves and pigeonholes, each one stuffed with books, tomes, scrolls and papyri. The library was one of his great pleasures, when all was said and done. It had been built carefully and over centuries, much like the rest of Karak Kadrin. 'Well, what are you thinking, hearthwarden?' he asked finally, looking back at Thungrimsson.

'It is a shame about the turnip festival,' Thungrimsson said. Ironfist growled wordlessly and the other dwarf raised his hands in a placating gesture. 'I'm thinking that Sylvania has been a boil on our hindquarters for more centuries than I care to contemplate. Whatever is going on in there bears keeping an eye on, if nothing else. And we should send word to the other holds, especially Zhufbar. The blood-drinkers have attacked them before.'

Ironfist gnawed on a thumbnail. Every instinct he possessed screamed at him to muster a throng and smash his way into that blighted land, axe in hand. There was something on the air, something that pricked at him, like a warning only half heard. There were other threats to be weighed and measured, but Sylvania was right on his hearthstone. He had been patient for centuries, waiting for the humans to see to their own mess. But the time for patience had long since passed. If the *zanguzaz* – the blood-drinkers – were up to some mischief, Ironfist was inclined to put a stop to it soonest.

His eye caught a golden seal on one of the more recently arrived message tubes. He recognised the royal rune of Karaz-a-Karak, the Pinnacle of the Mountains, the Most Enduring. He flicked the tube open and extracted the scroll within. He frowned as he read it. When he was done, he tossed it to Thungrimsson. 'We'll have to settle for keeping watch. At least for now. The Grudge-bearer has called together the Council of Kings.'

Thungrimsson's eyes widened in surprise as he read the scroll. 'Such a council hasn't been convened in centuries,' he said slowly. His eyes flickered to the scrolls and maps. He met Ironfist's grim gaze. 'It's worse than we thought, isn't it?'

Ironfist pushed himself slowly to his feet. He tapped the map again. 'It seems I'll be able to alert my brother-kings as to the goings-on in Sylvania in person,' he said softly.

🝓 *Lothern, Ulthuan*

Tyrion's palms struck the doors of the meeting chamber of the Phoenix Council like battering rams, sending them swinging inwards with a thunderous crash. Eltharion of Yvresse winced and made to hurry after his prince.

The latter's haste was understandable, if not strictly advisable. Then, the Warden of Tor Yvresse had never been fond of haste. Haste led to the mistakes and mistakes to defeat. A slim hand fastened on his arm. 'Give him a moment. He's making an entrance.'

'That's what I'm afraid of, Eldyra,' Eltharion grated, brushing the hand from his arm. He turned to glare at the woman who followed him. Eldyra of Tiranoc had once been Tyrion's squire; now she was a warrior in her own right, albeit an impetuous one. She was a vision of loveliness wrapped in lethality. She had learned the art of death from the foremost warrior of their race, and her skill with blade, bow and spear was equal to, or greater than, Eltharion's own, though they had never put that to the test.

'No, you're afraid he's going to kill someone.'

'And you're not?'

'Better to ask whether I care,' she said pointedly. 'The idea of our prince taking off the head of that pompous nitwit Imrik fills me with a warm and cheerful glow.'

Eltharion shook his head and followed Tyrion into the council chamber. Tyrion had interrupted the aforementioned Imrik, Dragon Prince of Caledor, in mid-speech. The Phoenix Council had been discussing the same thing they'd been discussing for months – namely Imrik's assertion that Finubar had ceded his right to the Phoenix Crown.

The Phoenix Council had been paralysed for months by disagreement among its members and disillusionment with the current wearer of the crown. Finubar had sealed himself in the Heavenlight Tower in order to divine the cause of the recent disasters that had beset Ulthuan, at a time when his people most needed his guidance. Eltharion could not help but wonder what was going through his king's mind; the longer Finubar sat isolated in his tower, the more that discontent spread through the halls and meeting chambers of the elven nobility. As Chrace and Cothique were overrun by daemon-spawn, and their peoples scattered or exterminated, Finubar had yet to reappear, and had, so far, allowed only one to impinge upon his solitude – Tyrion's brother Teclis. Teclis had come out of that meeting certain that Tyrion must take command of Ulthuan's armies.

Tyrion, however, had taken some convincing. Not that Eltharion blamed him for being preoccupied. He and his companions had only just returned from the citadel of abomination known as Nagashizzar, where they'd failed to rescue Aliathra, firstborn daughter of the Everqueen, from her captor, Mannfred von Carstein. Aliathra had been captured earlier in the year by the vampire while she had been on a diplomatic mission to the High King of the dwarfs at Karaz-a-Karak. Dwarfs and elves both had been slaughtered by Mannfred in pursuit of Aliathra, and when word reached Ulthuan of her fate, Tyrion had been driven into as wild a rage as Eltharion had ever seen.

The reason for the sheer force of that rage was known to only two others, besides Eltharion himself. Eldyra was one and Teclis the other. The three of them shared the weight of Tyrion's shameful secret, and when he'd made it known that he intended to rescue Aliathra, Eltharion, Eldyra and Teclis had accompanied him. But the expedition to Nagashizzar had been a failure. Mannfred had escaped again, and taken the Everchild with him.

Teclis's spies, both living and elemental, had confirmed that the vampire had taken Aliathra into the lands of men, and Belannaer, Loremaster of Hoeth, had sworn that he could hear the Everchild's voice upon the wind, calling from somewhere within the foul demesne known as Sylvania. Failure ate at Tyrion like an acid, making it impossible for him to focus on anything else. He had been planning for a second expedition when Teclis had forced him to see sense. Now his rage at Aliathra's fate had been refocused, and for the better, Eltharion hoped.

'Our lands are in turmoil, and you sit here arguing over who has the right to lead, rather than doing anything productive. No wonder the Phoenix King hides himself away – I would as well, had my advisors and servants shamed me as you now shame him,' Tyrion said as he stalked into the chamber, the stones echoing with the crash of the doors. Clad in full armour, armed and flanked by the armoured forms of Eltharion and Eldyra, the heir of Aenarion was an intimidating sight. At least if you had any sense.

'Ulthuan needs leadership. Finubar is not fit to be king. Not now, not when we are on the precipice of the long night,' Imrik growled. He glared at Tyrion as fiercely as one of the dragons his homeland was famous for. 'Speaking of which, where were you? First Finubar locks himself away in his tower, and then the Everqueen vanishes to gods alone know where. The Ten Kingdoms heave with the plague of ages and you, our greatest champion, were half a world away!'

'I am here now,' Tyrion said. He drew his sword, Sunfang, from its sheath and swept it through the air. The ancient sword, forged to draw the blood of the daemons of Chaos, burned with the captured fires of the sun. Runes glowed white-hot along its length and the closest members of the council turned away or shaded their eyes against the sword's stinging promise. Only Imrik continued to glare, undaunted.

Tyrion looked at the council, his eyes blazing with a heat equal to that which marked the runes on his sword. 'You will cease your nattering. You will take up blade and bow as befitting lords of Ulthuan, and marshal your forces to defend the Ten Kingdoms. Any who wish to quarrel further can take up their argument with the edge of my sword and see what it profits you.'

Imrik shot to his feet and slammed his fist down on the table. 'How dare you?' the Dragon Prince roared. 'What gives you the right to speak to this august council in such a disrespectful manner? We are your betters, whelp! Who are you to demand anything of us?'

Tyrion smiled humourlessly. 'Who am I? I am the Herald of Asuryan, and of the Phoenix King, in whose names I would dare anything. That is all the right I require.' He pointed Sunfang at Imrik and asked, 'Unless you disagree?'

Imrik's pale features tightened and his lean body quivered with barely restrained rage. 'I do,' he hissed. He circled the table and strode past Tyrion. 'Strike me down if you dare, boy, but I'll not stay here and be barked at by you.'

Tyrion did not turn as Imrik stalked past him. 'If you leave, prince of Caledor, then do not expect to be included in our councils of war. Caledor will stand alone,' he said harshly.

Imrik stopped. Eltharion saw his eyes close, as if he were in pain. Then, his voice ragged, he said, 'Then Caledor stands alone.' Imrik left the chamber without another word. No one tried to stop him. The remaining council-members whispered quietly amongst themselves. Eltharion looked at them and frowned. Already, they were plotting. Imrik's star had been in the ascendancy, and now it had plummeted to earth. Those who had supported him were revising their positions as those who had been arrayed against him moved to shore up their influence. None of them seemed to grasp the full extent of the situation.

He saw Tyrion looking at him. The latter crooked a finger and Eltharion and Eldyra moved to join him.

'Thank you for watching my back,' Tyrion said quietly. 'But now that the council has been tamed, I need you two to do as you promised. Make ready, gather what you need for the expedition, and set sail as soon as possible.' His composure evaporated as he spoke, and his words became ragged. Eltharion could see just how much it was costing his friend to stay in Ulthuan. There was pain in his eyes and in his voice such as Eltharion had never seen.

'You have my oath as Warden of Tor Yvresse,' Eltharion said softly. He hesitated, and then placed a hand on his friend's shoulder. He looked at Eldyra, who nodded fiercely. 'We shall rescue Aliathra, or we will die trying.'

La Maisontaal Abbey, Bretonnia

The three men descended down the dank, circular stone steps, following the woman. She held a crackling torch in one hand, and its light cast weird shadows on the stone walls of the catacombs. 'The abbey was built to contain that which I am about to show you,' the woman said, her voice carrying easily, despite the softness with which she spoke. 'Rites and rituals went into the placement of every stone and every slather of mortar to make this place a fitting cage for what is imprisoned here. And so it has remained, for hundreds of years.'

'But now?' one of the men asked. They reached the bottom of the stairs and came to a vaulted chamber, which was empty save for a wide, squat stone sarcophagus the likes of which none of the men had ever seen. It had been marked with mystical signs, and great iron chains crossed it, as if to keep whatever was within it trapped. The woman lifted her torch and let its light play across the sarcophagus.

'Now, I fear, we are coming to the end of its captivity. Something is loose in the world, a red wind that carries with it the promise of a slaughter undreamt of by even the most monstrous of creatures that infest our poor, tired land. Or those of its greatest heroes, Tancred of Quenelles.'

'This is what he was after,' Tancred, Duke of Quenelles, said staring at the stone sarcophagus. His breath plumed in the damp, chill air. Part of him yearned to touch the sarcophagus, while a greater part surged in revulsion at the thought. The thing that lay inside seemed to draw everything towards it, as though it weighed more than the world around it. Tancred felt the weight of his years settle more heavily than ever before on his broad shoulders. 'This is what Arkhan the Black was after, then, my Lady Elynesse?'

'Perhaps,' Lady Elynesse, Dowager of Charnorte, said. Her voice was soft, but not hesitant. She was older than even Tancred, whose hair and beard had long since lost the lustre of youth, though her face was unlined and unmarred by time. 'Such a creature weaves schemes within schemes, and concocts plots with every day it yet remains unburied.' She held her torch higher and circled the sarcophagus. 'This could be but one goal amongst many.'

'What is it?' one of the others asked. His hands were clamped tightly around the hilt of his blade. Tancred wondered whether the other knight felt the same pull towards the sarcophagus as he did. Though Fastric Ghoulslayer was a native of Bordeleaux, he had shed blood beside Tancred and the third knight, Anthelme of Austray, in defence of Quenelles in the civil war. The Ghoulslayer was a warrior of renown and commanded a skylance of Pegasus knights, and there were few whom Tancred trusted more.

'Whatever it is, I'd just as soon it stays in there,' Anthelme said nervously.

'And so it shall, if we have anything to say about it,' Tancred said, looking at his cousin. Anthelme, like Fastric, was a trusted companion, even beyond the bounds of blood. There were none better with a lance or blade in Tancred's opinion. 'Our kingdom lies broken and bleeding, and the one who struck that blow will return to capitalise on our weakness. The Dowager has seen as much. Arkhan the Black wanted this sarcophagus and its contents, even as the Lichemaster did in decades past. But we shall see to it that La Maisontaal's burden remains here, in these tombs, even if we must die to do so.'

'But surely whatever is in here is no danger to us? The true king has returned. Gilles le Breton sits once more upon the throne of Bretonnia, and the civil war is over. We have passed through the darkest of times and come out the other side,' Anthelme said. Those sentiments were shared by many, Tancred knew. When Louen Leoncouer had been felled at the Battle of Quenelles by his treacherous bastard son, many, including Tancred, had thought that the kingdom's time was done.

Then had come Couronne, and Mallobaude's last challenge. The Serpent had challenged the greatest knights in the land on Quenelles, Gisoreux, Adelaix and a hundred more battlefields, and had emerged victorious every time. But at Couronne, it was no mortal who answered his challenge; instead, the legendary Green Knight had ridden out of the ranks, appearing as if from nowhere, and had met Mallobaude on the field between the armies of the living and the dead. In the aftermath, when the surviving dukes and lords inevitably began to turn their thoughts to the vacant throne, the Green Knight had torn his emerald helm from his head and revealed himself to be none other than Gilles le Breton, the founder of the realm, come back to lead his people in their darkest hour. The problem was, as far as Tancred could tell, the darkest hour hadn't yet passed. In fact, it appeared that Mallobaude's rebellion had only been the beginning of Bretonnia's ruination, the return of the once and future king or not.

'And so? Daemons still stalk our lands, and monsters burn the vineyards and villages. Mallobaude might have lost his head, but he wasn't the only traitor. Quenelles is in ruins, as are half of the other provinces, and home to two-legged beasts. Borde-leaux is gone, replaced by a daemonic keep of brass and bone that even now blights the surrounding lands. No, we are in the eye of the storm, cousin. The false calm, before its fury strikes again, redoubled and renewed. I fear that things will get much, much worse before it passes,' Tancred said firmly. He looked around. 'Come, I would leave this place.'

He led them back up the stairs and out of the abbey, ignoring the huddled masses of peasants, who genuflected and murmured respectful greetings. More and more of them came every day, seeking the dubious sanctuary of the abbey's walls as the forests seethed with beasts and the restless dead, and the sky blazed with blue fire or was split by the fiery passage of warpstone meteors.

As they got outside, Tancred gulped the fresh, cold air. It was a relief, after the damp unpleasantness of the catacombs, and the close air of the abbey, redolent with the odour of the lower classes. He looked about him. His father, the first to bear the name of Tancred, had funded the fortifying of the abbey in the wake of the Lichemaster's infamous assault some thirty years earlier. The Eleventh Battle of La Maisontaal Abbey had been a pivotal moment in both the history of his family and Bretonnia as a whole.

The fortifications weren't as grand as Tancred's father had dreamed, but they were serviceable enough. There were garrison quarters, housing hundreds of archers and men-at-arms, as well as scores of knights, drawn from every corner of Bretonnia. The abbey sat in the centre of an army.

Somehow, he doubted that would be enough.

He turned as he heard a loud voice bellow a greeting. The broad, burly form of Duke Theoderic of Brionne ambled towards him, his battle-axe resting on his shoulder. 'Ho, Tancred! They told me you were slinking about. Come to inspect the troops, eh?' Theoderic had a voice that could stun one of the great bats that haunted the Vaults at twenty paces. He was also the commander of the muster of La Maisontaal. He'd come to the abbey seeking penance for a life of lechery, drunkenness and other assorted unchivalric behaviours, and had, according to most, more than made up for his past as a sozzle-wit.

They clasped forearms, and Tancred winced as Theoderic drew him into a bear hug. 'I see that the Lady Elynesse is here as well,' he murmured as he released Tancred. He jerked his chin towards the Dowager, who swept past them towards her waiting carriage. She had come to show them what was hidden. Now, having done so, she was leaving as quickly as possible. Tancred couldn't blame her. Lacking even the tiniest inclination to sorcery, he could still feel the spiritual grime of the thing that lurked in the depths of the abbey. He could only imagine what it must be like for a true servant of the Lady. 'Has she foreseen trouble for us?'

'Arkhan the Black,' Tancred said.

'I thought we sent him packing, didn't we?' Theoderic grunted.

'Do such creatures ever stay gone for as long as we might wish?'

'Ha! You have me there. Never fear, though – if he comes, we'll be ready for him,' Theoderic said, cradling his axe in the crook of his arm. 'Some of the greatest heroes of our fair kingdom are here. Gioffre of Anglaron, the slayer of the dragon Scaramor, Taurin the Wanderer, dozens of others. Knights of the realm, one and all. A truer gathering of heroes has never been seen in these lands, save at the court of the king himself!'

Tancred looked at Theoderic's beaming features and gave a half-hearted nod. 'Let's pray to the Lady that will be enough,' he said.

 Somewhere south of Quenelles, Bretonnia

The voices of the Dark Gods thundered in his ears and Malagor brayed in pleasure as his muscles swelled with strength. He snapped the gor chieftain's neck with a single, vicious jerk, and snorted as he sent the body thudding to the loamy earth. He spread his arms and his great, black pinioned wings snapped out to their full length. Then, he looked about him at the gathered chieftains. 'Split-Hoof challenged. Split-Hoof died. Who else challenges the Crowfather?' he bellowed. 'Who else challenges the word of the gods?'

None of the remaining chieftains stepped forward. In truth, Split-Hoof hadn't so much challenged him as he had voiced a concern, but Malagor saw little difference between dissension and discomfort. Neither was acceptable. The gods had commanded, and their children would obey, whether they were inclined to do so or not. He snarled and pawed the ground with a hoof, glaring about him to ram the point home. Only when the chieftains looked sufficiently cowed did he allow them to look away from him. They wouldn't stay cowed for long, he knew. The children of Chaos did not have it in them to be docile, even when it served the gods' purpose. In their veins was the blood of the gods and it was ever angry and ambitious. Soon, another chieftain would voice dissent, and he would have to fight again.

His goatish lips peeled back from yellowed fangs. Malagor looked forward to such challenges. Without them, there was no joy in life. Taking the life of an enemy with the sorceries that hummed in his bones was satisfying, in its way, but there was no substitute for feeling bone crack and splinter in his grip, or tasting the flesh and blood of an opponent.

Malagor folded his wings and looked about him as he idly stroked the symbols of blasphemy that hung from his matted mane and leather harness. Icons plucked from the bodies of human priests dangled beside twists of paper torn from their holy books, all of them stained and soiled and consecrated to the gods, who even now whispered endearments to him as he pondered his next move.

The forest clearing around him echoed with the raucous rumble of savage anarchy. Beastmen yelped and howled as they danced to the sound of drums and fought about the great witch-fires, which burned throughout the clearing. All of this beneath the glistening gaze of the titanic monolith that had sprouted from the churned earth months earlier. The strange black stone was shot through by jagged veins of sickly, softly glimmering green, and it pulsed in time to the thudding of the drums.

Ever since the dark moon had waxed full in the sky, and the great herdstones had risen from their slumber beneath the ground, so too had the voices of the gods hummed in his mind, stronger than ever before. And they had had much to say to their favoured child. They had demanded that he join the beast-tribes south of the Grey Mountains, and lead them into war with a man of bone and black sorcery. But his fractious kin had been preoccupied with battling their hated enemies, the wood elves.

It had taken Malagor months to browbeat, bully and brutalise a number of tribes and herds into following him into the war-ravaged provinces of Bretonnia, only to find that his prey had already slipped over the mountains and into the north. But all was not lost. The gods had murmured that Arkhan would return. And that he would fall in Bretonnia. That was their command and their promise. The skeins of fate were pulled taut about the dead man, and there would be no escape for him again.

'The Bone-Man must die,' Malagor bellowed. 'The gods command it! Death to the dead! Gnaw their bones and suck the marrow!'

'Gnaw his bones,' a chieftain roared, shaking his crude blade over his horned head. Others took up the chant, one by one, and soon every beast in the clearing had added its voice to the cacophony.

Malagor's muscles bunched and he thrust himself into the air. His black wings flapped, catching the wind, causing the witch-fires to flicker, and bowling over the smaller beastmen. He screamed at the sky as he rose, adding his howls to those of his kin.

The liche would die, even if Malagor had to sacrifice every beastman on this side of the Grey Mountains to accomplish it. The Dark Gods demanded it, and Malagor was their word made flesh. He was the black edge of their blade, the tip of their tongue and their will made into harsh reality. He flapped his wings and rose high over the trees. Overhead the sky wept green tears and crawled with hideous shapes, and Malagor felt the blessings of his gods fill him with divine purpose. He roared again, this time in triumph.

Arkhan the Black would die.

 Near the King's Glade, Athel Loren

The gor squealed and staggered back, grasping at its sliced belly with blood-slick paws. Araloth, Lord of Talsyn, darted forward to deliver the deathblow before the beast recovered. The ravaged glade rang with the sound of blade on blade, and the death-cries of elves and beasts. Blood, both pure and foul, turned the churned soil beneath his feet to mud.

A shadow fell over him, while his sword sent the beastman's brutish head spinning from its thick neck. Araloth glanced up and saw a minotaur raising its axe over him, its bestial jaws dripping with bloody froth as it gnashed its fangs. Its eyes bulged from their sockets, and it whined and lowed in mindless greed. The minotaur stumped forward, reaching for him with its free hand. He tensed, ready to leap aside, a prayer to Lileath on his lips.

Then a second, equally massive shape slammed into the bull-headed giant from the side, bearing it to the ground. The two enormous figures ploughed through the fray that swirled about them, scattering elves and beasts alike as they smashed through the trees of the blood-soaked glade. Araloth could only watch in awe as Orion, the King in the Woods, rose over the fallen minotaur, a hand gripping one of its horns.

Orion dragged the dazed beast to its feet and locked his arm about its throat. He grabbed its horns and threw his weight to the side. The glade echoed with the crack of crude, Chaos-twisted bone, and then Orion threw down his opponent and let out a roar of victory that caused the trees to shiver where they stood.

The beastmen began to retreat, streaming back the way they had come, first in ones and twos, and then in a mad panic, bellowing and braying in fear. Orion put his horn to his lips and sounded a long, wailing note. Glade Riders galloped off in pursuit of their fleeing enemies. Orion met Araloth's gaze for only a moment, before turning away and loping after his huntsmen. Araloth shivered and sheathed his blade.

There had been nothing but rage in his king's eyes. Even sorrow had been burned away, and reason with it. Only the battle-madness remained.

Despite his fear, Araloth could find no fault in that. Ariel was dying, and the forest with her, and there was nothing Orion or anyone could do. He understood the king's rage better than most, for was he not the queen's champion? 'Much good I did her,' he murmured, looking about him. Every muscle in his body ached, and his hands trembled with fatigue. He had been fighting for days on end, trying to drive back this latest assault on the deep glades of the forest.

The source of the sickness that afflicted the Mage Queen was not readily apparent, but in its wake came a rot on the boughs of the Oak of Ages, and then a sickness that spread through the forest, twisting and tainting everything. Glades that had gone unaffected by the shifting seasons since the first turning of the world now withered, the trees cracking and splitting, their roots blistering and turning black as the forest floor heaved with decay. Madness swept through the ranks of the dryads and treemen, making dangerous, unpredictable enemies of ancient allies as the children of Chaos poured into these now-desolate glades in their thousands.

These were not the usual herds who perennially spent their blood beneath the forest canopy, but bray-spawn and mutant filth from hundreds of leagues away, migrating from every direction, as if drawn to the weakened forest by some unvoiced signal.

Araloth looked about him, at the piles of twisted bodies that littered the ground, and the pale, slim shapes that lay amongst them. No matter how many they killed, no matter how many times they repulsed them, the creatures continued to pour into the forest. He leaned forward on his blade, suddenly feeling more tired than he had in centuries. He wanted to sleep for a season, but there was no time for rest, let alone slumber.

He opened his eyes and began to clean his sword. There would be another attack. The king and his Wild Hunt might have driven off this one, but there were more herds in the vicinity, and all of them were moving towards the King's Glade. Eventually, they would get through. And when that happened...

He turned as he heard the thud of hooves, dismissing the dark thoughts. A rider burst into the glade, and headed for Araloth. The wood elf swung down out of her saddle and thrust the reins into Araloth's hands. He blinked in surprise. 'What–' he began.

'The council requires your presence, champion,' the rider gasped, breathing heavily, though whether in excitement or fear he couldn't say. 'The Eldest of the Ancients has awoken, and he speaks words of portent. You must go!'

Without further hesitation, Araloth swung up into the horse's saddle and dug his heels into its lathered flanks. The horse reared and pawed the air with its hooves before turning and galloping back the way it had come, carrying Araloth into the depths of the forest.

As he rode, he wondered why Durthu had chosen now to awaken, and whether it had anything to do with their visitor. Several months after Ariel had fallen ill, an intruder had somehow navigated the worldroots and penetrated the King's Glade. The newcomer had allowed the startled sentries, including

Araloth himself, to take her into custody and asked only that they grant her an audience with the Council of Athel Loren. Araloth, bemused, had agreed, if only because it wasn't every day that Alarielle, Everqueen of Ulthuan, visited Athel Loren.

His bemusement had faded when he had learned of her reasons for braving the dangers of the worldroots. The forest was dying, and it seemed that the world was dying with it. The balance of the Weave was shifting, and all that his folk had fought so long to prevent was at last coming to pass. The doom of all things was upon them, and no one could figure out a way to stop it. Araloth bent low over the horse's neck and urged it to greater speed.

But if Durthu had at last risen from his slumber, if the Eldest of the Ancients had decided to address the council, as he had done so infrequently in recent decades, then perhaps that doom could still be averted.

And perhaps the Mage Queen could still be saved.

Hvargir Forest, the Border Princes

'Die-die filthy man-thing!' Snikrat, hero of Clan Mordkin, shrieked as he fell out of the tree onto the panting messenger. The man – a youth, really – died as soon as the skaven struck him, the weight of the rat-thing landing on his neck and the bite of the cruel, saw-toothed blade the latter clutched, serving to tumble him into Morr's welcoming arms before he knew what was happening. Snikrat bounded to his feet, tail lashing, and whirled about excitedly, hunting for more foes.

Relief warred with disappointment when he saw nothing save the hurrying shapes of his Bonehides scrambling over the thick roots and between the close-set trees of Hvargir Forest. The clawband of black-furred stormvermin swarmed towards him, chittering in obsequious congratulations. Snikrat tore his blade free of the messenger's body and gesticulated at his warriors.

'What good are you if you cannot catch-quick one man-thing?' he snapped. 'It is a lucky thing that I was here, in this place where you see me, to dispose of the creature whose body I now stand on with this blade I hold in my paw.'

Beady black eyes slid away from his own bulging, red-veined ones, and the stink of nervous musk filled the immediate air as his warriors bunched together and the front ranks shuffled back. Snikrat knew that he cut an imposing figure. He was bigger than any two of his Bonehides put together, and clad in the finest armour warpstone could purchase. His blade had belonged to a dwarf thane, once upon a time, and though it had changed hands and owners several times since, it was still a deadly looking weapon, covered in dolorous runes and smeared with several foul-smelling unguents, which, to Snikrat's knowledge, did nothing – but better safe than sorry.

He spat and looked down at the messenger. 'Search the man-thing there on the ground and the clothes that he wears for anything of value, by which I mean things of gold and or conspicuous shininess, and then give them to me, your leader, Snikrat the Magnificent, yes-yes.' He kicked the body towards his followers, the closest of whom immediately fell upon it in a frenzy of looting. A squealing squabble broke out. Snikrat turned away as the first punch was thrown.

He scrambled back up the tree he'd been hunched in before the messenger had disturbed his well-deserved meditation. From its uppermost branches, he could take in most of the forest, as well as the distant stone towers and wooden palisades that dotted the region. The lands the man-things called the Border Princes was cramped with duchies and fiefdoms, most no bigger than a common clanrat's burrow. The messenger had likely been heading for one of them, sent out to bring aid to the keep the rest of Clan Mordkin was, at the moment, busily sacking.

Snikrat hissed softly as he thought of the slaughter he was missing. Warlord Feskit had led the assault personally, from the rear, and he had wanted Snikrat around while he did it. Snikrat grunted in grudging admiration – no one had ever accused Feskit of being stupid. Indeed, the leader of Clan Mordkin was anything but, and under his beneficent rule, the clan had recovered much of the wealth and prestige it had lost over the centuries since its ousting from Cripple Peak. Though he was growing older and less impressive with every year, he had managed to avoid every serious challenge and assassination attempt made on him.

Perched on a branch, anchored by his hairless tail, Snikrat hauled a flap of tanned and inked flesh out from within his cuirass and carefully unfolded it. The map wasn't much, but it served its purpose. Carefully, his pink tongue pinched between his fangs, he used a stub of charcoal to draw an 'x' over the keep they'd just come from. There were still six more between them and Mad Dog Pass, which meant plenty of chances for him to add to his own meagre pile of campaign spoils. Idly, he reached up and plucked an egg from the bird's nest that sat in the branches above. He'd eaten the mother earlier, and it seemed a shame to let the eggs go to waste. As he crunched on the delicate shell, and eyed the map, he considered his fortunes, such as they were.

It was a time of great happenings and glories, from the perspective of an ambitious chieftain, such as he, himself, Snikrat the Magnificent. The sky wept green meteors and the ground vomited up volcanoes as unnatural storms swept the land. It was as if the great Horned Rat himself had opened the door to the world and whispered to his children, 'Go forth and take it, with my compliments.'

Granted, that was easier said than done. True, the man-thing kingdoms of Tilea and Estalia, as factitious in their own way as the skaven themselves, had fallen quickly enough to the numberless hordes that had surged upwards from the network of subterranean tunnels. Every city between Magritta and Sartosa was now a blasted ruin, over which the ragged banner of one clan or another flew. But there were other victories that proved more elusive.

Snikrat scratched at the barely healed mark on his throat. A gift from Feskit, and a sign of his mercy. Snikrat hunched forward and ate another egg. It had been his own fault, and he, Snikrat, was pragmatic enough to admit that, in private, in his own head. He had thought that the omens were a sign that he, Snikrat, should attempt to tear out Feskit's wattle throat. Instead, it was he who felt his rival's teeth on his neck.

Still, there was plenty of time. The world was the skaven's for the taking, even as Clan Mordkin was for his, Snikrat's. And then, the greatest treasures of the clan would be his... Including the Weapon – that oh-so-beautiful sword of glistening black warpstone that Feskit kept hidden behind lock and chain. Even he, Snikrat, had heard of the Fellblade, the slayer of kings and worse than kings, on whose edge the fortunes of Clan Mordkin had been honed. With a weapon like that in hand, there would be no stopping him, and he, Snikrat, would be a power to be reckoned with in the Under-Empire.

Snikrat chattered happily to himself and ate another egg.

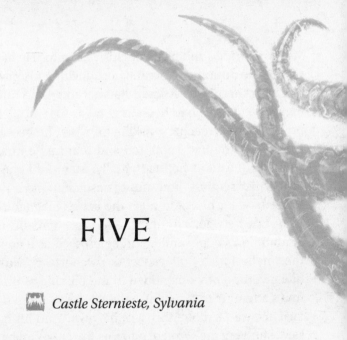

FIVE

Castle Sternieste, Sylvania

The woman who knelt before Mannfred von Carstein was pale and beautiful, and deceit oozed out of her every pampered pore. She claimed to speak for the Queen of the Silver Pinnacle, but so too did half a dozen other similar women, all of whom were mingling with his guests in a manner he found somewhat amusing. He accepted the scroll and waved a hand. She rose gracefully and retreated, leaving the garden behind. As she left, the guards crossed their blades, blocking any further entry.

Mannfred tapped the scroll against his lips. His eyes slid to his cousin, Markos, as the latter refilled his goblet from a jug of magically warmed blood. 'Where is the liche? He practically demanded that I include him in these meetings. I find myself slightly disappointed that he chose not to show up.'

Markos hesitated. His eyes went unfocused for a moment, and then snapped back to their usual keenness. He finished filling his goblet. 'He's in the old library in the west wing, poring over those books and scrolls you lent him.'

Mannfred frowned. It had been weeks since the battle at

Valsborg Bridge and its inconclusive climax. He had played the part of the dutiful aristocratic host, inviting his new... ally back to Castle Sternieste. Arkhan had accepted the offer with grating sincerity, and had been as good as his word. He had made no attempt at treachery, asking only that he be allowed to see those relics he had come for, and that he be included in any councils of war, as befitted an ally. Mannfred had yet to grant the former request, both out of suspicion and a perverse urge to see how far he could push the liche's magnanimity.

The line between ally and enemy was often only the thickness of ambition's edge, and could be crossed as a consequence of the smallest act of disrespect or discourtesy. Thus far, Arkhan had given no obvious notice to the passing of time, or Mannfred's attempts to evade his request. He wondered if the liche's absence was a subtle thrust of his own. 'And his creatures?' he said, studying the scroll of papyrus the Lahmian had given him. Arkhan's coterie of necromancers were as untrustworthy as their master, but they had enough raw power between them to be useful. 'What of them?'

'They've settled in nicely. Several of their fellows reached us weeks ago.' Markos tapped his chin. 'We have quite the little colloquium of necromancers now. Enough to raise a host or six, I should think.'

'You shouldn't, cousin,' Mannfred said. He hefted the scroll and it curled and blackened in his hand, reduced to ashes.

'Shouldn't what?' Markos asked.

'Think,' Mannfred said. He ignored Markos's glare and looked at Elize. He gestured to the ash that swirled through the air. 'What of the handmaidens of the mistress of the Silver Pinnacle? Can they be trusted, or will they seek to sabotage my efforts for lack of anything else to do, if they haven't already?'

Elize blew an errant crimson lock out of her face and said, 'They're cunning, but cautious. Overly so, in my opinion. Without word from their queen, they seem content to watch and nothing more.' She frowned. 'If the barrier of faith falters, even for a moment, they'll make for the mountains as quickly as possible. We may want to inhume them somewhere out of the way, if for no other reason than to deny the Queen of Mysteries what they know.'

Mannfred paused, considering. It was a pleasant thought. But that was for the future. He shook his head. 'No. As amusing as that thought is, the Queen of Mysteries is too dangerous an opponent to antagonise needlessly.'

'Besides which, for every one of her creatures you see, there are at least two you don't,' Erikan said. He sat in the tree, whittling on a length of femur with a knife. Mannfred glanced up at him.

'You are correct,' Mannfred said. 'And they're not the only maggots hidden in the meat.' He looked at Nyktolos. 'What of Gashnag's representatives? Will the Black Prince of Morgheim throw in with us, or will I be forced to bring him to heel like the brute he truly is? And can we trust those creatures of his, who currently enjoy my hospitality?'

'Those who hold true to the banners of mouldy Strigos are, for the moment, with us.' Nyktolos hesitated, and then amended, 'That is to say, with you, Lord Mannfred.' Nyktolos took off his monocle and rubbed it on his sleeve. 'And the beasts you brought from Mousillon are as content as such creatures can be. Nonetheless, it is my informed opinion that we cannot trust them, being as they are snake-brained, weasel-spined, marrow-lickers, fit only to be staked out for the sun.'

'Well said,' Alberacht grunted from where he perched on the high wall, wings drooping over the stones like two leathery curtains. His lamp-like eyes sought out Mannfred. 'We cannot trust the spawn of Ushoran, Count von Carstein. They are animals, and unpredictable ones at that,' he growled, with no hint of irony.

Markos nearly choked on a swallow of blood. Mannfred glanced at his cousin disapprovingly. While mockery was a game he enjoyed, Nictus was deserving of more respect. He was a monster, and addle-brained, but loyal. And, in his own way, the Reaper of Drakenhof was as much a power in Sylvania as any von Carstein. Nictus had been of the old order, a cousin to Isabella and a nephew of Otto von Drak. Von Drak had ordered Nictus chained in an oubliette for some unspecified transgression, and only Isabella's pleas had moved Vlad to bother digging him out. Nictus had served Vlad faithfully in life and then in undeath, with a dogged, unswerving loyalty that Mannfred had, at the time, found amusing. Now, centuries after his own betrayal of Vlad, he found Nictus's continued, unquestioning, loyalty almost comforting.

He heard a sibilant chuckle inside his head and felt a flash of anger. He pressed his fingers to his head and waited for it to pass. Pushing his thoughts of Vlad and loyalty aside, he asked, 'What of the others? The so-called Shadowlord of Marienburg? Cicatrix of Wolf Crag? Have they sent representatives or missives?'

'No, my lord. Then, Mundvard was never one to be accused of knowing his place. When Vlad died, he went his own way, as so many of us did,' Alberacht said. He shook his head. 'Marienburg is his place now, and he'll not leave it or invite us in, if he can help it.'

'And Wolf Crag, even ensconced as it is within our borders, has not responded. If Cicatrix still lives, she may well have decided to throw in her lot with von Dohl, given their past history. She was ever fond of that perfumed lout,' Anark said.

Mannfred sighed. Not all vampires in the world congregated in Sylvania, but Mannfred saw no reason that they shouldn't be made aware of what he had wrought. And if they chose to come and venerate him as the natural lord of their kind for it, why, who was he to turn them away? Granted, he tempered such musings with a certain cynicism. He had travelled among his farther flung kin, journeying through the stinking jungles of the Southlands and the high hills of Cathay, and knew that, whatever their land of origin, vampires were all the same. Uniformly deceitful, treacherous and arrogant.

They could be allies – but subordinates? He smiled to himself at the thought. There was little humour in the expression. Soon, however, he thought, they would have no choice. He felt the weight of destiny on his shoulders such as he never had before, even during those heady months when he had first taken control of Sylvania. The time was fast coming when all of the descendants of the bloody courtiers of long-vanished Lahmia, whether they lurked in jade temples, insect-filled jungles or mouldering manses, would have to bend knee to the new master of death.

And are you so sure that master is you, my boy? Vlad's voice murmured. Mannfred closed his eyes, banishing the voice. For all of the old ghost's attempts to undermine his surety, Mannfred felt all the more certain of his path. The world would be broken to the designs laid out by the Corpse Geometries, and made a thing of unflinching, unfailing order, ruled over by one will – his.

'Did you hear me, my lord?' Anark asked, startling him. The big vampire had grown into his role as the Grand Master of the Drakenhof Order, bullying and, in one case, beheading, any who might challenge him. In the weeks since Tomas's charred head had been relegated to a stake on the battlement for the amusement of the crows, Anark had weeded out the favour-curriers and courtiers, leaving only a hardened cadre of blood knights equal to any produced by the drill field of Blood Keep. Mannfred looked forward to employing them on the battlefield.

'What?' Mannfred blinked. He shuddered slightly. He felt as if he'd been lost in a dream, and was slightly ill from the sweetness of it. He felt the eyes of the inner circle on him, and he cursed himself for showing even the briefest of weaknesses. It wouldn't take much to incite a cur like Markos, or even lovely Elize, to start sharpening their fangs, and he could ill afford to have them start scheming against him now.

'I said that we have reports that the Crimson Lord has returned to Sylvania, and is claiming dominion over the citadel of Waldenhof,' Anark said.

Mannfred waved a hand. 'And so? What is that to me? Let that dolt von Dohl pontificate and prance about in that draughty pile if he wishes. He knows better than to challenge me openly, and if he chooses to do so... Well, we could use a bit of fun, no?' He clapped his hands together. 'See to our strategies for the coming year. Everything must go perfectly, or our fragile weave is undone. I must speak with our guest.'

He left them there in the garden, staring after him, and was gone out the door before they could so much as protest. He knew what they would say, even if they hadn't been saying it every day for weeks. The incessant scheming, strategising and drilling was wearing on them, even Anark, who lived for the tourney field. Vampires were not, by nature, creatures of hard graft. They were predators, and each had a predator's laziness. They exerted themselves only when the goal was in reach, and had not the foresight to see why that path led only to a hawthorn stake or a slow expiration under the sun's merciless gaze.

All save me and thee and one or two others, eh, boy? Vlad murmured encouragingly. *I taught you to see the edges of the canvas, where one portrait ends and another begins, didn't I?*

'You taught me nothing save how to die,' Mannfred hissed. He quickly looked around, but only the dead were within earshot. The truly dead these, rather than the thirsty dead, wrenched from silent tombs and set to guarding the corridors of his castle. He paused for a moment, eyes closed, ignoring the shadows that closed in on him. It was no use; he could feel them, winnowing into his thoughts, clouding his perceptions.

Vlad had indeed taught him much, his words aside. The creature who had given him his name had been as good a teacher as any Mannfred had had up until that point in his sorry life. He had learned from Vlad that the only true path was the one you forged for yourself.

In their centuries together, Vlad had taught him to change his face, and the scent of his magics, so as to hide his origins from prying forces who would seek to use the secrets of his turning against him. Vlad had taught him to trust only his instincts, and to be true to his ambitions, wherever they led, to use his desires like a blade and buckler. And, in the end, Vlad had taught him the greatest lesson of all – that power alone did not shield you from weakness. It crept in, like a thief in the night, where you least suspected it, and it slit your throat as surely as any enemy blade – Nagash, Neferata, Ushoran and, in the end, Vlad himself had all been humbled by their weaknesses. And so too had Mannfred.

But unlike them, he had risen from the ashes, remade and all the stronger for his failure. And he would not fall prey to his weaknesses again. 'I learned my lessons well, old man,' he murmured as he opened his eyes. 'I will be beholden to no man or ghost, and ambition is my tool, not my master.'

Something that might have been laughter floated on the dank air like particles of dust. Mannfred ignored it and continued on through the halls, his mind turning from the past to the future and what part his newfound ally would play in assuring that it came about.

He found the liche in the library, as Markos had said. Arkhan sat at one of the great tables, his fleshless fingers tracing across the page of one of the large grimoires that Mannfred had collected over the course of his life. His pet sat curled over his shoulder, its milky orbs slitted and its ragged tail twitching. He peered over Arkhan's shoulder, and saw the complicated pictographic script of lost Nehekhara. 'Dehbat's *Book of Tongues*,' he said. The cat hissed at him and he replied in kind.

Arkhan didn't turn as he reached up to scratch the cat under the chin. '*I knew Dehbat. He was one of W'soran's pets, in better days*,' he said, as he carefully turned the page. The book was old, older even than Mannfred, and was a copy of a copy of a copy.

'He was wise, in his way, if unimaginative,' Mannfred said, circling the table and heading for the great windows that marked the opposite wall. It was dark outside, as ever, but the sky was alive with a hazy aurora of witch-light. The light was not of his doing, and he knew that it was bleeding through his protective magics from the world outside. Time was running short. Eventually, Sylvania would be shorn of its protection, but still trapped by the wall of faith.

'*W'soran did not choose his apprentices for their creativity,*' Arkhan said. He closed the book. '*I cannot say why he chose them at all, frankly. They were all disreputable, undisciplined overly ambitious vermin, without fail.*'

'So speaks Arkhan the Black, gambler, murderer, thief, sorcerer, and secret animal-lover,' Mannfred said. 'I know of your history, liche. You are hardly one to speak of disrepute and discipline.' He looked at Arkhan, and the latter's jaws sagged open in a wheezing laugh that caused Mannfred's teeth to itch in his gums. 'Did I say something funny? Why are you laughing?'

'*I am laughing, von Carstein, because your misapprehension amuses me,*' Arkhan said. He hefted the book and tossed it to Mannfred, as if it were nothing more than a penny dreadful from a street vendor's stall.

'Enlighten me,' Mannfred said. He caught the book easily and set it back gently on the table. His fingers curled in the fraying hairs that hung lank and loose on the cover. The scalp had belonged to some night-souled shaman from one of the tribes in the Vaults, who had copied the book into its current form, and then been gutted and scalped at his own command by the savages whom he'd ruled. It was a lesson in the fine line between dedication and obsession.

'*You assume that I am Arkhan the Black,*' Arkhan said.

Mannfred froze. Then, slowly, he turned. He said nothing, merely waited for Arkhan to continue. Arkhan watched him, as if gauging his reaction. The liche's skeletal grin never wavered.

'*Arkhan the Black died, vampire,*' Arkhan rasped. He touched one of the other tomes. His skeletal fingers clicked as they touched the ancient bronze clasp that held it shut.

'And was reborn, as I was,' Mannfred said, trying to read something, anything, in the flicker of the liche's eye sockets.

'*Was I? Sometimes, I wonder. Am I the same man I was then, the man who drank of Nagash's potions, who chewed a drug-root until his teeth turned black, who loved a queen – and lost her? Am I him, or am I simply Nagash's memory of him?*' He tapped the side of his head. '*Are my thoughts my own, or his? Am I a servant – or a mask?*'

Mannfred said nothing. There was nothing he could say, even if he had wanted to. He had never had such thoughts himself. They smacked of philosophical equivocation, something he had no patience for. He saw a flash of something out of the corner of his eye, heard Vlad's dry chuckle, and bit down on a snarl. 'Does it matter?' he snapped.

Arkhan cocked his head. '*No,*' he said. '*But you asked what I found so amusing. And I have told you. You are missing several key pieces, are you not?*' He rubbed the cat's spine, stroking the bare bone and causing the foul beast to arch its back in a parody of feline pleasure.

'I am aware of the gaps in my collection, yes, thank you,' Mannfred said acidly. He threw up his hands. 'And were I not trapped here, I would have those items in my hand even now.'

'*The staff, the blade, the armour,*' Arkhan said.

'And two of the Nine Books,' Mannfred said slyly. 'Or are you offering those to me, as a gesture of our newfound friendship?'

'*You said that with a straight face. Your control is admirable,*' Arkhan said. Mannfred grunted, but said nothing. Arkhan inclined his head. '*And I am, yes.*'

Mannfred's head came up sharply, and his eyes narrowed. 'What?'

'*The books are yours, should you wish,*' Arkhan said. He stood and drifted towards the window, hands clasped behind his back. '*This place is as safe as any, for the time being, and we both desire the same end, do we not?*'

Mannfred stepped back and looked at the liche. 'Nagash,' he said. Shadows tickled the edges of his vision, and he heard what might have been the rustle of loose pages as a draught curled through the library.

'*Nagash must rise. As you promised the sorcerer-wraiths of Nagashizzar, the black cults of Araby, and the ghoul-cabals of Cathay, when you sought their aid in gathering your collection, as you call it.*' Arkhan pressed a bony digit to the window, and frost spread around the point it touched the glass in a crystal-line halo. He looked at Mannfred. '*For you, he is a means to an end. For me, he is the end unto itself. Yet we move along the same path, vampire. We tread the same trail, and follow the same light. Why not do it together?*'

'We are,' Mannfred said. 'Have I not opened my castle to you? Have I not given shelter to your creatures?' Though he meant the necromancers, he gestured to the cat, which glared at him with dull ferocity.

'*Yes, but you have still denied my request to gaze upon those items that are necessary to our shared goal. You have denied me my request to see those prisoners whose blood is the base of the sorceries that protect Sylvania – and trap you here.*'

Mannfred tensed, as he always did when the wall of faith that caged the laughable cess-pit he called a realm was mentioned. Arkhan scraped his finger along the window, cracking the glass. He had allowed Mannfred to play the genial host for long enough. It was past time for action. The world was cracking beneath the weight of warring destinies.

Arkhan had felt it, as he crossed the mountains and journeyed to Sylvania, though it had taken him the quiet weeks since to process those ephemeral stirrings into something approaching a conclusion. They were approaching a pivotal moment, and they were not doing so unobserved. Eyes were upon them, even here, in this place. Arkhan could feel the spirits of Chaos whis-pering in the spider-webbed corridors and rumbling far below the earth, and he had cast the bones and understood the signs. There were powers gathering in the dark places, old powers, no longer content to simply watch.

Time was their enemy now. And he could not allow Mannfred to cede any more ground, not if their shared goal was to be accomplished. '*They are part of it, you see. The magics used to bind you here, like a cur in a kennel, are your own, twisted back upon you.*' He decided to sweeten his bitter draft with a bit of flattery. '*Why else did you think it was so powerful, vampire? The living have no capacity for such magics, not on their own. You have made your own trap and you can break it, if you so desire.*'

Mannfred twitched. His eyes narrowed and he asked, simply, 'How?'

'*There is a ritual,*' Arkhan said.

'What sort of ritual?'

'*I doubt that you would agree to it.*'

'Let me be the judge of that,' Mannfred hissed. 'Tell me!'

Arkhan said nothing. He scratched the cat's chin. Mannfred's upper lip curled back from his teeth and he glared at Arkhan furiously. Arkhan met the glare patiently. He could not force Mannfred into what needed doing, not without fear of provoking the vampire. No, the easiest way of getting a vampire to do something was to tell them not to do it. Mannfred snarled and struck the stone sill of the window with his fist, cracking it. 'What sort of ritual, damn you? We do not have the time to play these puerile games of yours, liche.'

'*A sacrifice,*' Arkhan said. He removed the cat from his shoulder and deposited it on the table. '*You possess nine prisoners, do you not? That is the number required for the blood ritual you enacted to seal Sylvania against threats divine and worldly, if my memory serves.*'

Mannfred started visibly. 'You know it?' he asked.

'*I know more than you can conceive, von Carstein. All such sorceries derive from a single source, like the rivers of the Great*

Land. And I am most intimately acquainted with that source, if you'll recall.' Arkhan gave a negligent wave of his hand. *'Sacrifice one of the ones whose blood you've used to anchor your rite, any one of them, and it will create a momentary breach in the wall of faith that encircles your land.'*

'Sacrifice?' Mannfred asked. He shook his head. 'Madness. No. No, I'll not cripple the very protections I worked so hard to create.'

'Then, we'd best get used to one another's company,' Arkhan said. *'Because we're going to be here for a very long time. Out of curiosity, how long can one of your kind last without blood? A few decades, I expect. After that, you'll be too withered and shrunken to do much more than gnash your fangs fetchingly.'* He cocked his head. *'By my calculations, your servants will have drunk this province dry within a month, at least. They glut themselves without consideration for the future, and you let them, to keep them distracted and under control.'*

'How I control my servants is my business,' Mannfred growled.

'Correct,' Arkhan said, *'I cannot force salvation upon you, von Carstein. I merely offer my aid. It is up to you to accept it, or to gnaw your liver in continued frustration. But you are correct. Time grows short. What happens in a month, or a week, when your prisoners are the only living things left in this place? How long will your control last then? How long before you face revolt from your servants, and from your own unseemly thirst? Is it not better to sacrifice one now, so that you might be free to utilise the others as you wish, unimpeded?'*

Mannfred turned away. 'Which one?' he asked.

'I will need to see them to answer that. I have ways of determining which of them is the least necessary for your pattern.'

'And now we come to it,' Mannfred snapped. 'All your offers of aid and books are nothing more than your attempt to burrow your way into my vaults, are they not? You could not defeat me in open battle, and now you seek to trick me. You came to

Sylvania to claim those items I won by my guile and strength, and to demand that I swear fealty to the broken, black soul whose cloak hem you still cling to. Well, you'll get neither!' Mannfred whirled and caught up the table, wrenching it up over his head in a display of monstrous strength, spilling books and the yowling corpse-cat to the floor. His lean frame swelled with inhuman muscle as his face contorted, becoming as gargoyle-hideous as that of any of his more bestial servants. 'Nagash is not my god, liche. He does not command me!'

Arkhan looked up at the table, and then at the face of he who held it. He could see, though just barely, an enormous, ghostly shape superimposed over Mannfred's own, and heard a rustle of sound in the depths of his own tattered spirit that might have been laughter. Mannfred's face twisted, and Arkhan knew that the vampire heard it as well. The tableau held for a moment, two, three... And then Mannfred set the table down with more gentleness than Arkhan had expected. He seemed to deflate. The library was as cold as a crypt, and frost clung thick on the windows, as if something had sucked all of the heat from the room all at once.

'*Which are you, I wonder – servant or mask?*' Arkhan asked.

'I am my own man,' Mannfred grated, from between clenched fangs. He closed his eyes. 'Nagash holds no power over me. I am merely in a foul humour and my temper is short. Forgive me.' The excuse sounded weak to Arkhan. The defiance of a mouse, caught in the claws of a well-fed cat. Mannfred was bowing beneath the weight of another's will, no matter how much he denied it, and he knew it too. The thing that held his soul in its talons had done so for far longer than Mannfred likely suspected, Arkhan thought. It battened upon him, like a leech, and only now had it grown strong enough to be felt.

Memories of his own life, in service to Nagash, before things went wrong, spattered across the surface of his mind, brief bursts of colour and sound that pulsed brightly and faded quickly. It had taken him years to understand the plague that was Nagash. How he infected his tools, both living and inanimate, with himself, with his mind and thoughts. He hollowed you out and took your place in your own skull, pulling the red rags of your psyche over himself like a cloak, emerging only when necessary. Mannfred had never had a chance... Vampires were the blood of Nagash. It was his essence that had transformed Neferata into the creature she now was, and from her had sprung fecund legions, whose veins ran with the black blood of the Great Necromancer. While creatures like Mannfred persisted, Nagash would never truly be gone.

Arkhan felt a pang of something that might have been sympathy for the creature before him. For all of them – puppets on the end of his master's strings, though they knew it not. Some were more wilful than others, with longer strings, but they were still puppets, still slaves to the song of blood and the Corpse Geometries that hemmed them in.

Mannfred's head came up sharply, and his nostrils flared. 'Ha!' he barked. He looked at Arkhan. 'You wanted to see the prisoners, liche? Well let us go visit them.'

'*What changed your mind?*' Arkhan asked.

Mannfred chuckled and swept for the door. 'They're trying to escape.'

'*You don't sound concerned,*' Arkhan said, as he hurried after Mannfred, his robes rustling. The liche's hand fell to the pommel of his blade, as he examined Mannfred's broad back. It would be no effort at all to simply slide the blade in. Well, perhaps some effort. Mannfred was no guileless peasant, after all. Destroying him now might spare grief later. Vampires were unpredictable at the best of times, and this was most assuredly not the best of times. Right now, Mannfred thought he was in control. Eventually, however, he would try to openly resist Nagash's return, especially once he realised what fate awaited him, should they be successful.

Nonetheless, he still required the vampire's aid. Many hands made for quick work. Arkhan let his hand slide away from the blade. No, the time to dispose of Mannfred had not yet come.

'I'm not. I want them to try,' Mannfred said. I want them to try again and again, and grow more desperate with every failure. Their spirits must be broken. There can be no resistance, come the day. Nothing must stymie us.'

'*I couldn't agree more,*' Arkhan said.

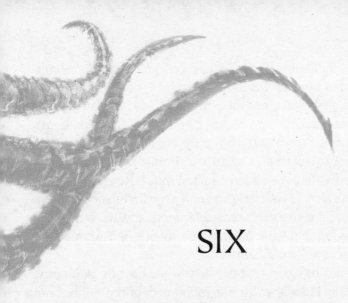

SIX

Volkmar stood knee-deep in ash and dust. Harsh smoke caressed his aching lungs and stung his weary eyes. Every limb felt heavy, and his heart struggled to keep its rhythm. He was bitterly cold and terribly hot, all at once. His hammer hung almost forgotten in his hand, its ornate head broken, and its haft soaked in blood and sweat. His breath fogged and swirled before his eyes, and he could see faces in it. Men and women, some he knew, others whom he found familiar though he could not say why or how.

There was blood on his face and hands, and his gilded armour was stained with tarry excretions and reeking ichors. The smoke that entombed him stank of funeral pyres, and he could hear the roar of distant battle. Weapons crashed against shields and bit into cringing meat. The air swelled and cracked with a riot of voices, echoing from unseen places. Screams of agony mingled with pleading voices and howling cries of pure animal terror. The air was choked by the smoke that curled about him; he could see strange witch-lights pulsing within its depths, and horrible, ill-defined shapes moving around him, either too slowly or too quickly. He could not say where they were going, or why. Something crackled beneath his foot.

The smoke swirled clear for a moment, and he saw that he stood on a carpet of bones, picked clean by the ages. Old bones and new bones, brown and white and yellow, clad in the shapeless remnants of clothing and armour from a span of centuries that boggled Volkmar's already addled mind. He saw weapons and tools the likes of which he had only seen in the most ancient of barrows, and those that seemed far more advanced than the ones he was familiar with. It was as if someone had emptied out all of the graveyards of history.

Volkmar did not know where he was, or how he had come there. He only knew that he was frightened, and tired, but not yet ready. Ready for what, he did not know, but the thought of it caused him to shudder in horror. He raised his hammer wearily, preparing himself for what he somehow knew came next.

All about him, the plain of bones began to tremble and clatter. Sparks of weird light grew in the empty sockets of every skull and a eye-searing green fire crackled along the length of every bone. The bones surged up with a cacophonous rattle, and something began to take shape – something immense and powerful, Volkmar knew, though he had never seen it before. A single voice suddenly drowned out all others, silencing them. It spoke in a language that Volkmar had only ever seen written down, and the words were carved into the chill air like sword strokes.

As the thing – *the daemon,* his mind screamed – grew and formed and spoke, the smoke above him cleared. He looked up at the cold, black stars that pulsed in the dead void above. A thought quavered in his head, like the tinny tone of a child's bell. Everything was dead, here. Nothing lived, save him. Nothing moved, or breathed, or laughed or loved, without the whim of the monstrous intelligence that guided the climbing, shifting pillar of bones rising up before him. It had conquered and covered and was the world about him. His world, for he could see the ruin of the great temple of Sigmar, there, rising from the sea of death, and the Imperial palace and a hundred other landmarks, barely visible through the smoke.

His heart sank. He saw the blackened skeletons of the Vagr Breughel Memorial Playhouse and the Geheimnihsstrasse Theatre, the broken ruin of Temple Street, and shattered remnant of the Konigsplatz. Altdorf, he was in Altdorf, and it, like everything else in this world, was dead and buried. The gods were gone, and only this cold, malignity remained.

The thought incited him, freeing him from his terrified paralysis. A hoarse roar slipped from his blistered lips, and he swung the hammer up, catching it in both hands as he forced himself forwards through the clawing tide of dead matter that swirled about him. A light, weak at first, and then growing stronger, suffused him. A corona of heat swirled into being about the shattered head of the hammer as he swung it.

The hammer smacked into a giant's palm. The sliding, slithering bones that made up the titan's claw gave slightly at the force of the blow. Then the massive claws curled down, enclosing the hammer completely, and, like a parent taking a toy from a child, snatched the weapon from Volkmar's grip. The arm was impossibly long, and attached to an equally out-of-proportion shoulder. The constant motion of the bones made it hard to discern the truth of the shape before him, but he saw enough to want to look away – *to run,* a voice screamed.

Volkmar turned and ran. It was not the first time he had done so, and he knew that it wasn't the first time he had faced this enemy either. He had fled from it before, and fought ineffectually against it and been buried by it again and again. He ran, and his hammer was somehow in his hand again, still broken, its weight slowing him down. The thing followed him, ploughing through the smoke and charnel leavings like a shark through shallow waters, absorbing and expelling the bones it rolled over. Sometimes it was beside him, and other times it loomed over him, its shadow enveloping him in a cloak of numbing cold. It outpaced him at times or fell far behind. He had the sense that it was in no hurry. That it was enjoying itself. But he did not stop, he could not stop. To face it, he knew, was to fall. Only in flight was there life, and Volkmar dearly wanted to live.

The courage that had sustained him throughout his long life, that had kept him on his feet through fire and ruin, that had seen him match his hammer against all manner of foes, had failed him. All of his training, all of his rhetoric, all of his faith, had fled him, leaving only the raw atavistic impulse to survive at all costs. So he ran.

He ran in pursuit of the wind. He heard a woman's voice, in the hissing sibilance of the breeze that stirred the smoke. He always heard it, as he ran. Sometimes he thought it was his mother, or an old lover, or the daughter he'd never had, but other times, he knew it was none of those. It was not a human voice. It was a voice that spoke to the wind, and to eagles, and it lent him strength, and propelled him on, easing the weight of his hurts and sweeping aside the dead shapes that lunged for him out of the smoke.

Run, she murmured.

Run, she whispered.

Run, she screamed.

Volkmar ran, and the dead world pursued him. And as his limbs failed, and his blood pounded in his ears, and the rattle of bones grew thunderous in his ears, he grasped at her words, her voice, grabbing for any shred of salvation, of hope, and, as all of the dead of Altdorf heaved beneath him, the Grand Theogonist woke up.

Volkmar's eyes sprang open, and he sucked in a lungful of stale, damp air. He shuddered and twitched, unable to control his limbs. His heels drummed on the stone floor, and his palms flapped uselessly against his battered cuirass. He moaned and tried to roll over, but the manacles about his wrists prevented it.

He was forced to squirm about and haul himself up into a sitting position. His body ached, much as it had in his dream. He coughed, trying to clear his throat, and looked around blearily.

'Still alive, my friend?' someone asked. Volkmar peered through the gloom, and caught sight of golden armour gleaming still beneath a layer of filth. He struggled to recall the Tilean's name, through the mugginess of his aborted sleep.

'If you can call it living,' Volkmar coughed. His throat was parched and drier than the deserts of Araby. He squinted at the knight. 'You've looked better, Blaze.'

Lupio Blaze, Templar of the Order of the Blazing Sun, laughed shallowly. 'As have we all,' he said, rattling his chains. His once-handsome features had been bludgeoned into a shapeless mass of dried blood and bruises, but his eyes were still bright, and his torn lips still quirked in a smile. 'Still, it could be worse. It could be raining.'

Overhead, thunder rumbled. The soft plop of water was replaced by the steady downbeat of falling rain. Blaze laughed again, and craned himself backwards, so that his head and torso was caught in the downpour. 'You see, Olf? I say that the gods still watch over us, eh?' Blaze called out, gulping at the rainwater. He made a cup of his hands, and caught a handful of the rain. Then he kicked the legs of the figure chained next to him. 'Up, Olf, have a drink, on me,' he said, pouring the handful of water into the cupped hands of the burly Ulrican priest who was chained to the lectern next to his.

Olf Doggert eagerly slurped the water, and then grudgingly passed the next handful of water to the next prisoner in line, the pinch-faced young priest of Morr, Mordecaul Cadavion. Cadavion drank his share and passed along the next handful, emptying his cupped hands into those of the wan-faced matron named Elspeth Farrier, a priestess of Shallya. Volkmar turned his attention to the figure of the man chained beside her. Wild haired and raggedly dressed even before their captivity, Russett, blessed of Taal looked like a living corpse now. He hadn't eaten in days, and he'd barely drunk anything. His flesh was mottled with bruises where he'd thrown himself at the walls, and bloody marks chafed his wrists where he continually yanked on his chains. One of his ankles had been gnawed to the bone, not by any of Mannfred's beasts, but by the man himself in an attempt to get free of an earlier set of chains.

The nature priest had suffered more physically in captivity than any of them, save Volkmar and Sindst, the sour-faced priest of Ranald, who'd lost a hand and several chunks of his flesh on their journey across Vargravia in Mannfred's bone cage. Russett crouched, wrapped in chains and silently rocking back and forth. Like an animal that had been caged too long, he had gone quietly mad. Now he stared at the cockroaches and rats that shared their prison, as if trying to communicate with them. But whatever esoteric abilities Taal had granted him were not in evidence, not in Sylvania. The voices of the gods, ever faint, might as well have been the only fevered imaginings of a flagellant, for all that they reached their servants here, Volkmar reflected.

He watched Elspeth help Sindst drink. He slurped greedily at the water in her hands, and nodded weary thanks when he'd finished. Volkmar looked around. After Mannfred's last visit, they had been moved from the walls to the lecterns, and had their chains shortened. The reason hadn't been shared, but Volkmar suspected that it was another of Mannfred's demented games. He knew that the vampire enjoyed their futile escape attempts, just as he knew that they couldn't stop trying. Wounded, exhausted and filthy as they were, none of them were yet ready to give up, save perhaps for poor Russett and the Bretonnian, Morgiana, whose mind and soul had been taken by Mannfred long before they had met her. She belonged to von Carstein now. She murmured to herself in the far corner of the room, unchained, but unmoving. She lay on her side on the cold stone, and stroked the floor as if it were a beloved pet, whispering constantly to it.

He caught a flash of a delicate fang as she muttered, and looked away, sickened by what she had become.

Volkmar caught Elspeth's eye, and the Shallyan priestess shook her head slightly. Volkmar sighed and winced, as the wound on his head split and began to leak blood and pus. He reached for it, but Elspeth hissed, 'Don't touch it. It's having enough trouble healing without you picking at it.'

'I don't think it's ever going to heal, sister,' Volkmar said. 'Mannfred won't give us that time.' He looked around. 'You can all feel it, can't you? That heaviness in the air? We're in the eye of a storm, and one that Mannfred wants to unleash on the rest of the world. He needs us for that.'

'Otherwise why keep us alive, right?' Sindst muttered, hugging his wrist-stump to his chest. 'We know all of this, old man. That's why we keep trying to escape. Badly, I might add,' he spat, glaring at Blaze and Olf.

'Keep talking, sneak-thief,' Olf growled. 'Seems to me, if Mannfred needs you alive, I'd be doing us all a favour by wringing your scrawny neck.'

'Do as you will, brute,' Sindst said, tonelessly. 'We're not getting out of here upright, none of us. We're all dead, even the pointy-eared witch over there.' He motioned with his stump to the elf maiden.

Volkmar looked at the elf. He pushed himself to his feet and moved as close as he could to the lectern where she was chained. Her eyes were closed, as they had been for the entirety of their brief, inhospitable association. Volkmar gathered water from Elspeth, and got as close to the elf woman as he could. 'Drink, my lady,' he croaked. 'You must drink.'

Her eyes flickered open. Volkmar realised that she was blind, and felt his heart twist in his chest. 'Aliathra,' she murmured. Volkmar blinked. He recognised her voice instantly as the same one he'd heard in his dream, urging him to run. A weak smile flickered across her face and was gone. She leaned forward, and he held his hands out. She reached up and took his hands in hers and bent her face. She drank deeply, and sat back, frowning. 'Tainted water from tainted skies,' she said. 'It tastes of his sorcery.'

'Funny, I thought it tasted of smoke, maybe with a hint of a Sartosan red?' Sindst said.

'Quiet,' Elspeth said sharply. 'That's quite enough out of you, servant of Ranald. If you can't be of use–'

Sindst's manacle clattered to the floor. He stretched his good arm and Volkmar saw a twist of metal sticking from the raw stump of his other wrist, poking through the filthy bandages. He grinned in a sickly fashion and said, 'It took a while. I had to hide it where the flesh-eaters wouldn't sniff it out. And wait for the flying fang-brothers to go wherever such creatures go when they're not watching us,' he added, referring to the two vargheists that Mannfred had left to guard them.

He heaved himself up and began to free the others. 'This is useless, you know,' he said, as he worked on Volkmar's manacles. 'We're all dying by inches – no food, no water, no weapons, sick, hurt and bled dry thanks to Mannfred and his cursed spell. We won't get far.'

'Then why bother?' Volkmar asked, looking up at him.

Sindst chuckled. 'Ranald is the god of luck, among other things. And you don't get lucky if you don't roll the knucklebones, Sigmarite.'

'I hope we have a better plan than last time,' Mordecaul said, as he was freed.

'Run faster,' Elspeth said.

'That's not a plan,' Mordecaul said.

'Die well,' Olf said, heaving himself to his feet.

'What part of the word "plan" don't you understand?' Mordecaul demanded.

Sindst chuckled. 'For the servant of the god of death, you're not very eager to make his acquaintance, are you, boy?'

Mordecaul hugged himself. 'I wouldn't be in his bower for

very long, would I? Death is not the end here.' He looked up, his pale face pinched with grief. 'I can't feel him. Morr, I mean. I can't feel him here.'

'None of us can feel our gods,' Blaze said, kicking aside his chains as Sindst freed him. 'That does not mean they are not there, hey?' He went to the younger man and clapped him on the shoulders. 'I knew a man, he was from Talabheim. His name was Goetz, and he was a brother-knight to me. He grew deaf to the words of Myrmidia, but he fought on, deaf and blind to her light. He still served. And when the time came, when he was at the end, suddenly – there she was!' Blaze made a flamboyant gesture. 'She had been there all the time, and he had been like a blind man standing in the sun, hey? That is what we are, newly blind. We must find the sun.' Blaze patted Mordecaul on the cheek. 'Find the sun,' he said again.

Volkmar watched the exchange silently. Blaze's overt display of faith made him feel ashamed, in some small way. His own faith had not so much been shaken as it had been uprooted. One did not become the Grand Theogonist on the strength of faith alone. Such a position was built on a bedrock of compromise. He had felt the power of Sigmar in his veins, but he had never spoken with his god, or gazed upon his face. He had never felt the need to do so. Sigmar provided him with purpose and the strength to carry out that purpose, and that was enough.

Or it had been. Now he wasn't so sure. He felt eyes on him, and looked around to see Aliathra gazing at him, her face like something carved from marble. In her eyes was something he could not define – sadness, perhaps. Or pity. Volkmar felt a flush of anger and shook off the cloud of doubt that had settled on him. Mannfred had called him 'Sigmar's blood'. Well, he'd show the vampire the truth of those words, when he pulled out the leech's unbeating heart and crushed it before his eyes.

Sindst had gone to the chamber door. 'I can't get it open,' he said.

'Then step back,' Olf growled. He flexed his long arms. 'Still a bit of strength left in this old wolf, I think. What about you, Blaze? What's that you Myrmidians always say?'

'We go where we are needed,' Blaze intoned. 'We do what must be done.' He grinned. 'See, I teach you something yet, yes?'

'Shut up and put your shoulder into it, you poncy pasta-eater,' Olf growled. Blaze chuckled and both men struck the door with their shoulders. Volkmar longed to help them, or to see to Morgiana with a sharp length of wood, but it was all he could do to stand. Instead, he kept an eye on the corner where Morgiana still lay, unheeding of their actions, as well as on the open roof above, just in case the vargheists decided to return. There was no way they could fight the creatures in their current state. It would be a miracle if they made the castle gates. But better a quick death in battle than whatever Mannfred had planned. He rubbed his blistered wrists and glanced down at the blood that flowed through the runnels that cut across the floor.

Then, his eyes were drawn to the gleaming iron crown, where it sat on its cushion of human skin. It seemed to glitter with a strange internal light, at once ugly and beauteous, attractive and repulsive in the same instant. He thought he could hear a soft voice calling to him, pleading with him, and he longed to pick it up.

I should, he thought. It was his duty, was it not? The Crown of Sorcery belonged in the vaults of the temple of Sigmar, in the Cache Malefact with the other dangerous objects. It should never have been brought into the light. How Mannfred had breached the vaults was still a mystery, but Volkmar's fingers itched to snatch up the crown and – *place it on my head* – carry it away from this fell place.

He froze, startled at the thought that had intruded on his own. It had not been his, and he knew it. His eyes narrowed and he mustered the moisture to spit on the crown, which seemed to flicker angrily in response.

'You can hear it, can't you?' the elf maiden murmured, from behind him.

Volkmar licked his lips. 'I can,' he hissed hoarsely. He looked away. 'But it says nothing worth listening to. It is nothing more than a trap for the unwary.'

'I saw Mannfred wearing it,' Mordecaul said. He looked at the crown and shuddered. 'It fit him perfectly.'

'It fits any head that dares wear it,' Volkmar grated. 'And it hollows out the soul and strips the spirit to make room for that which inhabits it.' He grinned mirthlessly. 'Let the von Carstein wear it, and bad cess to him. Let it drain him dry, one parasite on another. A better fate for him, I cannot imagine.'

'That is not his fate,' Aliathra said. Her blind eyes sought Volkmar's. 'He will burn in the end. As will we all.'

'I see the stories of the good cheer of the folk of Ulthuan were just that,' Sindst said. He hefted a broken length of bone in his good hand. 'If we're going, let's go.'

'The door is giving,' Olf said. The door shuddered on its hinges as the Ulrican and the knight struck it again. Even half starved and beaten bloody, both men were still strong, as befitted the servants of war gods.

Volkmar was about to reply, when a cloud of char and splinters cascaded down from above. He looked up and then turned, caught up Aliathra and Mordecaul and hurled them aside as the vargheist landed with a shriek and a crash. It reared up over Volkmar, wings filling the confined space of the chamber. It screamed again, jaws distending as it lunged for him. Then it jerked back as something soft struck Volkmar's shoulder and hurled itself into the creature's face. A second rat leapt from Volkmar's other shoulder, and then a third leapt from the floor, and a fourth, a fifth – ten, twenty, until it seemed as if every rat and cockroach that had shared the chamber with the prisoners was crawling over the vargheist, biting and clawing. The monster staggered back, crashing into the lecterns with a wail as the tide of vermin knocked it sprawling.

Volkmar turned and saw Russett watching him blankly. The nature priest was surrounded by rats, and his lips moved silently as he sent his furry army into hopeless battle with the vargheist.

'Come on,' Olf roared as he grabbed Volkmar and propelled him into the corridor. 'Leave him and let's go!'

Erikan swept the femur out, and the holes he'd cut into it caught the breeze, making an eerie sound. He leaned back on his branch and placed the femur to his lips. The tune he piped out was an old one; he didn't know what it was called, only the melody.

'Very lovely,' Markos said. 'But weren't you supposed to be helping us see to these strategies, Crowfiend?'

'I am,' Erikan said, not looking down. 'I'll take my hounds of night and silence the watch-posts along the Stir, as soon as we are able to leave. If we strike quickly enough, no one will have any idea that we are out and about.' He whirled the femur again, enjoying the sound it made.

'And by "hounds of night", you mean those mouldering wolves and chattering ghouls that you seem content to spend your time with? What sort of warrior are you?' Anark sneered, glaring up at him, his fists on his hips.

'An effective one, Anark, and a reliable one – Elize, keep your trained ape muzzled, please,' Markos said, poring over the map unrolled across the bench.

'Ape, am I? I am your Grand Master, Markos, and you had best not forget it!' Anark said, reaching for his sword. Elize caught his wrist and prevented him from drawing it. Which was wise, in Erikan's estimation. Markos was just looking for an excuse to humble Anark. Then, so was everyone else. Anark was fine in small doses, but they'd been cooped up with him for weeks, and he was champing at the bit to bully someone into a fight. Mostly he seemed to want to fight Erikan, but anyone would do,

THE END TIMES | THE RETURN OF NAGASH

by this point. Erikan looked down at Anark and smirked, then he brought the femur up and recommenced playing his tune.

'Oh believe me, I have not,' Markos purred, without turning around. 'You deserve your new position as surely as poor, late Tomas did.'

Alberacht cackled where he crouched, gargoyle-like, on the wall. Anark glared at him, but the monstrous vampire didn't even deign to return it. Instead, he dropped from the wall and ambled towards Markos. He tapped the map with one of his claws. 'Heldenhame, that's where our trouble will come from, you mark me, children.'

'The Knights of Sigmar's Blood,' Nyktolos said. He was running a whetstone along the length of his sword as he leaned against the garden wall. 'Master Nictus is correct. I have encountered them before. They are dreadful creatures, pious and murderous in equal measure.' He looked up and frowned. 'And Heldenhame is a tough nut indeed. High, thick walls and an armed populace do not for an easy siege make, should we get that far.'

'But it has its weak points. Everything has a weak point,' Elize said. Hands behind her back, she paced back and forth. 'We simply need to find it.'

'And hit it,' Anark added. Elize smiled and stroked his cheek. Erikan, still in his branch, rolled his eyes. He played an annoying little tune, causing her to look up at him. Her expression was unreadable.

'Are you ever sorry that you taught him how to speak, cousin?' Markos asked. Anark's face flushed purple and he made a half-hearted lunge for the other vampire, only to be stopped by Elize and Alberacht.

Erikan made to play accompaniment to the farce below, but lowered his femur as the sound of bells shook the air. He tossed aside the bone and dropped from his perch. 'The bells,' he said.

'Yes, thank you, Erikan. Any other blindingly obvious statement you'd care to make?' Markos snarled as he swept aside his maps and shot to his feet. 'It's why the bloody bells are ringing that I'm interested in.'

A pack of yowling, slavering ghouls surged past the garden entrance, accompanied by slower-moving skeleton guards, clad in rusty armour and brown rags. 'The prisoners are making another escape attempt,' Elize said. She spun and pointed at Alberacht and Nyktolos. 'Get to the courtyard. That's the quickest way out of the castle.' She turned to Markos. 'Rally the rest of the order. We'll need to search the castle, if it's anything like last time.'

'And who put you in charge, cousin?' Markos purred.

'I did,' Anark growled, drawing his blade. 'You will obey her as you would me, *cousin.*'

'She's right, Markos,' Erikan said, striding past the three of them. 'And we have no time for arguments regardless. The prisoners are too valuable to risk either their escape or their deaths at the hands of Lord Mannfred's other guests.' Markos made a face, but fell silent. In the last few weeks, more than one attempt had been made on Mannfred's inner sanctums by various vampires and necromancers enjoying his hospitality. If it wasn't the Lahmians, it was the Charnel Circle, or one of the lesser von Carsteins, seeking, as ever, to supplant their betters.

And while no one liked to mention it, food had been getting scarce. While Strigany caravans were still trundling along the old Vargravian road, bringing wagons full of kidnapped men and women to Castle Sternieste, pickings in Sylvania itself were growing distinctly thin. Only the Strigany or other human servants could pass through the barrier of faith, and fewer of them returned every day. Some likely fell to the Imperial patrols that guarded the hinterlands of the neighbouring provinces, but others had, perhaps, simply decided not to come back.

Erikan was out of the garden a moment later, the others trailing in his wake or splitting off to do as Elize had commanded. Soon it was just himself and Elize and Anark, hurrying in pursuit of the ghoul pack they had seen earlier. The dead that stood sentry in every corridor and stairwell were all moving in the same direction, directed by their master's will.

Volkmar and the others had tried to escape before, with predictable results. Once, they had even made it as far as the stables. But as more and more vampires had flocked to Sternieste, so too had the likelihood grown that another such attempt would lead to more than a beating for Mannfred's amusement. Hungry vampires had all the self-control of stoats in a hen house. Regardless, there were only so many ways that the prisoners could go. Erikan thought that it was likely that they would simply try to bull their way out this time. Subtlety had got them nowhere, after all.

His conclusion was borne out by the trail of shattered bones and the twisted bodies of fallen ghouls that littered the stairs leading down to the lower levels of the keep. Erikan felt a grim admiration for the prisoners. That admiration only grew stronger when they found one of their own, a Drakenhof Templar, with his skull caved in and a jagged length of wood torn from a postern shoved through a gap in the side of his cuirass and into his heart. Anark cursed. Elize shook her head. 'They know us of old, these mortals.'

'Well, you know what they say... Familiarity breeds contempt,' Erikan murmured. He didn't recognise the vampire. Then, there were many in the order he didn't know. Elize had kept him by her side at all times. That was one of the many reasons he'd left, and sought out Obald again.

They heard the clash of arms and followed the screams of dying ghouls. Volkmar and the others had made it through Sternieste to the inner courtyard that separated the main keep from the outer. It wasn't hard to figure out how they'd made it that far – though the castle's population had increased, it was night, and almost all of its inhabitants were out hunting. Those who were left were likely trying to either avoid getting involved, or were waiting to see how far the escapees got. You had to make your own entertainment, in times like these. But it wouldn't be long before certain vampires got it in their heads to try to get in on the fun.

Erikan sprang out into the rain-swept courtyard and took in the fight roiling about him. Only seven of the prisoners had made it this far, but they were giving a good account of themselves. Most of that was down to Mannfred's command that they not be harmed. A matronly woman swung a brazier about her with determined ferocity, sending ghouls tumbling and scrambling to get out of her way. A one-handed man guarded her back, a polearm held awkwardly in his good hand.

Volkmar himself led the way, watching over the elf maiden, who sagged against the shoulder of the young priest of Morr. And the Ulrican and the Myrmidian kept the group's flanks protected. The Myrmidian had found a sword from somewhere, and laid about him with enthusiasm and skill, crying out to his goddess all the while. The Ulrican had a spear, and as Erikan watched, he impaled a skeleton guard, hoisted it, and sent it flying towards the courtyard wall. Volkmar was leading the group towards the portcullis that separated the inner and outer keeps, where Count Nyktolos waited, leaning on his blade, his monocle glinting in the torchlight.

Above them all, shapes, lean and a-thirst, ran along the walls, keeping pace but not interfering, not yet. Erikan recognised a number of Mannfred's more recent hangers-on in that group, their eyes glazed with hunger and ambition as they looked down on the Grand Theogonist. Erikan understood that look, though he didn't feel it himself. Volkmar was the living embodiment of the church that had made the scouring of Sylvania and the destruction of its bloodthirsty aristocracy a central tenet of its dogma. To see him like this, running frightened, dying on his feet, must be like a gift from the gods that Mannfred had barred from his kingdom.

They wouldn't be able to resist the chance to see the old man scream, command from Mannfred or no. He glanced at Elize, and he saw by her expression that she was thinking the same thing. She nodded sharply and sprang for the wall. Anark made to follow her, but Erikan stopped him. 'No, we need to recapture them,' he said. Anark snarled, but didn't disagree.

They split up, each approaching the prisoners from a side. Erikan hurtled the rolling body of a disembowelled ghoul and drew his sword. He arrowed towards the knight, reckoning him more dangerous than the Ulrican, so long as he had a sword in his hand. Even as their blades connected, Erikan saw Nyktolos lunge forward, his sword chopping into the haft of the spear the Ulrican wielded.

The Myrmidian whirled his blade and stamped forward, moving lightly despite his wounds. He still wore the tattered remnants of his armour, and Erikan could smell the pus dripping from the sores beneath the metal, and the blood that had crusted on its edges. Their blades slammed together again. The man was smart – he didn't intend to pit his strength against Erikan's. He was simply trying to drive him back. Erikan allowed him to do so, trying to draw him away from his comrades. If he could get him alone, the ghouls could swarm him under through sheer numbers.

A wild cry caused him to glance up. Mannfred's pet vargheists circled the courtyard, screeching fit to wake whatever dead things had managed to ignore their master's summons. Alberacht swooped between them, looking almost as bestial. He had obviously gone to rouse the beasts into helping with the hunt.

Volkmar cried out as one of the vargheists plummeted down and plucked the elf from the ground. She screamed and struck out at the beast that held her, but it merely screeched again and carried her upwards. Volkmar cursed loudly and turned. Erikan saw Anark rush towards him with his sword raised. He cursed the other vampire for an idiot, albeit silently. The old man ducked aside and looped the length of chain he carried around the vampire's throat. Anark snarled as Volkmar hauled forwards with all of his weight, pulling him off his feet. He fell with a clatter, and his sword flew from his grip. 'Get the blade!' Volkmar roared.

The Ulrican snatched the sword up and spun on his heel, gutting a leaping ghoul. Erikan lunged to meet him, as Nyktolos blocked a blow from the Myrmidian meant to split Erikan's spine. He forced the Ulrican back with a slash. The burly warrior priest swept his stolen blade out in a wild, looping blow. Erikan weaved back with serpentine grace, not even bothering to block the attack. He heard Nyktolos laugh and saw the other vampire back away from his opponent as a mob of ghouls surged forward.

The knight, freed of Nyktolos, came at him from the side, hoping to flank him, even as the ghouls chased after him. Erikan pivoted, and avoided the knight's lunge. He flipped backwards, evading the Ulrican's blade a second time. The ghoul that had been pressing forward behind him wasn't so lucky. It fell, choking on its own blood. More of the cannibals rushed into the fray, trampling their dying comrade in their haste to reach the enemy.

Erikan sprang to the wall and dropped back behind the ghoul pack. Nyktolos had the right idea. There was no sense in risking himself. The two men fought hard, with desperate abandon. Bodies and blood slopped the floor. He saw that Volkmar had managed to get atop Anark and was hauling back on the chains, trying to snap his enemy's neck. The vampire's mouth was wide, and a serpentine tongue jutted from between his fangs as he writhed beneath the Grand Theogonist. Erikan hesitated. It was the perfect moment to be rid of Anark. He might not get another one. He heard Elize cry out and, almost against his will, began to move.

Then, the second vargheist had Volkmar in its claws, and it hauled him upwards to join its fellow. Erikan lowered his sword. 'He who hesitates is lost,' he murmured as he rushed to help

Anark to his feet in an obsequious show of concern.

Above, Volkmar cursed and tore at the vargheist holding him, to no avail. The beast had him, and there was no escape. Erikan watched as his struggles became weaker and weaker, until at last he ceased entirely, and hung in its grasp like a corpse. The vargheist dropped him onto a parapet, and sank down on him, like a cat crouching atop its kill.

The sound of applause swept across the courtyard, cutting through the sound of the rain and the whimpers of dying ghouls. Mannfred von Carstein stood on the parapet above the portcullis, Arkhan behind him. 'Well,' he said. 'Look how far you got. I am quite impressed, as I'm sure my comrade is.' He gestured to Arkhan. 'Aren't you impressed?' he asked, over his shoulder.

Mannfred didn't give Arkhan a chance to reply. Instead, he leapt down from the parapet and dropped lightly into the courtyard, drawing his blade as he rose. The torches that flickered, hissed and spat in the rain seemed to dim slightly, as if Mannfred's presence were draining the heat and light from them. 'I'm impressed,' he said again, looking up at the gathered vampires who crouched or slunk about above the courtyard. 'And yet, something puzzles me. Where did you think you were going to go? This castle is mine. This land is mine. I rule everything from horizon to horizon, every mountain, every bower, every ruin and river. All mine,' Mannfred went on. He waved aside the ghouls, who retreated from him with undignified speed. 'Where were you going to go?'

'Back into the eyes of our gods,' the knight said. His voice sounded thin and weak to Erikan's ears. 'Back to the light.'

'There is no light, unless I will it,' Mannfred said, extending his blade. He looked at the Ulrican and the Myrmidian. They were the only two left, save for the priest of Morr, who crouched nearby. The woman and the one-handed man had been knocked sprawling and pinned to the wet ground by Alberacht in the confusion. 'There are no gods, save me.' Mannfred smiled, and

Erikan felt a cold wind sweep through the hollows of his soul. Mannfred turned his blade slightly, so that the light caught the edge. 'If you bow, I will not hurt you too much. If you crawl to me, I will not take your legs. If you beg me to spare you, I will not take your hands.'

The stone, when it came, was a surprise, even to Mannfred, Erikan thought. The young priest had torn it from the ground and hurled it with such force that it drew blood when it caromed off Mannfred's skull. He whirled with a cry that put his vargheists to shame and his blade nearly took the young priest's head off. The young man fell back, face twisted in fear and defiance. Mannfred stormed towards him, but before he could reach him, a swirling storm of spirits erupted from the ground and walls of the courtyard and surrounded the man. Mannfred spun, and glared up at Arkhan, who lowered his staff silently, but did not call off the ghosts he had summoned.

Mannfred turned back in time to block the Ulrican's attack. The big man came at him in a rush, silent and determined. His sword drew fat sparks as it screeched off Mannfred's cuirass. Mannfred stepped back and his fist hammered into the man's chest. Erikan heard bones crack, and the Ulrican slumped, coughing redness. Mannfred caught the back of his head and hurled him to the ground hard enough to add to the tally of broken bones.

The Myrmidian hacked at him, and Mannfred caught the blow on the length of his blade and surged forward, driving the knight back against the hall. He pinned him in place. 'We need to sacrifice one, eh?' Mannfred asked, glancing at Arkhan. The liche nodded slowly. Mannfred looked back at the knight, as the latter strained against his strength, trying to free himself. 'This one, then. He's been more trouble than he's worth.' He tore his blade away from the wall, and the Templar staggered forward, off balance. He recovered quickly, and lunged. The blade skidded off Mannfred's side, staggering him. But before the knight could capitalise, Mannfred batted his guard aside and sent him flying backwards to bounce off the wall and topple to the ground, unconscious.

Mannfred looked down and then up, letting the rain wash the blood from his face. And for a moment, just a moment, between the shadows and the rain, Erikan thought he saw something terrible looming over Mannfred, shaking in silent glee.

SEVEN

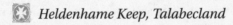 *Heldenhame Keep, Talabecland*

The empty bottle shattered as it struck the wall. Wendel Volker scrambled to his feet and darted out of the commandant's grimy office. Otto Kross stormed after him, as quickly as a man on the wrong end of a three-day drunk could manage. Kross was bald, with a thick beard and sideburns, which hid his heavy jowls, and a neck that was more an unsightly outgrowth of shoulder than anything else.

'I told you that I'd have you, popinjay, if you countermanded me again. Those men deserved a lashing! Their hides were mine,' Kross bellowed as he lunged, red-faced, after Volker, fists windmilling.

'I didn't countermand anything,' Volker yelped, scooting across the courtyard on his backside, trying to get enough room between himself and his commandant so that he could get to his feet without receiving a faceful of Kross's scarred knuckles. 'I simply placed them on punishment detail. How was I to know you meant they needed a flogging?'

That was a lie, of course. He had known, and hadn't approved.

Punishment was all well and good when the men in question had committed an actual infraction or crime. But flogging was a step too far, especially when their only real crime had been to be in the wrong place at the wrong time. He'd placed them on night soil duty, reckoning that would keep them out of Kross's sight until he'd sobered up and forgotten why he wanted them punished in the first place. Unfortunately, someone had spilled the beans. The next thing Volker knew, he was dodging bottles and Kross's fists.

'I'll stop your squawking, popinjay,' Kross snarled. He lurched drunkenly for Volker, tripped over his own foot, and fell face-first to the ground. Volker took the opportunity to get to his feet and made to flee, until he noted the gathering crowd of men. It looked as if every trooper assigned to the Heldenhame garrison was piling into the wide, long courtyard that linked the Rostmeyer and Sigmundas bastions.

It wasn't surprising. The past few weeks had seen a steady increase in tensions among the men. There was something growing in Sylvania, behind those blasted walls; they could all feel it. Not to mention the reports coming from the north. For every ten men who'd marched for the Kislev border, only seven reached their destination, thanks to beastmen, greenskins and plague. The fighting along the border had spilled into Ostermark and Talabecland, and the armies of those provinces were hard-pressed to hold the tide back.

Many men wanted to travel north, to fight the enemy. Others wanted to stay put, out of the way, safe behind Heldenhame's walls. Luckily for the latter, Leitdorf was obsessed with keeping his eyes firmly fixed on Sylvania. Or, as some lackwits whispered, he just wanted to stay good and close to the centre of the Empire, in order to take advantage of what many were coming to see as the inevitable conclusion of recent events.

Sometimes, Volker thought that was why Thyrus Gormann had come. It would be difficult for Leitdorf to get up to any mischief with the Patriarch of the Bright College looking over his shoulder.

Volker heard a voice growl, 'Two bits on the commandant.' He looked over and saw the scowling features of Captain Deinroth. Kross's second-in-command had never warmed to Volker. He shared his commandant's opinion, and indeed that of most of the other captains, that Volker was a man who had bought his rank with gold, rather than blood, and was thus no sort of man at all. Which was a bit unfair, Volker thought; it had been his father's gold after all, not his.

Deinroth, he thought, was the likely instigator of the current situation. In his years as Kross's second-in-command, Deinroth had learned well the art of winding his belligerent superior up and setting him loose like a demigryph in a glassblower's shop. He'd been poking and prodding at Kross to lay in to Volker for weeks now, and it looked as if he'd finally got his wish.

'Three on the popinjay,' a second voice cut through the rising tumult like the peal of a hammer on an anvil. Men fell silent as a robed figure strode to the front of the growing crowd. Stern-featured and grizzled by decades of service on the Sylvanian frontier, Father Janos Odkrier was a welcome enough face. Odkrier wasn't quite a friend, but he was as close as Volker had in Heldenhame.

Odkrier winked at Volker. Around him, money changed hands and men shouted out bets. Kross staggered to his feet, face flushed, teeth bared. He swayed slightly, but didn't fall. He raised his fists. 'I'll wipe that smirk off your chinless face, Volker,' he spat.

'There's no need for this, commandant,' Volker said hurriedly. A brawl wasn't quite as bad as a duel, but the knights frowned on it regardless. Especially in times like these, with northmen howling south in ever-increasing numbers, green comets raining down out of the sky, and a great bloody wall of bone towering over Sylvania's borders. The whole world was coming undone around them. 'If Leitdorf finds out, we'll both get our necks stretched,' he said. He cut a glance towards Deinroth, who was smirking in his usual unpleasant fashion, and wondered if that was what Kross's right hand man wanted. 'You know how he feels about his officers brawling in front of the rank and file.'

Kross smiled maliciously. 'Leitdorf isn't here, popinjay.' He shuffled forward and threw a blow that would have broken Volker's jaw, had it connected. Volker slid aside, the way his swordmaster had taught him, and drove his fist into Kross's side. The big man spun, quicker than Volker had expected, and caught him a stinging blow on the cheek. Volker fell back onto his rear, and only just managed to bob aside as Kross's iron-shod boot slammed down where he'd been sitting.

Volker's hand flew to his sword. As much as the thought turned his stomach, he knew that he could draw it and have it through Kross's fat gut in a wink and a nod. He was a better swordsman than any of those present. Indeed, he fancied he could even match one of Leitdorf's armoured thugs in a fair bout. But killing a superior officer was even worse than getting into a round of fisticuffs with one. Leitdorf already despised him; Volker had spent the months since his arrival avoiding the Grand Master of the Knights of Sigmar's Blood at every opportunity. Sigmar alone knew what Leitdorf would do to him if he pinked Kross even slightly. He pulled his hand away as Kross gave a bull bellow and charged towards him.

He caught Volker and swept him up in a bear hug. Volker groaned as he felt his ribs flex. Fat as he was, Kross was still strong enough to knock a dray horse off its hooves with a punch. The commandant's alcoholic breath washed over his face, and Volker was suddenly reminded that he had been headed to the tavern, before Kross had called him in. The crowd was cheering and catcalling in equal measure, their faces a blur as Kross spun him about. Volker slithered an arm free and poked Kross in the eye with his thumb. Kross roared and released him. The commandant stumbled back, clawing at his face. He belched curses and snatched his dagger from his belt. Volker backed away, hands raised. Kross staggered after him, blade raised.

Then came the sharp, savage sound of a cane striking something metal and all the cheering ceased. Both Volker and Kross turned as a lean, broad-shouldered figure stumped through the crowd. The newcomer leaned on a cane, and was dressed in the heavy furs and coarse jerkin that all of the members of the Knights of Sigmar's Blood wore when not in armour. His face bore the sort of scars that came from getting pulled off a horse and into a knot of orcs and summarily trodden on. His name was Rudolph Weskar, and he was the closest thing to the word of Sigmar made flesh this side of Leitdorf in Heldenhame.

All of the fire went out of Kross, and he hastily put away his blade. Volker swallowed as the limping man approached them. Deinroth and the other captains were already melting away with the crowd. 'Brawling without prior permission is a pillory offence, gentlemen,' Weskar said, leaning on his cane. His hard, dull eyes pinned Kross. 'Commandant Kross, I can smell the reek of alcohol on you from here. Do not make me regret recommending you to the Grand Master for promotion, Otto. Go sober up, and keep that potato peeler you call a knife in its sheath from now on.'

Kross hesitated. He glared at Volker one last time, then nodded tersely and slunk away. Volker didn't watch him go. He kept his eyes on Weskar. He licked his lips, suddenly dying for a drink. Weskar stumped towards him. 'Wendel, Wendel, Wendel. You disappoint me, Wendel. When I heard what was going on, I was hoping you might finally spit that hog, and thus deliver yourself to the hangman, freeing me to promote a more congenial pair to your positions. Instead, here we are.' He came close to Volker, and the latter tensed. A discreet cough caused Weskar to glance around. Father Odkrier alone had remained where he was, when Weskar's arrival had caused everyone else to scatter. The old Sigmarite wasn't afraid of anyone or anything.

Weskar turned back to Volker. 'Why?' he asked simply.

Volker swallowed. He knew what Weskar was asking. 'Kross was drunk, and bullying an innkeeper. When the man refused him further service, he tried to gut him. The lads intervened. Kross was still drunk when he ordered that they be flogged for laying hands on a superior officer. I thought if I could keep them out of sight until he sobered up...' He trailed off. Weskar grunted.

'That he might regret it, and not punish them further,' he said. 'You know a little something about the regrets overindulgence brings, I think, eh, Wendel?' He leaned forwards again, like a hound on the scent. 'You're dying for a drink now, I'd wager.' Volker didn't answer. Weskar twitched a hand. 'Go,' he said.

Volker hurried past him, his hands trembling. Odkrier caught him around the shoulders and shoved a flask into his hands as they left Weskar standing there, staring after them. 'Drink up, my boy. I'd say you've earned it.'

Karaz-a-Karak, Worlds Edge Mountains

Ungrim Ironfist sat on his stone bench and listened to the basso rumble of dwarf disagreement as the Kingsmeet entered its fifth hour. King Kazador of Karak Azul pounded upon the stone table with a heavy fist, and King Alrik of Karak Hirn crossed his brawny arms and scowled at his fellow monarch. Belegar of Karak Eight Peaks sat hunched and silent in his seat, looking at no one, his face sagging with the weight of constant worry. And glaring at them all, from the far end of the table, sat the High King, Thorgrim Grudgebearer.

As Kingsmeets went, this one wasn't as bad as Ungrim had begun to fear, on his journey to Karaz-a-Karak. He'd learned that the occurrences in Sylvania were already well known, at least by Thorgrim, and that the von Carstein was one of the problems under discussion. One of many problems, in fact. The reports he'd received had only been the tip of the proverbial anvil, and the world seemed to be intent on coming apart at the seams, all at once.

Ungrim didn't find that as distressing as the others. Indeed, it filled him with a bitter enthusiasm. He had long been torn between two fates – that of king, and that of a Slayer. To prioritise the one over the other was impossible, and as the centuries progressed, he had begun to feel as if he, like his father before him, would die still cloaked in dishonour, and that his son, Garagrim, would be forced to tread the same line. Ungrim closed his eyes for a moment, as the old pain resurfaced. Every time he thought it buried and gone, it clawed its way back to the forefront of his mind. Garagrim was dead now, and free of the shame that still held Ungrim. He had died as a warrior, and as a Slayer, though he'd had no dishonour of his own to expunge. He'd thought his blood could buy his father's freedom, but such things were not proper.

Garagrim had meant well, but he had been a foolish boy, with a beardling's bravado and his mother's stubbornness. At the thought of the latter, he felt a pang. He missed his wife's quiet counsel. His queen had a mind second to none, and a clarity of thought that cut through even the most rancorous preconceptions. It was she who should be sitting here. He had no mind for politics, and no patience for querulous oldbeards like Kazador.

Ungrim contented himself with examining the table. It had been carved long before the Time of Woes, and a map of the ancient dwarf empire at its height sprawled across its surface. Holds that had not existed for untold centuries were still marked there, as if to deny their destruction, as if to shout, *'What has been still is and will always be'* into the void. Then, that was the way of his people. Like mountains in the stream of time, they sat immoveable and intractable, but worn down bit by bit, over the span of aeons.

He sighed and looked about the chamber, scanning the gathered faces that watched from the ascending rows of benches that surrounded the table and its occupants. Courtiers, thanes, advisors, second cousins twice removed of the aforementioned thanes, and anyone who could get past the chamber wardens was watching. Politics was a spectator sport among the *dawi*. Like as not, someone was collecting bets on when the first punch would be thrown, or the first head-butt delivered.

'The Underway swarms with ratkin and *grobi*,' Kazador said, drawing Ungrim's attention as he cut the air with his hand. 'But they do not attack. Something is afoot. Something is growing in the deep darkness, something foul, that threatens to drown us all when it finally surges to the surface.'

'Or maybe they're simply warring with one another as they are wont to do,' Alrik said. He looked at Thorgrim. 'Their numbers swell and their filthy warrens abut one another in most places. They seek the same holes, and like the vermin they are, they fight over them. If they have gone quiet, it is because they are busy doing our work for us!'

'Then explain the new access tunnels my miners have found,' Kazador snarled, slapping the table. 'Explain the skaven-sign splashed on the walls of the lower levels. Explain the sounds echoing up from the far depths – not of battle, but of *industry*.'

Alrik settled back in his seat, silent and frowning. For several moments, no one said anything. Then, Thorgrim spoke. 'I too have heard these reports, and more besides. I have seen the glowering skies and heard the growl of the stones. Beasts stir in mountain caves, and our northern kin, in their strongholds in the mountains of Norsca, send word of daemons scouring the lands, and of the mobilisation of the barbarians who worship the Dark Gods.' He looked around. 'But these are not new tidings. These are merely old tidings on a new day. Our people are still strong. Our enemies still break themselves on our walls and are swept away by our throngs. Did not the Ironfist shatter such a horde in years past? Did he not take the head and pelt of the Gorewolf?'

Ungrim grimaced. In truth, he hadn't taken the Chaos warlord's head. The Gorewolf had been killed by the renegade Gotrek Gurnisson. In doing so, Gurnisson had saved Ungrim's life, which only added to the Slayer King's already weighty grudge against the other Slayer. Years later, when Gurnisson had returned to Karak Kadrin on the trail of a dragon, Ungrim had considered clapping him and his pet poet in irons and dumping them somewhere unpleasant, to repay the indignity. He had restrained himself then, as before. Gurnisson wore chains of destiny that not even a king could shatter, more was the pity.

'Horde after horde has poured into these mountains and we have shattered them all, be they northmen, orcs or ogres,' Thorgrim went on. 'To seal our gates is to admit defeat before we have even seen the enemy.' He sat back on his seat and looked around. 'I see by your faces that some of you agree, and others do not. Belegar, speak...' He motioned to the king of the Eight Peaks, who looked up, startled. Ungrim realised that he'd been lost in his own gloomy thoughts. He cleared his throat.

'I have little to add, High King,' he said. 'Siege is not new for those of us who make our home in the Eight Peaks. We war with grobi and ratkin both, and they war with one another when we retreat to lick our wounds and entomb our dead. In truth, these tidings mean little to me. I know my enemies, and I fight them daily. I fight them in the tunnels and on the peaks, and what does it matter if the sky above is blue, red or green, when a skaven is looking to gut you with a rusty blade? What does it matter if the earth shakes, when your halls are swarmed by goblins? What do the affairs of the far northern holds matter, when your own is swamped by enemies?'

He held up his hands. 'I have only two hands, brother-kings. I have only a third of a hold – aye, a great hold, and greater still when I have wiped it clean of the remaining filth that infests it, but still... only a third.' He looked squarely at Thorgrim. 'For my part, I am here because I owe you a debt, High King. You helped to defend my meagre holdings against the orcs, when the beast known as Gorfang came knocking at my gates. For your part, I suspect that I am here out of courtesy only, though you would shave your beard before you admitted it, I wager. I am here, because you are worried – all of you.' He turned, taking in the whole of the table. 'We are small for a grand council. Where are the others? Where are the kings of Zhufbar and Karak Izor? Where is the king of Kraka Drak or the lord of Barak Varr?' He sat back and shook his head. 'They did not – or could not come. They are worried. More worried than ever before. The sky weeps and the world heaves, and our enemies have gone silent. They are right to be worried.'

'Well said, brother,' Kazador grunted. He looked at Thorgrim. 'Alrik might be blind, but you are not, Grudgebearer. And if you will not heed me, you might heed another.' He gestured. From out of the throng of watching advisors and hangers-on stepped a thick-set figure who all immediately recognised. A rush of whispers and mutters swept about the chamber as Thorek Ironbrow, Runelord of Karak Azul, stepped forward, one hand resting on the anvil-shaped head of his rune hammer, Klad Brakak, which was thrust through his belt.

'Karag Haraz, Karag Dron and Karag Orrud all belch smoke into the sky, High King,' Ironbrow said portentously. He gestured in a southerly direction with one gnarled hand. The runelord's hide looked like leather, and was puckered by burns and pale scars.

Even by Ungrim's standards, Thorek Ironbrow was a conservative. He was a dwarf who held fast to the oldest of ways, and his words were heavy with the weight of uncounted centuries. He had ruled over the weapon shops of Karak Azul for as long as Ungrim had been alive, and even the sons of kings dared not enter his domains without his prior approval – almost all of the kings in the council chamber had felt the lash of Ironbrow's tongue or the hard, calloused palm of his hand on the backs of their heads as beardlings. That was why he could get away with lecturing them now. The runelord looked about him as he went on, his hard gaze resting on each king in turn, as if they were a group of particularly dull-witted apprentices. 'Mountains that have not erupted in millennia now vomit forth fire and smoke and death. The world shudders beneath a horrible tread, my kings, and unless we are prepared, we will be ground underfoot.'

Ungrim had heard that argument before. Every time a horde swept south, out of the Wastes, or west out of the Dark Lands, Ironbrow made some variation of it. He knocked on the table with his knuckles, interrupting the runelord's rehearsed speech. He grinned as Ironbrow glared at him for his temerity, and asked, 'And by prepared, you mean close the gates?'

Ironbrow hesitated. Then, solemnly, he nodded. 'We must put our faith in strong walls and shields, rather than squandering our strength upon wayward allies.' Another murmur arose at that. Everyone with half a brain knew what the runelord was referring to by that comment.

Thorgrim had earlier spoken of the kidnapping of the Ulthuani Everchild out from under the noses of the warriors of Karaz-a-Karak, and the subsequent battle at Nagashizzar: a battle that had failed to free her from Mannfred von Carstein's clutches, despite the aid the High King had rendered to the *elgi*. Ungrim glanced at Thorgrim, to see if he'd noticed the dig. It was hard to tell, given the High King's ever present sour expression.

Ironbrow was still talking. He gestured to King Kazador. 'My king has already heeded my council and sealed the main gates of Karak Azul. Will you not do the same, *Slayer* King?'

Ungrim sucked on his teeth, stung by Ironbrow's tone. 'No,' he said bluntly. He cut his eyes towards Thorgrim. 'Not unless so commanded by the High King, I won't.' He swivelled his gaze back towards Ironbrow. 'Karak Kadrin has ever been the edge of the axe, as Karaz-a-Karak is the shield. Let the world shake, and rats gnaw at our roots. We shall reap and slay and strike out as many grudges as Grimnir allows in what time we have.'

'You would doom your people, your hold, and for what? Has your inherited dishonour driven you that mad?' Kazador asked, heaving himself to his feet. 'Our people stand on the precipice of destruction, and all you see is an opportunity for war.'

'And so?' Ungrim asked hotly. He rose to his feet and slammed his knuckles down on the table, causing it to shiver. 'My people know war. And that is what is coming. Not some indecipherable doom, or irresistible event. No, it is war. And every warrior will be needed, every axe sharpened, every shield raised, for our enemies are coming, and our walls alone have never stopped them, as my brother-king knows to his cost.'

There was a communal intake of breath from the crowd above them as the words left Ungrim's lips. Kazador's eyes bulged from their sockets, and his teeth showed through his beard. Ungrim thought for a moment that the old king would launch himself across the table and seek to throttle him.

'Enough,' Thorgrim rumbled. 'That grudge has been settled, and by my hand. Every king here must do as he considers best for his hold and people. But there are other grudges to be settled and the Dammaz Kron sits open and impatient. I have vowed to strike out every entry in the Great Book of Grudges, and it seems that time to do so is running thin. If the throng of Karaz-a-Karak is mustered, I must know who will muster with me. Who stands with the Pinnacle of the Mountains?' He looked at Ungrim first.

Ungrim grinned. 'Do you even need to ask, High King?'

Thorgrim inclined his head slightly, and looked at the others in turn. Alrik stood and nodded belligerently. Belegar too stood and said, 'Aye, the Eight Peaks will march, to our enemies' ruin or our own.'

Thorgrim sat back. The High King seemed tired. Ungrim did not envy him the weight of responsibility he bore. Heavy sat the crown of the High King, and it was very likely that he was now watching the sun at last set on the empire of the dwarfs. Ungrim smiled humourlessly. Even so, if they were to die, then it was best done properly.

That was the only way dwarfs did anything, after all.

Adrift on the Great Ocean, sailing due east

The great beak snapped shut inches from Eltharion's nose, and a rumbling hiss filled the hold. The horses in the nearby stalls shifted nervously as the griffon hunched forward, its claws sinking into the wood of the deck. Eltharion reached up as the beast's chin dropped heavily onto his shoulder and stroked the ruffled feathers that cascaded down its neck. 'Shhh, easy, Stormwing,' he murmured. He felt one of his mount's heavy forepaws pat clumsily at his back, and heard its inarticulate grunt of contentment.

Around them, the ship made the usual noises of travel. Not even the graceful vessels of Lothern were free of those, though elvish craftsmanship was the finest in the world, and their ships second to none. If he listened, he could hear the waters of the Great Ocean caressing the hull, and beneath that, the melodic hum of the whales that occupied the sea. Their song was one of beauty and peace, but tinged with fear. Even the most isolated of animals could sense that the world was sick.

As he stroked the griffon's neck and head, he looked about him. The horses who shared Stormwing's hold belonged to the Knights of Dusk, a noble family of Tor Ethel. More accurately, the only family, noble or otherwise, of Tor Ethel, which was all but abandoned these days. It sat on the western coast of Tiranoc, and each year coastal erosion took more of that once shining city into the sea, claiming gardens, sanctuaries and palaces alike. The Knights of Dusk hailed from the ever-shrinking group of the city's remaining inhabitants. They were valiant warriors, as were the others who had accompanied him and Eldyra on this journey.

Besides the Silver Helms of Tor Ethel, there were the Sentinels of Astaril, mistwalkers of Yvresse, in whose company he had honed his archery skills as a youth, and the Faithbearers of Athel Tamarha, a company of spearmen who had fought at his side in every campaign but one. A small enough host, but tested, and experienced. They would need to be, to survive what was coming. They were entering unknown territory. The last time he'd set foot in the lands of men, they still hadn't quite grasped the concept that hygiene wasn't a mortal offence. He doubted much had changed in the intervening centuries.

He didn't hate them. He simply didn't see a reason for their existence. They caused more problems than they solved, for all that they were barely more than chattering apes. It had been men, after all, who had allowed the goblin, Grom, to pass through their lands in order to reach Ulthuan. Teclis doted on them, in his acerbic way, something that had always puzzled Eltharion. Men were the cause of the problems facing them now. Men fed Chaos a constant stream of souls, whether they knew it or not. And if they weren't doing that, they were turning themselves into abominations like Mannfred von Carstein. Men couldn't leave well enough alone. Some small part of Eltharion hoped that whatever was going on would swallow mankind whole before it ended, and that the Dark Gods would choke on their grubby little souls.

As if sensing the direction his thoughts were taking, the griffon grumbled into his ear, its hot, foul breath washing over him. He pushed the thoughts aside and concentrated on calming the animal. Once, when Stormwing was no more than a squalling cub, he'd have taken the beast in his arms like an infant, and carried it about until it was soothed to sleep by the rhythm of his heartbeat. Now the griffon was bigger than the largest of the horses who occupied the remainder of the hold, and a good deal more skittish about the confined space it found itself in.

'I see Stormwing is no more fond of the sea than his master,' a voice said. Eltharion didn't turn. He dug his fingers into the strange spot where feathers met fur on Stormwing's body and gave it a good scratch. One of the griffon's rear paws thumped the deck, and its spotted tail lashed in pleasure.

'Come to check on your own mount, then, Eldyra?' he asked. 'He misses you. I can tell.'

'I doubt that. He's asleep, the lazy brute,' Eldyra said, crossing to the stall where her stallion, Maladhros, stood dozing. The big, silver dappled animal was the only one who showed no concern at Stormwing's presence, though whether that was because they had been stabled together before, or because Maladhros had fewer wits than a thick brick, Eltharion couldn't say. The stallion was strong and fierce, and Eldyra swore that it was a canny beast as well, but Eltharion thought she vastly overestimated its problem-solving capabilities. When he'd come down into the hold, it had been eating an empty bucket.

She clucked and rubbed the stallion's nose, stirring it to wakefulness. Eltharion watched as she fed it an apple, and it crunched contentedly. 'He's taking the trip well,' he said.

'He knows it's important,' she said. She stroked the horse's mane.

'Does he now?' Eltharion smiled.

Eldyra looked at him. 'As a matter of fact, yes, he does. How is Stormwing?' she asked. She stepped across the hold towards him, light on her feet despite the pitch of the deck. She was the perfect blend of grace and lethality, much as Tyrion was, Eltharion reflected. He wondered if the latter was aware of just how much he'd shaped the princess of Tiranoc in his image, and whether he'd find that worrisome. Probably not; in Eltharion's opinion, Tyrion didn't worry as much as he should, at least not about the right things.

'Nervous. He doesn't like confined spaces. He prefers to fly,' he said. The griffon grumbled and eyed Eldyra balefully. Stormwing didn't care for anyone other than Eltharion getting too close. He had a tendency to snap.

'Why not let him?'

'There's no guarantee he'd remember to come back, rather than fly home,' Eltharion said, rubbing his palm over the curve of Stormwing's beak. The creature butted his chest and made a sound halfway between a purr and a chirp. 'He's not very bright.' He hesitated. 'Then, perhaps he's smarter than both of us.'

'Do you truly hold so little hope?' she asked, quietly.

He smiled thinly. 'I am not known as "the Grim" for nothing,' he said.

'That's not an answer.'

'No, it is not.' He looked at her. 'There is no hope. She is as good as dead, or worse. We are not heroes... We are avengers.'

'Tyrion doesn't think so,' she said.

'Tyrion lies to himself,' he said softly. 'Just as he lied to himself that there would be no consequences for his indiscretion. Those lies are the source of optimism, and his downfall.'

'You think that, and yet here you are,' Eldyra said. She said it as if it were an accusation. And perhaps it was, he thought. He nodded agreeably.

'I am, yes.'

'Why?'

'Why are you here?' he asked.

'My lord Tyrion ordered it,' she said stiffly.

'I was under the impression that he was your friend,' he said. 'Just as he is my friend.' He tasted the word as he said it. It wasn't one he used often, or, indeed, at all. But it seemed fitting, in reference to Tyrion. Tyrion was his friend, and that meant that there was nothing Eltharion wouldn't do to help him. 'And I, like you, am smart enough to know that if we were not here, he would be, and Ulthuan would suffer for it.'

'Or at least worse than it already has,' Eldyra said. 'Do you think...?'

'I do not think. I do not worry. I trust. We have our mission. Tyrion and Teclis will drive the daemonic hosts from our shores, as they did before. And we will find Aliathra, for good or ill, whether she is alive or...' He trailed off.

'She is alive. Of that much, I am certain, Warden of Yvresse,' a new voice cut in. A blue-robed shape descended the steps down into the hold. Pale eyes looked about from beneath a diadem of emeralds, and a thin mouth quirked in disgust. 'Why you two insist on spending so much time in this makeshift stable, I'll never understand. It smells awful.'

'It'd smell worse if someone didn't see to the animals occasionally,' Eltharion said, turning to face the newcomer. He cocked his elbow up on Stormwing's flat skull. 'And you could have waited until we came back up on deck.'

'Probably, yes, but then I wouldn't have been able to interject my opinions so smoothly, now would I?' Belannaer groused. He tapped the side of his head. 'It's all about the seizing the moment.'

'What is?' Eldyra asked, smiling crookedly. She enjoyed teasing the Loremaster of Hoeth, and Eltharion couldn't find it in his heart to blame her. Belannaer had once been the High Loremaster of Ulthuan, before ceding the title and its responsibilities to Teclis. Many, including Eltharion, thought Belannaer had been only too happy to do so, making him a rarity among the Ulthuani. In the years since, he'd found contentment amongst the tomes of yesteryear, forgoing the crudity of politics and war, for a life devoted to study and contemplation. But he'd set such prosaic workings aside when he'd learned of the Everchild's capture. Belannaer knew, better perhaps than anyone else save Teclis, what such an event meant to the fate of Ulthuan. But though he'd shed his reclusive ways and taken up his sword once more, he was still a scholar, with a scholar's stuffiness and a pedant's obliviousness.

'Everything,' Belannaer said. He gestured airily. 'History is made of moments and the people who seized them.' He looked at Eltharion. 'Aliathra has seized hers. I can hear her voice on the wind, stronger now than before, for all that she's growing weaker. Time is running short.'

'We can only sail as fast as the wind takes us, loremaster,'

Eltharion said. He knew what Belannaer was feeling, for he'd felt it himself. The growing impatience, the anxiety of uncertainty. There were still hundreds of miles of overland travel between them and Sylvania. They would make up time by keeping to the river, but even then, there was no telling what might arise to stymie them.

'I know, which is why I stoked the winds with my sorcery, so that we might move faster,' Belannaer said. Eldyra looked at Eltharion.

'I wondered why the ship was creaking so,' she murmured. Eltharion shushed her with a quick look and said, 'Something is different, isn't it?'

'Aliathra has shown me... flashes of what awaits us,' Belannaer said. 'There are dark forces on the move, and this is but the smallest shred of their plan. We will need allies.' He said the last hesitantly.

Eltharion tensed. 'Allies,' he repeated. 'You mean men.'

'And the dwarfs, if they can be convinced,' Belannaer said.

'No,' Eltharion said. 'No, the dwarfs are the reason that Aliathra was captured in the first place. I'll not surrender her fate to their hands again.' He felt a surge of anger at the thought of it. 'Neither will I entrust it to men.' He shook his head. 'They are worse even than dwarfs. They cannot be counted on.'

'And yet we must, if we are to have any hope of rescuing the Everchild,' Belannaer said. 'I've ordered the fleet to sail due east, for the Empire of Sigmar. They know Teclis of old, and will be open to our entreaties. We gave them aid, once upon a time, and they owe Ulthuan a debt.'

'You ordered?' Eltharion shook his head, astounded at Belannaer's arrogance. 'I lead this expedition, loremaster, not you,' he said softly.

'You do,' Belannaer said. 'And I am sure you will come to the right decision eventually.'

Eltharion glanced at Eldyra. 'Did you know about this?'

'No, but he's right,' she said.

Eltharion's eyes narrowed. Eldyra spoke quickly, 'Think about it, cousin... Our army is small and we will have to cross lands held by men sooner or later. Better to do it with permission, and perhaps even with allies, than to fight our way through.' She held up a hand as he made to protest. 'We could do it. Our army, small as it is, is better than anything they can muster. But elves will die in the doing of it. And for what – pride? Better to sacrifice pride than warriors, especially where we're going.'

Eltharion listened silently. Some of Teclis had rubbed off on her as well, he thought. Then, given how closely the twins' fates had been linked these last few centuries, that wasn't surprising. Eldyra had learned the art of battle as Tyrion's squire. But she had learned something else entirely by watching Teclis's crooked mind at work.

Regardless, she wasn't wrong, save about his pride. It wasn't pride that motivated him, but caution. What profit could be gleaned from faithless allies or worse, useless ones? They would hamper the clean, quick strike, and slow them down. He was certain their host could cross quickly into Sylvania, before the men could mobilise to question them. But could they then get out again, once victory had been achieved? It would be unfortunate if they succeeded in rescuing Aliathra from one savage, only to fall prey to another.

Finally, Eltharion nodded. 'You are right, cousin, loremaster,' he said. 'Better we ally ourselves with willing primitives than stand alone in defeat.'

'Then the fleet will continue east?' Belannaer asked.

Eltharion nodded. 'East – it is time to see if the Empire of Sigmar remembers its debts.'

 The King's Glade, Athel Loren

Durthu, Eldest of Ancients, spoke in a voice like the rustling of branches and the cracking of bark. It filled the King's Glade, travelling through the branches of every tree and slipped from every leaf, until the air throbbed with the sound of his voice. '*The cycle of the world begins anew, and just as the forest once aided the folk of Ulthuan in days now slid from mortal memory, it shall do so again.*' Durthu shifted his immense weight as he spoke, and the air was rent by the squeal of twisting branches and the dull, wet crunch of popping roots. The treeman was the oldest of his kind, and his mind was like the forest itself: vast, wild and unpredictable.

Araloth watched as a ripple of murmurs spread through the assembled ranks of the Council of Athel Loren where they sat. It was rare that Durthu spoke, and rarer still that he spoke so lucidly. More and more often these days, his mind was awash in the forest's rage, and he spoke words of war and madness. But here was the calm Durthu of old, the wise spirit who had so often guided his folk in ages past. Araloth felt a twinge of sadness as he watched the ancient tree-spirit speak. The forest was dying, glade by glade, rotting from within and falling to the madness that had poured forth from the Vaults of Winter. Soon enough, if it was not halted, Durthu would join many of his kin in either decay or madness. And that would be a terrible moment indeed.

Araloth pushed the thought aside and concentrated on Durthu's words. '*But as in those days, there will be a price for the forest's aid, Everqueen of Ulthuan,*' Durthu said, his ageless eyes fixed on the proud figure of Alarielle. She stood before the council, bound in chains of leaves and vines, as was customary.

The Everqueen lifted her chin and said, 'I know nothing of these events, revered ancient, but whatever your price, know that I will pay it willingly and in full.' Her voice possessed a liquid musicality to it that, in other circumstances would have seemed the epitome of beauty to Araloth. But now, he could hear the sadness that tainted its harmonies, and the desperation that had driven its owner to this point.

At her words, the trees of the glade seemed to sigh, though

whether in sadness or triumph, Araloth couldn't say. Nor did he wish to guess. The forest had a mind of its own, one that no elf could attempt to fathom, not if they wished to remain sane.

Durthu receded back into his place. Having said his piece, the Eldest of Ancients had fallen silent. The bargain had been struck, and there was nothing more to be said. The Council was quick to act. One of them stood and met Araloth's gaze. 'You heard?' he asked.

'I did,' Araloth said. He knew what was coming next, for it was the only reason that he would have been summoned to witness what had just occurred.

'You, Lord of Talsyn, and champion of the Mage Queen, will assemble a host to pierce black Sylvania, and lend our cousins aid in their rescue attempt.'

'I will,' Araloth said, simply. Nothing more needed to be said. His mind was already hard at work on the logistics of such an undertaking. Axe Bite Pass would be the quickest route. They would head north, through Parravon. There would be dangers aplenty, but he had little doubt that it could be done. He would request volunteers. He would not order any to follow him into such a place.

The chains of vines and leaves fell from the Everqueen as the audience ended. Two of the Mage Queen's handmaidens, Naestra and Arahan, waited to take Alarielle to the place of reckoning, where her part of the bargain, whatever it was, would be fulfilled. Araloth did not envy her the task to come. She glanced at the handmaidens, and then strode towards him. 'My daughter,' she said.

'I will do all that it is in my power to do for her,' he said quietly.

'As will I,' she said, looking into his eyes. She took his hand and squeezed it. He felt a shock as something passed between them. When she released his hand, he saw that she had pressed a locket into his palm. He looked at her questioningly.

'It will lead you to my daughter,' she said. 'Let us hope, for the sakes of those we love, that you reach her in time.'

EIGHT

Castle Sternieste, Sylvania

Mannfred felt a hum of satisfaction ripple through him as he watched Arkhan take in the room, and its treasures. There, the lecterns that held the damned tomes of Nagash. Nine, now, rather than the seven they had been, thanks to Arkhan.

And amidst them sat the Crown of Sorcery, pulsing softly with its weird light. Arkhan stood before the crown, and reached out a hand. Mannfred was possessed by a sudden urge to rip him away from it, but he wrestled the feeling down. It would not do to start a fight. Not now.

From above, the vargheists growled warningly. They hissed and snarled as the liche ran his fingers over the crown, but fell silent at Mannfred's gesture. Arkhan traced the wicked iron points that topped Nagash's crown, and then let his hand drop. He did not look at Mannfred when he said, '*You have the Claw as well.*' It wasn't a question.

Mannfred crossed his arms and smirked. 'Indeed.'

'*Where?*'

'Not here,' Mannfred said.

Arkhan turned. *'Even now, you do not trust me.'* The liche cocked his head. *'You are wise, in your generation.'* He turned towards the prisoners. *'I thought you enjoyed their escape attempts. Why torture them?'*

The prisoners hung in their chains, broken and beaten. They stank of death now, as much as anything else in the castle. Their flesh had been gouged and burned and flayed, and all remaining armour had been stripped from those who wore it. They had been crippled and hobbled, and hovered on the brink of death. Only Mannfred's sorcerous artifice kept them from tipping over entirely into the void. Mannfred strode past Arkhan and wrenched up Volkmar's head. Of the nine, only the old man and Aliathra were still conscious. The vampire looked at the elf woman. Her eyes were closed, but her lips moved silently. He wondered whether she, like the nature priest, had slipped at last into madness. Or worse, into damnation like Morgiana.

Volkmar glared defiantly up at him with exhausted, pain-clouded eyes. Mannfred leaned close, drinking in his captive's pain and helplessness. 'Because the time for games is done. If you can do as you claimed, then it is time to put away childish things and get to work,' he said, staring at Volkmar. He leaned close to the old man. 'Don't you agree, Volkmar? Aren't you tired of this never-ending game of ours? Don't you want to see it end, finally, once and for all?'

Volkmar hawked a gobbet of bloody spittle into Mannfred's face. Mannfred released the old man's head and stepped back. He wiped the spittle from his face and smiled. He felt no anger at the gesture. It was nothing more than the defiance of a peasant on the block. He looked at Arkhan and gestured. 'Well – I allowed you in here for a reason, liche. Tell me... Which one?'

Arkhan picked his way carefully across the blood-stained floor, and he gazed at each of the nine in turn. His hell-spark eyes lingered on the elf woman for a moment, and Mannfred felt himself tense, though he could not say why. Arkhan motioned to the unconscious form of the Myrmidian knight, Blaze. *'You were correct, earlier. This one. His blood is powerful, but not as much as that of the others. It is diluted, and thus perfect for our purposes.'*

Mannfred nodded slightly. 'As I suspected.'

'You have already assembled much of what is required. But we still lack three things.' Arkhan turned. *'Three items tied to the Great Necromancer's death. All lie within reach of Sylvania, and all require but the proper application of force to acquire. Neither guile nor cunning will be necessary. Luckily for you,'* Arkhan said.

Mannfred twitched. He closed his eyes and fought to control his temper. Arkhan was baiting him, but he would not give the liche the satisfaction. 'I know all of this, you black-toothed hank of gristle. What I do not know is how you intend to help me acquire them.'

'I told you – the secret is in the blood,' Arkhan said, motioning to the floor. *'The true question is, how are we to divide the work to come?'*

Mannfred ran his hands over his bare head. 'Ah, well, there I think is my contribution. Before your – ah – *timely* arrival, I was already concocting stratagems for that very purpose. Heldenhame is too obvious a target, and too close. If we strike there first, our enemies will surely know that we have escaped the cage they made for me. For us,' Mannfred said. 'I suggest we divide our forces. You came close to acquiring Nagash's staff, Alakanash, from La Maisontaal Abbey once... Best you succeed this time.'

Arkhan didn't react to his dig. *'And the Fellblade?'*

'Not far from here, as you said. My spies have brought word that it is in the possession of the skaven somewhere in Mad Dog Pass, as you yourself are likely already aware.'

Arkhan inclined his head. *'And you will acquire it?'*

'I will.' Mannfred gestured down at the map. 'We will depart via the western border, I think. It will give you the quickest path into Bretonnia, and me the quickest into the Border Princes. Speed is of the essence, but it will still take us most of the year. I suggest that we save Heldenhame for our coming out party, as it were.'

Arkhan looked down at the map. He looked up. '*Agreed. It will take me some time to prepare. A few days, no more than that.*'

'Excellent. It will take me that long to see to raising a proper host, to carry us in style to our respective destinations.' Mannfred spread his hands. And to ensure that you return on your shield, rather than behind it, ally-mine, he thought. 'If you were capable of drinking, I'd raise a toast to you, oh mighty Arkhan.'

'*And if I had any interest in drinking with you, Mannfred, I would accept. Go, you may leave me here. I must attune myself to your sorceries and find the right strands to pull and those to cut.*' Mannfred hesitated, and Arkhan gave a rasping laugh. '*Fear not, vampire. Leave your dogs to guard me, if you wish. Summon ghouls or assign your pantomime Templars to stand sentinel over me, to ensure that I do not steal your treasures. I care not.*'

Mannfred bowed shallowly. 'You cannot fault me for being overcautious, Lord Arkhan. Allies, in my experience, are as the shifting sands – untrustworthy as a matter of course. But you shame me with your generosity of spirit, and courtly manner. I leave you, sir, to do as you must. And I go to do as I must.' Mannfred swept his cloak up about him and turned and left.

As he stalked through the corridors of Castle Sternieste, Mannfred forced aside the worries that gnawed at him. He didn't trust Arkhan, but he had little choice at this juncture. As old and as learned as he was in the arts of sorcery, Arkhan was older still. The liche had likely forgotten more about magic than Mannfred would ever be able to learn. He had been present at the birth of necromancy, and he was as good as Nagash's will given form.

But that wouldn't save him, once he'd outlived his usefulness.

Something yowled, and he paused. He looked up and saw Arkhan's detestable cat slinking through the ancient support timbers above. It glared down at him with milky-eyed malevolence, fleshless tail twitching. Mannfred's eyes narrowed. Was it watching him – spying for its master? He raised his hand, ready to blast it from existence, when something stopped him. He caught a glimpse of a massive, gaunt shape, twitching and flickering with witch-fire, out of the corner of his eye, like a giant squatting to fill the corridor behind him, and he whirled with a snarl. But there was nothing there. No giant and no shadow, save his own.

When he looked back up, the cat had vanished.

Mannfred looked around once more, and then continued on his way. He soon arrived at the high garden that he had made his war chamber for the coming campaign. He could not say why he had done so; he had rarely visited the high garden in all the months he had made Sternieste his home.

And do you remember why you avoided coming to Sternieste? Vlad purred softly. *This was my garden, wasn't it? Where I held my councils of war, in that golden age between conquest and damnation, while Sylvania was still to be won. I am honoured that you have chosen to honour my memory in such a way, my most attentive student.*

Mannfred stopped. He ran his hands over the crown of his head. He had had hair once, a luxuriant mane of hair, the hue of a raven's wing. He had been beautiful, and proud of that beauty. But after rising from the sump of Hel Fenn, he had shaved his head. His return was a rebirth. In death, he had been purged of old failings and faults, and vanity was discarded with the rest. Or so he'd thought.

Really, though, it had been to mark himself as different to Vlad. Vlad, with his icy mane and aristocratic mien; Vlad who held to the noble traditions of a long-gone empire – including the superstition that councils of war should be held in the open air, beneath the eyes of the gods so as to gain their favour.

Mannfred felt a chill course through him. Was that why he had been drawn to Sternieste, to the garden? Was he unconsciously imitating Vlad?

How many of Nagash's detestable tomes did I gather again?

One or two, surely. Your initiative in that regard is impressive, I must say. Then, you never did know how to quit while you were ahead, did you? Vlad laughed.

No, no, he had chosen Sternieste for the strategic advantage it provided. And the garden... Well, few others even knew it existed, which made it the ideal spot to confer with his subordinates without danger of eavesdroppers.

Am I so poor an example, then? Vlad whispered.

'You're dead. You tell me,' Mannfred muttered. Vlad's laughter accompanied him into the garden, where the inner circle of the Drakenhof Templars sat or stood, arguing loudly amongst themselves. Well, Anark and Markos were arguing, which had become an annoyingly regular occurrence. The two vampires snarled and cursed at one another, and Mannfred thought they might come to blows. He paused, waiting, amused now, his previous uncertainties forgotten.

'Oh very good,' he said, after the spectre of violence had passed on, thwarted. 'I do so enjoy a spirited debate. I hope it was about something important.'

'He refuses to acquiesce to my authority,' Anark growled. Elize had one hand on his shoulder and her other pressed flat to Markos's chest.

'When you show me a reason to respect the puerile demands that flutter from your flapping lips, perhaps I will,' Markos snapped.

Mannfred sighed and strode between them. Elize retreated as Mannfred's hands snapped out and his fingers fastened on the throat of either vampire. Unliving muscle swelled as Mannfred hauled them both up and off their feet and into the air. 'This debate, while amusing, is most assuredly moot, my friends. The only authority here to which you must acquiesce is mine own.' Point made, he dropped them both. Anark, with a beast's wisdom, scrambled away. Markos sat and glared, rubbing his throat. Mannfred ignored him.

'The liche thinks that he can shatter the mystic cage that holds us,' he said, pushing aside the flicker of anger that accompanied those words. 'Out, all of you. Rouse the barrow-legions and draw the souls of the cursed dead from the stones where they sleep. The muster of Sternieste marches to war, and I would have every muck-encrusted bone and ragged shroud ready. Go, fly, rouse my army,' Mannfred said, sweeping out a hand.

Markos and the others filed out of the garden. But before Elize could follow them, Mannfred stopped her. As he did so, he noticed that her pets hesitated. Brute and shadow, Anark and the Crowfiend. Anark hesitated more obviously, waiting like a loyal hound. The Crowfiend lurked outside the entrance to the garden, as if he were only stopping to admire the mouldy tapestries that dangled from the walls there. Mannfred looked at Elize and she motioned delicately to Anark. He turned and left, visibly reluctant. The Crowfiend drifted away a moment later, silent and seemingly unconcerned.

'The loyalty you inspire in your get awes me, Elize,' Mannfred said. He clasped his hands behind his back and strode towards the tree. 'Do I inspire the same devotion in any creature?'

'I am your loyal servant, my lord,' Elize said softly.

'So you have shown again and again, sweet cousin.' Mannfred glanced at her. 'You are one of the rocks upon which my foundations stand.' He looked away. 'We are sallying forth from this besieged province, cousin, and I would have the Drakenhof Templars in the vanguard.'

'We have ever stood at the narrowest point, my lord,' Elize said.

'That point, I'm afraid, is going to become narrower still.' He lifted a hand, and spoke a single, shuddering syllable. The air thickened and the light dimmed, as if a fog had settled over the garden. 'There,' Mannfred said. 'Now we can speak freely with one another, without curious ears eavesdropping. Anark will accompany Arkhan into Bretonnia.'

'Bretonnia,' Elize repeated. She hesitated, and then nodded. Mannfred had not told his inner circle just what he was after, but he had no doubt that the brighter sparks among them had already guessed. 'Are you certain now is the time, my lord?'

'Was that a question, or a suggestion?' Mannfred asked. 'Arkhan's usefulness is finite. Can your pet be trusted to do this thing for me, sweet cousin?' Mannfred asked, looking up at the tree. It seemed to be flourishing anew, its limbs growing gnarled and strong, as if it were feeding on the mortal energies of the dead things gathered at Sternieste. He traced the jagged contours of its crumbling bark with a finger.

'He can, my lord,' Elize said.

'You sound confident.'

'In Anark's strength and willingness? Yes, cousin, I am. I chose him for those qualities.'

Mannfred smiled. 'Ah, cousin, my cousin, you were ever the darling of dear, sweet, mad Isabella's eye, in those glorious times now gone to dust and memory. She relied much on you, in those final days, while Vlad was occupied with the war.'

Elize said nothing, but silence was as good an answer as anything she might have chosen to say, to Mannfred's way of thinking. He glanced over his shoulder at Elize, studying her. 'You were alone among her handmaidens in your practicality and – dare I say it? – your sanity. A mind second only to my own, I have often said.'

'Have you, my lord? I have never heard you say such about anyone,' Elize said mildly. Mannfred raised his brow in surprise. Elize was normally quite circumspect. He expected such comments from Markos, but Elize...

'You are worried, then,' he said, turning to face her. 'Should I send another of your creatures? The Crowfiend, perhaps? Erikan of Mousillon,' he continued, and his smile turned feral as a brief look of consternation crossed her perfectly composed features. 'Oh yes, I smelt the stink of that particular demesne on him, the poor boy. He is the last surviving pup of the Cannibal Knight of Mousillon, of infamous memory, isn't he? The Bretonnians burned that lot in their sewer palaces. The Cannibal Knight, his princess of Bel-Aliad, and their squalling retainers. Royalty, that one, at least insofar as the Bretonni judge these things. He has no idea, of course, and I shall not tell him.' He crossed the space between them and caught her chin. 'That shall be my gift to you, hmm? From one loving cousin to another.' He lifted her chin, so that her eyes met his. 'Shall I send him instead of Anark, perhaps? Or both together?'

'As you wish, my lord,' Elize said.

Mannfred released her and stepped back. He chuckled. 'What game are you playing, sweet cousin, that you will not share your moves with me?'

'It is but a small one, to amuse myself,' she said.

'I've often wondered... How did you woo him? Or did he woo you, the necromancer's apprentice trailing after the beautiful lady without mercy?' Mannfred turned away. 'He angered you, though, your cannibal prince. I know that much. He left to follow his own path, without a word of thanks for all your efforts to groom him into something greater. What was your plan then? Was he to be a stepping stone to influence elsewhere?'

'As I said, my lord, it was but a small amusement,' Elize said.

She was lying. Mannfred nodded nonetheless, as if he believed her. 'Then you will not mind if I send both. If one of your creatures fails, then the other will not.'

Elize's face might as well have been a marble mask. 'As you will, my lord. Who, dear cousin, will accompany you? And who will be castellan here?'

'The latter is easy enough – you,' he said.

She blinked. Then, she inclined her head. 'You honour me, cousin.'

'I know. See that you do not disappoint me. I'd hate to accomplish my goals, only to return to a burned-out ruin, and a scattered army.' He ran his palms over his head and said, 'As for who shall accompany me... Markos and our good Vargravian count, Nyktolos. Both have warred in the Border Princes before, and their experience is required. Master Nictus will stay with you, to act as your good right hand.'

Elize hesitated. Then, 'Are you certain you wish to take Markos?'

Mannfred looked at her. 'Concerned for my wellbeing, sweet cousin?'

'If I were not, would I have warned you of Tomas's intentions, all those months ago, before this affair even began? Would I have warned you that he'd made an agreement with von Dohl, that he was promised command of the armies of Waldenhof, if he took your head?'

'As I recall, you warned me so that I might allow you to choose the next Grand Master of the Drakenhof Order. A straight bargain, Elize.' Mannfred laughed. 'And even if I hadn't known, Tomas would have failed. He was a maggot, nothing more, just like von Dohl, and the cursed Shadowlord and all the others who defy my blood-right.'

'Like Markos?'

Mannfred paused. 'Markos has never been... comfortable in a subordinate role. Vlad spoiled him. He had a peculiar fondness for acerbity in his servants.'

And you would know, wouldn't you, boy? Vlad's voice murmured. Mannfred ignored it and continued, 'It is a fondness that I do not, on the whole, share.' *Of course not. You never could stand to be questioned could you, young prince*? Vlad needled him. Mannfred felt his cheek twitch as he sought to restrain a snarl of frustration. 'I am giving Markos a chance. He will serve, or he will make his move,' he said. 'Either way, I am too close to victory to allow him to remain undecided. We are coming to the sharp end of all things, sweet cousin. The time when sides must be chosen, and banners unfurled for the last time. All games save mine must be put aside, for the good of all who bear the von Carstein name.' He looked at her. 'Including yours, my sweet Elize.'

'*Do you dream, old man?*' Arkhan asked. He examined Volkmar from a distance, head cocked. He had stood in the same place since Mannfred had left, soaking up the miasma of the place, drinking in the concentrated essence of his master's earthly remains. All that had been Nagash, save for certain pieces, was here, and he could feel the Great Necromancer's presence beating down upon his brain like a terrible black sun. '*I think you do. You can hear his footsteps in the hollows of your heart, and his voice in the sour places of your memory, even as I can.*'

Volkmar said nothing. He glared at Arkhan as silently as he had Mannfred. Arkhan leaned against his staff. He was not weary, but sometimes he felt what might be the ghost of such a feeling, deep in his bones. '*I see the skull beneath your skin, old man. It's no use denying it. He has chosen you.*'

'He *is* chosen, and by Lord Mannfred,' Morgiana hissed. She rose from where she'd been crouching in the corner and sauntered towards Arkhan, as far as her chains would allow. Unlike the others, she hadn't been beaten to within an inch of her life. She no longer had a life to lose. She glowed with the cold fire of undeath to Arkhan's eyes, and he did not wonder why she was still chained. She had been threat enough in life. In death she was even more dangerous. Or she would be, once she learned the new limits of her power.

Arkhan examined her curiously. She was kept with the others both because she made for a cruelly amusing gaoler, and because even Mannfred wasn't so foolish as to let a creature like Morgiana Le Fay wander loose. Her blood still pulsed with the raw stuff of life, as did her magics. It was only her presence that kept the other captives from slipping over the precipice into death's domain. Mannfred had truly wrought something abominable when he'd turned her. Still, there was yet a sliver of the woman she had been within the beast he'd made of her.

'*How did he acquire you, I wonder?*' he murmured, drawing close to her. She hissed and retreated, her eyes narrowing with pain. Arkhan stopped. Some vampires, those with an unusual sensitivity to the winds of death, felt pain in his presence. He was little more than the power of necromancy given form, and for some vampires, that was the difference between being warmed by flames and burned by them.

Morgiana's beautiful features twisted into an expression of bestial malice. 'Drycha,' she spat. Arkhan nodded. The branchwraith of Athel Loren had ever been a changeable and unpredictable factor. It did not surprise him that she had brought Morgiana to Mannfred. That sort of malevolent caprice was what Drycha was best at.

'Free me, liche, and I shall aid you in whatever way you wish,' Morgiana said, the mask of humanity slipping back over her face. She rattled her chains for emphasis. 'I shall abet you and comfort you. My magics – all that I am – will be at your disposal.'

Arkhan let a raspy laugh slip between his fleshless jaws. '*I doubt that, woman. Mannfred keeps you chained for good reason. You are more dangerous now than you were in your enchanted Bretonnian bower.*'

Morgiana snarled and sprang for him. Arkhan didn't move. He had stopped just out of the reach of her chains, and she tumbled heavily to the floor, where she rolled about, writhing and shrieking like a she-wolf in a trap. She spat bloody froth at him, and where it struck the floor, green patches of moss flourished, before swiftly withering and dying.

He turned away from her display, focusing his attentions on the Everchild, where she hung in her chains, eyes closed, lips moving in a silent song. And it was a song, for Arkhan could hear it, even if Mannfred could not. It was a hymn, a sorcerous prayer, subtle yet powerful enough to pierce the bindings Mannfred had placed about Sylvania. It was a thing of intricate beauty to his eyes and sorcerous sense, a crystalline web that stretched upwards from Aliathra, growing in strength and size, as she powered the spell with her own life essence.

'*I wonder if they have heard you yet, child?*' he asked as he approached her. '*I think they have. I can feel the burden of gathering destinies. Your song calls your kin to your side. Perhaps you have wondered why I have not stopped you?'*

The elf did not reply. Her eyes remained shut, and her lips continued to move. Arkhan brushed a strand of her hair from her face, and he felt her clammy skin quiver at his touch. *'It serves the ends of the one whom I serve, you see. I tell you this so that you understand that we are both pawns, and that there is no malice in my actions.'*

Her eyes flashed open. Arkhan lowered his hand. There was fire there, and rage. It crashed against the coldness of him, and he almost flinched back. As much power as inundated his cracked and ancient bones, the fury that lurked in the elf maiden's blood was greater by far. It was power enough to shatter continents and crack the world's core.

For a moment, Arkhan felt fire and pain. Then it passed, and he was himself again. He found that his cat had returned, its maggoty body pressed tight to his shoulders. Its weight had come upon him unnoticed, and it hissed at the elf maiden with feline disdain. He reached up and stroked the animal's decaying throat. Aliathra's eyes were closed. Arkhan turned away, disturbed.

That disturbance did not lessen in the coming days, as he prepared for the ritual that would allow for escape from the caged province. He saw Ogiers and the others but little over the following days. The trio of necromancers he'd scavenged from the ruins of Mallobaude's army had scattered the moment they arrived, slipping his reins to find newer, more pliable partners or masters. It would have been a matter of moments to summon them back to his side, but for the moment he left them free to pursue their whims. Morgiana, despite her madness and untrustworthy nature, still had an able mind, and she proved an able replacement, in between pleas for release and demands for blood. It was fitting that she was such, for she was, herself, one of the cornerstones of the very ritual that formed the root of their current predicament.

He had faced Morgiana only briefly on the field of Couronne during Mallobaude's revolt, but that confrontation had shown him the nature of the power that lurked beneath Bretonnia's barbaric facade. That Morgiana was still somehow connected to it, despite her current state only confirmed his suspicions. Necromancy, at its base, had been born in elven minds, or so Nagash swore. He had altered it, and forced it into a shape more to his liking, but its seed had been planted in the wisdom of Aliathra's dark kin, even as Morgiana's own had its roots in the secret glades of Athel Loren.

The collegial magics that had been used to create the wall of faith were similar, albeit watered down, and altered still further to account for the frailty of the human frame. Luckily, that was something Arkhan no longer had to worry about.

As the weeks progressed, he eventually ordered Morgiana unchained, to better aid him in preparing his form for the rite to come. His bones had to be carved with the proper sigils and runes, and the ritual knife he would use had to be soaked in the blood of each of the nine captives for a certain amount of time. The proper bindings had to be prepared, as well as the unguents and powders that would be used to mark the circle and feed the braziers. Many hands made for light work, and Morgiana had proved to be pliable enough, once freed.

Time passed strangely for the dead. It moved in fits and starts, as slow as tar and as fast as quicksilver. Arkhan could only keep track of the days by the puddles of melted candle fat, so engrossed was he in studying the Books of Nagash, as well as the other grimoires he ordered brought to him by the whining ghoul pack Mannfred had given him to act as his dogsbodies. He read and studied and read still more, and as they always did in such times, the unoccupied portions of his mind drifted into the depths of memory, and were reluctant to return. He had once spent a decade brooding on his throne in his black tower in the desert, lost in the grip of his memories. They were all that he had of himself that was not of Nagash's crafting. Or so part of him hoped.

On the last day, when the last mark was added to his scrimshawed bones and the last powder mixed and all preparations made, Arkhan stood in the centre of the chamber, admiring his handiwork. Over the centuries, he had carved and shaped his own bones more than once. Unlike his long-abandoned flesh, his bones always healed, and his work faded eventually. They would not have long before the marks he and Morgiana had so painstakingly made would vanish, necessitating that they start the whole purification rite over again. He sent the ghouls scrambling to alert Mannfred and turned to Morgiana. '*It is time, enchantress. I thank you for your service.*' He paused, and then asked, '*Would you see your land again, one last time? As payment, for services rendered.*' Even as he spoke he wondered when such a thing had occurred to him.

Morgiana looked at him and then away. 'I do not think so. I know what you intend, and I know that I cannot stop you, but I would not see it.'

'*Very well.*' Arkhan looked at her.

'You are going to kill me, aren't you?' Morgiana asked, suddenly. Arkhan hesitated. '*You are already dead,*' he said.

'No, I am not. If I were, this would not work,' she said, gesturing to the runnels of blood that cut across the floor. 'If I were, I would not feel the way I do.' She ran her hands through the ratty tangles of her once luxurious hair. 'How can anything dead be so hungry?' Her eyes, fever-bright with barely restrained madness, turned towards her fellow captives. All but Aliathra were unconscious, even Volkmar. Morgiana had been feeding on all of them, save those two, to keep them docile while Arkhan completed his preparations. It was the first taste of blood she'd had in a long while, and it was that which had shocked her back to something approaching lucidity. 'It's always with me,' she said. 'I can hear the Lady's voice, but only faintly, as if I am on the opposite shore of a vast, red lake. Sometimes her words are entirely drowned out by the crash of the crimson waves on the white rocks.' She looked at him. 'Can you even understand, dead thing that you are?'

'*I... can,*' he said. He crossed to her as faint echoes of memory were stirred from the sludge of ages and rose unencumbered to the surface of his mind. Of another woman, of another time, of another ritual, marred by poison and betrayal. Unthinkingly, he brushed a strand of hair from her face. '*My spirit will never know peace. I must play my part until the end of time.*'

'I thought I would as well, but the world had other plans,' she whispered, not looking at him. 'My path changed. And I cannot bear to see where it is taking me.'

'*I... knew a woman like you, once,*' he croaked, wondering as he spoke why he was bothering to do so. What matter to him the travails of a madwoman? Then, perhaps his unlife had simply given him perspective. Even as a man, he had never been given to torture. '*She too was afraid, and had lost the voice of her goddess.*' He fell silent.

She looked at him, and for a moment he saw the face of another superimposed over hers. A pale face, framed by hair the colour of night, with eyes like molten pools and lips that could change from kind to cruel with the merest twitch. Even now, when his mind was not otherwise occupied, he could see her face. Her hands reached up to stroke his jawbone. 'What happened to her?' she murmured.

'*She persevered,*' he said. '*She was a queen, and queens do not know fear for long.*'

Morgiana closed her eyes. 'I do not think I will have that opportunity. You will kill me, won't you?' she asked again.

'*I will,*' Arkhan said. '*In the end, nine are required for the final ritual, though eight will suffice. But no less than that.*' He stroked her cheek. Some part of him snarled in warning, but he ignored it. The chamber had been replaced by another in his mind's eye, of cool marble and sandstone. He could smell the ocean, and hear the rustle of silk curtains. *'There will be no pain... That I swear.'*

'Good,' she said. 'That is what I needed to know.' Her hand dropped. A moment later, his knife was jerked from its sheath and Morgiana had its tip pressed to the flesh over her heart. The flesh of her hand sizzled as·the malign enchantments wrought into the blade resisted her touch. Marble and silk again became mouldy stone and the stink of abused flesh.

Arkhan lunged forward, hand outstretched. *'Neferata,'* he rasped, momentarily uncertain what was memory and what was reality. She shoved him back, her vampiric strength taking him by surprise. He staggered. *'No, please...'* he said, still caught in the tangled strands of memory. He saw Neferata writhing on her bed, caught in the throes of an agonising death. He felt Abhorash's blade, as it cut him down. The full weight of the last, worst moment of a life badly spent crashed down on him for the first time in centuries, and he could not bear it. *'Please don't!'* The words were ripped from him before he even realised that he'd said them.

Morgiana smiled in triumph. 'My path was changed. But I can change it back.' She wrapped both hands around the hilt, and thrust it into her own heart. Black smoke boiled from the wound, and blood gushed as she toppled forward into Arkhan's arms.

The liche screamed. The sound was one of frustration, rage and despair. As her blood coated his arms and chest, he knew what she had done. It had taken her weeks, but she had ensnared him in her glamour, making him see... and feel. Rage burned through him, and then guttered out. He cradled her close as the last wisps of the glamour faded and he was himself again. No longer Arkhan the gambler, Arkhan the dread lord, now only Arkhan the Black.

He tore the knife from her chest and hurled it aside. He hesitated. Her face was peaceful, in death. But some part of her yet remained. Vampires could not truly die. He could bring her back with but a touch, to stir the black sorceries that flowed through her tainted blood. But still, he hesitated.

From behind him came a yowl. He turned and saw his cat crouched atop Nagash's crown. Its starved, crumbling frame was draped over the iron points, tail lashing. Its empty eyes met his own and he nodded slowly. He looked back down at Morgiana and said, *'No, my lady. Escape is not so easy as all that, I fear.'*

He placed a hand against the wound, and dark lightning crackled briefly from his fingers to course through Morgiana. Her body twitched and her eyes opened wide. Her lips spread and a scream escaped them. It was a sound empty of all hope. She clawed uselessly at him, and he jerked her to her feet. In moments, she was chained once more. She crouched against the wall, sobbing. Arkhan watched her for a moment, before turning away.

He felt eyes on him, and looked around to meet Aliathra's gaze. *'Were you amused, Everchild? I have heard that your folk drink deep of the cup of mortal suffering, finding it to be exquisite.'*

'No,' she spoke, her voice soft. 'I was simply surprised that it worked. I thought dead things could not be ensnared thus. Then, you are not truly dead, are you?' Arkhan said nothing. The elf smiled sadly. 'For that to have worked, there must be some kernel yet of the man you once were, trapped in the husk of you, Arkhan the Black. Some small touch of mercy.'

The cat shrieked, and Arkhan turned away. *'No. There is not,'* he said, finally. He picked up his staff and slammed it down. The chamber echoed with the sound, and he heard the howl of the vargheists who lurked in the shadows above drift down in reply. The cat leapt onto his shoulder. The vargheists dropped down heavily, snarling and snapping at one another. Arkhan pointed his staff at the unconscious form of Lupio Blaze. *'Unchain him, and bring him. I grow weary of Sylvania. It is time to leave.'*

Sylvania, the western border

'We are still agreed, then?' Mannfred asked, hands crossed on his saddle's pommel as he leaned over his mount's neck. The horse-thing was all bone and eldritch fire, and it stank of char-nel pits and mouldering ashes. 'West for you and east for me.'

'*As we agreed,*' Arkhan said. He stood at the centre of his care-fully prepared ritual circle. At his feet, pinned to the ground by crudely forged bronze spikes, was the pain-contorted shape of Lupio Blaze. Black candles, with tallow rendered from human flesh, surrounded the circle, as did a number of smoking iron braziers.

And in the distance, the only obstacle between them and the return of the Undying King. Gelt's wall of faith rode dips and curves of the border; the symbols of Morr, Sigmar, Ulric and a dozen other gods, some real, some not, hung suspended in the air, glowing with a terrible, painful light. The western border was one of the few places where the cursed barrier was visible to the naked eye, and thus the perfect spot to ensure that the spell had actually worked.

Behind Mannfred, the army of Sylvania waited. Arkhan would take only a small bodyguard of Drakenhof Templars and his dis-solute cadre of necromancers into Bretonnia, while Mannfred would lead the vast bulk of the waiting army into the Border Princes. Above the silent army, the Drakenhof banner fluttered like a dying snake.

'Excellent,' Mannfred said. He leaned back in his saddle and slapped his thigh. 'Well... on with it, liche. I have a world to con-quer and no time to dally.' He jerked on his mount's reins and galloped off to rejoin his waiting blood knights.

Arkhan watched him go and then looked down at the knight. '*Any last words, warrior?*' Arkhan asked softly. Blaze glared up at him defiantly, and spat something virulent in Tilean. Arkhan nodded respectfully. '*As it should be. A brave man's final words ought to be unrepeatable,*' he said.

Arkhan began to chant, slowly at first, and then faster, the words bursting from him like a cascade of rocks down a cliff-face. He spoke in the tongue of Nehekhara, and it came as easily to him as the memory of his first death. He spat the words into the teeth of the growing wind, and the vast faces, bloated and loathsome that leered down at him through the tattered veils of reality. The words were as much promise as invocation, and the world squirmed about him as his voice tore great wounds in the air. Thunder rumbled overhead. Black lightning, blacker than the dark sky, split the air, creating jagged cracks in the firmament full of squamous, daemonic shapes, which writhed and fought.

Ghostly shapes, half formed and inhuman, spiralled madly about Arkhan and his captive, and wolves, both dead and alive, began to howl. The bitter air grew thick and poisonous, as the weight of the forces Arkhan was invoking settled on the world. He drew the bone dagger from the jewelled sheath on his belt with his free hand and dropped down to crouch over the knight. The same dagger that had almost taken Morgiana's life would now spill the blood of her fellow captive. '*Rest assured that your sacrifice will help to save the world, warrior. Take that thought with you into the embrace of your goddess, for however long it lasts.*'

Then, with two swift movements, he slit the knight's wrist and thigh, releasing twin sprays of red blood to splash onto the thirsty ground. Blaze's struggles grew weaker, and his curses quieter, as his life emptied itself into the soil of Sylvania. Arkhan stood, and raised his hand. His fingers snapped closed and the candles tumbled over, setting the pooling blood alight. The fire raced about the circle, spiralling upwards with a loud roar, consuming everything within, save for Arkhan, who stood untouched by the greedy flames. His robes whipped about him as he raised his hand, and the flames tore at the heavens in reply. The fire whirled about him in a flickering typhoon of destruction, and in the coruscating surface of the flames he could see the faces of his enemies, gnashing their teeth and cursing him silently. Arkhan let the flames spill upwards into the sky.

And then he snuffed them with a snap of his bony fingers. The fire went out, leaving him in a circle of char and ash. He stood for a time, as the magics he had raised coursed through him. He had taken the power that had hidden in the knight's blood into himself, and he could feel it roil in his nonexistent veins. Its fury had momentarily silenced the voice of his master within him, and he felt as if an indescribable weight had been lifted from his old bones. He looked at his hand, considering the power he now held. It would be so easy to use it for himself, to do as he wished, for once. He could dispatch his rivals here, take Mannfred's acquisitions for himself and remake this blighted land into something that would ride out the coming storm better than the eternal abattoir the vampire imagined. A land of order and perfect, beautiful silence, where no daemon or dark power, save himself, held sway.

He looked up and met Mannfred's cool, calculating glare. A giant shadow hung over the vampire, looming above him, its black gaze on Arkhan. He knew that he was the only one who could see it, who could feel the impatient malevolence that boiled off it like steam. Who was it looking out of the vampire's eyes right now? What black brain drove Mannfred in his efforts?

Arkhan knew the answer well enough. He had seen it before, on the Valsborg Bridge, and in Castle Sternieste. The world buckled beneath the weight of a dark fate, and one that he knew better than to try and avoid. '*Nagash must rise*,' Arkhan murmured. He motioned slowly, and the ashes at his feet stirred, rising as if caught in a hot wind. They played about his fingers as he gestured with his knife and called out, '*Bring your standard forward, vampire.*'

Mannfred gestured. A blood knight rode towards Arkhan, carrying the Drakenhof banner. Arkhan anointed the ancestral banner of the Sylvanian aristocracy with a handful of ashes. '*Carry the banner to the wall.*'

The standard-bearer glanced at Mannfred, who motioned towards the partition. The blood knight grimaced visibly, and then kicked his coal-black steed into motion towards the wall of faith. As the armoured vampire extended the standard towards the hovering holy symbols, there was a flash, and one by one, the sigils and symbols tumbled from the air to land heavily on the ground. Mannfred stood up in his saddle and waved his hand. 'Forward!' he shouted. 'For Sylvania, and for the world to come!'

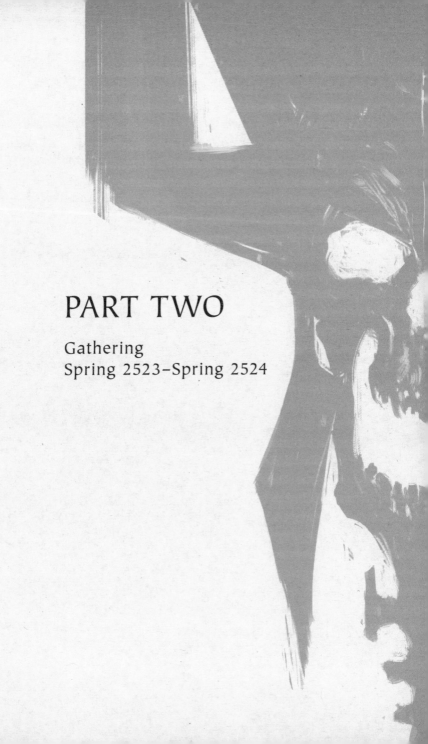

PART TWO

Gathering
Spring 2523–Spring 2524

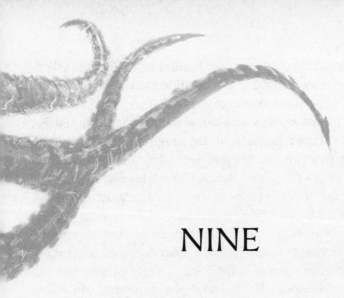

NINE

Hvargir Forest, the Border Princes

Mannfred lifted the pale arm from his lap and sent it and the bloodless body it was attached to thudding to the ground with a negligent gesture. The body had belonged to a young woman: a peasant from one of the villages they had taken the night before, he thought. Now it belonged to the worms, until he decided to add her pitiful carcass to his legions. He brushed his thumb across his lips and said, 'Bring Duke Forzini forward, if you please. I would speak with our host.'

Count Nyktolos nodded shallowly and stepped out of the tent that Mannfred had claimed for his own. The Vargravian's features were a distorted parody of a man's – too wide and flat by far, his flesh the colour of a bruise. A shark-like mouth stretched from pointed ear to pointed ear, and his eyes bulged unpleasantly. He resembled a puppet, with his monocle and his hair greased flat against his stoat-like skull. Looks aside, he was deadly with a blade and had a keen mind, two things Mannfred appreciated. Even better, his ambitions were just petty enough to be amusing, rather than annoying.

'Since when do you palaver with food, cousin?' Markos asked, from where he stood, examining the hide map stretched across a wooden frame in the corner of the tent.

'Speak of the annoyingly ambitious,' Mannfred murmured. He looked around the tent, taking in the rough decor. It had all the pomp and panoply he expected of the frontier nobleman he had borrowed it from two nights before. Tapestries and animal furs hung from the support poles of the tent, and a quadrupedal, low-slung iron brazier, filled with coals which had long-since gone cold, occupied the centre beneath the smoke hole cut into the top of the tent. A rack of spears – boar, wolf and other more esoteric varieties – stood behind the crudely carved wooden stool he now occupied. He looked down at the staff laid across his lap, and the withered, iron-wrapped thing that had been lashed to the top in ages past: the Claw of Nagash. The thing was a hand – or, more accurately, a claw. It was larger than a man's, and it seemed to ooze a sorcerous miasma. As he looked at it, the long, skeletal fingers seemed to twitch, as if they yearned to grasp his throat. And perhaps they did. Something of Nagash's spiteful spirit was trapped in this claw, just as it was in his crown and his books.

He'd brought the Claw so that it might lead him to the object of his search – the skaven-forged Fellblade – the very weapon that had severed Nagash's hand from his wrist and ended his Great Work the first time. There was a sympathetic vibration between the two, and with a bit of coaxing, the one pointed the way to the other. The Claw whispered to him, and he listened and set his legion marching towards Mad Dog Pass.

It had taken him centuries to discover Kadon of Mourkain's staff and the Claw, hidden as it had been, in the vaults of that lost city. Ushoran, fearing its power, had sealed it away in the deepest, blackest pit he could find, though he'd taken the Crown for himself. Then, perhaps the ancient vampire had thought that he could master one artefact of Nagash's but not two, more fool him. Ushoran's will had not proved equal to the task, though he'd come closer than any save Mannfred himself. Mannfred stroked the staff, and the Claw curled and twitched like an appreciative cat. 'Poor Ushoran. If only you had listened to me,' he murmured. 'I told you that she couldn't be trusted.'

'What?' Markos asked. He sounded annoyed.

Mannfred glanced at him lazily. 'Nothing, brave cousin. Merely talking to myself.'

'An old family trait,' Markos muttered.

'What was that?' Mannfred asked, even though he'd heard Markos quite clearly. 'You have something to say, Markos?'

'I said that this map is out of date,' Markos replied smoothly.

'It's Tilean. What did you expect? Cartography is one of the few arts that they do not claim to have invented,' Mannfred said. 'And in answer to your impertinent query, cousin... This is no mere hunting party, whatever our host claims. Why else bring a troop of armoured horsemen and spearmen?'

'Spears are used in hunting,' Markos said. Mannfred could tell from the glint in his eye that he was being deliberately obtuse. Markos's mood had been positively acidic since they entered the Black Mountains, and hadn't abated with battle. They'd encountered the small force as they descended the mountains and entered the Hvargir Forest. Mannfred had obscured the movements of his forces through sorcerous means as they travelled through the mountains, but Markos and the others had been growing restive when the unfortunate Duke Forzini had crossed their path with his simple 'hunting party'. Forzini was one of a multitude of minor, self-proclaimed counts and dukes who ruled the petty fiefdoms of the Border Princes.

'True,' Mannfred said. 'But what hunting expedition requires a hundred such, as well as cuirassiers, fully armoured knights, and what I believe is called a – ah – "galloper gun", hmm? What were they hunting *for*, cousin?'

Markos opened his mouth to retort, but Nyktolos returned,

and shoved a bedraggled figure through the tent flap. The man, bound in chains, and stinking of blood and fear, fell onto the ground at Mannfred's feet. Mannfred clapped his hands. 'Ah, and here he is now! The man of the hour, Duke Farnio Forzini, of the demesne of Alfori. They make a fine millet in Alfori, I'm told. Of course, the prime export, as with so many of these tiny mountain realms is violence.' Mannfred smiled. 'Something I myself am well acquainted with.' He stood and hauled his prisoner to his feet. 'Up, sirrah, up – on your feet. I am a count, and you a duke, and neither of us should kneel.'

Forzini flinched away from Mannfred's grin. The Tilean was a big man, with the muscle of a trained knight. He had fought hard, even after he realised what it was he faced. It had taken two days to beat a sense of fear into him. Forzini saw the dead body of the maid and his face went pale. Mannfred followed his gaze and asked, 'Oh, was she one of your peons? My apologies. I was peckish, you understand. I so rarely allow myself to indulge, but, well, you put up quite a fight and I built up a hellish appetite.'

He looked at the beaten man. He had to reach Mad Dog Pass before the first snows of the season, and that meant moving quickly through the Border Princes. He had no time to indulge in unnecessary battle. If the petty aristocracy of these lands had learned of his approach, and were mobilising to meet him in battle, he needed to know, and sooner rather than later. 'Where were you marching to?' Mannfred hissed. 'Tell me, and I won't gut you and feed you to my horses.'

'S-skaven,' Forzini mumbled, his eyes tightly closed.

Mannfred grunted. 'How many?'

'Thousands – more maybe,' Forzini said. He looked at Mannfred. 'We were riding to aid my neighbour, Count Tulvik, at Southern Reach. His fortress had come under siege.'

'Then you were going in the wrong direction,' Nyktolos said mildly, cleaning his monocle on his sleeve. 'I was once a... guest of old Tulvik.' He blinked. 'Well, his grandfather, actually.'

Mannfred growled. He caught Forzini by the throat. 'I don't care for lies, Forzini.'

'W-we were! I swear!' Forzini choked out. 'But then, a runner brought word that my own hold was under siege. So I turned back – my wife and children, my people!' The last exploded out and Forzini broke free of Mannfred with a convulsive surge of strength. Mannfred let him go. Forzini lunged for the hilt of Mannfred's sword. 'I have to save them!'

Mannfred casually dropped his fist onto the back of Forzini's skull and knocked him sprawling to the ground. He pinned the cursing duke in place with his foot and looked at Markos. The other vampire nodded grudgingly. 'That would explain what we've seen, wouldn't it? This isn't an isolated raid we're talking about, cousin. It's an invasion.'

When they'd descended into the foothills of the Black Mountains, the plains and fenland and forest should have been dotted with proud, if small, cities and fortified outposts as it always had been. What they had seen instead was a land in ruins. Castles were scorched piles, and towns were reduced to smouldering embers. And everywhere, the signs of plague – bodies choked the ditches and mass graves lay full, yet uncovered.

At first, Mannfred thought it was simply the aftermath of one of the interminable border wars, which occasionally flared up and then died away. But the devastation was too extensive. Memories of the portents of doom that he had witnessed in his scrying so many months ago had come rushing back, of the fates of Tilea and Estalia, and he knew that the end that he had witnessed was drawing closer. The weft and weave of the world was realigning and time was running out. That was the only thing that could draw the skaven from their twilight burrows in such numbers as Forzini and his own scrying had described.

He had faith enough in Elize's ability to maintain control of Sylvania in his absence, but he knew that no other could defend his realm better than he could. If the skaven were truly massing in such numbers in the Border Princes, he couldn't count on his sorceries seeing him unmolested to his goal. Better then not to even try, now that he had passed beyond the borders of the Empire.

'How many prisoners did we take?' he asked, after a moment.

'Ah, one, two, three... Fifty or sixty,' Nyktolos said, ticking off his fingers. 'Mostly the duke's household guard. They fought hard for a band of jumped-up bandit-knights.'

'Due to my friend Forzini here, I have no doubt,' Mannfred said. He caught hold of the chains binding Forzini and pulled him close. 'I am not ordinarily in the habit of giving choices, Forzini. It sets a bad precedent, you see, for royalty to allow the dregs to think that they get a say in their own fates. But, if there are thousands of skaven slumping and sneaking through these lands, I'll need every sword I can get, dead or... otherwise.' Mannfred licked his lips. Though the girl's blood had quenched his thirst, he could still detect the erratic thump of Forzini's pulse. Mannfred tightened his grip on the chains. 'Swear fealty to me, Duke Forzini, and I shall save your lands for you. Indeed, you can be the hero who saves the entirety of the Border Princes, if that is your wish. Or die here, and ride at my side regardless as a nameless and mindless thing. Serve me in life, or in death. But you shall serve me. Name your preference.'

He heard Vlad's sibilant chuckle as he gazed down into the flushed, sweating features of the duke. *Those are familiar words. You honour me, my son,* Vlad murmured. Mannfred could almost see him out of the corner of his eye. He blinked, and Vlad vanished. 'Well?' he snarled, hauling Forzini close. 'Make your choice.'

'Y-you will save my people?' Forzini asked.

'I will save everyone,' Mannfred said.

Forzini closed his eyes and nodded jerkily. Mannfred gave a satisfied growl and sank his fangs into the Duke's throat. As he drank, his eyes met Nyktolos's and the ugly vampire nodded sharply and left the tent. When he had finished, he let the duke's body slump to the ground. Crouching over him, Mannfred used a thumbnail to slit his palm, and then squeezed several drops of blood into the ragged wounds he had made in Forzini's throat.

As he rose, his hand was already healing. 'Is this wise, cousin?' Markos asked, looking down at the not-quite-dead man. 'Also, I hope you aren't expecting us to turn his servants. Such a thing is below even my slight dignity.'

Mannfred smiled. Screams echoed from outside. 'The Vargravian is already handling it. By the time we reach our destination, I shall have a bodyguard worthy of an emperor of the dead, cousin.'

Markos was about to reply, when the air was suddenly split by the howl of a wolf. The sound ratcheted through the tent, drowning out even the scream's of Forzini's men. Markos drew his blade and rushed to the tent opening. 'The alarm,' he barked.

Mannfred followed more sedately, wiping his lips with his fingers. It seemed he wasn't going to have to go looking for the skaven – they had come to him.

💀 *Brionne, Bretonnia*

The castle on the crag had once been one of the great bulwarks upon which the might of Brionne had been built, guarding the province's border against all enemies. Now, it was a fire-blackened ruin, long since picked over by scavengers of all varieties, human or otherwise.

Heinrich Kemmler, the Lichemaster, lifted his staff and thumped the end of it on the ground, calling the dead of the ruined keep to attention. The crackle of bones pushing through the ash and the wreckage of their own flesh filled the air, and Kemmler closed his eyes and moved his hand and staff like the orchestral conductor at the Imperial opera. The dead rose at his cajoling, reaching towards him like penitents in a temple, and a harsh, croaking laugh slipped from Kemmler's lips.

Arkhan watched the Lichemaster draw the dead from their too-brief slumber, and felt no little surprise at the obvious power the elderly necromancer now seemed to wield. When he had last seen Kemmler, in the waning months of the Bretonnian civil war, the Lichemaster had been a mumbling, muttering wretch, barely cognisant of the world around him. Now, Kemmler resembled the Lichemaster of old, full of cold, dark reservoirs of power.

Those reservoirs had barely been tapped in the Vaults, Arkhan knew, when he and Kemmler had cracked open the web-strewn, elf-sealed tombs that lined the high reaches of those mountains months earlier. Kemmler had swept aside the antediluvian magics that chained the wild, selfish spirits that clustered in those mausoleums as if they had been nothing more than cobwebs. Arkhan had done the same, but he knew the origins of his own strength. He knew what lay at the bottom of the inner wells from which he drew his power. Kemmler's newfound strength, on the other hand, was a puzzle and a concern. His wrinkled frame swelled with the winds of death and dark magic, and the dead responded to his smallest gesture. Kemmler's glittering gaze met Arkhan's, and the old man smiled widely, exposing a crooked cemetery of brown and black tombstone teeth.

Arkhan gave no sign that he had noticed the smile. Instead, he let his gaze slide past the puppet to the puppetmaster. Krell the Undying. Krell of the Great Axe, who Arkhan knew of old, and who had served as Nagash's right hand, as Arkhan was his left. The ancient wight, clad in his ornate armour, which was stained a rusty hue by the oceans of gore that he had waded through over the centuries, loomed over Kemmler, his terrible axe hanging from his hand. Krell met Arkhan's gaze, and his great horned helm twitched slightly. Had that been a nod of greeting, a gesture of respect, or simply an idle shudder of the wretched berserker spirit that fuelled the wight, Arkhan wondered. There was no way to tell. Krell's mind was a roiling storm of battle-lust and blood-greed at the best of times.

If Kemmler was a worry, then Krell was a fixed point: the unassailable rampart upon which the future could be erected. Nagash had wrested Krell's mighty soul from the clutches of the Dark Gods, and bound it to him as inextricably as he had Arkhan's. They were his hands, his sword and shield, and his will made flesh.

But was that all they were? He thought again of the Everchild's taunt – had it been a taunt? – that he was, in some way, still the man he had been. He leaned against his staff, gnawing over her words. The effects of Morgiana's glamour had long since faded, but he could still feel the wounds it had wrought in his psyche. It had stirred the embers of a fire he'd thought long since extinguished. And if those embers still existed within him, what of Krell?

He gazed at the armoured bulk of the enormous wight. If there was some part of Krell as he had been left in that powerful husk, what might it do if it awakened? Would even Nagash be able to control such an entity, if its ire was aroused?

And what if it already had been? Krell met his gaze, and the two dead things stared at one another across the courtyard. Whose puppet are you? Arkhan thought. Kemmler laughed, and Arkhan turned towards him. The Lichemaster was directing two of the newly risen dead to fit a scavenged bridle and saddle onto the resurrected body of the lord of the keep. Then, if Krell broke his leash, he suspected he knew where the Great Axe would fall first. The thought was almost amusing. If anyone deserved to be savaged in that way, it was Kemmler.

'What is he doing?' Ogiers asked. 'Is he mad?' Arkhan looked back at his coterie of servants. The necromancers stood nearby in a nervous cluster, watching as Kemmler worked his sorceries. Even amongst the desecrators of the dead, the Lichemaster was in a league of his own. None of them had wanted to come, and Arkhan could tell that even the normally phlegmatic Fidduci was bothered by the company he now found himself in.

'You have eyes. What do you think?' the latter asked. The Tilean was furiously cleaning his spectacles, something he did when he was nervous. 'Of course he's mad. He's always been mad.'

'But useful, yes?' Kruk tittered, stroking his wispy beard. He hunched forward over his cousin's rotting shoulder and stroked the dead man's mouldering features affectionately. 'And it is no strange thing. A horse is a horse, of course – two legs or four, yes?' The crippled midget bounced in his harness and laughed at his own words.

Across the courtyard, Kemmler forced the dead lord to fall onto all fours. Kemmler laughed again, and raised his staff. Dark energy crackled along its length and bodies shuffled towards the kneeling lord. They knelt, linking arms and legs, and his intended mount climbed atop them. The whole twitching mass resembled nothing so much as an awkward pyramid for a moment. Then Kemmler swept his staff out and barked a guttural phrase, and the dead men began to sink and slide into one another with a variety of unpleasant sounds. Bones burst through sloughing meat and crashed into one another, splintering and reforming as flesh melted into flesh, and organs were discarded in splashes of blood and fluid.

A moment later, a conglomerate horror that reminded Arkhan of a spider, if a spider were made of writhing human bodies, pushed itself up on its multitude of hands and feet. Kemmler climbed into the saddle and hauled on the reins, forcing the thing to rear. He laughed again as it dropped down, and leered at Arkhan. 'Well, liche? What do you think of my new pet?'

'*Very pretty, Kemmler. You're welcome, by the way. A less genial master might not have allowed you to indulge your appetites for flesh-craft,*' Arkhan said. He was rewarded by a scowl from the necromancer. While Krell's loyalty was certain, Kemmler had a distaste for servitude that bordered on mania.

'Allow? We are partners, Nehekharan,' Kemmler said. 'You need me.' He grinned at Ogiers and the others. 'My power far outstrips that of your cat paws. Between them, they might just manage to summon a small horde, but you'll never take La Maisontaal Abbey without me.' He spat the name of their destination like a curse. Then, for Kemmler, perhaps it was. He had tried to assault the abbey more than once in his sordid career, and failed every time. Arkhan wondered if Kemmler could feel the call of the artefact hidden in the abbey's vaults even as he himself could. He suspected that Nagash whispered in the Lichemaster's ear, whether Kemmler knew it or not. Else how could he have controlled Krell – if he truly did.

'*Whatever you need to tell yourself, so long as you do as I say,*' Arkhan rasped. Kemmler made a face. He was different. Arkhan could not say why, or how, but it was as if something had been awakened in the necromancer. And Arkhan did not like it. He did not like Kemmler's newfound lucidity, or the threads of power that ran through him. '*We are both servants of a higher power. All of us here serve that power, lest anyone has forgotten.*'

He turned, taking in the other necromancers, and the lazing vampires, who met his gaze with glittering red glares. '*Do not think that you can stray. Time runs slow for the dead, but it runs all the same,*' he said, his voice carrying to every corner and ear capable of hearing and comprehending. He raised his staff and gestured to the sky, which boiled like a storm-tossed sea of green and black overhead. Sickly coronas rippled across the shroud of the night, and green scars carved through the black, streaking down towards distant mountains. It reminded Arkhan of the pearlescent flesh of a corpse succumbing to decay.

The world was rotting inside and out. It was dying. But it would linger on its deathbed for millennia, if the thrones and dominations that stood arrayed in his path had their way. The gods of men and daemons fought to own a world that had one foot in its grave. Only in death would it be redeemed. Only by the will of the Undying King.

The cat, in its usual place on his shoulder, stretched, bones and ligaments popping audibly as it dug its claws into his robes. He felt a surge of purpose in him as he continued to speak, though he wondered, deep in the secret places of his mind, whether those words were his, or those of Nagash. '*We all serve the will and whim of the Undying King, and it is his hand that guides us on this road. It is by his will that we all exist. Vampires were born from his black blood as surely as you walkers of the deathly way follow his wisdom and hearken to his teachings, as certainly as it was by his will that I persist in my task. We owe him our service, our loyalty, for without him, we would be dust and forgotten. Instead, we stand at the threshold of the world's heart and knock. We were the meek, and now we are the mighty. We serve the King of the World.*' He looked at Kemmler. '*All of us. Remember that.*'

Kemmler snarled and opened his mouth to reply, when a black horse galloped into the courtyard, hurtling through the shattered portcullis with preternatural grace. Its rider slid from the saddle as the horse came to a stop near Arkhan. The vampire gestured over his shoulder and barked, 'Company!' The vampire was one of a number Mannfred had insisted he take as an honour-guard. This one was called Crowfiend, he thought, though he resembled neither a crow nor a fiend as far as Arkhan could tell. Nonetheless, Arkhan preferred his company to that of Anark, the brutish commander of the armoured blood knights. That one stank of ambition and impatience, two things that Arkhan no longer understood or tolerated.

Arkhan cocked his head. '*Beastmen?*' His scouts had reported that a sizeable herd of the Chaos creatures were nearby, laying waste to a village in the valley below. Whether they desired battle, or merely wanted to scavenge in Arkhan's wake, he couldn't say.

'Bretonnians,' Erikan Crowfiend said. 'They're flying the flag of Quenelles.'

Arkhan felt a twinge of surprise. His forces had skirted Quenelles's southern border despite the fact that their goal lay in the strand of the Grey Mountains that marked the eastern edge of that province. Instead, Arkhan had led his followers further south, coming down out of the mountains into Carcassonne, rather than risking the wrath of Athel Loren.

The southernmost provinces had been the most heavily devastated in the civil war, stripped of foodstuffs and able-bodied men. He'd done so intentionally, hoping to leave himself a clear path to reach the abbey when he wished. But evidently, the province had not been as devastated as he thought.

'Tancred,' Kemmler snarled. There was an eagerness in that sound that disquieted Arkhan. He recalled suddenly that it had been a previous Duke of Quenelles who had defeated the Lichemaster during one of his periodic attempts to take La Maisontaal Abbey. It was the same duke, or perhaps his son, who had harried the Lichemaster out of Bretonnia and into the Grey Mountains.

'Possibly, or it could be any one of a hundred other displaced aristocrats from that province,' Arkhan said, gesturing sharply. *'It matters little. They are in our way. We will smash them, and continue on. Nagash must rise, and none will stand in our way.'*

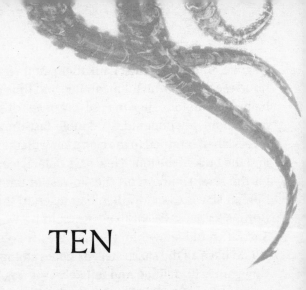

TEN

 Hvargir Forest, the Border Princes

When Snikrat saw the tents, arrayed so temptingly on the blighted plains that hugged the edge of the forest, he immediately began to salivate. It looked like yet another of the petty man-thing princelings was attempting to flee. It was the perfect target – big enough to give a fight, small enough that the fight wouldn't last very long, thus presenting him, Snikrat the Magnificent, with the perfect opportunity to cement his heroism in the minds of his followers, without actually risking himself too much.

'Forward, brave warriors,' he chittered, flourishing his blade. 'Forward for the swift-glory of Clan Mordkin! Forward, at the command of me, Snikrat the Magnificent.' Clanrats stampeded past him, most of them already intent on looting the collection of tents and supply wagons, the latter seemingly unprotected. His stormvermin bodyguard, the aptly named Bonehides, knew better than to leave his side. Partially it was because it was their job to see that he survived, and partially because the wiser among the black-furred skaven knew Snikrat's reputation for sniffing out the best loot. Snikrat grinned and gestured towards the supply wagons. 'There! We must flank them, in their side, there, so that none escape, by which I mean flee and thus possibly evade us,' he hissed out loud, just in case any of Feskit's spies were listening. 'Come, my Bonehides – double-fast-move-move!'

Feskit had returned to the clan's lair with the bulk of their army, and the bulk of the loot a few days before, leaving Snikrat to pilfer the scraps and escort the slowest of the hundreds of filthy human slaves Clan Mordkin had taken in their ravaging of the Border Princes. Feskit likely thought he was being generous. Snikrat would show him true generosity soon enough – Feskit would have all the sharp steel he could stomach. The thought of vengeance, ill-defined and unlikely as it was, filled Snikrat with a surge of confidence. First he would kill any humans who tried to flee, as they inevitably did, being inveterate cowards, then he would loot the wagons – and then, yes, then, at some point, inevitably, after a suitable period of time, he would kill Feskit and wrest control of Clan Mordkin from his unworthy paws.

Granted, there were probably some steps in there he was missing, but he'd work those out when he came to them.

He led his stormvermin towards the wagons, looking forward to the screams of the man-things. But instead of screams, all he found was... Quiet. He stopped, and his warriors clattered to a halt around him. Snikrat's hackles itched, and he sniffed the air. It stank of blood and rot, which weren't the usual odours one associated with humans.

Snikrat heard the sounds of his warriors attacking the camp. To his finely attuned ears, it did not sound like a slaughter. At least, not the good kind. His musk-gland tightened and he fought down a sudden surge of irrational fear. What was there to be afraid of? Was he not Snikrat the Magnificent, heir to Feskit, whether the latter admitted it or not?

'Come-come, let us take the wagons, by which I mean these wheeled conveyances here, for the greater glory of skavenkind,' he said. His next words died in his furry throat as the air quivered with a low, harsh growl. That growl was joined by several more. Black, lean shapes moved across the top of the wagons or behind them, and Snikrat looked about, suddenly aware that the wagons weren't as undefended as he'd assumed.

Wolves crouched on the wagons or slunk from beneath them. Each bore numerous wounds, any one of which should have laid such beasts low, Snikrat saw as he extended his blade warily, his stormvermin clustering about him. Yet they didn't seem bothered by the broken shafts of arrows and spears that poked from their sagging hides. 'Dead-dead things,' a stormvermin squealed.

'Nonsense,' Snikrat blustered. 'Spears!'

His warriors levelled their cruelly barbed spears and locked shields, forming a rough hedgehog. He'd learned the tactic from a Tilean slave when he was but a pup. Sometimes he regretted eating the old man as quickly as he had. Nothing alive could break a Bonehides square, especially not a pack of quarrelsome curs.

Something laughed.

There was a promise implicit in that sound. Snikrat recognised it, for he himself had often laughed such a laugh while advancing on wounded or unwary prey. It was the laugh of a wolf-rat on the hunt, and his fur bristled with barely restrained terror as his eyes rotated. There, on the top of the wagons, something purple-faced and dead crouched, eyeing him through the lens of a monocle. The thing grinned, displaying row upon row of serrated, sharp teeth. Snikrat swallowed.

'Oh happy day. A-one, a-two, a-three... So many little rats for me,' the vampire snarled. Then, faster even than Snikrat the Magnificent could follow, it sprang upon them, its sword whistling down like the stroke of doom.

 Brionne, Bretonnia

The spear thrust out at Malagor from the depths of the hay loft. He swatted the rusty head aside with his staff and thrust one long arm into the hay, seizing the spear-wielder and dragging him screaming into the firelight.

The village had already been burned once, but that hadn't stopped the beastmen from trying to burn it again. Malagor drew the wailing man towards him and calmly silenced him by slamming his head into a nearby post. Then, with a flap of his wings, he flew up and out of the barn, carrying his prize.

He caught an updraught, and rode the hot wind above the burning village. It had been prosperous, as such places went, before the war that had recently rocked this land. Malagor's lips peeled back from his fangs in a parody of a smile as he looked down and saw his warriors pursuing frightened peasants. There was little enough sport in this land, and he was glad enough to provide his followers with some small bit, before they went into battle.

The herds he led had been growing restless for lack of entertainment or battle. They chafed beneath his will, and he had been forced to meet more than one challenge in the days preceding the slaughter below. The village had been a gift from the Dark Gods; he'd been running low on chieftains, forced as he was to kill any who brayed a challenge.

But the gods were watching over their favoured child, and he felt their hands lift him up and their breath fill him, as they lent him strength and clarity. Their whispers had only grown stronger as he led the herds away from Athel Loren and into the human lands of Carcassonne, burning and pillaging the pitiful remnants of a once proud province along way. At their whim, he had held fast to the reins of the herd, and not unleashed them against Arkhan's forces when the bone-man and his followers had crossed the Vaults and into Carcassonne. Instead, he had followed them, keeping pace but never allowing the forces under his command to attack the dead legions marching across the landscape. He had been confused at first, but he now saw the truth of the gods' plan, and found it good.

His captive squirmed and Malagor tightened his grip. The man was screaming still, and pleading with him in the incoherent babble of the man-tongue. Malagor ignored it. He hadn't brought the creature up into the sky for a conversation. He had brought it to send a message.

Malagor growled in pleasure as his wings carried him out over the village and away. He saw the serpentine length of the River Brienne and the slumped ruin of the fortress that occupied the crags above the village. A column of smoke extended above the latter, blacker than the night sky it rose to meet. The screams of the dying carried on the wind, sped along by his sorceries. After all, what use a beacon if no one noticed?

And the village *was* a beacon. A signpost for the army that even now advanced towards it, riding west from Quenelles. Malagor could hear the horns of the Bretonnian host, and knew that they were close. His wings flapped, carrying him to meet them. The gods whispered to him, telling him what he must do, and he did it, happily. He swooped upwards, wings beating, and tore open the belly of his captive. Its screams were like music, and he howled in accompaniment as he gutted the squirming, hairless thing.

The bone-man and his creatures were close by, in the castle on the high hill overlooking the village and the river. They had been there for some time, and to Malagor's eyes, the ruin glowed with the faint phosphorescence of necromantic sorceries. He could feel the dead stirring, and something else as well – something that drew the attentions of the gods. Whatever it was, it was powerful, and the gods approved of that power. A surge of envy washed through him as he went about his task, and he bit and tore at the now limp body with more ferocity than was necessary. Blood splattered his muzzle and chest, and gore matted his hair.

Butchery complete, he plunged down, wings folded, cutting through the air like a missile fired from a ballista, his burden dangling behind him, its slick intestines looped about his gnarled, hairy fist. At the last possible moment, he banked, hurtling upwards again even as he released the mutilated corpse, and let it tumble gracelessly to the ground before the front ranks of the approaching army. Then Malagor was streaking upwards, across the face of the moon and back towards the village. His warriors would need to be on the move when the Bretonnians arrived, or they would become bogged down in battle.

They would lead the humans on a merry chase, and right into the bone-man's army. The will of the gods caressed his thoughts, soothing his envy and anger, as if to say, *See? See what we do for you, oh best beloved child? See how we spare your lives? See how we deliver victory unto you? And all we ask is that you claim it, as we command.*

The bone-man's army would be weakened by battle, like a stag after it has fought off a rival, if it was not destroyed outright. Malagor could smell the stink of strange magics on the human army. But if the bone-man triumphed, then, like wolves, Malagor and his followers would harry them as they marched on. The gods whispered of living men amongst the dead, whose will kept the legions marching. They would be Malagor's prey. Without them, Arkhan would be forced to use more and more of his power to keep the dead moving, and less of it to protect himself.

And then, when he was stretched to his utmost, Malagor would strike. The bone-man would die again... And this time, he would stay dead.

Tancred spurred his horse forwards, his heart hammering in his chest. He felt weighed down by fear and excitement, by glorious purpose. He let his lance dip and it rolled in his grip as he angled it towards the massive, red-armoured shape of Krell of the Great Axe, one of a pair of curses that had haunted the ducal line of Quenelles for centuries. The lance struck like a thunderbolt and exploded in a cloud of splinters. The remnants of it were ripped from his hand and he let it go as his destrier galloped past the reeling wight. Krell roared like a wounded lion and made a flailing grasp for his horse's tail.

Tancred and his men had left La Maisontaal Abbey weeks earlier, in an effort both to conserve what supplies the abbey-garrison had, and to hunt down a particularly pernicious band of beastmen, which had been haunting the border country since the end of the civil war. The survivors of their attacks spoke of one with wings, which had interested Tancred. Such a beast was bound to be important in some fashion, for obvious reasons.

He put little stock in the whispers of the peasantry, who murmured the name of Malagor, for that creature was nothing more than a fairy tale. While the beastmen did have their war-leaders and shamans, they were brute things, no more dangerous than the orcish equivalent. To think that there was one whom all such dark and loathsome creatures would bow to was laughable.

Tancred had brought Anthelme with him on the hunt, leaving the defence of the abbey in the hands of Theoderic and the others. He had had his misgivings at first, but he knew that such a hunt might help ease the chafing boredom of garrison duty his restive knights were already complaining of. Now it was beginning to look as if he were being guided by the Lady herself. When they'd sighted the motley horde of braying beastmen, the creatures had broken and fled rather than giving honest battle, and in pursuing them, Tancred and his warriors had crashed right into the mustering forces of the very enemy he had been preparing the abbey's defences against.

Arkhan the Black had returned to Bretonnia, as Lady Elynesse, Dowager of Charnorte, had foretold, and he'd brought with him an army of the dead: an army that was Tancred's duty, and honour to destroy here and now, before it reached the abbey. He had ordered his men to charge before the undead could organise their battle line, and, like a lance of purest blue and silver, the knightly host of Quenelles had done so, driving home into the sea of rotting flesh and brown bone. He had lost sight of Anthelme in that first, glorious charge, but he could spare no thought for his cousin, not when the cause of so much of his family's anguish stood before him.

Tancred bent and snatched up his morning star from where it dangled from his saddle. It had been his father's, who had wielded it in battle against Krell and his cackling master decades ago. Now it was the son's turn to do the same. 'Father, guide my hand,' Tancred growled as he jerked on his warhorse's reins, causing the animal to rear and turn. He spotted Krell immediately. The wight was already charging towards him, bulling aside the living and the dead alike in his eagerness to get to grips with Tancred. The black axe flashed as Tancred rode past. He slashed at the beast with his morning star.

Krell roared again, a wheezing wail that nearly froze Tancred's blood in his veins. The dreadful axe came around again, braining Tancred's mount even as the animal lashed out at the dead man with its hooves. Krell staggered. The destrier fell, and Tancred was forced to hurl himself away from it and avoid being caught under the dying beast. He landed hard, his armour digging into him. He clambered to his feet as Krell lunged over the body of his horse.

Tancred stumbled aside, narrowly avoiding Krell's blow. The axe hammered into the ground. Tancred whirled back and sent the head of the morning star singing out to strike Krell's wrist. The wight let go of his axe and grabbed for the mace. He seized the spiked ball and jerked it from Tancred's grip. He hurled it aside as he grabbed for Tancred with his free hand. Armoured fingers dug into Tancred's helmet, causing the metal to buckle with an ear-splitting whine. Tancred clawed for the sword at his waist as Krell forced him back, his heels slipping in the mud. The wight was impossibly strong, and when he fastened his other hand on Tancred's helmet, Tancred knew he had to break the creature's grip before his skull burst like a grape. He drew his sword and slashed out at Krell's belly in one motion. Blessed steel, bathed in holy waters by the handmaidens of the Lady herself, carved a gouge in the bloodstained armour.

Krell shrieked and stepped back, releasing Tancred. The latter tore his ruined helm from his head as Krell turned to retrieve his axe. 'No, monster! You've escaped justice once too often,' Tancred bellowed. He cut at the wight's hands, forcing Krell to jerk back. Tancred knew that if the undead warrior got his hands on his axe, there would be little chance of stopping him. He slashed at him again, driving the monster back a step. He felt the strength of purpose flood him, washing away his earlier doubts and spurring him on. His father had gone to his grave, cursing the names of Krell and Kemmler. They had been a weight on his soul that had never been dislodged, and it had dragged him down into sour death at the Battle of Montfort Bridge. But now, Tancred could avenge his father, and Quenelles as well.

He hammered at Krell, and witch-fire crawled up his blade with every blow. He heard the singing of the handmaidens of the Lady, and felt their hands upon his shoulders, guiding him. Every blow he struck was with her blessing, and Krell staggered and reeled as strange fires crawled across his grisly armour and ichors dripped from the sharp, jagged plates like blood. His flesh-less jaws gaped in a bellicose snarl and he swatted at Tancred, like a bear clawing at leaping hounds. Men joined Tancred. He still saw no sign of Anthelme, but he had no time to worry. All that mattered was Krell. Spears stabbed at the beast from every side, digging at the wounds Tancred had already made.

The wight flailed about like a blind man, splintering spears and driving back his attackers, but more pressed forward. Tancred growled in satisfaction and looked around. Kemmler would be close by. If he could find the madman, and put an end to him, then Krell would be easier to dispatch once and for all.

'Tancred!' a voice shrieked. Tancred spun, and only just

interposed his sword as a stream of crackling, sour-hued fire swept towards him. The flames parted around the blade. A wizened, crooked figure strode through the press of battle as if it were no more important than the squabbling of vermin. 'Duke of Quenelles, I thought you gone to the worms at Montfort Bridge,' Heinrich Kemmler snarled. He swept out his staff and his blade. The skull atop the former chattered like a berserk ape as Kemmler drew close.

'My father, necromancer,' Tancred said. He felt strangely calm. It was as if every moment of his life had led to this point. As if this single moment of confrontation were his reason for being. He felt a weight upon him that he had never felt before, save the first day he had taken up the burden of his ducal duties and privileges. 'I am the son, and it falls to me to see that you at last pay your debt to the world.'

Kemmler cackled and weird shadows wreathed him, obscuring him from sight as Tancred attacked. Tancred struck out at him, but his blade bit nothing but air again and again. 'What's the matter, Tancred? Too long off the tourney field?' Kemmler hissed, as though he were right beside him. A blow caught Tancred in the back and he lurched forward. He turned, but the flickering shadow-shape was gone before he could so much as thrust. More blows came at him. One of his pauldrons was torn from his shoulder, and rags of chainmail were ripped from his torso. His surcoat was in tatters and his pulse hammered in his head painfully. He couldn't breathe, could barely see for the sweat, and his muscles trembled with fatigue.

'I've been waiting for this for centuries,' the necromancer said, circling him, his form rippling like a rag caught in a wind. 'Your father and grandfather – your whole stinking line – has harried me from the day I first had the misfortune to set foot in this pig's wallow of a country. Again and again I have been forced to flee from you, but no more. Today your line ends screaming...'

Out of the corner of his eye, Tancred saw the old man's shape waver into solidity. The necromancer raised his sword for a killing blow, his face twisted in a leer of satisfaction. Tancred spun and his blade pierced the old man's side, tearing through his flickering cloak. Kemmler screeched like a dying cat and he flailed at his enemy with his blade. Tancred avoided the wild blows and moved in for the kill. He could hear Krell roaring behind him, but he concentrated on the hateful, wrinkled, fear-taut features of the necromancer before him. He drove his shoulder into the old man's chest and knocked him sprawling. 'No, old devil, this is the end of you,' Tancred said. He stood over Kemmler, and raised his blade in both hands. 'For my father, and in the name of all those whom you have slain and defiled, you will die.'

Before he could strike, however, he felt a sudden ripping pain, and then everything was numb. The world spun crazily. He struck the muddy ground, but felt nothing. He couldn't feel his legs or his arms. He saw a headless body – *whose body was that?* – totter, drop its sword, and fall nearby. Everything felt cold now, and he couldn't breathe. He saw Krell, axe dripping with gore, kick the headless body aside, and drag Kemmler to his feet. *Whose body?* he thought again, as darkness closed in at the edges of his vision. *Whose body is that?*

Then, he thought nothing at all.

Heinrich Kemmler watched as Tancred's head rolled through the mud. He tried to smile, but all he could muster was a grimace of pain. He levered himself awkwardly to his feet with his staff, its skulls, hung from it with copper chains long ago gone green with verdigris, dangling grotesquely. It was a potent artefact, his staff, and he drew strength from it as he gazed down at the wound Tancred had left him as a parting farewell. Blood seeped through his coat and dripped down into the dirt. The wound hurt, but he'd suffered worse in his lifetime. He scrubbed a boot through the dirt. 'That's the last taste you'll have of me,' he hissed. He looked up as a shadow fell over him.

Krell, coming to check on him, like a faithful hound. Or perhaps a hound-master, checking on his pet. As he gazed up at the scarred and pitted skull of the wight, Kemmler wondered, and not for the first time, if he was fully in control of his own fate. He thought of the shape he sometimes saw, that seemed to lurk in Krell's shadow – a phantom presence of malevolent weight and titanic malice. He thought that it was the same shape that padded through his fitful dreams on those rare occasions when sleep came. It whispered to him, indeed had been whispering to him all of his life, even as a young man, after he'd first stumbled upon those badly translated copies of the Books of Nagash in his father's haphazard ancestral library.

Those books had started him on his journey, the first steps that had seen him defy death in all of its forms, benign or sinister. He had fought rivals and enemies alike, striving to stand alone. The Council of Nine and the Charnel Congress – rival consortiums of necromancers – had faded before his might, their petty grave-magics swept aside by his fierce and singular will. He had pillaged the library of Lady Khemalla of Lahmia in Miragliano and driven the vampiress from her den and the city, and in the crypts beneath Castle Vermisace he had bound the liches of the Black Circle to his service, earning him the sobriquet 'Lichemaster'.

He had counselled counts, princes and petty kings. He had gathered a library of necromantic lore second only to the fabled libraries of forsaken Nagashizzar. He had waged a cruel, secret war on men, dwarfs and elves, prying their secret knowledge from them, and with every death rattle and dying sigh the voice in his head, the pressing *thing* that had encouraged him and driven him, had purred with delight. Until one day, it had gone silent.

It had abandoned him to a life of scurrying through the hills, a broken, half-mad beggar, his only companion a silent, brooding engine of destruction, whose loyalties were unfathomable. He had thought, once, that Krell was his. Now he knew better. Now he knew that they had been at best, partners, and at worst, slaves of some other mind.

Kemmler's eyes found the tall, thin shape of Arkhan the Black, as the liche oversaw the rout of the remaining Bretonnian forces. With Tancred's death, they'd lost heart. In some ways, the living and the dead were remarkably similar. He glared at the liche and then stooped to retrieve his sword. He grunted with pain, but hefted the blade thoughtfully.

Arkhan heard the same voice he had, Kemmler knew. Krell as well; both liche and wight were slaves to it. And that was the fate it intended for Kemmler. Just another puppet. He could hear it again, though only faintly. But it was growing louder, becoming a demanding drumbeat in his fevered brain. It was inevitable that he would surrender.

Kemmler looked at Krell. He spat at the wight's feet and sheathed his sword. 'Inevitability is for lesser men.'

ELEVEN

Skull River, the Border Princes

Mannfred brought his blade down on the rat ogre's broad skull, cleaving it from ears to molars. The beast slid away, releasing its grip on Mannfred's mount, as he jerked his blade free in a welter of blood and brains. Two more of the oversized vermin lumbered towards him, growling and giving high-pitched bellows. He spurred his mount towards them, his teeth bared in a snarl. As his skeleton steed slipped between the two creatures, he swept his sword out in a single scythe-like motion, sending the heads of both monsters flying.

'A heady blow, cousin,' Markos crowed, from nearby. The other vampire's armour was drenched in skaven blood, and his blade was black with it from tip to the elbow of his sword arm. Markos, like the other Drakenhof Templars, had been at the centre of every recent battle.

'Shut up and see to our flanks, Markos,' Mannfred snapped, shaking the blood from his sword. 'I tire of this.' He stood up in his saddle and looked around. When his scouts had brought him stories of the lands ahead literally swarming with the rat-things, he had thought they were exaggerating. But in the past weeks, he had seen that, if anything, his spies had been conservative in their estimates of the number of skaven running roughshod over the Border Princes. This was the fifth – and largest of them all by far – horde in as many weeks to bar his path, and he was growing frustrated.

It was as if some unseen power were seeking to block him from getting to Mad Dog Pass. He'd thought it was the skaven, at first, but the hordes he faced were more intent on pillage and loot than on stopping him. They inevitably attempted to retreat when they saw the true nature of the forces at his disposal, as had the first such band they'd encountered.

He had taken the time to question the spirits of the deceased ratmen, and had found the dead ones no less deceitful than the living vermin. In his frustration, he had torn apart more skaven souls than he had slain living ones. But in the end, his suspicions had been confirmed – the Under-Empire had risen, and the skaven were at last united. They had eradicated Tilea and Estalia, and Araby was even now under siege from above and below.

No, it wasn't the skaven; it was something in the air itself. Arkhan was right. Forces were moving in opposition to them, and not merely those from the expected quarters. Mannfred was playing dice with the Dark Gods themselves. The thought did not frighten him. Rather, it invigorated him. If the Chaos gods were taking a hand in affairs so directly, then he was on the right path. He had faced the servants of Chaos before, and emerged triumphant. This time would be no different.

He looked up at the dark sky, where strange green coronas still swirled and crawled, like flies on the flesh of a corpse, and laughed. 'Come then,' he said. 'Come and set yourselves against me, oh powers and principalities of madness. Let the heavens themselves crumble in, and the earth turn to mud beneath my feet, and I will still triumph. Send your daemons and proxies, if you would, and I will show you that in this fallen world there is one, at least, who does not fear you. I have beaten gods and men before, and you will be no different. The veil of perfect night shall fall on this world, and order and perfection shall reign, according to my will and no other.'

The air seemed to thicken about him for a moment, and he thought he saw cosmic faces stretched across the sky above, glaring down at him in tenebrous fascination. He felt the weight of their gaze on his soul and mind, and he swept his sword out in a gesture of challenge.

A screech alerted him to the skaven retreat, and he looked down. The ratkin were fleeing with all the orderly precision of their four-legged cousins. He fancied that more of the pestilential vermin died in the retreat than in the battle itself. Then, considering the sheer size of the horde in question, perhaps that wasn't all that surprising.

'They flee, my lord,' Duke Forzini said as his horse trotted past. His armour, like Markos's, was dripping with blood, and his sword dangled loosely in his grip. 'If we press forward, we might catch them.' The duke had taken to vampirism with admirable rapidity, and his mouth and beard were matted with gore. Forzini had personally inducted most of his household knights into a state of undeath, binding them to him with blood where before they had been loyal only to his gold.

'No need,' Mannfred said. He sheathed his blade. 'They are going in the same direction we are, and the fear they carry with them will infect those who stand between us and our goal.' He looked about him, and smiled cruelly. Then, with a gesture, he drew the corpses of the two rat ogres he'd slain to their feet. 'Besides, we have a wealth of new recruits to add to our ranks.' More skaven followed the rat ogres' example, their torn and mutilated bodies sliding and shuffling upright.

Despite his bravado, and despite the sheer number of skaven corpses that were even now being washed away down the roaring waters of the Skull River, the battle had been a close one – this swarm had been the largest his forces had yet faced. An ocean of squealing bodies and ramshackle war engines that had momentarily blanketed the horizon. Mannfred had been forced to rouse the dead of three ravaged fortress towns to throw at the horde.

Speed and subtlety alone was no longer going to serve, he thought. The closer they drew to Mad Dog Pass, the greater the likelihood that he would find himself facing similarly sized hordes of skaven. He needed every corpse he could find to throw at them.

He felt a tremor, and glanced up at the Claw of Nagash, where it sat atop the staff strapped to his back. The fingers twitched and stretched, as though gesturing towards the mountains rising in the distance. It seemed that its movements were becoming more agitated the closer they came to Mad Dog Pass, almost as if it were impatient to be reunited with the blade that had severed it from Nagash's wrist, once upon a time. Mannfred could almost feel the dark magics radiating from the Fellblade. His palms itched to hold it, and he could sense the hum of its deadly energies. His hand clenched.

You don't have it yet, boy. You still have a million ratmen between you and that dark blade, and you'd best not forget it, Vlad said. Mannfred opened his hands and looked resolutely away from the shifting shadow-shape that scratched at the edges of his attention. Vlad's voice had only become stronger as they came closer to the Fellblade. When he fought, there was Vlad, watching him as though he were still a boy on the proving ground, fumbling with his blade. Vlad had always watched him that way.

'Nothing I did was ever up to your standards, was it, old man? I never measured up to you or your blasted queen, or the bloody champion. And you wonder why I stole that cursed bauble...' he muttered, running his hands over his scalp. 'Yet here I sit, on the cusp of victory. And where are you? Ash on the wind.'

Better ash than a body rotting in a bog, Vlad said. *Did you enjoy it? Sunk in the mire, a hole in your heart, unable to move or scream. I wonder, did something of that tainted place creep into your veins? Is that why you changed? You were always so vain, and now, you are as foul and as bestial as any of those treacherous animals I locked away in the vaults below Castle Drakenhof. Why, you'll take to wing any day now, I'd wager. You'll shed all pretence, just like Konrad, and succumb to the madness in your blood...*

Mannfred snarled. His hand flew to the hilt of his blade and he drew the sword, twisting around in his saddle to face the shade of his mentor. The tip of his blade narrowly missed Markos's nose as he rode up. The other vampire jerked back and nearly fell from his saddle. 'Are you mad?' he snarled.

'Mind your tone, cousin,' Mannfred growled. He fought to control his expression. 'You shouldn't sneak up on me while I am concentrating.' He looked about, and saw that every dead thing around was standing at attention, empty eyes fixed on him. He could feel the power of the Claw mingling with his own as it spread outwards and roused the inhabitant of every grave for miles around, be it skaven, human, orc or animal. More, he could feel them stumbling forwards at his call, answering his summons. Thousands of rotting corpses and tormented spirits were coming in response to his command.

'How many more cadavers do we require?' Markos muttered, looking around at the swaying dead who surrounded them.

Mannfred smiled nastily. 'Enough to drown the skaven in their burrows, cousin. I will bury them in the bodies of their kin. Come – time slips away, and I would not have my prize do the same!'

🕱 *Quenelles, Bretonnia*

When it came time to make camp, the village had seemed the best spot. It was still mostly intact, if all but abandoned. They had seen smoke rising up into the overcast and cloud-darkened sky, and Anark, the Crowfiend and the other vampires had ridden pell-mell to claim whatever living blood remained in the village. Unfortunately for them, all of the villagers who had not fled were piled up on a pyre in the centre of the market square, burned to a crisp.

Luckily, the vampires had glutted themselves during the battle several days before. But Arkhan had been hoping to add the inhabitants to his host. Too many of the dead had been irretrievably lost in that battle. If they were to take La Maisontaal Abbey, and then escape Bretonnia in the aftermath, they would need a host of considerably larger size than they currently had.

'No blood, no corpses of any worth – it's almost as if someone got here ahead of us,' Erikan Crowfiend said as he rode up to Arkhan to deliver his report. A gaggle of ghouls gambolled after his horse. The Crowfiend had an affinity for the flesh-eaters and he had begun to assert some control over the numberless cannibals that haunted the meadows of Quenelles. 'I've sent out scouts, but none of them have come back yet.'

Arkhan pondered his comment silently. Every graveyard and town they had come to since crossing the border into Quenelles had been razed to the cellar stones, and the bodies of the dead mangled or burned beyond use. Some of that, he knew, was down to the ghouls, who spilled across Bretonnia like locusts, feeding on the dead left behind by the civil war. But he could not escape the feeling that potential lines of supply were being cut one by one by unseen enemies.

In all the centuries of his existence, Arkhan had learned much of the arts of war. The back-alley gambler had become a hardened battlefield general, who knew the way of the refused flank, the feint and the coordinated onslaught. He knew when he was facing a planned attack, even if it looked like coincidence or random chance.

There was a mind working against his, and he suspected he knew where it hid. More than once, he had caught the creeping moth-wing touch of dark magics at the edges of his senses. Not necromancy, but something older and fouler by far. The magics of ruination and entropy. The magics of the Dark Gods. He could taste them on the air, as he had when he'd breached the wall of faith in Sylvania. They were gathering their strength, as the winds of magic writhed in torment. Even now, the air stank of the breath of the Dark Gods. It hung thick and foul and close, obscuring his sorcerous senses.

He glanced up, and saw a shape, circling far above. For a moment, he mistook it for an unusually large carrion bird. Then, he realised that he had seen that dim, flapping form before. It had harried his host for leagues. It never drew too close, but it had pursued them relentlessly. It was this thing that radiated the magics he sensed, he was certain. It followed him, and a horde of beastmen followed it, the very beastmen who had led the Bretonnians upon him, and now loped in his wake like wolves haunting the trail of a dying stag. They had been shadowing the undead since the battle with Tancred's forces.

Arkhan had dismissed the creatures at first, thinking them little better than the ghoul packs that now loped in the wake of his host. But his scouts had brought him reports that the creatures had followed them from the battlefield, shadowing his forces, never engaging in conflict, and always fleeing if challenged. The herd was also growing in size. Worse, it was doing so more quickly than his own forces. He felt as if he were being driven forwards, like the beast before the hunters, and there was nothing for it but to run as quickly as possible.

'Bah, we will find blood and corpses aplenty if we but follow Tancred's army and destroy it. They'll make for Castle Brenache. With the forces at our disposal we can tear it down stone by stone,' Kemmler said. Arkhan ignored him. 'Are you listening to me, liche?' Kemmler snapped. He grabbed Arkhan's arm.

Arkhan knocked Heinrich Kemmler sprawling. '*You are a fool, old man. Your obsession has almost cost us everything. We are done with your fantasies of vengeance.'* The liche pinned Kemmler in place with his staff. Krell moved towards them, axe not quite raised. Arkhan fixed the wight with a glare, and the cat perched on his shoulder hissed at the wight. Krell hesitated, seemingly uncertain who to strike. Arkhan decided not to press the issue.

He lifted his staff and stepped back. *'You have cost me an asset, and burdened us all, in the name of bruised pride and ego.'* Kruk had died in the battle with the Bretonnians. Kemmler had abandoned his position to attack his old enemy, leaving Kruk exposed to the lances of the knights, and the little necromancer had been dislodged from his harness somehow. He'd subsequently been trodden into a red pulp by the galloping hooves of the knights' horses. Ogiers and Fidduci had been able to keep those dead under the little man's control upright, but only just. With Kemmler distracted by Tancred, Arkhan's army had nearly disintegrated.

If the Bretonnians had not routed when they had, Arkhan knew, it was very likely that his mission would have been over before it had even truly begun, so devastating had their initial charge been. Luckily, the core of his army was still intact – the wights and skeletons he'd drawn from the molehills and tombs of the Vaults, and the blood knights who Mannfred had foisted on him. And he too had recovered the ancient canopic jars that he had cached on the border of Quenelles, which housed the dust and ashes of the Silent Legion.

Over the course of centuries, Arkhan had carefully seeded many desolate and isolated places with unliving servants, so that should he ever find himself in need, he would have warriors to call on. The Silent Legion were one such group. In ages past, they had served Nagash, and it was only the increasing strength of the winds of magic that would enable Arkhan to restore them to fighting vigour and control them. But he needed time to prepare the proper rites to do so. Time that Kemmler had cost them.

'You promised me Tancred's head,' Kemmler snarled as Krell

helped him to his feet. The old man stank of blood and indignation, and he pressed a hand to his side, which was stained dark. Tancred hadn't died without leaving his enemy a painful reminder of their dalliance. That wound had weakened Kemmler, and slowed down their advance considerably. 'I was merely taking my due, and I won you the battle in the process.'

'*It should not have been a battle,*' Arkhan said. '*It should have been a slaughter. We should have drowned them in a sea of rotting flesh and mouldering bone, and swept them aside in minutes. Instead, we were drawn out into a pointless struggle that lasted more than a day. We have no time for this.*'

'Maybe you don't,' Kemmler spat. 'But Bretonnia owes me a pound of flesh and I intend to collect!' He gripped his staff so tightly that the ancient wood creaked.

'*What you think you are owed is of no concern to me,*' Arkhan said. '*La Maisontaal Abbey is only a few days' march from here, and I would give our enemies no more time to prepare. I care nothing for Brenache, or your grudge. We have wasted enough time.*'

'Time, time, *time,*' Kemmler mocked. 'You act as if you still live, and that one day is different from another. What matters when we do it, so long as it is done. Let Nagash wait.'

The zombie cat twitched and fixed Kemmler with a glare that the old necromancer didn't seem to notice. Arkhan reached up to stroke its head. '*Nagash isn't what I'm worried about. How long do you think we have before the new king of this ravaged land notices that we've invaded? Or the rulers of Athel Loren? They are occupied, for now, but that will not last forever. And there are more enemies abroad than just men and elves.*'

'Who would dare challenge the most mighty and puissant Arkhan, eh?' Fidduci broke in, before Kemmler could spit what was certain to be an acidic reply. The Tilean took off his spectacles and began to clean them on the hem of his filthy robe.

The spear caught him just between his narrow shoulder blades and punched through his chest in an explosion of gore. Ogiers, who'd been standing beside him, fell back with a yelp. Arkhan looked up as a howl echoed through the air. The flying shape had drifted lower, and he saw then that it was no bird, but instead a winged beastman. It swooped upwards with a triumphant roar and he knew then that it had thrown the spear. Kemmler had distracted him, and he had not seen the beast's approach.

Fidduci coughed blood and reached out, weakly, towards Arkhan. The liche ignored him, and began to ready a sorcerous bolt. He intended to pluck the flying beast from the sky for its temerity. A shout drew his attention before he could do so, however. He saw Anark and the other vampires riding back towards him, smashing aside zombies in the process. 'Beware!' Anark bellowed. 'It's a trap!'

Horns wailed and Arkhan cursed as beastmen came charging out of hiding in a rush, exploding from the meadows around the village, and out of the seemingly empty shacks, howling and snarling. They tore through the ranks of the unprepared dead like starving wolves, with crude axes and chopping blades. Arkhan whirled around, and black lightning streaked from his eyes, incinerating a dozen of the malformed creatures. It wasn't enough. A gor, foam dripping from its muzzle, leapt over the burning, smoking remains of its fellows and brought a blade down on Ogiers's skull, splitting the Bretonnian's head from crown to jaw.

As the necromancer fell, Arkhan obliterated his killer. Power roiled within him, and spewed out in murderous waves, laying beastmen low by the score. But still they came on, their eyes bulging and froth clinging to their lips. They had been driven beyond the bounds of madness, and there was no fear in them. Magic had hidden their presence from him, magic wielded by the flying creature that even now circled above him, its jeering laughter drifting down like raindrops. It was all Kemmler's fault. The Lichemaster had tarried too long, playing his games of spite with Tancred, and been wounded for it. They'd lost half of their army at a stroke, as Fidduci fell, bleeding and hurting. And now, the children of Chaos were attempting to take advantage of their weakened state. He could almost hear the laughter of the Dark Gods, echoing down from the storm-stirred heavens.

Arkhan was forced to fall back. The cat yowled and hissed as it clung to his shoulder, and he drew his tomb-blade, only just in time to block a blow aimed at his skull. He spun, crushing his attacker's head with the end of his staff. For a moment, he won clear. But it didn't last.

The minotaur was the largest of its brutish kind that Arkhan had ever had the misfortune to see. It rampaged towards him, bellowing furiously, bashing aside its smaller cousins heedlessly as it came closer to him, the great axe in its hand licking out towards him. Arkhan thrust his staff and his blade up, crossing them to catch the blow as it fell. The axe was the same size as his torso, and it was all that he could do to catch the blade. The force of the blow drove him down to one knee. He strained against the weight of the axe as the minotaur hunched forward, trying to break his guard through sheer brute strength.

Then, suddenly, a red-armoured form bulled into the creature from the side, rocking it away from Arkhan. The minotaur stumbled back, lowing in confusion. Krell stomped forward, pursuing the creature. The two axes met in a crash of steel again and again as beast and wight fought. The minotaur was the stronger of the two, but Krell was by far the better warrior, and the wight's greater skill with the axe began to tell. The minotaur staggered in a circle, pursued by Krell, who opened wound after wound in its hide. Blood splashed onto the ground as the giant, bull-headed beast sank down onto all fours and gave a piteous groan. Krell planted a boot against its shoulder and sent it flopping over onto its back.

As Krell finished off the minotaur, Arkhan shoved himself to his feet and looked up, hunting for the flying creature he'd seen before. That one was the true danger, he knew. That one had the ear of the Dark Gods, else why would it be able to fly?

But the creature was nowhere to be seen. It had vanished, and, as Arkhan watched, its followers departed as well. Crude horns wailed and the beastmen began to retreat in ragged disorder, streaming back into the night, not altogether reluctantly. They had been eager enough for a fight when they'd arrived, but the dead made for bad sport.

He looked around. Fidduci had finally succumbed to the spear that had pinned him to the earth. His spectacles had fallen from his nerveless fingers to shatter on the ground, and his black teeth were wet with blood. Ogiers lay nearby, still twitching in his death throes. Arkhan felt the weight of his army settle on his shoulders, like a sodden blanket.

He wondered, as he leaned against his staff, if this had been his enemies' intent all along. His trusted servants were dead, and his effectiveness lessened. Now he had only Kemmler to help him. Kemmler, who had already proven himself as unreliable as ever. Kemmler, who was more powerful now than Arkhan had ever seen him.

Kemmler cackled nearby as he jerked Fidduci's and Ogiers's bodies to their feet. He appeared unconcerned about the state of affairs, and his coarse, chilling laughter echoed over what had, only moments before, been a scene of slaughter.

Arkhan watched him, pondering.

✦ Castle Sternieste, Sylvania

Volkmar was on the plain of bones again, the stink of a hundred thousand charnel fires thick in his nose and lungs. His hammer hung broken and heavy in his hands, and his armour seemed to constrict about him like a giant hand clutching his torso. He was tired, so tired, but he couldn't give up. He refused to surrender.

Catechisms sprang unbidden to his lips and rattled through

the stinking air. Passages and entire pages from holy books shot out into the grey emptiness. He shouted out Sigmar's name, and shrieked out the story of the Empire's founder.

Sigmar.

Sigmar.

Sigmar!

The name pierced the emptiness like a well-thrown spear, and it hung quivering there for a moment, gaining strength. Then, as it had before, the ground began to move and shift, as if something vast were burrowing beneath it. The bones rattled and fell as the thing drew closer to the surface and ploughed after him.

He heard Aliathra's voice, somewhere far above and behind him. Though he could not make out her words, he knew that she was calling out to him, pleading with him not to fight this time, but to run.

Volkmar hesitated, and then did as she bade. The thing, the force, the daemon, wanted him to fight. He knew it in the marrow of his bones. It wanted him to fight, so that it could sweep over him and bowl him under. So he ran. And it followed him. A hideous voice, as loud and as deep as the tolling of the monstrous bells of Castle Sternieste, smashed at him, trying to force him to make a stand.

Instead, he ran harder, faster, forcing his body to keep moving. And he shouted Sigmar's name as he ran. Every time the word left his lips, the terrible voice seemed to weaken a little bit. But it did not cease its hunt.

Bones slipped and rolled beneath his feet. The hands of the dead clawed at his legs as they always did, dragging him down. Fleshless jaws bit down on him, and bony fingers tore at him, and he swung about with his hammer, trying to free himself. Too late, though. Always too late.

A mountain of bones rose over him, blotting out the grey light. The bones shifted and squirmed, shaping themselves into a vast countenance, titanic and loathsome. Eyes like twin suns blazed down at him, and a breath of grave-wind washed over him, searing his lungs and withering his flesh. He felt his skin shrink taut on his bones, and his marrow curdle as the wind enveloped him. He lifted his hammer, too weak to do anything else.

And then, Volkmar the Grim woke up.

Volkmar stirred groggily in his chains. Sleep still held him in its clutches, and the faintest ghost of a distant howl rippled through the underside of his mind. He felt the air stir, and knew that they had a visitor. He smelt the stink of old blood, and stale perfume, and knew that the new mistress of the castle had come to visit.

Mannfred was gone. Where, he could not say, but he had suspicions aplenty. That left a castle full of vampires still, and there was no hope of escape. That realisation had come to him slowly but surely, with insidious certainty. There was no hope, of escape or even survival. But perhaps whatever Mannfred was planning could still be thwarted. Perhaps the Empire could be spared whatever monstrous evil the vampire sought to unleash.

Then, perhaps not.

He heard the vampire as she drew close, passing amongst Mannfred's collection. Did she linger over the Crown, perhaps, and let her fingers drift over the books?

'What would you give me, if I were to kill one of you?' the vampire asked, without preamble. She looked up at Volkmar with something approaching loathing. The Grand Theogonist hung in his chains like a side of beef, his eyes not quite closed, his breathing shallow. 'That being the only way to defeat our lord and master, of course. He had nine. Now he has eight. He can do nothing with seven.' She cocked her head like a falcon sighting prey, and her eyes slid towards Aliathra, who hung nearby, head lolling, her blonde locks spilling over her pale face, matted with blood and filth. 'I know that you are conscious, elf. I know that you are listening.' Her eyes slid back to Volkmar. 'As are you, old man. Pretending to be unconscious will avail you nothing.'

'Your kind only bargains for two reasons,' Volkmar rasped. *He had nine...* Lupio Blaze was dead, then. They had come and taken the knight in the evening. They had not brought him back. He had suspected that the Tilean was dead. 'Either you are bored... or afraid,' One blood-gummed eyelid cracked wide. 'Which is it, Elize von Carstein?' The old man laughed as her eyes widened slightly. He allowed himself to feel a brief surge of pleasure at her momentary discomfiture. 'Oh yes, I know you, witch. I know all of your cursed clan, root and branch. The witch hunter Gunther Stahlberg and I even made a chart, before Mannfred killed him. The Doyenne of the Red Abbey, Handmaiden of Isabella von Carstein, cousin to Markos von Carstein, of the red line of Vlad himself, rather than by proxy. You are as close to royalty as your kind gets.'

'Then you know that I can give you what you wish,' Elize said. 'I can help you, old man.' She turned towards Aliathra. 'I can help you as well, elf. I can free you. I can kill you now, to spare you pain later. I can kill your fellow captives, if you are too proud to ask for yourselves. All I require is that you ask.' She glided towards him and leaned close, her palms to either side of his head. Volkmar glared at her with his good eye. 'Ask me, old man. Beg me, and I will put you out of your misery, like an old wolf caught in a trap.'

'Frightened, then,' Volkmar coughed. His lips cracked and bled as he smiled. 'You are frightened, and I think I know of what. Something so dark and hungry that you pale in comparison. You can feel it, can't you? In whatever passes for your heart,' he said. He closed his eye. 'Mannfred has left you here, and now, like a rat that scents a snake, you want to squirm away. So be it woman. Kill us, and run.'

'Beg me,' she growled.

Volkmar wheezed hoarsely. It wasn't quite a laugh, but it was as close as he could manage. 'No, no, I think not. Run away, little rat. Run and hide before the snake gobbles you up.'

Elize raised a hand, as if to tear out his throat. It trembled slightly, and then fell. Volkmar said nothing. He opened his eyes to watch the vampire leave. 'You should have let her do it, priest. You should have asked her to kill you,' someone croaked, as the chamber door rattled shut. 'You should have *begged*.'

'Be quiet, witch,' Volkmar rasped. It was hard to get air into his lungs, hung on the wall as he was. It was all he could do to speak. The manacles bit into his flesh, and he felt his blisters pop and weep as he shifted in his chains.

'Your arrogance has doomed us, Volkmar. And you most of all – I am damned, but you will be doubly damned,' the Bretonnian witch yowled. Volkmar heard her chains rattle. 'He is coming for you, old man.'

'I said be silent,' he snarled, trying to muster something of his former authority. He knew he'd failed when she began to laugh and wail.

There was no hope.

Volkmar closed his eyes and tried not to sleep.

Elize stood staring at the wall opposite the door to the chamber for some time. She could feel the burning gazes of the two wights, who now guarded the chamber, on her back, but she didn't move away. They were no threat to her. Mannfred had seen to that.

She considered simply going back in and killing one of them – the nature priest, perhaps. He was little more than a mindless husk, after all this time in captivity. There were ways that it could be done that would leave no one the wiser. Mannfred would assume that he'd simply expired, despite the sustaining spells he'd etched into the prisoners' flesh. Unless he didn't, in which case she'd have some explaining to do.

Elize didn't fear Mannfred's wrath any more than she had feared Isabella's incandescent and unpredictable tantrums, or Vlad's quietly menacing disappointment. She knew which strands to pluck to see her safely out of the von Carstein web, and which to pull in order to get back in, should it be necessary. Mannfred was guileful and cunning, but not especially subtle. He strode across the landscape like a warrior-king, and expected his opponents to fall at his feet in awe of his majesty and political acumen.

He was, in short, a barbarian. Vlad had been much the same – a man out of time. The difference between them lay in the fact that Vlad had had an almost childlike delight in learning the ways of the Imperial court, and navigating the choppy political waters of the Empire. Vlad had been subtle: patient and unswerving. Mannfred was not patient. He never had been. He was a creature of passions and selfish demands, and he only understood those things in others. Patience, to Mannfred, was simply fear. Dedication was foolishness. Subtlety was hesitancy.

But this time, Mannfred had bitten off more than he could chew. They could all see it, even if the sisters of the Silver Pinnacle hadn't been whispering it into every ear. It was madness, what he planned, and in everyone's best interests to see that he failed.

Elize looked back at the door, thoughtful now. The old man hanging on the wall in there was no different, really. An obstinate, obdurate relic, sitting athwart the stream of history, determined to bend it to his will. Again, the temptation to simply kill him rose. But... no. Best to wait, until there was no other option. Best to wait until all of the pieces were in place.

'Think carefully, child. Think, before you do something we will all regret.'

Elize turned. Alberacht Nictus lumbered down the corridor towards her, more or less a man. His wings had shrivelled to flaps that could easily be folded in the narrow corridors and he wore a set of armour purloined from somewhere. His face was still a tale of horror, but his eyes shone with kindly madness. He held out a taloned paw. 'Come away, my sweet girl. Come away, and let the Sigmarite rot in his tomb.'

Elize took his claw gingerly. Alberacht pulled her close, like a doting uncle. 'You always were a risk-taker, my little stoat. Always going for the throat,' he gurgled. 'That is why Isabella loved you best.'

'Unlike Mannfred,' Elize said. She allowed Alberacht to guide her away from the chamber. The big vampire chuckled harshly.

'Mannfred heeds your words,' Alberacht said. 'After all, we are here, are we not?'

Elize tensed. 'What do you mean? Speak plainly, Master Nictus.'

'Oh, is it Master Nictus now? Have I offended you, cousin?' Alberacht peered at her owlishly, and showed his teeth in a ghastly smile. 'You were here, at Sternieste, before the wall went up, and before Mannfred made his bid for secession. It was you who advised him to raise the Drakenhof banner and call the order to war. You asked him to set the black bells to ringing, while you rode out to find your pet and Markos.'

'Anark is hardly my pet,' Elize murmured.

'Was I speaking of him?' Alberacht leaned over and kissed the top of her head. 'You are as clear as glass to these old eyes, my girl.'

Elize pushed away from him carefully. They had come to one of the places where the wall of the keep had crumbled away, and she leaned against the gap, looking out over the courtyard far below and the plains beyond. The dead were still mustered amongst the barrows, waiting for an invasion that might never come. Screams echoed up from the courtyard, where Mannfred's court were engaged in their early evening amusements. She'd had to put a guard on the larder once Mannfred departed, to keep the greedy parasites from emptying Sternieste's dungeons of every breathing human in an orgy of indulgence and slaughter.

'He left me,' she said softly, after a few moments.

'Aye, he did,' Alberacht said. He loomed behind her, his claws on her shoulders. 'Though I think he regrets it. I think the Crow-fiend regrets many things.'

'I care not whether he regrets it,' she hissed. 'He. Left. Me. I made him and he *left*. No one leaves me. I leave. I go where I will. Not him!'

'Ah,' Alberacht breathed. He was silent for a time. Then, he said, 'Sometimes, I think that Vlad did us a disservice. There is something in the von Carstein blood that encourages duplicity and madness. Konrad, Pieter, Nyklaus with his ambitions of admiralty... Isabella.'

'I am not mad,' Elize said.

'I am,' Alberacht said. 'Then, I was a von Drak, and they were all mad.' He leaned close. 'I was speaking of your duplicity, in any event. All of this, simply for the Crowfiend?' He leaned around her, so that he could peer up into her face. 'Tomas – dead. Anark elevated to a position he is unsuited for. Markos's predilections with succession encouraged, and Mannfred warned of that burgeoning treachery. Are any of us out of your web, my child?'

'You and the Vargravian,' she said, smiling slightly.

'Ah,' he murmured. 'Am I to feel slighted, then?' She tensed again. There was no way of telling which way the old monster would jump at the best of times. His mind was lost in a red haze.

'No,' she said carefully. 'But you are impossible to predict. And the Vargravian is an unknown quantity. I know him only by reputation. Tomas elevated him to the inner circle. The others I know.' She pounded a fist against the crumbling edge of the gap. 'They are fixed points, and I can weave my web, as you call it, about them.' She smiled thinly. 'Mannfred taught me that.' She looked at Alberacht. 'It is not all for Erikan. It is for us, as well. For the future. For too long we have clung to this place. Sylvania was a prison even before the wall of faith surrounded it. There is a whole world out there, past the borders, where we can spread and take root. But before we can flourish, certain branches must be pruned.'

'And what of Mannfred's plans, child? You know what he intends. You know what awaits us, when they return.'

Elize turned away. 'It will not come to that. Even Mannfred is not so blinded by ambition that he would risk unleashing the Undying King upon the world.' She smiled. 'Anark will do his part, and Markos as well. Nagash will not rise, but when this farce is done... *we will.*'

TWELVE

 Beneath Mad Dog Pass, the Border Princes

The skaven screamed and died as the bodies of the Iron Claw orcs, torn and savaged by the ultimately futile battle that had seen the entire tribe decimated by the forces under Mannfred's command, launched themselves through the crude pavises of wood and rope, and hacked down the clanrats manning the ballistae behind. More zombies shoved through the gap created by the dead greenskins, flooding the tunnels beyond the chamber where the skaven sentries had chosen to make their stand.

Mannfred urged his skeleton mount through the sea of carnage that his servants had left in their wake, his face twisted in an expression of disdain. This was the tenth such cavern he had ridden through in as many hours, and impatience was beginning to eat at him like acid.

Never before had he felt so pressed for time. It had always seemed a limitless commodity for him. But he felt it closing in on him now, cutting off his avenues of manoeuvre. It was as if he were being surrounded by enemies on all sides, trapped in an ever-tightening noose. He clutched Kadon's staff to him, and took comfort in the Claw of Nagash, its withered fingers twitching and gesturing mutely.

Power. That was what it was all about. That was what it had always been about. The power to see his journey to its end. The power to control his own destiny. Too often had he been at the mercy of others, his desires supplanted by the whims of those who considered themselves his superiors. Vlad, Neferata, his father... They had all tried to keep him from achieving his destiny. But no longer. He had outlived, outfought, outschemed them all. He had thwarted his enemies at every turn, and thumbed his nose at every empire.

That you have, my boy. Your famed subtlety has deserted you, it seems. Or perhaps you deserted it, eh? The skies are blood-red, the gallows scream hungrily and Mannfred von Carstein has come into his own, Vlad murmured.

Mannfred snapped his reins, causing his mount to gallop through the cavern. The drumming of its hooves blocked out Vlad's voice. Nevertheless, he could hear the quiet conversation of his Drakenhof Templars behind him, as they urged their steeds to keep up with his. They were talking about him, he knew. Scheming most likely, but then, they were von Carsteins. None of them would dare try anything, save perhaps Markos.

He scanned the cavern and caught sight of the latter, dispatching a squealing skaven warrior with a casually tossed sorcerous bolt. Markos was almost as good a sorcerer as Mannfred himself. He, like Mannfred, had learned much under the tutelage of the bat-faced nightmare known as Melkhior, when Vlad had employed the latter to teach them the finer arts of necromancy. Mannfred remembered the thin-limbed horror, in his stinking rags, with his fever-bright eyes as he showed them the formulas of the Corpse Geometries. There was much of W'soran, Melkhior's primogenitor, in him, from the way he spoke, to his apparent disdain for even the most basic aspects of hygiene.

It was from Melkhior that he had discovered the origin of the dark magics that empowered the ancient ring that Vlad wore, and it was from the old monster that he learned of how it held the secrets of the resurrection of the Undying King. Melkhior had whispered of certain rites that might stir Nagash, and of the shifting of the Corpse Geometries that had seen Nagash come back and wage an abortive campaign to reclaim his pilfered crown. Then the Night of the Restless Dead, in which Nagash's ravening spirit had managed only a single night of terror. Even diminished and shrunken, Nagash was the sort of power that caused the world to scream in horror. But he was a power without true thought. Nagash himself, as he had been, was long gone to whatever black reward awaited such creatures. All that was left of him was something less even than Arkhan the Black – blind impulse, and the fading echo of a once mighty brain.

Or so Melkhior had sworn. Mannfred knew better than to trust the words of any of W'soran's brood. He had felt a great sense of relief when Melkhior's student, Zacharias, had put paid to whatever subtle schemes his master had been weaving. Not that Zacharias was an improvement; if anything, he was just as devious and as arrogant as Melkhior, and W'soran before him. Indeed, Zacharias had openly opposed Mannfred's schemes from the moment of Melkhior's death, striving to unravel stratagems that had taken him centuries to forge. He could not fathom the other vampire's intent, save that Zacharias feared what Mannfred might do once he gained the power of Nagash. Or, perhaps he feared what would happen should Mannfred fail.

Mannfred frowned. He considered the Claw of Nagash, where it lay across his saddle. He could feel the power it held, power enough to carve out a nation, if he wished. Once, that would have been enough for him. He had vied for thrones before. But something had changed in him. A throne, a city, a province – these were no longer good enough. Even an empire was but a drop in the ocean of his ambition.

Those ambitions were the root of every plan he had concocted since he had dragged himself from the mire of Hel Fenn, revivified by the blood of a dying necromancer. They drove him on, into the reeking tunnels, and he, in his turn, drove on the dead with the lash of his will. Vlad was right. He had discarded subtlety; there was no use for it here. The only tools of worth were the press of bodies and the savage tactics of attrition.

In the hours that followed, Mannfred willed wave after wave of zombies into the labyrinthine network of tunnels. Through the eyes of his flesh-puppets, he mapped out the safest route for him and his Drakenhof Templars to take towards the heart of the festering pit. He lost hundreds of zombies, but gained twice their number in new recruits from among the skaven dead. Entire squealing tribes of the vermin were stifled and silenced beneath the tide of rotting meat, and then dragged upright to serve beside their slayers. It was necromancy as applied brutality, sorcery wielded like a blunt object, as Mannfred battered himself a path through the enormous burrow.

He led his knights deeper into the tunnels, which grew grand in scale. The burrow was a tumour of stone and darkness. Foul poisons dripped from filth-encrusted stalactites, and the rough walls of rock were marked by generation upon generation of crude skaven-scrawl; the caverns were choked with ramshackle structures of warped wood and rust-riddled metal. And everywhere, the skaven. Some fled his approach, others tried to resist. Sometimes they even fell upon one another in vicious displays of compulsive betrayal that startled even Mannfred, who took advantage of such incidents with bemusement.

Deeper and deeper he pushed his forces. He could feel the Fellblade now, like a wound in the world, pulsing, calling to the claw it had hacked from Nagash's wrist. It called to him, and Mannfred went gladly, driven by the devils of his ambition.

The Fellblade would be his, and with it, the power of Nagash.

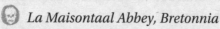 *La Maisontaal Abbey, Bretonnia*

'It's a fairly innocuous sort of place,' Erikan Crowfiend murmured. He leaned over his horse's neck and ran his fingers through the matted mane of the ghoul crouched beside him. The rest of the pack swirled about him, yapping and snarling like dogs on the scent. There were hundreds of them, drawn from all over Bretonnia to the meadows of Quenelles by the scent of death. The other vampires seemed perturbed by the presence of so many flesh-eaters, especially Anark von Carstein, who glared at the Crowfiend with barely repressed fury.

'It is nothing more than a slightly fancy tomb,' Kemmler said. The ghouls gambolling about the legs of Erikan's steed avoided the Lichemaster and Krell, who stood just behind him, his Great Axe in his hands.

'*A tomb whose inhabitants are barred to us, thanks to Bretonnian witchery,*' Arkhan said. He stood on the back of his chariot and looked at his commanders, examining each one in turn. Then, he turned his attentions back to the object of their discussion.

La Maisontaal Abbey sat on the slopes of the Grey Mountains, its walls the same hue as the tumble-down stones of the cliffs around it. Its walls were half finished, but it was an imposing structure nonetheless, built to protect its inhabitants from any who might wish them harm. It had been built in the early years of Gilles Le Breton's first reign, its construction funded by a mysterious nobleman from the east, who had claimed that the abbey was the repayment of a debt owed. Arkhan, who had once lost his head to the sword of the nobleman in question, suspected that there was more truth to that tale than not.

In the fading, grey miasma of the day, the abbey was a flickering nest of fireflies as torches, lanterns and bonfires were lit. He wondered if the inhabitants thought that firelight would be enough to keep back the host he had arrayed on the plains before La Maisontaal. '*What do your spies tell you, Crowfiend?*' he asked, after a moment.

The vampire glanced down at one of the ghouls, who gave a warble and licked broken fangs in the parody of smile. The Crowfiend looked at Arkhan. 'Much meat,' he said, with a shrug.

'Asking them to count is useless. Past one, it goes "many", "much" and "most". That's as accurate as they get.' He straightened in his saddle. 'They're keeping close to the walls and the torches, however. That much they could say. Plenty of weak points, jammed with frail, trembling meat, ready to be torn and squeezed dry of life.' The Crowfiend smiled crookedly. 'A better sort of battlefield than Couronne, I will say.'

'If you must,' Arkhan said. He looked at Anark. *'You, vampire. Mannfred spoke of your military experience. Analyse and explain,'* he said.

The vampire grunted and shook himself. 'Traditional Bretonnian tactics. A shieldwall of peasantry in front of artillery, knights on the flanks to crush the attack once it becomes hung up on the fodder.' Anark lifted himself slightly in his saddle, and his brutal features slackened into something approaching consideration. 'Trebuchets and archers. The bonfires mean fire-arrows,' he added, his lip curling away from a fang.

'What is fire to the dead?' Kemmler asked, running his fingers through his tangled beard. 'Let our army carry an inferno into the heart of their army, if that is the fate they choose.'

Arkhan ignored the necromancer. He let his gaze drift across the ragged ranks of his army. The vast majority of it was composed of the graveborn victims of war and plague. He disliked relying on such chattel – zombies were little more than ambulatory shields for better, more reliable troops. Unfortunately, he had precious few of the latter.

The Silent Legion stood ready for battle, clad in ancient armour and bearing weapons not seen since the height of the Nehekhara. He had seen to their resurrection from their essential salts upon his arrival on the fields before La Maisontaal Abbey, and Nagash's nekric guard stood ready to wage war on the living once more.

Arrayed about the Silent Legion were the warbands Arkhan and Kemmler had dragged from their slumber in the Vaults.

Composed of wights and skeletons, the warbands were possessed of a savage bloodlust second only to Krell's, and without
the sorcerous chains that compelled them to obey Arkhan, they
would have already begun the attack.

Beyond them, and scattered before and around the host were
the ghoul packs that had followed them from the borderlands
and into the hills. A harsh winter and a bloody spring had added
to their numbers, as villages throughout southern Bretonnia
became little more than haunts for newly christened cannibal
clans. Such pathetic beasts were drawn to the stench of necromancy like iron filings to a lodestone. Like the zombies, they
were of little practical use, but Arkhan was confident that they
could readily take blows meant for more valuable troops as easily as any staggering corpse.

And last – the Drakenhof Templars. The armoured vampires
were eager for war, none more so than the brute Mannfred had
named Grand Master. Anark met his gaze and looked away
quickly. Was he nervous, Arkhan wondered, or bored? Neither
would surprise him. That Anark intended treachery was almost
certain. The creature was barely competent, save in military matters, and openly defied Arkhan at every opportunity, eliciting
chortles from his fellow leeches. All save the Crowfiend, whom
he seemed to despise even more than Arkhan.

Arkhan dismissed the thought. He had no time to worry
about traitors. He looked up at the night sky, and for a moment,
immense, terrible shapes seemed to claw down towards him, like
hungry birds. The cat on his shoulder hissed softly. He'd almost
forgotten that the animal was there, so quiet had it become since
they'd arrived. He stroked its greying flesh gently.

No time, he thought. There was no room for error now, not
with the delays and losses they'd suffered. The beastman attack
they'd fought off some days before had taught him that. Though
they had driven the creatures off, the damage had been done.
The unassailable horde he had assembled had dwindled to its

current state. It was still an ocean of corpses, but he was forced to see to their control himself, along with Kemmler.

His options had been forcibly limited. There was no time for grand strategy now, only brute speed. '*So be it,*' Arkhan rasped. He swung his staff out and pointed it at Krell. '*Krell will take the fore. He will lead the Silent Legion, and the tribes of the dead into the centre of the enemy line. They shall be the head of my spear and the stumbling dead shall be the haft, driven forward by Kemmler and me.*'

'That is exactly what they are counting on,' Anark protested. 'Even a dried up old thing like you should have the wit to see that. The knights will fold into your flanks like the jaws of a trap!'

Arkhan looked at the vampire. '*That is what you are for, von Carstein. Besides, it would be rude of us to ignore such a heart-felt invitation, would it not?*'

Kemmler cackled wildly. 'Oh, there's hope for you yet, liche! Come, hurry! I have waited centuries to tear this rotting heap of stone apart, and I can wait no longer.' He gestured sharply, and Krell broke into a trot. As the wight moved, the Silent Legion fell into step with him. The skeletal warbands joined them, rasping battle-cries issuing from the long-withered throats of their chieftains.

Arkhan stepped down from his chariot and made to join Kemmler, where the latter waited amidst a knot of zombie knights, still clad in bloodstained armour and clutching broken weapons. He paused as the Crowfiend interposed his steed. Arkhan looked up at him.

'A word of advice,' the vampire said, not looking at him. 'Kemmler stinks of ambition.'

'*As does your companion Anark,*' Arkhan said.

'Not my companion,' the Crowfiend said. The vampire looked at him. 'The Drakenhof Templars were ordered to escort you to La Maisontaal Abbey. And that is what we shall do.'

'*And afterwards?*'

The Crowfiend kicked his horse into motion. He galloped away, followed by his ghouls. Arkhan watched him go. Then he joined Kemmler.

'What did the leech want?' the old man grunted.

'*Merely to pass on the compliments of Mannfred von Carstein,*' Arkhan said. The dead twitched into motion, lurching forwards. Arkhan and Kemmler moved with them, lending sorcerous speed to the slower corpses.

'Ha! That's a poisoned chalice if there ever was one,' Kemmler spat. He peered after the Crowfiend, eyes narrowed. 'I remember that one. He served in Mallobaude's army. He followed that fool Obald around. Fussed over the old pig-farmer like a nursemaid,' he sneered. He smiled nastily. 'If he's here, the Bone-Father must have finally died.'

'*You sound pleased,*' Arkhan said.

'Merely satisfied, I assure you,' Kemmler said, and tittered. 'Obald was a fool. Just like the idiot Ogiers, or that black-toothed sneak, Fidduci.' He glanced at Arkhan, his eyes sly. 'They were but pale imitations of their betters. Useless chattel, fit only to be used and discarded.' He made a fist. 'Power belongs only to those strong enough to wield it. It belongs to those who can survive its use, and those who can take it for themselves. I'm a survivor.' He licked his lips. 'Pity Nagash wasn't, otherwise we wouldn't be in this mess, would we?'

Arkhan said nothing. Kemmler laughed and turned his attentions back to the dead. The vampire had been right – Kemmler was up to something. He couldn't help but to boast. He resolved to keep an eye on the old man, even as the night sky above was suddenly lit up by a rain of fire.

'*Arrows,*' he said, raising his staff. A quickly conjured wind plucked away those missiles that drew too close to him and Kemmler. But even as Arkhan readied himself to deal similarly with the next volley, he saw that they were not the target.

The forward elements of the undead host had crossed no more

than half the field before the Bretonnian bombardment began. A second volley of flaming arrows pierced the darkness and tore into the ranks of skeletons and wights. Again and again, the Bretonnian archers fired. Only scant seconds passed between each volley, testament to the skill of the longbowmen. Peasants though they were, Arkhan was forced to admit that their skills were on par with the archers of Lybaras.

With a flick of his fingers, he willed those of his minions who possessed them to raise their shields. Nonetheless many were still set alight by glancing or lucky shots, and the shields were of little help against the larger fireballs launched by the massed trebuchets. As the great war engines found their range, more and more impacts occurred, tearing great ragged holes in the undead ranks.

But the undead marched on, driven forwards relentlessly by the combined wills of Arkhan and Kemmler. Dark magic flowed from the fingers of both necromancer and liche, rousing the fallen dead to continue the march, no matter how badly damaged they were. There were few in the world more attuned to the winds of death than he and his troublesome comrade, Arkhan knew. Dieter Helsnicht, perhaps or Zacharias the Ever-Living, but no others possessed the mastery of broken bone and torn flesh that he and Kemmler did.

The dead fell around him and rose again; shattered skeletons swirled and danced back into motion, to rejoin the unwavering advance. The attrition caused by the bombardment slackened, drew to a crawl and then ceased. Arkhan spat black syllables into the greasy air, and every iota of concentration he possessed was bent to thrusting his warhost forward, as if it were a single weapon, and his the hand that wielded it.

It would have been easier with the others – the battle-line more fluid, the tactics less primitive. But Arkhan was forced to admit that it would not have been nearly as satisfying. It had been decades since he had dirtied his hands with war in this fashion. He had stayed on the sidelines of Mallobaude's rebellion, a fact he regretted, if only for the squandered opportunities.

His attention was drawn by screams. Krell had reached the enemy. With a roar audible only to sorcerers and lunatics, Krell unleashed the Silent Legion upon the Bretonnian lines.

The killing began.

THIRTEEN

 Mordkin Lair, the Border Princes

'The dead-things... followed you,' Warlord Feskit hissed. He was old, for a skaven, and his fur was the colour of ash. He tapped the hilt of the wide, jagged-bladed cleaver that was stabbed point first into the bone dais supporting his throne. The latter was a trophy taken from a fallen dwarf hold in years past, and it overflowed with pillows and cushions made from the hair and beards of men, elves, dwarfs and unlucky skaven. Feskit himself wore a necklace of orc tusks, goblin noses and human ears, all of which he'd pilfered from the various battles he claimed credit for. 'You ran, and they followed.' Every word was enunciated slowly, drawn out like the flick of a torturer's knife across cringing flesh.

'No-no, Snikrat the Magni– Snikrat the *Loyal* came to warn you, mighty Feskit,' Snikrat chittered. He knelt before the throne, his loyal Bonehides arrayed behind him – far behind him – and gestured towards Feskit imploringly. 'They seek to invade our lair, oh perspicacious one, by which I mean our tunnels, the very heart of our fortress, this place here,' he continued, sweeping his arms out. 'That they followed me is only incidental, by which I mean unrelated, to my own headlong plunge to assure myself of your wellbeing, because you are my warlord and I am your loyal champion.'

In truth, Snikrat had no idea whether or not the dead had followed him. It was certainly possible, but he suspected otherwise, given his cunning and the stealthy nature of his retreat across the plains, back to the mountains. He had seen other clans attempt to match claw and blade with the undead, and he had, briefly, considered lending aid. But it was imperative that he warn Feskit about the enemy; and if that enemy was destroyed before he got back... Well, the credit would be ripe for the claiming, wouldn't it?

As it happened, he had managed to lead what was left of his warband past the undead at the entrance to Mad Dog Pass, while the charnel horde was otherwise occupied with the Iron Claw orcs. The greenskins hadn't been faring particularly well, the last Snikrat had seen. He decided not to mention it. Clan Mordkin and the Iron Claws had waged a war for control of the pass for decades, and Feskit respected their strength inasmuch as he respected anything. If he knew that they had been beaten, he might decide to abandon the lair, rather than fight, and Snikrat's continued survival hinged on the latter.

'Hrr,' Feskit grunted. He sat back, his eyes narrowed to mere slits. Snikrat tensed. He glanced at the armoured stormvermin, who crouched or stood arrayed about Feskit's dais, ready to lunge forward to slaughter at their claw-leader's command. The Mordrat Guard were Feskit's personal clawband and they were loyal to a fault, thanks mostly to Feskit's generous patronage, which ensured that they saw little in the way of actual combat while claiming the bulk of the loot. Feskit was too smart to risk them in open combat, where they couldn't protect him from treacherous rivals, or, in certain cases, each other. They were also indolent, lazy and far from as skilled as most thought them.

Snikrat knew all of this because he had, once upon a time, been the commander of the Mordrat Guard. He had profited from Feskit's indulgence, and then, when he had climbed as high as he could, he had made the obvious decision. Granted, it had been the wrong decision, and it had ended with him flat on his back and Feskit's teeth in his throat, but it had seemed obvious at the time. Snikrat rubbed his throat nervously. Feskit had spared him that day, though he'd never said why.

Snikrat thought – Snikrat *hoped* – that it was because Feskit was canny enough to know that he was getting old, and that if Clan Mordkin were to continue to flourish, it would need a suitable skaven to lead it. A magnificent skaven, a great warrior and cunning to boot. But that skaven had to prove himself worthy of Feskit's patronage. He had to acquire victories, follow orders and serve the clan in all those ways that most skaven simply could not, whether due to their inherent untrustworthiness or simple weakness.

As Feskit stroked his whiskers, deep in thought, Snikrat surreptitiously took in the gathered chieftains. Those Feskit considered the most loyal sat near the dais, surrounded by their bodyguards. The rest were scattered throughout the great cavern or hadn't been invited. There were more than a dozen missing. Some were likely still out plundering the Border Princes, he suspected. Which was just as well – more opportunities for him. He needed to reclaim his place at the foot of the throne, if he was to have any chance of successfully challenging Feskit a second time. He scratched at his throat again. Unless Feskit simply had him executed.

A sudden, discordant clamour of bells echoed through the caverns. The upper tunnels had been breached, Snikrat knew. A wave of relief washed aside his worries. He'd timed his return perfectly. Death shrieks drifted down from the vaulted roof of the cavern, slithering through the numerous flue holes that marked the rock. They echoed and re-echoed about the cavern, and a nervous murmur swept through the gathered chieftains. Snikrat, who was already far too familiar with the enemy even now bearing down on them for his liking, shivered slightly.

Feskit glared at him. Then he waved a paw at the knot of trembling slaves who cowered at the foot of his throne. 'Bring me my armour and weapons.' He gestured to the black-clad gutter runners who lurked nearby, waiting to carry forth Feskit's decrees to all of the small clans within his realm. 'Summon the conclave of chieftains. The burrow must be defended.' His eyes found Snikrat again, and his lips peeled back from his fangs. 'It is lucky that you returned when you did, Snikrat. Where would I be without my greatest champion?'

Snikrat stood, his chest swelling. 'Snikrat the Magnificent lives only to ensure the greater glory of Clan Mordkin, mighty chieftain,' he said.

'Of that I am certain, yes-yes,' Feskit said. He flung out a paw. 'Go then! Defend our lair from these intruders, Snikrat. Prove yourself worthy of my faith, yes,' he chittered.

Snikrat hissed in pleasure and whirled, gesturing to the gathered chieftains. 'You heard our most merciful and wise clanleader! Gather your warriors and war engines. Awaken the beasts,' he snarled. 'It is time to drive these dead-things from the lair of Mordkin!'

Quenelles, Bretonnia

Anthelme slumped in his saddle, aching, exhausted beyond all measure, burdened by tragedy and fear alike. Nonetheless, the newest, and perhaps last, Duke of Quenelles led his companions north, to war.

He closed his eyes as he rode. His cousin's face swam to the surface of his thoughts, and he banished it with a curse. He had failed Tancred. It hadn't been for lack of trying, but it had been a failure regardless. At the battle's height, his steed had been struck with terror and had fled, taking him with it. By the time he'd brought the beast under control, Tancred was dead, and his muster shattered and shoved aside by the undead host as it made its way north.

Anthelme had made his way to Castle Brenache, where he'd found Fastric Ghoulslayer and Gioffre of Anglaron and the rest of the Companions of Quenelles attempting to rally the remaining knights. Their joyful greetings as he'd ridden shame-faced into the castle courtyard had torn his heart worse than any blade. They'd thought him dead; he wished that were so. More, he wished that Tancred were alive and that he had fallen in his cousin's place.

Instead, Quenelles was his, and the weight of it felt as if it would snap his spine. The province was in ruins – beset by beastmen and worse things. Calls for aid came every hour, and Anthelme was inundated with inherited troubles. He did not know what to do. Would the defences of the abbey hold, or would aid be required? He had sought the counsel of the Lady of Brenache, the Dowager of Charnorte. She had warned Tancred so many months before, and he'd hoped that she might help him now. And she'd tried.

Her scrying had proven a troublesome affair, marred by what he could only describe as daemonic interference. Anthelme shivered in his saddle as he remembered how the clear waters of her scrying bowl became as dark as a storm cloud, and leering faces formed in the ripples. Fell cries had echoed from the stones and the Lady's voice had been drowned out by the laughter of the Dark Gods.

He had been ushered from her chambers then, with a promise that she would find an answer for him, and for three days she took neither food nor drink. Her chamber had rocked with the sounds of madness – strange laughter, scratching on the stones and foul smells that lingered in the corridors of the castle. The knights began to mutter that the Lady had deserted them – why else would Tancred have fallen? Why else would the realm be beset by so many enemies at once?

As Anthelme sat and waited for the Lady Elynesse to come out of her room, knights had demanded that he ride out to face one foe or another. Anthelme refused them all, though it hurt him to do so. Some knights left, sallying forth alone to confront the horrors that afflicted their ancestral lands. Others stayed, their natural impetuousness tempered by the memory of Tancred's fall.

On the third day, their patience was rewarded. Lady Elynesse staggered from her chambers. The Lady's voice had at last pierced her fevered dreams, and given her a dire warning to pass on – if Anthelme did not go to La Maisontaal, Bretonnia itself would fall.

'Stop thinking,' a voice said, rousing Anthelme from his reverie.

'What?' he asked. Gioffre of Anglaron grinned at him, and slapped him on the back, causing his mail to jingle.

'I said stop thinking so hard. You're spooking the horses.'

'That doesn't make any sense.' Anthelme looked around.

'No, but it got you to pay attention, didn't it?' Gioffre said. 'We're but a day's hard ride from the abbey, and you look as if you'd rather be anywhere else.'

'It's not that,' Anthelme said quickly. Gioffre laughed.

'Oh I know. Anthelme, you are a true knight, as was Tancred. I fought beside you during Mallobaude's rebellion, remember? I know that you are no coward. Just as I know that you only fear failure.' He smiled. Gioffre wasn't especially handsome, but his face became almost pleasant when he smiled. 'We will not fail. Troubadours will sing of the day the Companions of Quenelles sent the dead back into the dark, and saved Bretonnia.' He clapped Anthelme on the shoulder. 'Now, heads up.' He pointed upwards. 'The Ghoulslayer and his flock of overgrown pigeons are back.'

Anthelme couldn't resist a smile. Gioffre had a distaste for the winged stallions that Fastric Ghoulslayer and his fellow pegasus knights rode. Anthelme suspected that it had less to do with the fact that he felt the surly beasts were unnatural, and more to do with their habit of befouling the ground beneath them as they swooped through the air. Horse dung wasn't pleasant, especially when it was coming at you from above, and very quickly.

'Ho, Duke Anthelme,' Fastric shouted as his steed swooped lazily through the air. The pegasus whinnied as it descended, and it tossed its head and trotted arrogantly towards Anthelme and Gioffre. Their own steeds snorted and pawed the ground as the beast fell into step with them. Normal warhorses didn't get along with pegasus, even at the best of times. Gioffre's stallion nipped at Fastric's steed, and the former planted a fist between his mount's ears. 'Keep that bad-tempered nag of yours under control, sirrah,' Fastric said.

'It'd be easier if that beast of yours didn't provoke the other animals,' Gioffre said.

Before the old, familiar argument could begin again, Anthelme said, 'What news, Ghoulslayer?'

'Beasts,' Fastric growled. 'Hundreds of them. They're moving north, but much more slowly than us.'

'Has Arkhan the Black made common cause with the creatures, do you think?' Gioffre asked. 'I wouldn't put anything past that creature, frankly.'

Anthelme frowned. 'They've been following us for days. If they were allies, wouldn't they have attacked us by now? Even creatures like that should have no difficulty in divining our destination.' He thought briefly of the beast-herd that had led Tancred into the ambush that had cost him his life, and wondered if this was the same one, before dismissing the idea. There were dozens of such warbands prowling the province now. 'No,' he said, straightening in his saddle. 'No, they're scavengers. They're following us in hope of an easy victory. Well, let them. All they'll find is death.'

He twisted in his saddle and looked back at the column of

knights that followed him. Standards of every design and hue rose over the assembled force. Warriors from every province and city were counted amongst the Companions of Quenelles, and for a moment, just a moment, Anthelme felt the shadow that had been on his heart since Tancred's death lift. He felt a hand on his shoulder, and looked at Fastric. 'He would be proud,' the older knight murmured. 'As are we all. Where you lead, Anthelme, Duke of Quenelles, your Companions will follow.'

Anthelme nodded brusquely. 'Then let us ride. La Maisontaal Abbey is in need of defenders, and I would not have it said that the Duke of Quenelles fell short in his responsibility.' He kicked his horse into a gallop, followed by Gioffre. Fastric set spurs to his steed and the pegasus sprang into the air with a neigh.

Horns blew up and down the column, and the Companions of Quenelles hurtled north.

La Maisontaal Abbey, Bretonnia

Theoderic of Brionne growled in satisfaction as the line of shields buckled, but did not break. 'Hold, you filthy pigs,' he rumbled as he watched the peasants resist the undead advance. 'Hold.' The peasants did not love him. He knew this, and accepted it as a consequence of his position. But if they did not love him, they at least feared him, and they would do their duty, dreading the price of failure.

Tancred had cautioned him against meeting the enemy in open battle, should they arrive in his absence. The dead could not be smashed aside so easily, he'd said. But Tancred hadn't heeded his own advice, and now, if the message his cousin had sent was to be believed, his body was somewhere out there in that lurching horde.

It was almost enough to make him doubt himself. The newly christened Duke of Quenelles had sent riders from Castle Brenache, where he was taking the counsel of the Lady Elynesse, the Dowager of Charnorte. The riders had only just managed to outpace the dead, and they had brought word of Tancred's fall and of Anthelme's intention to ride to La Maisontaal's aid with the Companions of Quenelles. Anthelme had advised him to retreat behind the abbey walls, and to hold the dead back, but not to meet them in pitched battle.

A sensible plan; behind the walls, the muster of La Maisontaal could more readily rely upon the magics of the three sisters of Ancelioux. At the thought of the trio of damsels, he glanced towards the shieldwall, where they stood, clad in shimmering damask and furs against the chill of evening. He knew little of the women, and what he did know, he didn't like.

It was rare to have three daughters chosen by the Fay Enchantress, as poor Evroul of Mousillon had, and even rarer to see them after the fact. It hadn't been a happy reunion, by all accounts – Evroul, unlucky in fortune as well as family, had chosen the wrong side in the civil war, and his own daughters had killed him. Nonetheless, their magics would come in handy in the battle to come, he thought.

Anthelme's advice aside, Theoderic had no intention of waiting for rescue. Right or wrong, he was a man of tradition. The darkness was not to be feared, or avoided. It was to be confronted head on, and smashed aside with blade and lance. Under his command, the garrison at La Maisontaal was more active than it had been, even under Tancred's father. It was larger, with more men than had ever before manned its walls.

As soon as his scouts had reported the host approaching the cleared plains before the abbey he had sworn on the tatters of his honour to guard, he had known that the moment he had been seeking since he had given up his ancestral lands and titles had arrived. Before him was a chance for redemption, a chance to atone for the failings of mind and body that had tarnished his family name.

'This... is a glorious day,' he murmured. He looked around at the knights who surrounded him. Anticipation was writ on every face, and their horses shifted impatiently, as eager as their riders to be at the charge. He knew that similar looks would be on the faces of the knights waiting for his signal on the opposite flank.

He rose up in his saddle and lifted his axe over his head. On the other side of the field, a horn crafted from the tusk of a great wyrm wailed. Theoderic knew that horn, and the man who wielded it – Montglaive of Treseaux, slayer of the wyrm Catharax, from whose cooling corpse he had hacked the tusk he had made into his horn. Montglaive commanded the right flank, as Theoderic commanded the left. As the horns on the right sounded, so too did the horns on the left, and Theoderic felt his soul stir.

He was not a man for speeches, inspiring or otherwise. It was not in him to rouse or incite, but he knew that something must be said. He felt the weight of the world's attention on him. The air vibrated with some inescapable pulse, some fateful pull, which sharpened his attentions and tugged at his heart. He might die this day, but he would not be forgotten. He would not be remembered as a sozzle-wit or a failed knight, but as a hero. As a champion of the Lady, and of the realm. Songs would be sung, and toasts raised, and the name of Theoderic of Brionne would stand through the ages to come.

That was all he had ever wished.

'This is a glorious day!' he roared, spreading his arms. 'We honoured few stand between holy ground and a black host, and the Lady stands with us! Our fair land writhes in pain, assaulted by daemon, outsider and ill-roused corpse. But we few stand here, to prove not simply our courage, or our honour, but that though all Bretonnia is besieged, hope has not yet forsaken the realm eternal! Hope, which echoes in the rattle of swords and the thunder of hooves! Ride, defenders of La Maisontaal! Ride, knights of Bretonnia! Ride and sweep the enemy before you – ride for the Lady and the world's renewal!'

All around him, his knights gave a great shout, and then thrust back their spurs and joined the battle, Theoderic at their head. The ground shook as the pride of Bretonnia hurtled towards their enemy, lances lowered.

Theoderic bent forward over his charger's neck. He carried no lance, but instead wielded his axe. The weapon was his only reminder of who he had been, before his disgrace. He had carried it in glory and in folly, and he would not be parted from it save in death. Its blade had been anointed in the holy font of La Maisontaal, and as it spun in his grip, it began to shine with a blessed light.

The darkness retreated before him, and he could see the dead where they stumbled, mindless and remorseless. To him, in that moment, they were a sign of all that had afflicted Bretonnia. He raised his axe, roared out an oath and struck out as his steed smashed into the flanks of the dead and pierced them like a spear. His axe licked out, shining like a beacon, and took the head from a zombie.

Then the rest of the knights struck home, and the twelfth and final battle for La Maisontaal Abbey began in earnest.

FOURTEEN

 Mordkin Lair, the Border Princes

Markos von Carstein did not consider himself unduly ambitious. Indeed, he liked to think of himself as something of an idealist. Vlad had been an idealist, and Vlad was his model in most things. Vlad was a paragon, the vampiric ideal made flesh. The King of Blood, the Emperor of Bones, his ghost was tangible in every speck of Sylvanian soil.

Markos bent away from the thrusting spear, and flicked his wrist, bisecting the squealing ratman's skull with his sword. He twisted in his saddle, chopping another in half, and swatted away a smoke-filled globe with the flat of his blade, sending it tumbling back towards the skaven who'd thrown it. It shattered and the skaven died, choking on its own blood.

It was Vlad who had elevated him from the common muck, and made him a Templar of the Drakenhof Order. It was Vlad who had nurtured his natural gifts for sorcery and strategy. It was Vlad who had given him purpose.

And it was Mannfred who had taken it all away.

Mannfred the liar. Mannfred the schemer. Mannfred the

acolyte. Mannfred, who had come from somewhere else to join Vlad, who was no Sylvanian, who sometimes spoke in an accent that Markos had yet to recognise, despite his travels.

Vlad should never have trusted him. But that too was part of the ideal. Vlad had worn his honour like armour, and it had dragged him down in the end. Markos had learned from Vlad's mistakes and when Mannfred had set his feet on the path of empire, Markos had absented himself. Mannfred was not Vlad, and he lacked Vlad's patience, something that inevitably led to his downfall. His attempt at conquest had ended with him sinking into Hel Fenn, and the shattering of the Drakenhof Order. They had all gone their separate ways, eager to put their defeat behind them.

Markos had spent years building up his own network of spies and informers. He had schemed and plotted dynastic marriages and political alliances, all to ensure his ultimate success. Elize, he knew, had been doing much the same, as had Tomas and the others. The Game of Night had lasted for centuries, as the remaining von Carsteins wove plot and counter-plot against one another and the Lahmians.

And then Mannfred had ruined it all by coming back.

Markos growled and parried a rust-edged cleaver. He thrust down, pinning the skaven to the cavern floor. There were seemingly thousands of the beasts, and they just kept coming in wave after wave of squealing fodder. He jerked his blade up out of the dying skaven and looked around. The cavern resembled the bowels of some vast, nightmarish engine – immense cogs, corroded pistons and acid-pitted flywheels projected from the walls at all angles, and rose from deep grooves in the cavern floor. The mechanisms were still in motion, despite the battle, and as Markos watched, a skaven warrior got too close to one and was whisked into a clanking maw, to be pulverised instantly.

The cavern was so choked with machinery that it was impossible for the combatants to fight more than five or six abreast, and the skaven suffered for this inability to bring their numbers to bear. Horns wailed and bells clanged somewhere far back in one of the tunnels, and those skaven closest to the exits began to flee the cavern.

Markos wheeled his horse about and galloped back towards the knot of undead horsemen who surrounded the Drakenhof Templars and Mannfred. As he passed through the ranks of the former, he examined them enviously. The Doom Riders had been legendary even in Vlad's time. Supposedly, they had first ridden forth from whatever barrow had held them at Nagash's command, and after his defeat at Sigmar's hand, they had ridden into the depths of the Drakwald, from whence they had haunted the surrounding lands for centuries until Vlad had sought them out and bent them to his will.

The undead horsemen wore corroded armour of a bygone age, and carried lances wreathed in cold flame. They watched him as he threaded through them, and his flesh felt as if it were covered in crawling spiders as they tracked his progress with hell-spark eyes. When he reached the others, Mannfred glanced at him. 'Well?'

'They're falling back,' Markos said. He leaned back in his saddle. 'We'll have the cavern cleared within the hour, unless they bring up reinforcements. Which they don't seem inclined to do, if you want my opinion.'

'I don't,' Mannfred said, turning away.

Markos bit down on the reply that sprang unbidden to his lips. He turned away from Mannfred and settled down to wait, one hand resting on the pommel of his blade. His anger simmered, but he wrestled it down.

Striking now would be disastrous, whether he succeeded or not. They were miles beneath the surface, and dependent on Mannfred for guidance to find their way through the seemingly endless labyrinth of twisted and reeking warrens. He'd considered trying his luck when the skaven had attacked Forzini's camp, but Elize's words of caution had restrained him. Mannfred was wary, ready for treachery right now. But, when he'd achieved his goal, Markos would have his chance, or so Elize swore. With the Claw and the Fellblade in his possession, Mannfred would be distracted, drunk on victory and his own power. It was a window of opportunity, albeit a narrow one.

Strike swiftly, before he has the chance to acclimate himself to the power of the artefact, she'd said, and he had to admit that it wasn't bad advice. Not that he trusted Elize farther than he could throw her. She was likely hoping that he and Mannfred would kill one another. So be it. He couldn't find it in his heart to blame her. Elize had her own games, just as he did.

Mannfred had ruined them all by coming back. Arrogant, assured of his superiority, he had smashed their delicately woven webs to shreds and tangles, and demanded that they kowtow to him, as they once had. As if their ambitions meant nothing compared to his own.

Well, Markos intended to show him the error of his ways.

Mannfred was as mad as Konrad had been. Oh his madness took a different form, to be sure, but he was just as much a lunatic. His time in the mire had rotted his brains, and he endangered them all with his current obsession. Markos shivered slightly as he looked at the staff Mannfred clutched, and the withered thing that occupied its head. He could feel the malignancy of the Claw in his bones.

Markos was not one to lie to himself. He knew what he was, and what he had done in his centuries of bloodletting. But there were things in the world far worse than him, and the Claw was the tool of one of them. Mannfred was caught up in its whispers and promises. They could all hear the voices – the voice – of the artefacts that Mannfred had gathered. A wheedling, demanding susurrus that permeated Castle Sternieste and haunted them. Every vampire felt the call of Nagash in their blood, whether they admitted it or not.

Most, however, knew better than to give in to it.

He looked at Mannfred again, and blinked. For a moment, in the flickering of the great globes of warpfire that hung from the roof of the cavern, he thought he'd seen something looming over the other vampire. A dark shape, far darker than any shadow, and colder than the depths of a mountain lake.

Markos shuddered and looked away.

 La Maisontaal Abbey, Bretonnia

Heinrich Kemmler didn't flinch as the knights struck the vast sea of the dead. He felt the reverberations of that impact in his bones, but he ignored it. He had more important matters clamouring for his attention. His magics were growing less precise, and less effective. At first, he'd thought the culprit was Arkhan. He wouldn't have put it past the liche to strike while he was otherwise occupied, and try to wrest control of the dead from him.

Arkhan didn't trust him, Kemmler knew. Nor did he blame the liche. Kemmler had no intention of allowing Nagash to return, whatever Arkhan's desires. Nagash's time had passed and good riddance to the creature. Hundreds of arch-necromancers had risen and fallen with the tide of years since the Undying King had been gutted on his own basalt throne, each of them worth more than any old dead thing.

The very thought of it incensed him. The drumbeat – the heart-beat of the Great Necromancer – in his head threatened to drown out all of his hard-won coherency. It had driven him mad, that sound. He knew that now. It had forged him, and fed his hungers. It had been the rhythm that had guided his steps, and set him on the path he had trod for centuries. It was the voice inside his head, whispering the secrets of power and the wielding of it; and then, when he had needed it most, it had taken all of it away. That was something Kemmler could not forgive.

Fresh rage flooded him, and he clawed at the barely visible

skeins of magic that flowed about him, trying to find the source of the interference. He could feel the heat of Krell's growing battle-lust, and he focused on it, using it as a touchstone. The wight had been his constant companion for more years than he cared to count, and he had woven innumerable spells with Krell at his side. The creature was at once a sump and a sponge for dark magic. Sometimes, he even thought that he could hear Krell speak. Or perhaps not Krell, but something that clung to his brutal husk like a shadow.

When Krell was near, the drumbeat was almost impossible to ignore. But that was not the only sound in his head. There were words as well, whispers and wheedling, plaintive murmurs, which rose and fell with the winds of magic. Kemmler had first heard those voices in the hour of Krell's resurrection, when they had offered him aid if he would bend the wight to certain tasks. And he had, and the voices too had grown quiescent. But now, as the drumbeat grew louder, so too did they, as if the initiators of each were attempting to drown out the other.

Strange currents of power flowed through him now, beneath the old familiar shroud of deathly sorcery. Like an adder beneath the water, this new power warmed him to his joints, and buoyed him. It had healed his mind and memory and soul, though it had taken centuries to do so. Centuries to clear out the rot of Nagash, Kemmler knew.

Nagash had used him. It was Nagash who had used him to build an empire, and Nagash who had guided him to Krell, but not for Kemmler's sake. That was what the whisperers had told him. And it was Nagash who wanted to use him now. It was Nagash who stalked him in the dark hollows of memory, hunting the tatters of his soul.

Fear, now, warred with rage. He flailed as a thread of magic slipped between his fingers. A nearby zombie flopped down, inert and inanimate. More followed suit, and Kemmler hissed in mounting frustration. Concentrate, he had to concentrate.

Between the hammer of the drum and the mounting agitation of the whispers, he heard the telltale cackle of the skull atop his staff.

Kemmler turned, and his eyes narrowed. He caught a pale wisp of rising magics – not the ashy smoke of the wind of death, but the gossamer effluvium of the raw stuff of life – and saw a trio of women standing behind the embattled shieldwall of peasantry. His lips writhed back from his teeth in a snarl of disdain.

The women were marshalling the magics of life to counteract his sorceries of death. Behind them, moss and flowers crawled across the stones of the abbey walls, and thick vines and roots crawled across the battlefield about them. The impertinence of it assaulted his sensibilities, and he slammed the end of his staff down, planting it like a standard.

'This is my ground, witches,' he hissed. And it was, in every way that mattered. He had bought it in blood and time. Every time he had made war in this place, on the abbey, he had shed his life's blood and soured the ground with the stuff of death. They could plant all of the trees and flowers they liked, remove all of the bodies, weave every protective enchantment known to elf or man, but the ground was still his and would be forever more.

As if they had heard his words, three pairs of eyes, violet and alien, met his own dark ones. He felt a jolt as three minds, trained to think inhuman thoughts and bent to inhuman goals, reached out to him. They were powerful, these witches. The cursed elves of Athel Loren had taken their natural gifts and forced them down unnatural paths, moulding them into weapons to be used against their own kind.

Thoughts like claws tore at his connection to the winds of magic, severing his links with brutal efficiency. He snarled and champed like a beast in a trap, and every vein stood out in his neck and arms as he reached for his staff with his free hand. A wind sprang from nowhere, tearing at him, hot and cold all at once. His bones felt heavy, but hollow, and things that might have been maggots squirmed beneath his flesh and dripped from the unhealed wound that Tancred had dealt him. The soil churned beneath him, as if in pain, and there was moss growing on his staff. He swept it off angrily.

They had minds like trees with ancient roots: anchored and arrogant. He lashed out at them, attacking them mind to mind, and was rebuffed. Kemmler ground his teeth in growing frustration. His rage turned incandescent and burned away all hesitation.

The whispers rose, drowning out the drumbeat. Warmth – true warmth – flooded him, filling the cold emptiness that Nagash had left in him all those centuries ago when his voice, his spirit, had abandoned Kemmler on the eve of the Battle of Ten Thousand Skulls. *Yes,* they whispered. *Yes, yes, yes, it is all yours for the taking. You do not serve us, but we will serve you.* And he knew that they lied, because they were crafted from the very stuff of falsehood; but he also knew that what they offered was real – and that Arkhan, and his phantom master, offered nothing at all save the very thing that Kemmler had fled from down through the long, winding nightmare road of years.

No, better damnation than oblivion.

Better madness than servitude.

Better to fight and fail than surrender and be nothing.

'Mine – the abbey, the air you breathe, the ground you stand on, all of it mine,' Kemmler snarled, as the fire surged in him. He dug the end of his staff into the ground the way a torturer might dig a blade into the flesh of his victim. 'So listen and listen well to the master of La Maisontaal, witches.' Power flooded through him as he gripped his staff with both hands and channelled the new, destructive magics that hummed through his veins into the earth. Pockets of dark magic and old, sour death awoke at its touch, and the ground lost its colour as he sent the awakened power burrowing through the soil. 'I am not the intruder here. *You are.*'

He felt, rather than saw, the panic begin to creep in and undermine their inhuman calm. They could feel the very earth beneath their feet rejecting their petty magics. Steam escaped from the cracked and dying soil, rising up to mingle with the smoke of the fires. Three pairs of hands began to weave a complicated counter-spell, but it was too late.

Kemmler smiled as he felt their mystical defences fall away, as if they had built them on sand. Then, the sky spoke harshly, and a bolt of black lightning lanced down through the dark sky to strike the three women and the men who protected them. Kemmler felt their deaths and he threw his head back and expelled a cackle.

'Thus to all who would deny me my proper due,' he roared. 'Heinrich Kemmler yet lives!' He swept out his hands and felt his ebullience fill the dead around him, driving them faster and lending strength to their faltering limbs.

For a moment, he stood in an eye of calm amidst the chaos of battle. He felt strong – stronger than he had ever felt before. He was cloaked in magic, and his wound was healed. He sucked in a breath.

The dead hesitated. Empty eyes turned towards him, and lipless mouths flapped as though in warning. His skull staff was silent. The rush of confidence, of self-assurance, faded. Kemmler licked his lips, suddenly nervous. Though many corpses were looking at him, they were all doing so with the same set of eyes. And they were neither as dead nor as empty as he had first thought. They were dark with anger, and with promise.

Kemmler pushed through their ranks. One or two reached out for him, but he clubbed them aside with his staff and his will. More and more of them turned to follow him, but not in the way they had before. He felt his control slacken, and knew then what he had given up.

It was time to get what he had come for.

It was time to put an end to things.

FIFTEEN

 Mordkin Lair, the Border Princes

'Again! Burninate them again – quick-rapid!' Snikrat shrieked, beating one of the warpfire gunners about the head with the flat of his blade. 'Immolate, by which I mean set fire to, the cursed twice-dead, but still somehow moving and, more importantly, *biting*, things!'

Things were not going as well as Snikrat had hoped.

The gunner chattered curses as he aimed the warpfire thrower and unleashed a second belch of crackling green flames into the mouths of the tunnels that opened up onto the cavern. The fire lashed out indiscriminately, spraying the walls and those skaven too slow in retreating as well as the inexorable dead. Skaven flooded out of the tunnel past Snikrat and his warriors, squealing and slapping ineffectually at their fur as they sought to escape the hungry grasp of the flames.

The undead came on at a remorseless pace, pushing through the flames. Some fell, but these were replaced by more. And those that had fallen continued to crawl or slither forward until they were consumed entirely by the snapping flames. They inundated the upper tunnels, marching blindly into the spears and swords of the skaven, dragging down their destroyers as they were hacked apart. No matter how desperately the skaven fought, no matter how ferociously or cunningly, they could not match the dead, nor the unbending will that forced them on, metre by metre, tunnel by tunnel. Little by little, the warriors of Clan Mordkin were being driven back to the very heart of their domain.

'More! More-more-*more!*' Snikrat wailed, battering away at the unfortunate gunner with his blade for emphasis. 'Hotter! Faster! Quicker! Don't look at me idiot-fool – look at them!' The warpfire gunner snarled and hunched, trying to avoid the blows. The warpfire throwers burbled and a third roar of green flame spewed out, momentarily obliterating the mouth of the tunnel. 'Yes! Yes! Yes!' Snikrat bounced on his feet, sword waving over his head as the front rank of corpses vanished, utterly consumed. 'Fall and cease, dead-dead things. Snikrat the Magnificent commands you in his most commanding and authoritative manner to die, by which he means die again, and to thus stop moving!' Behind him, his Bonehides began to cheer in relieved fashion. The stormvermin hadn't been looking forward to fighting the undead again, especially in the cramped tunnels.

The cheers died away abruptly as the first stumbling, staggering torch lurched blindly out of the tunnel mouth. It was followed by another and another and another, until it seemed as if hundreds of burning corpses were squirming towards Snikrat's ragged battle-line. A snorting undead boar, still girded with the legs of the orc who had ridden it in life, barrelled towards the warpfire throwers.

Snikrat yelped and, in his haste to scramble out of the way, his sword accidentally chopped through the hose. Green liquid sprayed everywhere as the burning pig lunged at the hapless gunners. The resulting explosion picked Snikrat up by the scruff of his neck and sent him hurtling away from the tunnel mouth, his fur crisping and his flesh burning.

He hit the cave floor hard and rolled, snuffing the flames that had caught him in the process. The cavern rumbled as fire washed the walls. Timber props, weakened by the gushing warp-fire, gave way, and some of the tunnels collapsed, burying the living and the dead alike.

As Snikrat scrambled to his feet, clutching his burned tail to his chest, he saw the few surviving warriors of the Bonehides fall, dragged down by the burning dead. The air stank of fear-musk as the remaining warriors began to stream away from the cavern, pelting into the various tunnels, swarming away from the groping dead.

The tunnels were lost. Feskit was not going to be happy. None-theless, it was Snikrat's duty to report on his sad failure, in person, to his liege lord. He ran with heroic alacrity, his injured tail whipping behind him as he pelted down the tunnel. He used his weight and strength to smash aside fleeing clanrats, and when the tunnel was so packed with squealing skaven that such tactics proved impossible, he scrambled up onto a clan-rat's shoulders and bounded across the heads of the others as they fought and bit for space.

Snikrat burst out of the crowded confines of the tunnel and sprinted towards the Mordkin lair's final line of defence – a vast chasm, which split the outer tunnels from the great central cav-ern that was the rotten heart of the burrow. A long and winding bridge spanned the chasm. Composed of planks, spars, tar-clogged ropes and other detritus fit for purpose, including but not limited to panels of metal, bones and sheets of filthy cloth, it was the very pinnacle of skaven efficiency and engineering, and the sight of it lent Snikrat speed.

There was no other way across the chasm, not for leagues in any direction. Feskit had long ago ordered all other routes under-mined to better prevent infiltration or attack by rival clans or ambitious greenskins. Skaven were clustered about the bridge, some trying to organise themselves into something approaching military readiness, while others were squealing and fighting to cross the bridge before their fellows. Snikrat charged headlong into the disorganised knot of clanrats, laying about him with his fist and sword until he reached the bridge and began to scramble across.

He heard the communal groan of their foes echo through the cavern as he ran. Skaven began to scream and the bridge swayed wildly as clanrats followed him, pursued closely by the swarming dead. Snikrat whirled as something grabbed his tail. A zombie, blackened by fire and missing most of its flesh, had lunged through the confusion and latched on to him. Snikrat shrilled in terror and lopped off the top of the thing's grinning skull. It slumped, and its weight nearly pulled him from the bridge. As he extricated himself, he saw that those skaven who had been following him had not been nearly so lucky. They fell or were hurled into the chasm by the stumbling corpses, as the latter pressed forward, crawling along the bridge. The whole ramshackle structure shuddered and swayed wildly, and Snikrat had a sudden vision of himself plummeting into the darkness below.

Fear lent him wings, and he fairly flew towards the opposite side. A small army of clanrat weaponeers were gathering there, beneath the watchful eyes of several other sub-chiefs. Warpfire throwers and jezzail teams assembled along the edge of the chasm, weapons at the ready. As Snikrat hurtled to join them, he screamed, 'Burn it! Burn the bridge – hurry, hurry, hurry!'

With somewhat unseemly haste, the warpfire throwers roared, the tongues of green flame barely missing him as they struck the centre of the span. He crashed onto solid ground and rolled to his feet, teeth bared and sword extended in what he hoped was a suitably heroic pose. 'Yes, yes! Watch, minions – my grand strategy unfolds! See how cunningly Snikrat the Magnificent wages war,' he cackled as the bridge began to groan and shift. Then, with a shriek of rupturing wood and tearing cloth, it toppled lazily into the chasm, carrying the dead with it.

Snikrat's cackles grew in volume, and he was joined in his triumphant laughter by the other skaven as more and more zombies flooded out of the tunnels and were pushed into the depths by the mindless ranks coming behind them. The dead were stymied by the chasm, just as he had cunningly planned. Now was the time to unleash the full fury of Clan Mordkin's arsenal. He shrieked orders to that effect, and the warpfire teams and jezzail gunners opened fire in a cloud of black powder and scorched air.

Snikrat watched in satisfaction as the dead were plucked from the opposite side of the chasm by a barrage of warpstone bullets, which whined and crashed across the divide. Zombies slewed off the edge and spiralled into oblivion, or collapsed burning. With a hiss of triumph, he sheathed his blade and strutted back towards the tunnels that led to the fortress-lair to inform Feskit of his triumph.

By the time Snikrat made it back through the gates of the fortress-lair, however, his ebullience had begun to sour. The clangour of alarms still choked the air, and clanrats scampered past him, running far more quickly than he would have expected. He could hear screams as well, and once, the dull crump of a warpfire thrower exploding.

Snikrat began to run. He had to explain to Feskit that whatever was happening wasn't his fault. The weaponeers had disobeyed his orders – the clanrats had broken and run – the chieftains were fleeing – only Snikrat was loyal enough to stand beside Feskit, as he had in times past. His hand clenched on the hilt of his blade, as, in the depths of his twisty mind, the thought surfaced that merciful Feskit would surely be distracted enough to accept Snikrat's blade at his back. He would need all of the loyal servants he could get, would old Feskit.

Snikrat had visions of himself courageously stabbing the tyrant of Mordkin in the back as Mordkin's arsenal of weapons and beasts exterminated the dead. They carried him all the way to Feskit's throne room, where chieftains and thralls scurried about in varying levels of panic. The alarm bells were deafening here, and they were ringing so ferociously that one snapped loose of its line and plummeted down, crushing a dozen slaves into a pulpy mess as Snikrat watched.

'You failed,' Feskit hissed from behind him. Snikrat spun, his paw still on the hilt of his sword. Feskit was surrounded by his Mordrat Guard, and Snikrat jerked his claws away from his sword as they levelled their halberds.

'No! Successes unparalleled, oh merciful Feskit! Snikrat the Faithful, Snikrat the Dutiful, was failed by faithless, cowardly clanrats and irresponsible underlings; I-I came to warn you that the dead-dead things advance towards the gates even now,' Snikrat babbled, his mind squirming quickly as he tried to stay on top of the situation. 'They-they have crossed the chasm somehow – magic! They crossed it with magic, foul sorcery – and Snikrat came back to see to your defence personally.'

'Did he?' Feskit said. 'I feel safer already.' His eyes glinted. He glanced at one of his stormvermin. 'Rouse the packmasters and the remaining weaponeers. Summon the turn-tail chieftains who enjoy my gracious hospitality, and scour the barrack-burrows for every stormvermin,' he snarled.

'And... and what of Snikrat, oh most kindly lord?' Snikrat squeaked hesitantly. He rubbed his scarred throat, and wondered if he should make himself scarce.

Feskit glared at him, and then said, 'You... Hrr, yes, I have a special task for you, Snikrat.' He turned and grabbed another stormvermin by his cuirass and jerked him close. 'You – tell the slaves to fetch... the Weapon.'

The stormvermin paled beneath his black fur. Feskit snarled again and shoved him back. 'Fetch it now, quick-quick!' Snikrat smelt the spurt of fear-musk that rose from the assembled stormvermin at the thought of the Weapon. The Fellblade, with its blade of glistening black warpstone. Could Feskit mean to give it to him to wield? He felt his courage return. With that blade in hand, Snikrat knew he would be invincible.

'I will not fail you, Lord Feskit,' Snikrat hissed, head full of the victories to come.

'No, you will not,' Feskit said. Then, with a lunge that would have put a wolf-rat to shame, he sank his yellow, chisel teeth into Snikrat's throat. Snikrat tumbled back, clutching at his ruined jugular. Through a darkening haze, he saw Feskit chew and swallow the lump of gristle and flesh. 'The Fellblade drains its wielder. You shall sustain me through the efforts to come, loyal Snikrat,' Feskit said, cleaning his whiskers as his stormvermin raised their blades over Snikrat, to complete his butchery. As everything went dark, he heard Feskit say, 'Thank you for your contribution.'

La Maisontaal Abbey, Bretonnia

Arkhan's mind was like a spider's web, stretched to its breaking point by a strong wind, covering the battlefield. In the north, he urged Krell on about his bloody business. In the south, he goaded the shuffling dead to keep pace with the rest of the army. What remained of his attentions were fixed on Kemmler, and when he felt the surge of power, he knew that his suspicions had been proven correct.

The Lichemaster was more powerful now than ever before, and that power had not come from Nagash. The decaying cat on his shoulder hissed as a bolt of black lightning cut down through the night sky and struck a point on the battlefield. '*What are you up to, necromancer?*' Arkhan said, out loud.

The winds of death suddenly thrashed about him, as if they were ropes that had been pulled taut. He felt the air pulse with indefinable motions and saw things not born of the world move through the shifting gossamer aurora of magics that hung over the battlefield. Daemonic voices cackled in his ear, and gloating phantom faces gibbered at him and vanished. His attentions snapped down, retracting to focus on Kemmler. But before he could do so fully, he was brutally interrupted.

'Death to the dealers of death!' the knight bellowed as his horse bulled through Arkhan's skeletal bodyguard and drove the blade of his axe down through the liche's ribcage, before the latter could react. The blow lifted Arkhan from his feet and sent him to the ground in a heap. The laughter of the Dark Gods roared in his head. He could see the trap now, in all of its crooked cunning. The beastmen, Kemmler, all of it... He was caught in the jaws of a hungry fate. Even now, with more than half of the knights who had crashed into the flanks of his host dead, there were still enough Bretonnians left on the field to carry the day, if Arkhan fell.

Something – not quite panic – filled him. It wasn't desperation either, but frustration. To have come so close only to be denied. He saw the cat streaking towards him. It had fallen from his shoulders when he was knocked down, and he felt bereft, though he could not say why. Above him, in the smoke, faces leered down at him, mouthing the vilest curses, and devilish shapes capered invisibly about the knight, kept at bay by the light emanating from his axe. The Dark Gods wanted Arkhan in the ground, and more, it seemed that they wanted to watch him being put there.

Under other circumstances, he might have felt flattered. As the knight urged his horse forward, Arkhan's shattered, brown bones began to repair themselves. The knight growled in satisfaction as he closed in. Arkhan tried to heave himself up. 'Oh no, evil one. That will not do. The Lady has tasked Theoderic of Brionne with giving you the long overdue gift of death, and you shall accept it in full,' the knight roared as he raised his axe. His armour was battered and stained, but the blade of his axe glowed brightly as the dawn broke over the battlefield.

Before the blow could fall, a blur of red iron interposed itself between axe and bone, and the knight was toppled from his saddle. Arkhan was somewhat surprised to see Anark von

Carstein there, blade in hand, armour torn and stained with the detritus of hard fighting. Another slash and the knight's horse screamed and fell, hooves kicking uselessly in its death throes. Arkhan watched in satisfaction as the knight gasped as he tried to gather his feet under him. His fall had broken something in him, the liche knew. The man spat blood and groped for his axe. He caught it up, while Anark's blade descended for his skull. He swatted the blow aside and dragged himself to his feet.

'Give me your name, devil, so that I might tell it to the troubadours who will sing of this day in years to come,' Theoderic rasped, hefting his axe. Anark lunged without speaking, his blade moving quicker than the knight could follow. He interposed his axe, audibly swallowing a groan as whatever had broken inside him shifted painfully, and the edges of both weapons bit into one another. Arkhan watched the battle, somewhat amazed that the mortal was still on his feet. A raw light seemed to infuse him, as it had his axe, and it forced him up and on, lashing at him like a slave-driver's whip. The Bretonnians called it a blessing, but Arkhan knew it for what it was. Nagash had used similar spells to invigorate and drive forward the Yaghur in those dim, dark days of the past. Whatever the Lady was, whether she was some goddess of elves or men, or something else entirely, she was as desperate as the Chaos gods to see Arkhan stymied.

Theoderic smashed the vampire in the face with his elbow and knocked him to one knee. He drove his axe down, crumpling a blood-red pauldron and gashing Anark's neck. He drew his axe back and swung, knocking the vampire sprawling. 'Tell me your name, beast! Let it ring over the field!' he roared, swinging his axe up to take a two-handed grip on the haft as the beast clawed for its blade. The vampire moved so quickly, Theoderic's words had barely left his lips before Anark launched a blow that severed both of Theoderic's arms and his head as well.

'My name is Anark von Carstein, meat,' the vampire spat as he glared down at his fallen foe. Arkhan dragged himself upright.

He touched the spot where the axe had caught him, and felt the bones click back into place. The weapon had been blessed, to do such damage, but he had survived worse in his time.

'*Indeed it is. It seems that I owe you a debt, von Carstein,*' Arkhan said as he retrieved his staff. The cat leapt up and hauled its way back onto his shoulder, its eyes glowing faintly. Most of the flesh was gone from its skull, and its spine rose above its sagging hide like a battlement. It felt as heavy as ever, and it gave an impatient miaow as it wrapped itself about his neck. He stroked its bony shoulder and set his staff. All around him the fallen dead, including what was left of Theoderic, began to slide and slither and stumble upright. Waste not, want not, after all.

'One that I will be only too happy to collect from you, but not until this affray is ended,' Anark growled. He gestured with his sword. 'Which shouldn't be too much longer, from the looks of things.'

Arkhan followed the gesture just in time to see the Bretonnian shieldwall shatter. Here and there, groups of men kept their order and fought against the tide that sought to overwhelm them. But most of them gave in to their terror and fled towards the dubious safety of the abbey walls. Krell's wights pursued, taking advantage of the breach in the line. The lines of archers and war engines were overrun by slavering ghouls, led by the Crow-fiend, and embattled knights were surrounded by skeletons and clawing zombies. The battle was breaking down, becoming a slaughter.

The greater part of the Bretonnian army was dead or fleeing. Those who remained would not survive long. La Maisontaal Abbey was as good as theirs. The staff of Nagash would soon be on its way back to Sylvania, to be reunited with the other relics. Satisfaction filled him such as he had not felt in centuries.

The end was coming. The end of his road, of all struggle and strife. Lamps extinguished, story finished and finally… sleep. Blessed eternal sleep. He swept his staff through a curl of smoke full of silently snarling faces. '*Arkhan still lives, little gods. You have failed. And Nagash will shatter your petty schemes and hurl you back into the void that gave birth to you,*' he rasped, hurling his bravado at the wispy shapes like a javelin.

But his moment of satisfaction was brief. Kemmler was nowhere to be seen. And Arkhan knew where he had gone. He saw hazy daemonic shapes, small, stunted things, scampering towards the grounds of the abbey, invisible to all eyes but his. He looked at Anark. '*Finish this. Kill everything that lives.*'

The vampire looked at Arkhan as he started towards the abbey. 'And what about you?'

Arkhan didn't stop or turn. '*I go to claim our prize.*'

SIXTEEN

 Mordkin Lair, the Border Princes

'It's really quite amusing, in its way,' Markos murmured as he leaned against the tunnel mouth, arms crossed. 'They just keep wandering into the flames, don't they?'

'It's a waste of materials,' Count Nyktolos grunted. He plucked his monocle from his eye and cleaned it on the scorched hem of his cloak. 'We only have three thousand, six hundred and fifty-three zombies left.'

'Did you count them?' Markos asked, brow arched.

'No,' Nyktolos said. Then, 'Yes, possibly.' He put his monocle back into place and sniffed. 'There is very little to do down here but kill skaven or count zombies.'

Markos shook his head, and looked at Mannfred, where the latter stood in the tunnel mouth, hands clasped behind his back, gripping the staff of Kadon with the Claw of Nagash mounted atop it, held parallel to the ground. 'Well, cousin? You heard the Vargravian – we're running short on fodder. How do you intend to get us across that chasm?'

Mannfred ignored Markos. His eyes were fixed on the chasm

ahead, rather than the group of vampires behind him. He heard the hiss of the bloodthirsty steeds of the Drakenhof Templars, and the soft clatter of his own skeletal mount. The former were as impatient to taste the blood of their enemies as their masters were.

He lifted the staff, and the Claw flexed. The power it radiated throbbed in him like the ache of a sore tooth. The Fellblade was close – too close to allow such a minor obstacle to stymie him. A slow smile crept across his face, as he came to the obvious conclusion. Ignoring Markos's pestering, he strode out of the tunnel, towards the chasm. The zombies ceased their mindless advance as he took control of them directly once more, the reins of his will snapping taut about the husks, and pulled them in his wake.

Mannfred could feel the dregs of raw magic that still lurked in the warpfire-blackened stones, and in the shards of expended warpstone fired from the skaven weapons. He went to the edge of the chasm, where the anchors for the bridge had been torn free of the rock. He held the staff in both hands, and focused on drawing the residual magics from the warpstone all about him. The air bristled with energy, which only grew as the skaven began to fire at him. Warpstone bullets whistled past his head, and he drew their energy from them as they drew close. A corona of crackling magics swirled about him, and the burned and shattered dead scattered in heaps and piles began to stir.

The dead behind him moved towards the chasm, their rotting bodies shuddering as Mannfred gestured sharply. The dead flesh of the zombies split and tore as their bones began to lengthen and grow. Hooks of bone sank into the rock as the dead toppled forward. More zombies, some little more than burned skeletons, climbed over these, their bones going through a similar transformation. A symphony of bursting flesh and cracking bone overshadowed the crack of skaven weaponry as the gruesome bridge took shape.

The skaven's rate of fire grew more intense, and Mannfred's smile grew as a warpfire thrower, pushed past its limits, exploded

MANNFRED VON CARSTEIN

The last of the original von Carsteins, the blood-children of Vlad himself, Mannfred is dangerous beyond measure. A powerful necromancer, skilled warrior and cunning tactician, his hunger for power is matched only by his thirst for blood. For years, Mannfred has watched the lands around his stronghold of Sylvania, biding his time and preparing to strike. Having gathered much of what he needs to resurrect Nagash, Mannfred is now ready to seize the Great Necromancer's power and create his kingdom of the dead. Allied with his old foe Arkhan the Black, Mannfred is wary of treachery, for he knows that Arkhan genuinely desires the dark lord's return, but Mannfred von Carstein will be servant to no one… Nagash will rise, but it will be on the vampire lord's terms.

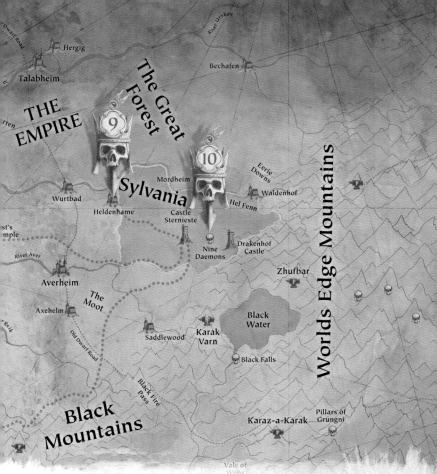

1. A CONCLAVE OF THE DEAD •••••
Arkhan reunites with the Lichemaster Heinrich Kemmler and Krell – his vassals during Mallobaude's abortive campaign.

2. THE VENGEFUL DEAD ARISE •••••
Arkhan and Kemmler raise the wights of Stonewrath Peak to form the core of the army they will lead into Bretonnia.

3. THE RAZING OF CARCASSONNE •••••
Arkhan's army advances across the plague-ridden southern counties of Bretonnia. Scores of villages and towns are overcome by his legions, which grow larger with every victory.

4. DUKE TANCRED'S FALL •••••
Duke Tancred II, recognising the work of his father's old foe, the Lichemaster, musters the survivors of ruined Quenelles to face him in battle. Tancred succeeds in dealing Kemmler a vicious wound, but is hacked down by Krell in return for his temerity. Tancred's army is routed soon after, and the duke raised as a zombie so that Kemmler might slay him again and again.

5. THE TWELFTH BATTLE OF LA MAISONTAAL •••••
Arkhan's forces breach the sanctified walls of La Maisontaal Abbey to reclaim Alakanash.

6. BARON CASGILLE RIDES OUT •••••
Baron Casgille receives word of a dark presence making its way across his lands. Summoning the knights of neighbouring villages, he rides out to challenge it. Casgille and all who follow him are slain when Arkhan raises a horde of plague-ridden dead to pull the horrified knights from their saddles.

7. ORION'S WRATH •••••
Athel Loren's Wild Hunt falls upon Arkhan's army as it crosses Parravon. Realising his minions are outmatched by the wood elves' fury, Arkhan escapes into the mountains whilst Krell's forces hold the Wild Hunt at bay.

8. BETRAYAL AT BEECHERVAST •••••
Anark von Carstein, commander of the Drakenhof Templars, attempts to destroy Arkhan and claim Alakanash (and Mannfred's favour). Arkhan defeats the would-be assassin, and leaves him manacled to the gatepost of Beechervast's Sigmarite Temple.

9. THE FALL OF HELDENHAME •••••
United once more, Arkhan and Mannfred lay siege to Heldenhame, and slaughter the Knights of Sigmar's Blood.

10. DEATH AT THE NINE DAEMONS
Eltharion the Grim leads an army of high elves in a desperate effort to stop Arkhan from resurrecting Nagash and rescue the Everchild. As Mannfred's undead host holds the elves at bay, the ritual begins…

Arkhan the Black

The first and most loyal of Nagash's followers, Arkhan the Black has spent centuries preparing for his master's return. With the End Times approaching and the hordes of Archaon the Everchosen poised to cover all the world in Chaos, he must accelerate his plans… Allying with the devious vampire Mannfred von Carstein is a source of frustration to Arkhan, but strangely fitting, as it was his actions in helping Neferata to create her blood elixir that created the race of vampires in long-lost Lahmia. Arkhan knows that Mannfred and his vassals cannot be trusted – they will betray him before the end – but that is an irrelevance as long as they assist him in his plans. Nagash will rise. Nagash must rise. And Arkhan will see it done.

and consumed its crew. Pistols and jezzails snapped and snarled, and bullets struck the bridge or hissed past Mannfred. More weapons began to misfire. The skaven began to retreat in ragged formation as the bridge drew closer and closer to the opposite ledge. Some continued to fire as they fell back, but most simply dropped their weapons and ran.

'Oh well done, cousin,' Markos said from behind Mannfred. He led his own mount and Mannfred's by their reins. 'Not subtle, mind, but we've dispensed with subtlety, haven't we?'

'Markos... shut up,' Mannfred growled, fixing Markos with a glare. He hauled himself up into his saddle. 'All of you, mount up. We are close to our goal, and I would tarry no longer. I want this business done. I grow tired of these reeking tunnels.'

So saying, Mannfred jerked his mount's reins and galloped over the bridge. Markos and the others followed suit. The bridge squirmed beneath the pounding hooves of their fiery-eyed horses. Seeing the onrushing knights, the remaining skaven turned to flee. But not one of the vermin made it to the dubious safety of the tunnels as Mannfred and his followers laid about them with their blades, lopping off heads and tails, and shattering spines as they crushed the ratkin to a red mulch beneath their hooves.

The dead flowed after them. Howling spectres led the way, filling these new tunnels as they had the others, flowing through every flue, nook and cranny that the skaven had dug. Hastily erected barricades of wood and metal were no barrier to immaterial beings, and skaven clanrats died in droves, unable to fight back or even flee. Zombies too pressed forward, flooding those passages wide enough to accommodate their sheer numbers. The dead skaven left in Mannfred's wake staggered up to join the advancing host, adding to the sheer bulk of corpses that choked the inner tunnels of the skaven stronghold.

As the dead fulfilled their function, Mannfred led his Templars on through the crooked burrow, Kadon's staff held out before him like a standard pole. The Claw of Nagash pulled him on, drawn inexorably towards its nemesis. Over the hours that followed, Mannfred and his warriors fought their way through waves of mutated beasts, armoured stormvermin and limitless ranks of skaven warriors. Some vampires were pulled down, but even outnumbered seven to one, Mannfred and the others were more than a match for the best that the ratkin could throw at them. Where blade and muscle would not suffice, Mannfred, supported by Markos, unleashed volley after volley of devastating spellcraft, scouring entire tunnels and caverns of all life before drawing their victims to their feet and sending them ahead to attack their fellows.

So it went for hours, until at last, Mannfred, at the head of his host, stood before the walls of the fortress-lair of the skaven. The walls were, like all skaven constructions, a derelict mismatch of materials, most of which had never been intended for such a purpose. The gates were a different, and much more interesting, matter. They were made from the bones of what appeared to be a great dragon, and as Mannfred examined them, he smiled.

'We can take the walls,' Count Nyktolos said, calming his restive steed. Mortar fire and warp lightning began to streak from the lopsided towers, as if in reply to his statement. He whistled. 'Or not,' he added.

'I lack the patience for a siege,' Mannfred said.

'Then what – surely you don't mean to parley with vermin?' Markos asked. Mannfred's smile spread. The other vampire sounded affronted.

Mannfred lifted the Claw of Nagash, and black lightning began to spit and spark from the twitching, spidery fingers. He chuckled. 'No, Markos. I have a more... elegant solution in mind.'

 La Maisontaal Abbey, Bretonnia

Erikan bounded through the line of trebuchets, his blade singing out to open up an unlucky peasant's throat. The man fell, gagging on his own blood, and the ghouls that had followed Erikan pounced on him, ending his troubles with a few well-placed bites. Erikan watched them feed for a moment, and then continued on, pursuing the fleeing peasantry. More ghouls followed him, baying hungrily as they knuckled across the uneven ground.

The true dead were barred from the abbey grounds for the moment, leaving only creatures like himself and the ghouls capable of crossing the boundary stones in pursuit of the peasants. He'd left his horse somewhere amongst the abandoned artillery pieces. He'd never been very comfortable fighting from the back of a steed. He felt like too much of a target. Let Anark and the others play at hammer and anvil with the flower of Bretonnian chivalry. He would hunt amongst the stones and take his share of scalps there.

The air sizzled with sorcery, and he heard a thunderclap, which shook the ground beneath his boots as he moved. In the next moment, Krell bulled into the line of archers, his great black axe chopping through armour, flesh and bone with ease. Men died screaming. Smoke coiled through the air, obscuring his vision for a moment.

When it cleared, he saw a hunched shape hurrying towards the abbey. Kemmler, he realised, after a moment. The necromancer was far ahead of them, and moving more quickly than Erikan had thought possible for such a broken-down wreck of a human being. Another curl of smoke obscured the Lichemaster, and when it cleared he was gone. Erikan considered pursuing him, and then decided that it wasn't even remotely his problem.

An armoured knight, unhorsed and bare-headed, charged towards him. He shouted unintelligible oaths and awkwardly swiped at the vampire with his blade. He was barely more than a youth, and his eyes were wide with fear and determination. Erikan parried his next blow, and for a moment, duelled back and forth with the young knight. He felt no satisfaction when his blade slid through his opponent's guard and crunched into his throat. He kicked the body off his sword and spun in time to chop an inexpertly wielded halberd in two.

He stepped back as the man who'd thrust it at him was bowled over by a ghoul sow and her mate. The two creatures smashed the wailing peasant to the ground, but didn't kill him. The sow shrilled a question at Erikan. He looked at her, and then at the cursing, struggling man she held down. Men just like him had taken Erikan from the only home he knew, and put his parents to the torch. The knights had ordered it, but men like this one... They had taken pleasure in it. They had enjoyed seeing his family die.

For a moment, as he stared down at the pale, frightened features, he remembered that night – the stink of torches cutting through the comforting miasma of the tunnels, his mother shrieking in anger and fear as his father bellowed and hewed at the invaders with his fine sword. He remembered his brothers and sisters fleeing into the darkness as men rode the slower ones down. He remembered a white sun on a red sky turning black. He remembered Obald saving him from the flames, and a red-haired woman – had it been Elize, even then? The memory was fuzzy and he couldn't be sure – tending his burns.

But mostly, he remembered fire and blood.

Erikan snarled and hacked the helpless man's head from his shoulders. He lifted his blade and licked the blood from it, as the ghouls fell to their feast. He looked about him, watching as the battle became a massacre. A new day was dawning, but the skies were mournful, as if the clouds were weeping for the fate of the defenders of La Maisontaal.

He smiled, amused at the thought. Let the world weep, if it wished. Crying never made anything better. The first drops of rain had begun to fall when he heard the horns. He turned, and his eyes widened. A curse flew from his lips as he saw the standards rising over the melee.

The new arrivals came by the south road, as if they'd followed in the footsteps of the dead. Ghouls scattered before them, and zombies were trampled beneath the hooves of their steeds as the column of knights plunged deep into the undead ranks, further fracturing an already divided army. The knights struck the dead like a battering ram, their lances thrust forwards to catch the enemy. When the lances had done their work, swords came into play, hacking apart rotting limbs and splintering ancient bone.

The undead reeled, and those with any spark of initiative converged on the newcomers. Erikan saw Anark and the other Drakenhof Templars fighting their way towards the knights, and Krell as well. Satisfied that he wasn't needed, he turned back, ready to order his ghouls into the abbey. Before he could do so, a shadow fell over him.

He looked up as the ghouls scattered, wailing. A lance crashed into his shoulder and knocked him sprawling. The pegasus swooped overhead as its rider released his shattered lance and drew his sword. 'Filthy flesh-eater,' the knight roared as his flying steed dived back towards Erikan. He scrambled aside, narrowly avoiding the blow. He snatched up his sword from where it had fallen and flung himself into the frame of a trebuchet. The pegasus galloped past, wings snapping like thunderclaps. More pegasus knights plunged through the air, attacking the ghouls and wights.

Out of the corner of his eye, he saw Krell swat one of the newcomers from the air, killing both pegasus and rider with a single blow. The wight was steadily chopping his way through enemy and ally alike as he fought his way towards the knight in the fanciest armour. From long, bitter experience, Erikan knew that one was likely the leader. He silently wished Krell luck, though he doubted the creature would either need or appreciate it.

Erikan skinned up through the frame of the trebuchet, climbing towards the arm. His attacker circled the trebuchet, rising back into the air as Erikan burst out into the open, and as quick as lightning, climbed the arm. He ran upwards, sword held low, and sprang into the air as the pegasus passed overhead. His hand snapped out and caught hold of the saddle.

With a twist of his shoulder, he flung himself up and landed on the back of the snorting, bucking beast. The knight twisted in his saddle but not quickly enough, and their blades locked. Erikan's lunge carried him and his enemy off the pegasus, and they hurtled towards the ground.

Erikan struck the earth first, and he shrieked as he felt bones crack. Thrashing wildly, he sent the knight flying. The man climbed awkwardly to his feet, his armour rattling. Erikan slithered to his feet, his body already healing. The knight had lost his sword in the fall, as had Erikan. The former scooped up a spear and lunged smoothly, faster than Erikan expected, and caught him in the belly. With a single, powerful thrust, he shoved Erikan back and up. Erikan howled and grasped at the haft of the spear.

'When you get to whatever damnation awaits you, tell them it was Fastric Ghoulslayer who sent you,' the knight roared, shoving the vampire back. The point of the spear burst out from between Erikan's shoulder blades, punching through his armour and pinning him to the frame of a trebuchet. He screamed in agony. The spear had only just missed his heart, but agony sizzled through him, causing his limbs to spasm helplessly.

'Do it yourself,' Erikan spat, through bloody teeth. He kicked out and knocked his enemy sprawling. He tore the haft of the spear to flinders and fell to the ground. With a snarl, he ripped the splinter of wood from his chest and flung himself onto the knight before the latter could get to his feet. He clawed at the man's helm as the latter struggled, and shoved the edge of it up, exposing a small expanse of flesh. With a triumphant howl, Erikan plunged the splinter of wood into the soft flesh just below his opponent's jaw, and shoved until the tip scraped metal. The man shuddered beneath him, and went still.

Erikan rolled aside and looked up into the cold, burning gaze of Arkhan the Black. '*Kemmler... Where is he?*'

Erikan pointed weakly towards the abbey. Arkhan nodded and stepped over him. Erikan watched the liche stalk towards the abbey. 'You're welcome,' he coughed, and shoved himself to his feet. Then he began to search for his sword, one hand pressed to the wound in his chest.

There was still a battle to win.

SEVENTEEN

 Mordkin Lair, the Border Princes

The gates twisted and then shrieked, the dark spirit that still clung to the ancient dragon's bones giving voice to its frustration and rage. Ropes snapped and wood ruptured as the creature tore itself free of the fortress walls that rested upon it, and the dragon's skeleton rose to its full terrifying height for the first time since its death at the hands of the skaven. The walls sagged and crumbled as the great beast thrust itself into the lair of its murderers, seeking vengeance on the descendants of those who had long ago feasted on its flesh. Skaven died in droves as they tried to flee.

The reanimated dragon reared up and ripped an artillery tower apart. Its whip-like tail curved out, the sorcerously hardened bone cutting through stone and wood like a scythe through wheat, and part of the outer wall exploded into ragged fragments.

'Elegant, he says,' Markos muttered, as he stared at the ensuing devastation.

'Perhaps we have different definitions of the term,' Mannfred said, smiling thinly. 'Regardless, we have our path.' He raised the staff. 'For Drakenhof! For Sternieste! For Sylvania – ride!' He drove his spurs into the fleshless flanks of his horse of bones, and it shot forward, galloping faster than any living creature. His knights, vampire and wight alike, followed in his wake. They charged towards the shattered walls and on through, riding hard amidst the dust and smoke. Zombies poured through in their wake, hungry for the flesh of the living, as Mannfred allowed his control to lapse. Let the dead go where they would, and cause what mischief they wished. The more confusion, the better for him.

Skaven weapons overloaded and exploded as the gunners on the walls tried to bring down the reanimated dragon. Warp lightning arced out, destroying the ramshackle buildings and obliterating knots of skaven who rushed to repel the invaders.

Mannfred gave vent to a primal howl as he rode down a mob of clanrats. In the days since he'd entered the tunnels, he'd refrained from engaging in battle more than was necessary. But now he was free to unfetter his accumulated frustrations. His knights scattered, similarly hungry for carnage. Their lances and swords tore the life from the clanrats and stormvermin who sought to keep them at bay, or else escape them.

Mannfred unleashed baleful magics and laid about him with his blade, following the pull of the Claw. The Fellblade was close. He could feel it, like an itch behind his eyes. He pursued the sensation, galloping down the central thoroughfare of the fortress-lair, eliminating anything that dared cross his path.

Then, at last, he saw it. The Fellblade seemed to blaze with a darkling light, as its wielder swept it through the air in a gesture of command. The skaven warlord – for so Mannfred judged the heavily muscled, grey-furred beast to be – crouched atop a heavy shield, carried by four of its black-furred bodyguards. It was surrounded by a phalanx of stormvermin, and as it caught sight of him, its eyes bulged with rage. It gestured at him and chittered shrilly. The stormvermin began to advance cautiously towards him. Mannfred brought his steed to a halt and watched them come.

He considered simply charging into their midst. Kill a few, and the rest would flee. And, as big as the warlord was, it was little more than a beast and no threat to him. But the presence of the Fellblade in its paw gave him pause. Craven though its owner might have been, the blade was still dangerous. Even a lucky blow might harm him greatly. So... the oblique approach, then.

Mannfred slid from the saddle. Then, mustering the quicksilver speed of his bloodline, he sped towards the advancing skaven. But rather than attacking them, he sprang aside, skirting them and winnowing through their ranks faster than their beady eyes could follow. He let his blade lick out, and the shield-bearers who held the warlord's makeshift palanquin aloft fell, blood spraying from their wounds. The warlord was spilled to the ground with a wail. The other stormvermin reacted much as he'd predicted, and panic swept through them. He ignored them, and circled the warlord as the beast struggled to its feet.

It whirled with commendable speed, launching a blow that, under other circumstances, might have split him crown to groin. But to Mannfred, the beast was moving in slow motion. He watched the blow descend before casually stepping into the arc of the swing. He grabbed the warlord's forearm, and snapped it with a twist of his wrist as he slid the point of his own blade through the creature's rusted breastplate and scabrous chest.

The skaven gave a shrill, agonised cry, and sank down to its knees. The Fellblade fell from its worthless paws and clattered to the ground. With a final whimper, the creature toppled forward, and kicked in its death throes. Mannfred watched it die, and felt little satisfaction.

Well, he was hardly a worthy opponent, was he? A bit anticlimactic, wasn't it? Vlad laughed. *More like pest control than a true battle.*

Mannfred ignored the shadowy presence and scooped up the

Fellblade. It seemed to writhe in his grip for a moment, like a spiteful cat, before it grew still. He peered down the length of the sword, studying the eerie patina of the black blade. Then he shoved it through his belt without flourish and remounted his steed.

He summoned his remaining knights and Templars to him as he rode back through the ruined gates of the fortress-lair, ignoring the battle that still raged all around him. The reanimated dragon and the zombies would serve to keep the skaven occupied for several days to come, until the magic he had used to reanimate them at last faded. After that, let the skaven do as they would. He couldn't care less whether they survived, flourished or perished. Whatever their fate, they were no longer of any importance.

Mannfred bent low over his steed's neck as he began the long trek back to the surface. He had his prize, and there was much work yet to be done.

Nagash would rise, and Mannfred would rule.

 La Maisontaal Abbey, Bretonnia

'*Kemmler!*'

The aged necromancer turned as Arkhan's challenge echoed through the darkened crypt that lay in the bowels of the abbey. The bodies of the brothers of La Maisontaal lay about him on the floor, slain when they'd made one last desperate attempt to defend the malevolent artefact long ago given into their care. Arkhan paid no heed to the crumpled corpses as he stepped into the chamber.

Kemmler smiled and lifted the Great Staff of Nagash, Alakanash, in triumph. 'Too late, puppet. Too late,' he said. 'I've found it, and I have claimed it.'

'*If I am a puppet, I am not alone in that,*' Arkhan rasped. He had foreseen Kemmler's betrayal. Subtlety had never been the

Lichemaster's strong suit. But he had never expected the old fiend to possess enough courage to take up Nagash's staff for his own. He could practically hear the shard of Nagash in the staff writhing in animal fury, and Kemmler's knuckles were white as he tightened his grip on his prize.

'Indeed. I have been a puppet for more years than I care to remember, liche,' Kemmler said. 'Not as long as you, but long enough to know that I do not wish to end up like you – a hollow, thin thing of ashes and scraps, haunting its own bones. Nagash is as much a vampire as the von Carsteins. He feasts on us, taking and taking, until there's nothing left. And then he drags us up to take yet more. Creatures like you and Krell might have no will of your own left, but Heinrich Kemmler is no dead thing's slave.' He circled the sarcophagus slowly, leaning on Nagash's staff. Even now, he was playing the tired old man, though Arkhan could see the power flowing through his withered frame, and the invisible daemons that capered about him like eager children. 'I am the master here. Not you. And certainly not Nagash. He might have his hooks in you and in the fanged fop, Mannfred, but the Lichemaster is no dogsbody. I have found new patrons.'

'*New masters, you mean,*' Arkhan said.

'Partners,' Kemmler said, flashing rotten teeth in an expression that was as much grimace as grin. It was a lie, and a vainglorious one, and Kemmler knew it. 'They recognise my power, liche. They see me for what I am, what I have always been, and they shower me with their gifts where Nagash would grind me under.' He smiled in a sickly fashion. 'And oh, they hate him. They hate him more than any creature that has yet walked this world. They hate him for his hubris, and they hate him for what he would do to this world.'

'*They hate him. And they fear him,*' Arkhan said. '*Otherwise, this conversation would not be taking place. They fear him, and you fear him. The Dark Gods are mice, scrabbling in the holes of time, and Nagash is the cat who will drive them out.*' As he moved forwards, his thoughts reached out to the freshly slain bodies of the monks, and they began to twitch and scrabble at the floor. If he was quick, he might be able to overwhelm Kemmler before he became attuned to the power contained within the staff.

'Not without this he won't,' Kemmler said. He lifted the staff and brought it down, so that the butt struck the floor. The stones hummed with a black note as mortar and dust cascaded down. Several of the bodies flopped back into motionlessness. 'Answer me honestly, Arkhan... Do you truly want him back?'

Arkhan stopped. '*What?*'

'It's a simple enough question,' Kemmler said. 'Do you want him back? Have you ever questioned that desire? Are you even *capable* of doing so?' He shook his head. 'What am I saying? Of course you aren't.'

Arkhan said nothing. Kemmler's words echoed through him. That was the question, wasn't it? He had never truly considered it before. He wanted to throw the Lichemaster's assertions back into his face, but he couldn't. The cat dug its claws into his shoulder. It seemed to weigh more than it had, as if death had lent it mass.

Before he could muster a reply, the beast yowled and sprang across the distance between Arkhan and Kemmler, raking the latter's wizened face. The necromancer screamed and batted the animal aside with the staff. The cat's body struck the wall and fell in a tangle of broken bones and rotting flesh, but it had accomplished its goal. Arkhan threw aside his staff and lunged with all the speed his long-dead frame could muster. Skeletal palms struck the staff in Kemmler's hands and, for a moment, liche and Lichemaster stood frozen. Living eyes met dead ones, and a moment of understanding passed between them.

Arkhan understood Kemmler's rage, his fear and his obsession. But he could not forgive it. Once, maybe. But not now. For now, Arkhan understood what was truly at stake. There were only two paths available to the world as it stood here in this moment – one led to madness and the destruction of the natural order, as the world was remade by the Dark Gods in their image; the other led to a cessation of everything before those horrific changes could be wrought. Had he not already had his destiny chosen for him, Arkhan knew which he would have preferred. At least Nagash might let him rest, eventually.

'*You have always been a selfish, short-sighted creature, Heinrich,*' Arkhan rasped. Kemmler grimaced and began to mouth a spell, but Arkhan swung him about and smashed him back against the sarcophagus that had contained the staff. '*Driven by petty desires, unable to see the bigger picture even when it is laid out before you. The Great Work must be completed, and no turncoat beggar with delusions of grandeur will stop it. Nagash must rise, and if you must fall to serve that end, so be it. You call yourself the Lichemaster... Well then, prove it.*'

Kemmler howled and the raw stuff of magic erupted from him, cascading over Arkhan, searing his bones and blackening his robes. But the liche refused to release his grasp on the staff. His will smashed against Kemmler's, probing for some weakness. The old man's will was like unto a thing of iron, forged by adversity and rooted in spite, but Arkhan's was stronger yet. He had conquered death more than once, clawing his way back to the world of the living again and again. '*Prove it,*' he said again, dragging Kemmler towards him. '*Prove your boasts, old man. Show me the fiend who almost cracked the spine of the world at the Battle of Ten Thousand Skulls.*'

'I'll show you,' Kemmler screeched. He shoved Arkhan back, and they strained against one another, the staff caught between them. 'I'll not be your slave! I am Kemmler – I have broken cities and empires. I have slain armies,' he shrilled. 'And I will kill you, once and for all!'

Spell clashed against spell and magic inundated the chamber, splashing across the stones like blood. Arkhan could feel it building, growing in strength as the magic fed on itself and its surroundings. There were too many dangerous artefacts here, and they all resonated with the power that poured from him and Kemmler, even while the staff did.

The chamber around them began to shake. There was a thunderous crash as the windows upstairs succumbed to the growing pressure and exploded outwards. Green fire licked out from between the stones, rippling around them as they struggled. A tornado of wild magic swirled, and La Maisontaal Abbey shuddered like a dying man. One of the holiest sites in Bretonnia was being ripped apart from the inside out, but Arkhan spared no thought for such trivialities. It was all he could do to maintain his grip on the staff. Kemmler shrieked and cursed as magical flames caressed his flesh, billowing up around him and from within him as his new gods filled him with their power. Arkhan held on grimly, ignoring the sorceries that tore at him.

Kemmler's flesh bulged and split like a blooming flower, and shapes squirmed in the dark within the raw redness of him. They were strange, terrible shapes that cursed and railed as they lashed Arkhan with fires of many hues and sweetly scented lightning. Kemmler's eyes protruded, and the determination in them faded, swallowed by fire and intent. The skull-headed staff, which had been screaming the entire while, fell silent as it exploded into fragments. Caskets exploded out of the crypts around them, wreathed in fire. Arkhan felt ethereal talons tear at him and hideous voices wailed in his head, but he ignored them all, concentrating on the staff and his enemy. Kemmler's eyes widened still further, as if he'd seen something over Arkhan's shoulder, but Arkhan ignored the sudden babble of his voice.

And then, it was done. There was a roar, as of ocean waves smashing across rocks, and a great, sudden motion as if all of the earth had been thrown into the sky; a fire without heat filled Arkhan's vision. He heard Kemmler wail, and it was a sound full of horror and hopelessness and frustration. Then he was on one knee, leaning against Alakanash, amidst the crater that had once been the vaults of La Maisontaal Abbey.

Arkhan chuckled grimly and rose to his full height. Ash drifted off his ravaged robes. He heard the thunder of voices and the blare of horns, and knew that what was left of the Bretonnian army was retreating.

He looked around, searching for the cat. There was nothing left of the beast, save a pile of ash and, rising above it, an enormous shadow, which had been burned into the ravaged stones. There was something unpleasantly familiar about that shadow, and Arkhan felt a pang of unease. Then, with a skill born of long experience, he brushed the feeling aside.

Nagash would rise.

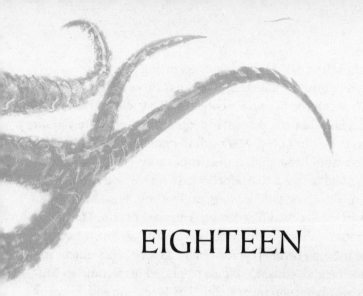

EIGHTEEN

 The Black Mountains, the Border Princes

Mannfred coughed and rolled over onto his back, smoke rising from where the sorcerous blast had caught him. His fur cloak was burning and his armour was scorched. He knew by the taste of the magic who had attacked him, and he cursed himself. He had expected it to come sooner, and he had become distracted by the thrum of power that emanated from the Claw and the Fellblade. The hum of the ancient sorceries had lulled him, and now he was paying the price. His attacker strode towards him, casting aside his cloak of elegant haughtiness.

'I expect Anark has made his move by now, the sullen fool. He won't succeed, you know. And Erikan won't help him. The Crow-fiend knows better than to get between creatures like you and the liche,' Markos said, stopping a short distance from Mannfred.

'A wisdom that you do not seem to share, cousin,' Mannfred said, as he rose to his feet. He cast a glance at the Fellblade where it lay, considering. Then, with a grunt, he turned away from it. He didn't need it.

'The Crowfiend knows his limits, as do I. Mine simply... extend a bit further than his,' Markos said, gesturing lazily.

'Have you chosen a side then, Markos? Picked a new master, perhaps?' Mannfred asked. He considered a spell, and then discarded the idea. Markos was not his equal, but there were certain traditions to be honoured. Markos had made his challenge, and the battle would be settled in the proper way – blade to blade.

'Hardly,' Markos said. 'If Anark fails, then I will see to the liche, never fear. Your rival will not long outlive you, Lord Mannfred.'

'My heart swells,' Mannfred said. 'You cannot win, Markos.'

'No? I rather fancy my chances.' He drew his sword. 'I had this forged for me, by a certain swordsmith in Nippon.' He smiled. 'You call yourself a god, cousin.' Markos extended his sword. 'In Nippon, they say that if you meet a god, if he is real, he will be cut by this steel,' Markos said. 'It is the finest, sharpest steel that can be made in this world. A man can be cut by it and not know for several hours, such is its keenness.' He smiled and spun the blade. 'Don't worry, cousin. I'll make sure you know when it's time to die.'

Markos moved forward smoothly, with a grace and poise that Mannfred couldn't help but grudgingly admire. He'd learned more than sorcery in his time in Cathay and Nippon, it seemed. His first slash came so quickly that it had opened up Mannfred's cheek before he saw it coming. Mannfred scrambled to his feet, the taste of his own blood on his lips. He drew his blade, blocking a second blow.

'You choose the most inopportune times to exert yourself, cousin,' Mannfred hissed as he and Markos circled one another. The other Templars were staying out of it, Mannfred noted. Vampires respected little, save for the sanctity of the challenge. 'We are on the cusp of ultimate victory, and you seek to rock the boat *now*?'

'*You* are on the cusp of ultimate victory, and so, yes, now seems like a good time,' Markos said. 'I've read the same tomes, cousin. I've read the scrolls and the grimoires, and what you're planning is madness. You can't control what you intend to unleash, and I'll not be the slave of some long-dead necromancer, first of his kind or otherwise.' He fell into a defensive stance, blade angled parallel to his body. 'You would damn us, and the world that is ours by right of blood, to servitude at the feet of a dusty god. For the good of all of us, in the name of Vlad von Carstein, I will gladly, and cheerfully, strike off your head.'

Hark at him, the supercilious little weasel, Vlad's voice murmured in Mannfred's ear, as if he were right over his shoulder. *Familiar bit of rhetoric, though, you must admit. It wasn't so long ago that you were framing similar arguments, right about the time my ring went missing, eh, boy?*

'Shut up,' Mannfred hissed. Vlad laughed. 'Shut up!' Mannfred howled, and flung himself at Markos. Their blades crashed together with a sound like a wailing wind, and sparks slid from their edges as they scraped against one another, separated and came together again. Markos laughed tauntingly and pressed Mannfred back.

'I'll be silent the day I lose my head, cousin,' he sneered. 'I was of Vlad's get, the same as you. My blood runs as pure as yours, and flows with the same power!'

'Your blood,' Mannfred spat. He caught a blow on the length of his blade and rolled into it, driving his shoulder into Markos's chest who staggered back. 'Your blood is gutter-froth, compared to mine. I was born in a palace, *cousin.* I was born the son of kings, and Vlad did not make me the creature I am. He merely honed me, the way that blade you boast of was honed.'

Vlad's laughter faded in Mannfred's ear drowned out by the sound of his own blood thundering in his veins, as he harried Markos back, wielding his sword as if it were a feather. His rage lent him strength, as it always had, and his arrogance as well.

He was not meant to fall here. He was meant for greater things. Better things. He had no illusions about the kind of man he was. He had sacrificed more on the altar of ambition than a guttersnipe like Markos could ever guess, all to reach this moment, this crossroads. He had been denied a throne once, in the dim, fell reaches of the past. And the world owed him a debt for that insult.

Markos's confidence began to crumble as they traded blows. He had squandered the advantage of surprise in order to grand-stand. That was the perennial flaw in Vlad's blood, the urge to monologue, to make the enemy recognise your superiority, before the first blow had fallen. Mannfred fell victim to it him-self, but he at least came by it honestly. Markos had been the son of a vintner, and not even a wealthy one.

'You think a sword, or a bit of knowledge, makes you special, Markos? You are not,' Mannfred said, sliding around a blow and catching Markos in the belly with a shallow slash. Armour peeled back like flesh as the blade danced across Markos's torso. 'You are no more special than Hans or Pieter or Fritz, or poor, sad Constan-tin, buried in his books. Just another funeral pyre to light the way of your betters.' He attacked Markos again and again as he spoke, striking him with all of the speed and strength he possessed. Blood poured down Markos's arms and legs, and his armour fell to tatters. Efficiently, ruthlessly, Mannfred cut ligaments and ten-dons, the way a butcher would ready an animal for sale.

Markos stumbled and sank to one knee, bracing himself with his blade. He coughed blood, and his free hand was pressed to his belly. His blood pooled about him, and the greedy earth drank it up thirstily. His lips began to move, and Mannfred felt the winds of magic stir. With a single word, he cut Markos off from them. He saw the other vampire's eyes widen. A pall of res-ignation crept over Markos's narrow features as he realised what had happened. 'I waited too long,' he said.

Mannfred nodded and said, 'The approach of death lends a certain clarity.' He caught Markos's chin with the flat of his blade and lifted his head. 'You went after me with a blade for the same reason Tomas did, all those months ago. You thought I was a better sorcerer than a swordsman.'

'No, I thought you were mad. I see no evidence to the con-trary,' Markos coughed. 'You will destroy us – all that Vlad built, and for what?'

'For me,' Mannfred said. 'Always, for me. This world is mine. It did not belong to Vlad and it does not belong to Nagash or the Dark Gods. It was promised to me in my cradle, and I will have what I am owed.' He lifted his blade in both hands. 'Close your eyes, cousin. No man should have to see his body after his head has left his shoulders.'

Markos continued to stare at him. Mannfred shrugged and let the blade fall. Markos's head came away, and his body slumped. *Do you feel better now? Konrad always felt a bit better after a good bloodletting,* Vlad hissed. Mannfred looked down, and saw something that might have been Vlad's face – or perhaps a skull – reflected in the blood spreading away from Markos's body.

He didn't reply to the taunting voice. He had given in to that urge entirely too often, of late. It was stress and nothing more. The ghost of his fears and worries. Vlad's spirit was gone from this world.

True enough, though you especially should know that beings like ourselves do not go gently into the darkness. You came back, after all, Vlad murmured. Mannfred could almost see him, circling, hands clasped behind his back, speaking the way a master speaks to a pupil. *Then, perhaps I am not Vlad at all, and perhaps you did not come back all on your own, hmm?*

Mannfred cleaned his blade on his cloak and sheathed it. The presence continued to speak, as if it took his silence for an invitation. He wondered, briefly, if there might have been some truth to Markos's words. Was he going mad?

Do you care? Vlad asked.

Mannfred had no answer.

 Beechervast, the Grey Mountains

The town had been called Beechervast. Now, it was nothing. Flames crackled and buildings collapsed with rumbling groans as the dead marched through the dying settlement, adding to their number. Erikan watched as a screaming woman was dragged from the ruins of a hostel by two of his order. Her screams faded to moans as the two vampires fed greedily.

Erikan let his gaze drift to where Arkhan the Black stood near his chariot, watching what his magics had wrought. After the wood elf ambush at Parravon, they'd lost most of what was left of their army, including Krell, who'd held off their attackers while Arkhan and the others made for the dubious safety of the mountains. Whether Arkhan had attacked Beechervast simply in order to replenish his forces, or to wait and see if Krell caught up with them, Erikan couldn't say, and hadn't asked.

They'd lost much to acquire the shroud-wrapped shape strapped to Arkhan's back. His eyes were drawn to it. It was a staff, he thought, much like the one Arkhan carried. To Erikan, it seemed to pulse with a sour light. It was like a wound in the world, and something in it pulled at the thing he was. There was power there, but he knew that if he tried to take it, it would consume him the way a moth is consumed by flame. Arkhan was welcome to it, whatever it was. He looked away from it, and saw Anark ambling towards Arkhan. Subtle as a brick to the head, he thought. He'd been wondering when Anark was going to give it a go.

Anark sprang into motion. He leapt towards the liche and shrieked a war-cry as he swung a wild, overhand blow. The liche whirled and swatted aside the tip of the sword with his staff and drove a bony fist into Anark's face, sending him flying backwards.

Erikan winced, as the Grand Master of the Drakenhof Templars hit the ground with a clatter. To his credit, Anark was on his feet a moment later. He charged towards Arkhan, who had stepped down from his chariot. Arkhan side-stepped the vampire's lunge and caught him in the back of the head with his staff, sending him stumbling to his hands and knees.

Arkhan looked at Erikan, who still sat atop his horse. '*Well, vampire?*' the liche croaked.

'Not me,' Erikan said, holding up his hands. 'Not my fight, Black One.'

'Traitor,' Anark snarled as he regained his feet.

'From here, it looks like you're the one attacking our ally for no reason,' Erikan said, settling back in his saddle, thumbs hooked in his sword belt. 'What would Lord Mannfred say, I wonder? Or Elize, for that matter?'

'*I could hazard a guess as to what Lord Mannfred would say,*' Arkhan said, planting his staff. '*Tell me, vampire... What did he offer you? What could possess you to act so foolishly?*'

'This is positively cunning for Anark, sad to say,' Erikan interjected. 'What happened, Anark? Did Elize bat her pretty lashes and ask you for one little favour? I remember those days, when I was her favourite.'

'Shut your filthy mouth,' Anark howled. He leapt for Arkhan again. There was no subtlety to him, only raw power. He was nothing but one big muscle, all killer instinct without the cunning to mediate it. His armour creaked as he swelled with murderous power. Arkhan caught the blow on his staff, and for a moment, liche and vampire strained against one another.

Then, the moment passed. Black lightning crackled along the length of Arkhan's staff and caught hold of Anark's sword. A moment later, the blade shivered into fragments, and its wielder was tossed back into the dust, bloody from the metal fragments that had spattered his face. Before Anark could get to his feet, Arkhan drove the end of his staff into his skull with all the precision of a trained spearman. There was a wet, unpleasant sound, and Anark went limp.

'Effective,' Erikan murmured.

'*I have dealt with treacherous vampires before,*' Arkhan said. He turned and looked at Erikan. '*I assume that you were not part of this less-than-devious stratagem, then?*'

'I had no idea that it was even in the offing,' Erikan lied. 'Thickheaded as he is, that blow won't keep him down long. Anark isn't much, but he's a fighter. I fancy he could keep going, even missing the whole of his head. And he won't give up.'

'*What would you suggest?*'

Erikan couldn't say why he was helping the liche. He thought, perhaps, it was simply that Anark had been a constant source of annoyance. Or maybe he'd grown tired of the way Elize seemed to shower the brute with affection. Let her get a new, hopefully smarter, pet. 'Chain him to the postern of the Sigmarite temple I noticed when we rode through the gates. Let the flames or the sun have him, and that'll be the end of it.'

'*A more merciful death than I intended,*' Arkhan said. He gestured, and a trio of wights came forward and hefted Anark's limp form. They carried him off.

'But still a death,' Erikan said.

'*Yes,*' Arkhan said. The liche examined him silently for a moment, and then turned away. They left Beechervast not long after, riding out at the head of an army newly swollen by the addition of the population of the town, slaughtered and resurrected.

No one seemed too put out by Anark's death. Then, he hadn't exactly gone to great lengths to make friends amongst the order. Neither had Erikan, but he supposed he was more tolerable than a swaggering bully any day. As a member of the inner circle, leadership of the remaining blood knights had fallen to him, and he rode at their head for lack of any better ideas. He wondered how Elize would receive the news of Anark's death. Would she be angry, sad, or... nothing. The latter, he thought, would be the most unpleasant. Vampires could love, but it did not come easily. And sometimes it was not recognised as such until it was far too late.

The Lahmians had songs, spread by the Sisterhood of the Silver Pinnacle, about lost loves and immortal tragedies. They turned troubadours and poets just to keep those songs and verses alive and circulating amongst the living. It made things easier, sometimes, if the cattle thought love, rather than thirst, was the norm for vampires.

As they rode towards the Sylvanian border, Arkhan communed with the spirits of the dead from atop his chariot, seeking any word on Krell. Wailing ghosts and shrieking spectres circled him like pigeons in an Altdorf plaza. Erikan rode beside him.

The spirits scattered abruptly. 'Any word?' Erikan asked.

'*Krell yet persists. He will rejoin us when he can. He is leading the Wild Hunt away from our trail.*' Arkhan shook his head, a curiously human gesture. '*Beastmen, wood elves, Kemmler... Enemies at every turn.*'

'Rats in a sinking barrel,' Erikan muttered.

Arkhan looked at him. Erikan shifted uncomfortably. '*Why do you serve the von Carstein, vampire?*' Arkhan asked suddenly. '*Love, fear... boredom?*'

Erikan didn't look at the liche. He didn't like the twin witch-fires that flickered in the dead thing's eye sockets. He'd only ever seen Arkhan at a distance; up close, the sheer wrongness of him, of something once human bent and twisted into something new, something abominable, something that should not walk upon the earth, was all too easy to see and to feel. Arkhan's presence, the undiluted necromantic energies that emanated from his skeletal form, made Erikan's head ache, as if he had a sore tooth.

But it wasn't simply the liche's noxious presence that made him hesitate. The question wasn't an easy one. Why had he answered the call? Why had he left Sylvania in the first place? The questions were like the strands of the same cloth; as he tugged each one, another came loose. Arkhan looked at him. '*Well? We have nothing but time, Crowfiend. Why not pass it in conversation, rather than silence?*' Arkhan cocked his head. '*Are you upset about the other? What was his name – Anark?*' The liche made a rattling sound that Erikan had come to associate with his attempts at humour. '*That one was not fated to find himself on the right side of history, I'm afraid. But you... You are a survivor, I think. A scrambler on the edge of destiny. When all is said and done, why do you serve von Carstein?'*

Erikan hesitated. And then, he said, 'Power. Not over the world, but over myself – my own fate. As long as others were stronger, I would never be master of my own fate. That is why I studied necromancy.'

'I smell no stink of grave sorcery about you,' Arkhan said.

'I was a terrible student,' Erikan said, smiling slightly. 'Plenty of inclination, but no aptitude. So I sought out the next best thing...' He bowed his head. Arkhan gave a raspy chuckle.

'A woman, was it? And then?'

'It wasn't enough. I climbed one tower, to find myself at the bottom of another. So... I left.' His smile faded. 'From the moment I was born it was a loveless life. I lived out of spite, and it wasn't enough. So I turned into something worse than death, and tried to take from the world until there was nothing left to take. But the world was bigger than I thought.' He looked up at the forest canopy overhead. 'I am tired of surviving. I am tired of the world. I want an end, and I want to watch it all fall into the grave with me. I do not want fire. I want ash, and silence. I want night, silent and eternal, stretching from pole to pole, heaven to earth.'

Arkhan looked at him for a long time. Then, as if uncertain of his own intent, he reached out and clasped Erikan's shoulder. *'You will have it. Nagash rises, and the world descends. We will all know the peace of oblivion.'*

'Will we?' Erikan asked softly. 'Or will we be puppets, for an eternity?'

Arkhan's grip tightened. *'No. Nagash despises anything that is not him, or of him. He hates and fears that which he did not create. We will be dust on a nightmare wind, vampire, when we have fulfilled our purpose. We will be nothing.'* He released Erikan's shoulder. *'Or so I hope.'* He turned away. *'I am tired, vampire. I am so tired, but I cannot lay aside my burden, until the end of all things. I was a gambler once. I gambled and lost. And this is my debt.'*

Erikan said nothing. Arkhan fell silent. They rode in silence, two weary souls, bound in chains of night and servitude.

NINETEEN

 Castle Sternieste, Sylvania

'Treachery,' Mannfred intoned grandiloquently. 'Treachery most vile.'

'*Which treachery are we speaking of – yours, or mine?*' Arkhan asked, not bothering to look at the vampire. Mannfred glared at the liche's back. The two stood at the top of Castle Sternieste's tallest tower. Arkhan had arrived a few days before Mannfred, and had awaited his return at the tower's pinnacle, as if in anticipation of a confrontation. Mannfred saw no reason to deny him such, if that was his wish.

Despite the fact that they had both been victorious in their respective endeavours, and that both Alakanash and the Fellblade were now in their possession, Mannfred saw little reason for celebration. Neither, apparently, did Arkhan. Mannfred wondered whether the liche was even capable of such an emotion.

On the ride back through the Border Princes, Mannfred had managed to half convince himself that Arkhan had somehow encouraged Markos's failed coup. He hadn't thought the liche would actually admit it, but he'd hoped to see some sign of concern. Instead Arkhan had seemed almost... relieved? He wondered what had happened on Arkhan's campaign in Breton-nia. The vampires who had ridden with the liche spoke of a rain-lashed battle on the Lieske Road with a herd of beast-men, and an attack by the fierce elves of Athel Loren, which had seen the loss of Krell. Whether the ancient wight had truly been destroyed, or merely separated from his master for the moment, Arkhan had not seen fit to share. Mannfred shoved the thought aside. 'Yours is the only treachery I see, liche,' he snarled.

'*Then you are as wilfully blind as you are ignorant, vampire.*' Arkhan glanced over his shoulder. '*Your assassin failed.*' Mann-fred let no sign of his annoyance show on his face. Elize had sworn to him that her pets could accomplish the task he'd set for them, but they'd failed. Anark was dead, and the Crowfiend had either thrown in with Arkhan or chosen discretion over val-our. If it was the latter, Mannfred found it hard to blame him. If it was the former, Mannfred fully expected Elize to deal with it before he next saw her.

'As did yours,' Mannfred hissed. Arkhan didn't react. Mannfred glared at the fleshless face, and wondered what he had expected. Denial, perhaps, or denunciation. That was how a vampire would have reacted. Instead, the liche simply turned away. Mannfred shook his head, frustrated. 'And I am not speaking of overly ambi-tious underlings, in any event, as you well know.'

'*Illuminate me then, I beseech you.*'

Arkhan stared out at the horizon, his fleshless hands clasped behind his back. He stood at the edge of the crumbling battle-ment, at his ease and seemingly unconcerned. Mannfred's hands twitched, and he considered unleashing a spell to send the liche tumbling from the tower like a skeletal comet. But he restrained himself. If Arkhan wanted to play the fool, fine. He would treat him as such.

'The protective spells I wove about my land are failing,' he ground out. 'You told me that losing one of the nine would have no effect.' Elize had reported as much to him as soon as his mount clattered into the courtyard of Sternieste. She had practically flown to his side to warn him that the omnipresent clouds that swirled overhead, blanketing his kingdom, had grown thin in places. The cursed light of day was returning to Sylvania. Slowly, but it was returning. And when it had, so too would come the zealous priests and fanatical witch hunters, to harry his subjects and tear asunder all that he had worked so hard to build. Worse, Gelt's wall of faith still stood as strong as it ever had, and showed no sign of failing.

'*I told you that it would have negligible effect. And such is the case. Your enchantments still hold – the sun is kept at bay and your empire of eternal night yet stands. Rejoice,*' Arkhan said. Mannfred snapped at the air unconsciously, like a dog provoked beyond endurance.

'With every day that passes, the spell grows weaker, and I can do nothing to stop it. We have weeks, or perhaps only days, before the enchantment fails entirely. And then what, bag-of-bones?' Mannfred demanded, pounding a fist into the battlement. Stone cracked beneath the blow and fell, tumbling down, down, to smash onto the courtyard so far below. Arkhan watched the stone fall, and then looked at Mannfred.

'*By then, Nagash will have risen. By then, it will be too late.*'

'You knew,' Mannfred hissed. He leaned towards the liche. 'You knew. You tricked me.'

'*I am but a bag-of-bones. I am dust and memory. How could I trick you, the great Mannfred von Carstein?*' Arkhan gave a rattling laugh. He looked at Mannfred. '*How it must have galled you to take that name, eh? How it must have pricked that monstrous pride, that abominable vanity that you wear like a cloak. Tell me, did you weep bloody tears when you surrendered your silks and steel for wolf-skin and crude iron?*'

Mannfred heard Vlad's chuckle. He had hoped that he'd heard

the last of the memory, or the ghost, or whatever it was, in the Border Princes. *You did. I remember it quite clearly. You whined for weeks – weeks! – and over a bit of frayed silk.*

'Quiet!' Mannfred snapped. He saw Vlad's face, hovering just behind Arkhan. His mentor's smile cut him to the quick, and he longed to unleash the most destructive spells he could bring to mind, just to wipe that mocking grin away.

'Were you talking to me, or to him?' Arkhan asked. The liche cocked his head. *'Who do you hear, vampire? I can hazard a guess, but I would not wish to offend you.'*

Mannfred spun away with a snarl, fighting to regain his composure. His hands balled into fists, and his claws cut into the flesh of his palm. 'You have already offended me,' he said, not looking at the liche. 'And I hear nothing but your hollow, prattling lies.'

'Then I shall continue... Time is our enemy. It has turned on us. The enchantments I laid upon the Drakenhof banner yet hold. But they too will eventually fade. And our work is not yet done.'

'The Black Armour of Morikhane,' Mannfred said. He closed his eyes. Somewhere behind him, he heard Vlad applaud mockingly. *Oh well done, boy. I see you were paying attention. Then, you always were a quick study,* Vlad said. Mannfred opened his eyes and turned. 'Heldenhame,' he said. He looked out over the battlements, towards the northern horizon, where Heldenhame Keep stood silent sentinel over Sylvania.

He felt a pang as he took in the realm he had claimed by right of blood and conquest. In the beginning, he had never truly thought of Sylvania as anything other than a stepping stone. It was a backwater, full of ignorant peasants, barbaric nobility and monsters. He had never seen its potential the way Vlad had. But as he waged war after war, shedding blood for every sour metre of soil, he had come to see what the other vampire had seen, all those centuries ago. He had come to understand why they had taken up new names, and sought to burrow into the vibrant, if savage, flesh of the young Empire.

There was a rough beauty to this land, with its dark forests and high crags. It was a cold land, full of shadows, as far and away from the land of his youth as it was possible to get. But where that land had cast him out, this one had taken him to its bosom, and he felt his pulse quicken as he gazed out over it.

This was his land now. He had died to defend his right to it, and its waters ran in his blood. Nothing would take it from him. Not Nagash, and certainly not Karl Franz. But they weren't his only enemies. He'd seen the portents, but hadn't truly believed, not until his march across the Border Princes. The world was in upheaval. Everything was changing. His spies had learned much while he prosecuted his campaign against the skaven. There was a war-wind blowing down from the north, and drums beat in the Troll Country, rousing the lost and the damned to war. Kislev was gone, and the northern provinces of the Empire were in flames.

As he stared out at his land, Mannfred thought of the being he had seen in his scrying, the one to whom even daemons bowed, and he felt a cold determination settle over him. If this was the end, better Nagash than nothing. 'Heldenhame,' he said aloud, again.

Heldenhame was the Empire's first line of defence against any army coming from his lands, and he had wasted more than one legion on its walls. But then, so had many others – including the barbarous orcs. 'Its walls are strong, but they have their weaknesses.'

'*And you know what they are?*' Arkhan asked.

'I have known what they are for the better part of a year. My spies within Heldenhame tell me that the city's western wall was badly damaged last year, during a greenskin attack. Leitdorf has spared no expense in conducting repairs, but such a thing cannot be rushed, especially when you have naught but frail men as your labourers. It will be easy to breach, with the proper application of force.' Before Arkhan could speak, Mannfred held up a hand. 'However, the garrison of that wall has been reinforced with cannons, fresh from the forges of Nuln, thus rendering any assault there costly.'

'*You have a plan,*' Arkhan said. It wasn't a question.

Mannfred chuckled. 'I have many plans. The western wall is the obvious point of assault. But to strike there is predictable, and sure to be more arduous than we would like. However, the appearance of predictability is as valuable as its absence, if properly employed. We must take the oblique approach to this.' He stretched out a hand, and curled his fingers. 'With one hand, we shall show them what they expect.' He raised his other hand. 'And with the other, we shall crack their walls.'

'*Your confidence is inspiring,*' Arkhan said.

'And your mockery is forgivable, this time,' Mannfred said, with a mildness he didn't feel. 'You were right before. We need each other, liche. We are surrounded by enemies, and time, as you said, is not on our side. So let us cease wasting it. We will march north, now. And we will rip the last piece of the puzzle from the guts of Heldenhame.'

He turned and set one foot on the battlement. He flung back the edges of his cloak, raised his hands and began to speak. Overhead, the clouds swirled as Mannfred cast his voice and his will to the winds. He called out to every creature, dead, alive or otherwise that owed him allegiance. In his mind's eye, he saw bat-winged monstrosities flop from dank caves and ghoul packs emerge from their burrows. He felt his mind touch the ephemeral consciousness of every chill-hearted spirit within his demesne, and rouse them to abandon their haunts and hurtle through the black sky towards Sternieste.

Before the ancient bells of Sternieste struck midnight, he knew that a mighty army would be assembled before the walls of the castle. And when it marched north, the world would tremble.

Amused by Mannfred's display of unbridled sorcerous dominion, Arkhan watched in silence as the vampire called his forces to war. He let his mind drift as Mannfred lashed the world with his will. He had more pressing concerns than Mannfred's petulance.

He had brooded on Kemmler's betrayal and what it meant since the obliteration of La Maisontaal Abbey. He had suspected Kemmler's treachery, but not the reasons behind it. Nagash's hold on the necromancer had not been as certain as Arkhan had thought, and that disturbed him. Kemmler's taunts haunted him.

That the Dark Gods would intervene so directly in order to prevent Nagash's resurrection seemed unbelievable. But he knew what he had felt and seen. And it hadn't merely been Kemmler. His return to Sylvania and Castle Sternieste had seen him lead what remained of his forces through the Great Forest. After departing Beechervast, Arkhan had taken the Lieske Road, and it seemed as if every Chaos-touched creature in those woods had been drawn to him, like moths to a flame. Howling, malformed monsters had pounced from the shadows, or swooped through the branches above. Chimeras and jabberslythes and worse things had thrown themselves into battle.

There had also been the beast-herds. Frothing, goat-headed beastmen had launched ambush after ambush, culminating in a final, bloody affray during a storm that Arkhan suspected was of no natural origin. During that battle, he had again seen the winged beast that he had first spotted in Quenelles. Clad in ragged robes, it had bellowed in a crude tongue as it tried to stem the inevitable retreat of the beastmen, once their courage had been broken by Arkhan's spellcraft and the ferocity of the Drakenhof Templars, led by Erikan Crowfiend.

Arkhan had recognised his winged foe, in that moment before it too had fled. Like Mannfred, he had his spies and for years he had gathered information about the powers that might place themselves in his path. The thing called Malagor was a true servant of the Dark Gods, in the same way that he served Nagash. Its presence would have spoken volumes as to their intentions, if he did not already suspect their meddling.

With betrayal, and obstacles, however, came clarity. Misfortune had dogged his trail for months prior to coming to Sylvania. And not only his. Every being, however removed or reluctant, who might serve Nagash had seemingly been marked for death by the Chaos gods. When he had first begun to groom Mallobaude for his task, even providing for the would-be king to receive the blood-kiss of vampirism from an old, long-established Bretonnian line of the creatures, his stronghold of Mousillon had been beset by a horde of daemons. Though the creatures had gone on to assail the realm at large, Arkhan's plans had nonetheless been interrupted. When he had arrived in Sylvania, he had learned that Mannfred had suffered similar attacks.

His study of the mystical wall of faith forged by Balthasar Gelt had also led him to wonder just how the wizard had come by the knowledge he'd used to forge the cage that now encompassed Sylvania. Brilliant as the Supreme Patriarch was, at least as far as mortals went, Arkhan couldn't help but question the timing.

Sylvania had been a thorn in the Empire's flank for centuries. Why suddenly move to contain it now? Unless, perhaps, Gelt was also an agent of the Dark Gods, in some capacity. Not an active, aware one of course, otherwise he could not have so effectively shackled the power of Sigmar. But he could easily be a pawn of other powers.

Had Kemmler been telling the truth – were the gods of Chaos so frightened of Nagash's return that they were actively attempting to prevent it? Was Nagash truly so powerful that he incited such terror in entities as vast and as unknowable as the Dark Gods? And if so, what was Arkhan truly bringing back into the world? Was it the Nagash he remembered, the petty, spiteful, stubborn Undying King, who had killed his own people because they refused to bow... Or was it something even worse?

Arkhan looked down at his hands. They had been free of flesh for more years than he could count. He had sacrificed his mortality, his flesh and his hope on the altar of Nagash's ambition.

If it came down to it, he knew that he would sacrifice all that remained. He had no choice in the matter.

Or did he?

Elize von Carstein traced the rough bark of the dead tree with her fingers. The garden was empty, save for a few carrion birds perched here and there on the battlements. The castle itself was a hive of activity, as it had been since von Dohl's failed assault a week earlier. The self-proclaimed Crimson Lord had ridden right up to the gates and demanded that Elize turn Sternieste and all of its treasures over to him.

Von Dohl had been accompanied by Cicatrix of Wolf Crag, and the heir of Melkhior, Zacharias. The Necrarch, in particular, had seemed unusually intent on getting into Sternieste's vaults. When Elize had denied them entry, von Dohl had been beside himself with rage. The battle that followed had been brief but brutal.

Long-dead warriors had clashed amidst the barrow-fields as the Drakenhof Templars held their lord's fortress against his enemies. She had duelled with Cicatrix atop the gatehouse, trading sword blows with the other woman. Von Dohl had ever let his harlot fight his battles for him, and he had only retreated when Elize had struck her shrieking head from her shoulders. What was left of Cicatrix still decorated one of the stakes mounted on the gatehouse battlements, and had greeted the master of Sternieste when he returned.

Arkhan the Black had returned a few days after the battle, and Mannfred not long before him. Their confrontation had been brief, and from what her spies claimed, heated, but now the great bells were tolling and the forces loyal to Mannfred were gathering. The time had come to take Heldenhame, and the murky air of the castle was tense with anticipation.

She heard Erikan Crowfiend enter the garden behind her. She

knew it was him by the sound of his footsteps and the scent of him, sweet like overripe flowers or spoiling meat. She recalled that she had once tried to teach him how to use perfumes to mask his predator's scent, but he had never taken to it. 'Markos,' he asked, simply. His voice tugged at her. It was not a purr or growl, but placid like the burr of treacherous waters.

'Dead,' she said. 'Just like Anark.' She dug her claws into the bark. Impossibly, the tree had begun to flower. Its skeletal branches were covered in putrid blossoms, which stank of rotting meat. She turned away from it, and fixed Erikan with her gaze. 'Why didn't you help him?' she demanded.

'And how would I have helped Markos? I wasn't with him.'

'Don't play the fool,' she snapped. 'I meant Anark. Why didn't you help him?'

'Why should I have? He was attacking our ally – the very ally we were sent to protect, in fact,' Erikan said. 'He's lucky I didn't kill him myself.'

Elize snarled. 'Are you truly so foolish? Do you understand what you've done? *The liche is dangerous!*' She took a step towards him, her hands curling into fists. 'What could possess you not to seize that opportunity?'

'I did,' he said, flatly.

'Then why is he still here?'

Erikan smiled. 'I would have thought that was obvious.'

Elize stared at him. For the first time in a long time, she was uncertain. She had thought that Erikan would have seized his moment and struck Arkhan down, as Anark kept him occupied. Surely, she'd thought, he would see what was so clear to her – if Nagash returned, they were doomed. Perhaps not immediately, but soon enough. She knew enough about the Undying King to know what it was he wanted, and how badly that would end for her kind. When the last mortal had died, what would they feed on?

Mannfred had likely never even considered that, she knew.

He thought he could control the force he sought to unleash. But Arkhan knew better, and that made him more dangerous. 'What do you mean?' she demanded. 'Speak sense!'

'Nagash must rise,' Erikan said. 'And I intend to see that he does. If that means I must keep the liche in one piece, so be it.'

Elize shook her head. 'Are you mad?'

He was silent for a time. She wanted to grab him, and shake him, to force him to speak. But something in his gaze held her in place. When he finally spoke, his voice was rough. 'I think I have been. But I'm sane now.' He reached for her, and she jerked back. He let his hand fall. 'For the first time, in a long time, I see things as they are, rather than how I wish them to be.' He looked up at the sky. 'Can't you feel it, Elize? Can't you smell it on the air?' He looked at her. 'Then, maybe it's only obvious to someone who was raised by the eaters of the dead.'

'What are you talking about?' she growled, shaking her head. A lock of red hair fell into her face and she blew it aside impatiently.

'The world is already dead,' Erikan said. He stepped forwards swiftly, before she could avoid him, and he took hold of her. She considered smashing him to the ground, but stayed her hand, though she couldn't say why. 'All of our struggles, all of our games, have come to nothing. Whatever purpose you conceived for me the day you bestowed your blood-kiss upon me will never be fulfilled. The petty schemes of Mannfred, von Dohl and even Neferata in her high tomb are done, though they may deny it.' He pulled her close, so close, as he had done so many times before he had gone, before he had left her. 'The world is dead,' he repeated. 'Let Nagash have it, if he would.'

She stared at him. She tried to find some sign in his face of the young man she had turned so long ago, thinking to make him a king in his land the way Mannfred had made himself king in Sylvania. What had happened to him, she wondered, in all their years apart? What had made him this way? She reached up and stroked his cheek. 'Why did you leave?' she asked softly. 'Oh my sweet cannibal prince, why did you leave me?'

He looked down at her, his face twisting into an expression of uncertainty. 'I... wanted to be free,' he croaked, with what sounded like great effort. Then, 'I *want* to be free.'

She grimaced. Her lips peeled back from her fangs and her claws dug into his cheek, drawing blood. He staggered back, a hand clapped to his face. She lunged forward with a serpent's grace and struck him. He tumbled onto his backside, his eyes wide with surprise and shock. 'Freedom,' she spat. 'Freedom to – what? – slide into oblivion? That isn't freedom, fool. That is *surrender*.'

He made to scramble to his feet, and she kicked him onto his back and pinned him in place with her foot on his throat. She glared down at him, her fingers dark with his blood. 'If I had known that you would give up so easily, I would never have bothered with you in the first place,' she hissed. 'Fine, fool. Have your freedom, and enjoy it while it lasts.'

'I–' he began. She silenced him with an imperious gesture.

'Since you feel so strongly about it, you will stay here and guard Sternieste. I will lead our brethren to war in your place, Crowfiend,' she spat. Then Elize left him there, staring after her. There was an army to ready for the march, and the castellan of Sternieste had much to do. As she stalked through the corridors, snarling orders to scurrying ghouls and lounging vampires, her mind pulsed with dark purpose.

The world was hers, and she would not surrender it – or anything of hers – without a fight.

Nagash would not rise. Not if she could help it.

TWENTY

Hans Leitdorf, Grand Master of the Knights of Sigmar's Blood, tossed the scroll aside with a weary curse, and rubbed his aching eyes. 'I'm not as young as I used to be,' he said.

'None of us are, old fellow,' Thyrus Gormann said, emptying a decanter into his cup. 'What was that one – bill of sale? An invoice for lumber, perhaps? Or something more interesting.' Gormann spoke teasingly. He was the only man who could get away with poking Leitdorf, and he indulged every opportunity to do so. He glanced towards the frost-rimed window. The sun was rising. It had been a long night, and they were almost out of ale. Still, it was nearly time for breakfast, a thought that cheered him considerably.

'Elves, actually,' Leitdorf said, leaning back in his chair. He and Gormann were in his office in the high tower of Heldenhame Keep. The office had a certain rustic charm, which spoke more to its owner's disregard for the subtleties of interior decoration than any longing for simpler surroundings. Gormann took a swallow of wine and gazed at the other man with keen eyes.

The Patriarch of the Bright College was, despite his bluff exterior, a man of quick wit and political acumen. It was something he shared in common with Leitdorf, who was more a political animal than he let on.

Gormann grunted. 'Elves... in Altdorf?' he guessed. 'Ulthuani, I'm guessing.'

'Yes. They've come to petition Karl Franz for aid, apparently.' Leitdorf said. He rubbed his face. 'Fill me a cup, would you?'

Gormann did so. 'Well, they picked the right time, didn't they?' he asked, as he handed the cup to Leitdorf. 'It's not like we have a war to fight, after all.'

'I don't think they particularly care about our little disagreements with our northerly neighbours,' Leitdorf said. He emptied half the cup and set it aside. 'Karl Franz is keeping them at a distance, for the moment. He placated them by sending a rider to Karak Kadrin – I'm guessing to see if the dwarfs were interested in taking them off his hands.'

'Ha! That I'd like to see,' Gormann laughed. He tugged on his beard. 'Old Ironfist is no friend to the elves, nor in truth to us. We're allies of convenience, nothing more.' He cocked his head. 'Did your spies happen to mention what it is they want?'

Leitdorf gave Gormann a hard stare. 'I don't employ spies, Thyrus.'

'My mistake. Did your... friends happen to say what the elves wanted?'

Leitdorf made a face. 'No. Nor do I particularly care. We have enough troubles of our own.' He swept a heavy, scarred hand out to indicate the stack of reports scattered across his desk. 'Reports from the Border Princes, Bretonnia, Tilea... It's all going to pot.'

'When isn't it?' Gormann asked.

'This isn't a joke, Thyrus,' Leitdorf growled. 'If I didn't know better, I'd swear von Carstein had escaped Sylvania somehow.'

Gormann's mouth twisted into a crooked smile. 'No such luck, I'm afraid. Gelt's wall of faith still holds.'

Leitdorf sighed. 'Admit it, Thyrus. That was the whole reason you came to visit Heldenhame, wasn't it? To examine Gelt's thrice-cursed enchantment.' He shook his head. 'I know what goes on behind the doors of your colleges. They're worse snake pits than the Imperial court.'

'Well, I admit, it wasn't for your company, splendid as it is, Hans,' Gormann said, opening a second decanter. He gave the liquid within a sniff and filled his cup. 'Gelt's a funny one – always has been. Powerful, but dodgy. Even Karl Franz, Sigmar bless and keep him, doesn't like the scrawny alchemist much.'

'Which was it that saw him usurp your position as Grand Patriarch? The power or the dodginess?' Leitdorf asked. He held up a hand as Gormann made to reply. 'I know, I know – it wasn't a usurpation. It was a transition. That's what wizards call it, isn't it?'

'He beat me fair and square, Hans. Truth to tell, I was getting tired of the job anyway. There's precious little fun in it. The uptight little alchemist is welcome to it.' Gormann took a drink. His duel with Gelt was the stuff of legend, though not for the reasons he'd wish. Gelt had been more cunning than he'd expected, though he'd heard plenty of stories about the younger man's little tricks – turning lead to gold and the like. When the dust had cleared, he'd been out of the job, and the Gold Order had outstripped the Bright Order in prominence.

He didn't bear Gelt a grudge – not too much of one, at any rate – but he'd come to learn that the new Grand Patriarch wasn't adverse to cutting corners. He was cunning but sloppy, with a compulsion to tinker when he wasn't cheating his creditors. That sort of man needed someone trailing after him, making sure he wasn't causing too much of a mess. Gormann chuckled to himself. That he'd been elected to that position by his fellow patriarchs would be amusing, if it weren't so sad. Then, if Gelt grew suspicious, they could simply claim that Gormann was driven by vindictiveness.

He'd come to Talabecland to study the wall of faith. The magics that Gelt had employed to create his wall were old, and far out-side of Gelt's area of study. Someone, it was assumed, had helped him. Gelt was keeping mum, but the other patriarchs, especially Gregor Martak, master of the Amber Order, were concerned, and Gormann didn't blame them. It wouldn't be the first time one of their own had used forbidden magics. Traitors like van Horstmann were few and far between, but their actions were indelibly engraved on the collective memory of the Colleges of Magic. Gormann didn't like to think of them, though. As much as he disliked Gelt, he didn't think the alchemist would willingly turn to the dark. He cleared his throat and asked, 'What news from the rest of the Empire?'

'The same as it's been for a year. Kislev is gone, and her people with her, save those who fled south to warn us of the invasion,' Leitdorf said. 'Only Erengrad remains yet standing, and that only because of von Raukov and the Ostlanders. Men from Averland, Stirland, Middenland and Talabheim march north to bolster our defences on the border.'

He looked tired, Gormann thought. Then, he always had. Being brother to a man like the deceased and infamously insane for-mer Elector of Averland had a way of ageing a man prematurely. Leitdorf had stayed out of the succession debacle, claiming that his duty was to the Knights of Sigmar's Blood. In truth, Gormann was one of the few who knew that it was actually because Leit-dorf was convinced that the Empire of his father and grandfather was being bled white by callow nobles and politicking aristocrats. He included Karl Franz among the latter, though he'd been wise enough never to say so where anyone important could hear him.

Gormann often feared for his friend. Leitdorf was a man of blood and steel, for whom patience and politesse were vices. Gormann had never been very good at the glad-handing his former position had required, but even his limited skills in that regard far outstripped Leitdorf's. If the Knights of Sigmar's Blood hadn't been so influential, it was very likely that someone would have put something unpleasant and surely fatal in Leitdorf's wine.

Leitdorf went on. 'Beastmen still rampage across ten states, including this one. Plague ravages the western provinces, and our sometimes allies across the mountains are beset by their own foes.' He drained his cup and stared at it. 'The dwarfs have shut their gates. Tilea and Estalia are overrun.' He smiled sadly. 'I fear that we are living in the final days, old friend.'

'Plenty before you have said as much, and as far back as Sigmar's time, I'd wager,' Gormann said. He drained his own cup. 'We're no more at the End Times than they were then.'

Before Leitdorf could reply, the clangour of alarm bells sounded over the town. The bells echoed through the room, and Leitdorf leapt to his feet with a curse. 'I knew it!' he snarled. He hurled aside his empty cup. 'I knew it! Gelt's wall has failed.'

'You can't know that,' Gormann said, but it was a half-hearted assertion. He could feel what Leitdorf couldn't – the rising surge of dark magic that caused a sour feeling in the pit of his gut. He knew, without even having to see, why the bells were ringing. He tossed aside his cup and snagged the decanter as he followed Leitdorf out of his office.

Outside, men ran through the courtyard of the keep, heading for their posts. Leitdorf stormed to the parapet, shoving men aside as he bellowed orders. Gormann followed more slowly. The sky was overcast, and a cold wind curled over the rooftops of Heldenhame. Flocks of carrion birds were perched on every roof and rampart, cawing raucously.

'You told me I didn't know that Gelt's wall had failed, Thyrus? There's your proof. Look!' Leitdorf roared as he flung out a hand towards the approach to the western wall. It was thick with worm-picked skeletons, clutching broken swords and splintered spears, and steadily advancing towards the wall. Further back, on the edge of the tree line, Gormann could make out the shape of catapults. Their silhouettes were too rough to be wood or metal, and Gormann knew instinctively that they were bone.

He took a long drink from the decanter. As he watched, the torsion arms of the distant war engines snapped forward with an audible screech. The air ruptured, suddenly filled with an insane and tormented cackle that cracked the decanter and made Gormann's teeth itch. Most of the missiles struck the wall. One crashed into the ramparts, and smashed down onto a regiment of handgunners who'd been scrambling to their positions. A dozen men died, consumed in eldritch fire or simply splattered across the rampart by the force of the impact.

'They're aiming for the blasted scaffold,' Leitdorf growled. 'The Rostmeyer bastion is still under reconstruction. There's no facing stone to protect the wall's core. It's nothing but rubble.' He whirled to glare at Gormann. 'If they destroy that scaffold, the whole wall will come down.'

'That's why you put the guns there, isn't it?' Gormann asked, taking another slug from the cracked and leaking decanter. 'See? There they are – happily blazing away.' And they were. The sharp crack of the Nuln-forged war machines filled the air, as in reply to the enemy's barrage. Round shot screamed into the packed ranks of skeletons, shattering many.

But even Gormann could see that it was like punching sand. Every hole torn in the battle-line of corpses was quickly and smoothly filled, as new bodies filled the breaches, stepping over the shattered remains of their fellows.

'Kross is a fool,' Leitdorf said, referring to the commander of the Rostmeyer bastion. 'They need to concentrate on those catapults. Infantry, dead or otherwise, will break itself on the walls. But if those catapults bring it down...' He turned and began shouting orders to his men. Gormann peered out at the battlefield. Gun smoke billowed across the walls and field beyond, obscuring everything save a vague suggestion of movement.

'I think they figured it out,' Gormann said. The smoke cleared for a moment, and the wizard saw one of the catapults explode into whirling fragments and flailing ropes as a cannonball struck it dead on. Men on the ramparts cheered. Leitdorf turned back, a fierce grin on his face.

'Ha-ha! That's the way!' he shouted. 'I knew Kross was the right man to command that bastion. Damn his pickled heart, I knew he wouldn't fail me!'

Gormann said nothing. He finished the bottle. His skin itched and his eyes felt full of grit as he sensed a tendril of dark magic undulate across the field. He heard the cheers began to falter and didn't have to look at the tree line to know that the shattered engine was repairing itself.

'By Sigmar's spurs,' Leitdorf hissed.

'All these years sitting on their doorstep and you didn't expect that, Hans?' Gormann asked dully. He examined the decanter for a moment, and then flung it heedlessly over his shoulder. He heard it smash on the cobblestones somewhere far below. 'This battle won't be as quick as all that.'

The cheering atop the battlements faded as the wind slackened and the fog of war descended on Heldenhame once more.

Wendel Volker staggered through the smoke, eyes stinging and his lungs burning. Flames crackled all around him. A shrieking fireball had crashed down onto the tavern, and it was ready to collapse at any moment. He resisted the urge to sprint for safety and continued to clamber through the wreckage, stumbling over bodies and searching for any signs of survivors. So far he'd found plenty of the former, but none of the latter.

The roof groaned like a dying man, and he heard the crack of wood surrendering to intense heat. Fear spurted through him, seizing his heart and freezing his limbs, but only for a moment. Then his training kicked in, and he whispered a silent prayer of thanks to the man who'd taught him swordplay. He knew the fear was good, and it had sobered him up. He had a feeling he was going to need to be sober. He could hear the bells of the keep, and the roar of the cannons on the western wall, punctuated by the harsh rhythm of handguns firing at an unknown enemy.

Kross would be up there, he knew, unless he was still sleeping off his drink from the night before. A brief, blissful image of Kross, asleep in his bunk as a fireball landed atop his quarters, passed across the surface of Volker's mind. His joy was short lived. A burning mass of thatch tumbled down, nearly striking him. Ash and sparks danced across his face and clothes, and he swatted at himself wildly. He heard someone scream, and a flurry of curses. He wasn't the only one in the tavern. He'd led as many as would volunteer into the burning building.

That they'd been close to hand was less luck and more circumstance – Volker and the men he'd led into the inferno had only just left the tavern, after all. He'd wasted an entire night swilling cheap beer rather than dealing with the stacks of make-work that the seneschal of Heldenhame, Rudolph Weskar, insisted his underlings produce. Those who could read and write, at any rate. Since Kross could do neither, his records and logs were handed over to Volker, who suspected that Weskar was still attempting to stir the pot. The seneschal had made his disdain for both men clear in the months since their last confrontation, and Volker had done all that he could to avoid Weskar and Kross, as well as Kross's lackeys, like Deinroth.

Volker saw a bloody hand suddenly extend from beneath a fallen roof beam and flail weakly. He shouted, 'Here!' He coughed into a damp rag and shouted again. Uniformed men swarmed forwards through the smoke and Volker helped them shift the roof beam. He recognised the barmaid from his previous night's carousing and scooped her up. Ash and sparks washed down over him as he grabbed her, and he heard the groan of wood giving way. 'Everyone out,' he screamed. The barmaid cradled to his chest, he loped for the street. Men bumped into him as they fled, and for a moment, he was afraid that he would be buried and immolated as the tavern roof finally gave way and the building collapsed in on itself.

Volker hit the open air in a plume of smoke. His skin was burning and he couldn't see. Someone took the girl from him and he sank down, coughing. A bucket of water was upended over him and he gasped. 'Get his cloak off, it's caught fire,' a rough voice barked. 'Someone get me another bucket. Wendel – can you hear me?'

'M-Maria,' Volker wheezed. 'Is she...?' More water splashed down on him. He scraped his fingers across his eyes and looked up into the grim features of Father Odkrier.

'Alive, lad, thanks to you.' Odkrier hauled him to his feet. 'Can you stand? Good,' he said roughly, without waiting for a reply.

'We're under attack, aren't we?' Volker asked. The streets were packed with people. Some were trying to put out the spreading fires, but others were fleeing in the direction of the eastern gate. Volker didn't blame them.

'Sylvania has disgorged its wormy black guts and the restless dead have come to call,' Odkrier said. Volker saw that he held his long-hafted warhammer in one hand.

Volker shuddered and looked west. The boom of the cannons continued, and he saw men in Talabecland uniforms hurrying towards the Rostmeyer bastion. He swallowed thickly, and wished that he'd managed to save a bottle of something before the tavern had gone up in flames. 'Kross isn't going to be happy.'

'No one will be happy if our visitors get in, captain,' a harsh voice said. Rudolph Weskar glared about him, as if he could cow the burgeoning inferno by sheer will. Then, Volker wouldn't have been entirely surprised if it had worked. 'Especially you, captain. Why aren't you at your post?' He raised his cane like a sword and tapped Volker on the shoulder. Excuses flooded Volker's mind, but each one died before reaching his lips. Weskar frowned. 'Never mind. Go to the eastern walls and bring as many men as you can. We'll need them if the western wall comes down.' Weskar's hard eyes found Odkrier. 'The men at Rostmeyer bastion are in need of guidance, father.'

'I'll wager they could use my hammer as well,' Odkrier growled. He slapped Volker on the shoulder. 'Take care, lad. And don't dawdle.' Then the warrior priest turned and hurried off.

Volker watched him go, and wondered if he would ever see the other man again. He looked at Weskar and asked, 'How bad is it, sir?'

Weskar looked at him, his eyes like agates. 'Get me those men, Volker. Or you'll find out.'

Hans Leitdorf cursed for the fourth time in as many minutes as a merchant's cart was crushed beneath the thundering hooves of his warhorse. The man screamed curses from the safety of a doorway as the column of heavily armoured knights thundered past. Leitdorf longed to give him a thump for his impertinence, but there was no time. Instead, he roared out imprecations at the running forms that blocked the path ahead. 'Blow the trumpets!' he snarled over his shoulder to the knight riding just behind him.

The knight did as he bade. Whether the blast of noise helped or hindered their efforts, Leitdorf couldn't actually say. He felt better for it, though. No one could say that the knights hadn't given fair warning. Anyone who got trampled had only themselves to blame.

Still, it was taking too long to reach the southern gate. When the messengers from the Rostmeyer bastion had reached him, Leitdorf had already been climbing into the saddle. A sally from the southern gate was the most sensible plan – it would enable the knights to smash into the flanks of the undead unimpeded. If they ever got there. A night soil cart was the next casualty of the horses, and Leitdorf cursed as bits of dung spattered across his polished breastplate.

He'd brought nearly the entire order with him. Those who

remained he'd left to watch over Heldenhame Keep, or were abroad on the order's business elsewhere. He felt no reluctance in bringing every man who could ride with him. He'd left the defences of the city and the keep itself in Weskar's capable hands. Even if the enemy got into the city, the keep would hold. The walls were thick, and the artillery towers manned. No barbaric horde or tomb-legion had ever cracked those defences, and this time would be no different.

Fireballs shrieked overhead, striking buildings. Bits of burning wood, thatch and brick rained down on the column as they galloped through streets packed with panicked people. Men and women were scrambling for safety like rats, and the roads were becoming progressively more impassable. The rattle of handguns echoed through the air. The dead had drawn within range then, which meant they were close enough to scale the wall.

The enemy had no siege towers and no ladders for escalade, but Leitdorf had fought the undead often enough to know that they had little need of such. If there was a way in, they would find it. 'Damn Gelt and his gilded tongue,' he spat out loud.

'You're not the first to say that,' Gormann said. Leitdorf looked at the Patriarch of the Bright College. The wizard rode hard at his side, clad in thick robes covered in stylised flames. He wore no hood, so his white-streaked red hair and beard surrounded his seamed face like the corona of the sun. He carried his staff of office, and he had a wide-bladed sword sheathed on his hip.

'Nor will I be the last, I think, before our travails are over,' Leitdorf said. 'I knew his blasted cage would fail. I knew it.' He looked away. 'I argued long and hard that his sorcery was only a temporary measure at best – that it afforded us an opportunity, rather than a solution. We should have seized the moment and swept Sylvania clean with fire and sword. And now it's too late. The muster of Drakenhof is at our gate, and the Empire is in no fit state to throw them back if we fail.' He pounded on his saddle horn with a fist.

'Doom and gloom and grim darkness,' Gormann said. A fruit vendor's stall toppled into the street as people made way for the knights, and cabbages and potatoes burst beneath his horse's hooves. He looked up as another fireball struck home. 'If this is an invasion, it's a fairly tentative one. A few mouldering bones and artillery pieces do not a conquering force make. Where are the rest of them? The rotting dead, the cannibal packs, the spectres and von Carstein's detestable kin?'

'Sometimes I forget that you've been living in Altdorf, getting fat all of these years,' Leitdorf said. He ignored Gormann's outraged spluttering. 'You are fat, Thyrus. I'm surprised you fit into your robes. Those dead things out there are to soften up our walls for the rest of them, when night falls. Then we'll be on the back foot, unless we smash them here and now, and send von Carstein back over the border with our boot on his rump.'

'You never told me you were a poet, Hans,' Gormann said.

Leitdorf growled and hunched his shoulders. 'Will you for once in your sybaritic life take things seriously?'

'I take everything seriously, Hans,' Gormann said. 'I'm more concerned about *how* von Carstein circumvented Gelt's cage. That enchantment was like nothing I've ever encountered, and if von Carstein managed to break it, then old Volkmar's wild claims about that leech getting his claws on the thrice-cursed Crown of Sorcery might be more than some dark fantasy.'

'Or Gelt's spell wasn't as permanent as he claimed. I ought to wring that alchemist's scrawny neck,' Leitdorf barked. He looked at Gormann. 'Of course, you've considered the obvious...'

Gormann made a face. 'I have.'

Leitdorf frowned. 'What do we really know about Gelt, Thyrus? I'd always heard that he cheated you of the staff of office, but you've never said what really happened.' He snapped his reins, causing his mount to rear as a pedlar scurried out of his path. 'Out of the way, fool!' he roared. He glanced at Gormann. 'There are rumours about Gelt. Dark ones... What if this is part of some scheme? He caged Sylvania, right after Volkmar – one of his most influential critics – vanishes into its depths, and then claims that nothing can escape. As soon as we've turned our eyes and swords north, that inescapable cage is suddenly no more effective than a morning mist.'

Gormann didn't look at him. Leitdorf had known the Bright Wizard for a long time. He could tell that what he was saying wasn't new to Gormann. Even knowing as little as he did of the internal politics of the Colleges of Magic, he knew that Gelt's eccentricities weren't as universally tolerated as Gormann's had been. Why else would they have sent Gormann to investigate the wall of faith, unless they suspected that something was amiss?

Before he had a chance to press his friend further, he saw the blocky shape of the southernmost gatehouse and barbican rising over the tops of the buildings to either side of him. His trumpeter blew another note, and the men manning the gate hurriedly began raising the portcullis. He spurred his horse to greater speed, and pushed aside his worries.

There would be time to worry about Gelt after the dead were successfully driven back.

'Well?' Mannfred hissed, from where he lurked beneath the trees. His eyes were pinpricks of crimson in the shadows, and his fingers tapped against a tree trunk impatiently.

'*Well what?*' Arkhan asked. He gestured and a shattered catapult began to repair itself. An easy enough task when the engine in question was composed of bone, dried flesh and hair. It was child's play for a creature like Arkhan – barely worth the effort it took to accomplish it. In fact, none of what he was now doing was worth his attention. Any halfway competent hedge-necromancer could keep the mass of skeletons attacking a wall, and the catapults and their crews functioning.

'Don't taunt me, liche.'

'I wasn't aware that I was. I am trying to concentrate, vampire. You are disrupting that concentration. Unless you have something pertinent to say, I'll thank you to keep quiet.' Arkhan gestured again, resurrecting a pile of shattered skeletons moments after a cannonball tore them to flinders.

He'd spent most of the night before stalking the steep slopes beneath the distant western wall of the city, drawing those self-same skeletons to the surface. The worms had fed well the previous year, and thousands of bodies, both human and orc, had been buried in mass graves on the field before the wall. Their spirits, only barely aware, were restless and eager to rise and fight again. Arkhan was only too happy to give them that opportunity.

The catapults had been a stroke of genius on his part. He had found a spot where the dead had lain particularly deep, and manipulated their remains to form his war engines, as he had so long ago in the Great Land. Frames of twisted bone and ropes of hair and stretched ligament worked just as well as iron and wood. His magics supplied the ammunition as well – great, cackling balls of witch-fire.

'Do not bandy words with me, sirrah,' Mannfred snapped. 'Have we drawn them out?'

'You can hear the trumpets as well as I,' Arkhan said. In his mind's eye, he could see what the dead saw. Balls of lead hammered into the dead ranks as they advanced up the muddy slope towards the western wall, fired by the increasingly desperate ranks of handgunners on the parapet. The men loaded and fired with an almost mechanical precision and, for a moment, Arkhan almost admired them. They displayed a courage and dedication that rivalled that of the legions of Khemri at their height. But it would buy them nothing. *'The knights are exiting through the southern gates, as you predicted. They will crush my flesh-less legion and the artillery with ease, when they get around to charging.'*

'Not too much ease, one hopes,' Mannfred said, glaring up at the sun. It was riding low in the sky, and obscuring clouds clawed at its edges. 'We need to keep them occupied for another few hours.'

'*Easily done. You know where the Black Armour rests?*' Arkhan looked at him. Mannfred's cruel features twisted into a smile.

'I've known for months, liche. It is sequestered in the vaults of the castle from which this detestable little pile takes its name. While you keep them occupied here, I shall seize my– Your pardon, *our* prize. My forces but await the weakening of the sun's gaze.'

'*Good,*' Arkhan said.

'That said, you should keep an eye socket tilted further west,' Mannfred said, watching the skeletons march into the teeth of a cannonade.

'*Reinforcements?*'

Mannfred's smile widened. 'Of sorts,' he laughed. 'A herd of beastmen are gambolling towards us, even as I speak. I have set wolves, bats and corpses on them, to occupy them for the nonce, but they are heading this way.' He examined his nails. 'They've come a long way, for such blissfully primitive creatures. Almost as if they were looking for something, or someone.'

Arkhan felt a cold rush of frustration. '*Was there a winged creature leading them?*' he demanded, after a moment's hesitation. Mannfred's gleeful expression told him that the vampire had been expecting that question.

'Oh yes, your crow-winged pet is amongst them. Why didn't you tell me you'd made a new friend in Bretonnia? My heart aches,' Mannfred said as he placed a hand over his heart. 'It simply bleeds for the distrust you continue to show me.'

'*Now who's mocking who?*' Arkhan said. Frustration lent strength to his magics. He raised his hands, the sleeves of his robes sliding back from the bone. Black smoke rose from the pores that dotted the bones of his forearms, and drifted towards the battlefield. Where it drifted, dead things moved with renewed vigour. '*I did not tell you because it was not important.*'

Mannfred drifted towards him. He drew his sword and Arkhan felt the edge of the blade rest against the bare bone of his neck. 'Oh, I believe that it is, liche. We are so very close to our goal, and to have it endangered thus... aggravates me sorely.'

'*Is the Grave Lord of Sylvania afraid of a few mutated beasts, then?*' Arkhan ignored the blade and kept his attentions fixed on the western wall. At a twitch of his extended fingers, the skeletons closest to the wall surged into fresh activity. Gripped by Arkhan's will, they climbed over one another like a swarm of ants, building ladders of bone that grew taller and taller by the moment. Soon, skeletal hands were grabbing the ramparts. Handguns and cannons barked and flamed, shattering sections of the growing constructs, but Arkhan's magics repaired them as quickly as they were broken. The pace of the ascent barely slowed.

'It is not the beasts that concern me, but what they represent,' Mannfred said. 'You were attacked by beastmen and the cursed inhabitants of Athel Loren on your journey, liche.' He did not lower his sword. 'We are seemingly beset by enemies.'

'*I told you that time was not on our side. The Dark Gods fear Nagash. They fear his power and his wrath. The events which even now grip this world are a sign of that.*' He looked at Mannfred. '*Did you think it was coincidence that saw Sylvania caged right at the moment that Kislev fell to northern steel? Did you think the daemon-storms that ravaged your lands were but an odd turn of weather? Those were distractions, just like this is a distraction. Of course we are beset, fool... We seek nothing less than the unmaking of the world, and the overthrowing of the old order. They will do everything in their power to delay and hinder us. They will send beasts and even men and elves to assail us. They will aid our enemies, and undermine our allies, all to buy a few more hours of existence.*'

Arkhan turned away. In his mind's eye, he saw what was taking place on the distant wall. A doughty man, old and steeped in faith, whose aura blazed like the light of a comet, had thrust himself into the fray, sweeping the dead aside with great swings of his warhammer. Men cheered, heartened by his presence. Arkhan knew him for what he was – a priest of Sigmar – and at his impulse, the dead turned their attentions to dealing with this new threat. The warrior priest was plucked from the bastion and torn apart. The defenders began to flee, in ones and twos at first; and then, all at once, organised fighting men became frightened cattle, stampeding for the dubious safety of the second bastion on the western wall. Satisfied, Arkhan turned his attentions back to Mannfred.

'*We are at war with life itself, vampire. All life, however corrupt and insane. Without life, the Dark Gods do not exist. Without life, they will gutter like candles in the wind, and as the gods of men and elves do. They must stop us, or they face extinction.*'

Mannfred stared at him. Then, almost absently, he lowered his sword. His head tilted, as if he were listening to some inner voice berate him. Mannfred shook himself. In a quiet voice, he said, 'I do not wish the death of all things.'

'*What you wish is inconsequential,*' Arkhan said, after a moment of hesitation. Mannfred looked at him, and for a moment, the mask of von Carstein slipped, and was replaced by an older, yet somehow younger, face. The face of the man who became the vampire. The face of one who had known grief and strife and eternal frustration. Of one who had seen his hopes dashed again and again. Some spark of pity flared in Arkhan. He and Mannfred were more alike than he had thought. '*Nagash must rise,*' he said.

The mask returned crashing down like a portcullis, and Mannfred's eyes sparked with fury. 'At the moment, Nagash is dust, liche. And my wishes are anything but inconsequential. He will rise, but at *my* behest, at *my* whim,' he snarled, striking his chest with a closed fist. He flung out a hand. 'Bring that damnable wall down. I would be done with this farce.'

'*As you wish,*' Arkhan said.

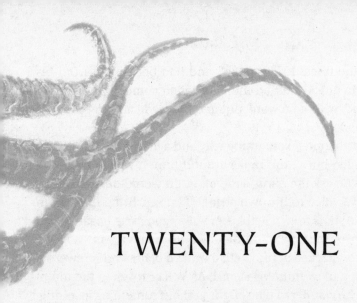

TWENTY-ONE

Volker and the men he'd procured from the eastern bastions reached the foot of the inner wall just in time to see the entirety of the western wall give way. The battlements lurched like a drunken giant, and Volker could only stare in mounting horror as, with a great rumble and an explosive gout of dust, the centre of the wall collapsed in on itself, scaffolding and all. Rubble and crushed bodies spilled across the ground in front of him.

'Back!' he yelped, waving at his men. 'Get back!' With the scaffolding's support removed, destruction rippled along the sturdier sections of the wall, buckling the ramparts and causing them to collapse. Men and skeletons alike were hurled from the battlements, their bodies vanishing into the ever-expanding cloud of dust and smoke.

Shock was replaced by fear, as Volker saw skeletons clamber through the dust-choked breach. He tore his sword from its sheath and lurched forward. His men followed, forming up around him more out of well-drilled instinct than inclination. As he moved over the rubble, he brought his sword up. It was made of the finest Kriegst steel, and had been a gift from his mother. He quickly kissed the twin-tailed comet embossed on the hilt and, without a word, pointed the blade at the approaching skeletons.

Someone shouted something vile, and a litany of epithets and curses boiled out of the ranks around him. It wasn't quite the sort of battle cry the bards sang of, but it would do in a pinch. Volker gave voice to his own string of curses, firing them from his lips like shots from a helblaster volley gun as he began to run up the newborn slope of rubble towards the invaders.

A skeleton hacked at him with a broken blade and he swept it aside with a blow from his sword. As Volker reached the top of the slope, he wondered if he ought to shout something inspiring. He opened his mouth and got a lungful of dust, so he coughed instead. His men followed him up, battering aside skeletons in order to join him at the crest of the breach, where they formed a ragged line of spears and swords. Sergeants bellowed orders and a defensive formation took shape. Volker, who knew better than to interfere with sergeants, settled for looking heroic. Or as close to heroic as he could get, covered in dust and blood, and smelling of the previous night's booze-up.

The line was barely formed when the next wave of skeletons ploughed towards them through the breach. Volker swung and chopped at the undead until his arm and shoulder were numb. For every three skeletons they hacked down, six more replaced them. They attacked in total silence, providing an eerie counterpoint to Volker and his men, who expelled curses, cries and wailing screams as they fell to ragged spears and rusty blades.

Volker stumbled, sweat burning his eyes, his lungs filled with dust. The rubble beneath his feet was slick with blood and covered in fragments of shattered bone. The enemy catapults continued to launch shrieking fireballs into what was left of the walls and the city beyond. Most of the artillery fire was directed at what was left of Rostmeyer bastion, where the surviving handgunners fired down into the melee in the breach. Volker felt bullets sing past his head and wondered which would get him first, the skeletons or his own comrades. He pushed the thought aside and concentrated on the work at hand.

A fireball struck the side of the breach and crackling flames washed over the line of men. Soldiers screamed and died. Volker screamed as well as fire kissed the side of his face and body. He staggered into a soldier, slapping at the flames that clung to him. The man stumbled as Volker fell, and nearly lost his head to a skeleton.

By the time he put the fire out, half of the men he'd brought were dead. Volker pushed himself to his feet, using his sword as a crutch. A skeleton lunged out of the smoke to thrust a jagged spear at the man Volker had fallen into. Volker intercepted the blow, catching the spear by the haft. He jerked the dead thing towards himself with a yell and smashed its skull with his sword. He heard men cheer, and looked around blearily, thinking Leitdorf or Weskar had finally arrived with reinforcements.

It took him a moment to realise that they were cheering for him. He shook his head, bemused. He dragged the man he'd saved to his feet and propelled him back into line. 'Form up,' he shouted. 'Back in line, back in line!'

More skeletons stalked through the breach, and many of the shattered ones began to twitch and rattle. The cheers died away. Volker spat and raised his sword. 'Sigmar give me strength,' he said, even as he wondered where Leitdorf was – where were the Knights of Sigmar's Blood?

'Sound the trumpet,' Leitdorf growled. 'Let the cursed dead know that the hand of the god is here to send them back to the grave.' He drew his sword and levelled it at the mass of thousands of skeletons advancing on the breach in the western wall. When the knights of the leading brotherhoods had rounded the southwestern corner of the city wall and beheld the horde that awaited their lances, not one had hesitated, which caused the gloom that enveloped Leitdorf to abate slightly.

The loss of the city's outer wall was a failure on his part. He had been too distracted to see personally to the repairs, as he should have done. He'd left it to the fat pig, Kross, and Weskar, when he knew the former was allergic to hard labour and the latter had no interest in such menial tasks. It was his fault that it had come to this. It was his fault that men – his men – had died. But he could see to it that no more did so. He could see to it that the dead were punished and thrown back across the border into their dark county once more.

Mannfred von Carstein's head would be his. He would take it in a sack to Altdorf and hurl it at Balthasar Gelt's feet, just before he took the alchemist's lying tongue as well.

'Sound the trumpet again,' he bellowed. 'The Order of Sigmar's Blood rides to war!' The world became a whirl of noise and sensation as the knights around him began to pick up speed. There were nearly twelve hundred warriors gathered, spreading to either side like the unfolding wings of an eagle as they urged their horses from a canter to a gallop. Once loosed to the charge, they were nothing short of a wall of destruction that could level anything in its path.

The ground shuddered beneath them. He caught sight of Gormann hunched over his horse's neck, his staff held up like a standard, a swirling ball of fire floating above it. The wizard caught his eye and grinned widely. Leitdorf couldn't help but return the expression. It had been too long since they had fought side by side – the Battle of Hel Ditch, he thought, and the razing of the Maggot Orchard – and he looked forward to seeing his old friend in action once again.

The closest skeletons had only just begun to turn when the charge struck home with a sound like thunder. To Leitdorf, it was as if he and his men were the curve of some vast reaper's scythe. One moment, there was an unbroken sea of bleached or browning bone, marching beneath ragged, worm-eaten banners; the next, a wave of shining steel crashed into and over the dead in a massive roar of splintering bone and pounding hooves.

Leitdorf roared out the name of Sigmar as he hewed a corridor through the dead, making way for the knights behind him. As he took the head of a grinning skeleton, he jerked his stallion about and raised his sword. His standard bearer, close by, raised the order's banner in response, and the trumpeter blew a single, clarion note. The men who'd been with Leitdorf wheeled about and smashed their way clear of the skeletal phalanxes that sought to converge on them. They would reform and charge again, each brotherhood picking their own targets in order to render the horde down to a manageable size and destroy it piecemeal.

He'd learned from hard experience that the dead didn't care about numbers, or morale. If his knights became bogged down amidst the mass of corpses, they'd be swarmed under in short order. The only way to defeat the dead was to pummel them to nothing with mechanical precision. To hit them again and again, until they stopped getting back up. He looked around for Gormann and saw that the wizard's horse had gone down in the first charge. Gormann was on his feet, however, and fire swirled about him, like silks about a Strigany dancer. His face was flushed, and his eyes looked like glowing embers as he spun his staff about, conjuring dancing flames. The air about him thickened, becoming the eye of a nascent firestorm.

Leitdorf found himself unable to tear his eyes away. It had been years since he had seen Gormann's power unleashed. Normally the wizard contented himself with parlour tricks – lighting his pipe or conjuring a fire in the fireplace. But here was the true majesty of the Bright College, the searing rage of an unfettered inferno.

He pulled his men back with oaths and furious gestures. The knights formed up and cantered to what he hoped was a safe range. The dead closed in all around Gormann, who did not appear concerned, and for good reason. Even at a distance,

Leitdorf felt the heat of what came next.

There was no sound, only fury. No flames, only incredible, irresistible heat. Bone and rusty armour fused into indeterminate slag as the heat washed over the ranks of the dead. Bleached bone turned black and then crumbled to fragments of ash as Gormann began to stride forward, encased in a bubble of devastation. The bubble shimmered and began to grow, as if every skeleton consumed by it was a log added to a fire. Tendrils of flame exploded outwards from his palms at Gormann's merest gesture, and consumed the dead in a maelstrom of fire and smoke.

Leitdorf looked up as one of the enemy catapults fired at the wizard. Without looking up, Gormann raised his hand and his fingers crooked like claws. The cackling fireball slowed in its descent and finally stopped right above its intended target. Gormann gave a great, gusty laugh, wound his arm up and snapped it forward, like a boy hurling a stone. The fireball careened back towards its point of origin, and the catapult and its crew were immolated instantly.

More catapults fired, and Gormann slammed his staff down. The fireballs jumbled before him like leaves caught in a strong wind. He raised his staff and they followed the motion of it. With a sharp gesture, he sent them hurtling back the way they'd come. Gormann turned as smoke rose from the tree line behind him and called out, 'Well? What are you waiting for, Hans? Get to work.'

Leitdorf laughed and signalled his trumpeter. Another note, and two unengaged brotherhoods galloped towards the tree line and the remaining artillery pieces, crushing any skeletons who tried to bar their path underfoot.

The catapults fell silent a few moments later, and he allowed himself to feel a flush of victory. The battle had been costly, but he had done it. He made to call out to Gormann when the wind suddenly shifted. The breeze, which had played across the city all morning, increased in speed and strength, becoming a roaring gale. The sun faded as dark clouds gathered, filling the sky. Instinct made him turn in his saddle.

The clouds were thickest and darkest around Heldenhame Keep. 'No,' he said, in disbelief. The enemy had got past them, somehow, some way, and they were in his city. He thought of Weskar, and the few men he'd left on the walls and knew that they would not be enough, brave as they were. 'Sound the retreat,' he snarled to his trumpeter, jerking his horse about and driving his spurs into its flanks. 'We have to get back to the city – *now!*'

But as he said it, he knew it was too late.

The vargheists went first, as was their right and their duty. They hurtled down from the teeth of the storm onto the battlements of Heldenhame Keep, unleashing a frenzy of blood-soaked death upon the men who manned them. Handguns flamed, and here and there, a bat-like shape plummeted with an animal wail. But such occurrences were few and far between. The remaining vargheists took the fight across the battlements and into the passageways and barrack-rooms of the towers, drawing defenders after them into a nightmarish game of cat and mouse, just as Mannfred had intended.

Astride his steed of twisted bone and leathery wings, Mannfred watched the battle unfold with a cruel smile. His strategy had worked to perfection. Leitdorf and his cursed knights had been unable to resist the bait Arkhan had dangled before them, like meat before a lion. They had denuded the castle of defenders, and he intended to make them pay for that error in blood. 'You thought me caged, Leitdorf? There is no cage built or conjured that can hold me!' he roared, spitting the words down at the battlements as his mount swooped over them.

Well that's simply not true, now is it?

Mannfred grimaced. Even here, amidst the fury of the storm, Vlad haunted him. Or perhaps not Vlad. Perhaps something else, something worse. He shook his head. 'I say what is true. I make my own truth, ghost. Go haunt Arkhan if you wish to play these games. I grow tired of them and you.'

Clouds billowed around him, and he could almost see the outline of a face, the same face he'd glimpsed so many months ago in the garden, and from out of the corner of his eye many times since. It smiled mockingly at him and he snarled in annoyance. Vlad's voice was loud in his head, as if the long-dead Count of Sylvania was right behind him. *This isn't a game, boy. It's a warning from a teacher to a student – do you remember that night? The night it all began, the night I opened the Book of Nagash and set us on this path? Do you remember what I said then?*

Mannfred twitched and tried to ignore the voice. At his unspoken command, spectral shapes descended through the storm or flowed up through the rocks of the castle. These were the ghosts of madmen, warlocks, witches and worse things, conjured by his skill and impressed into his service by his will. He felt their cruel desire to abate their own sufferings by inflicting pain and death, and encouraged it. At a thought, they swept into battle with those who still manned the walls and artillery towers, killing them in droves. Such things could not be harmed by mortal weapons and as such made effective shock troops.

I asked you a question, little prince... Maybe you didn't hear me. Or maybe you are afraid to answer...

'I am fear itself, old man. I cause fear, I do not feel it,' Mannfred hissed, watching as the defenders of Heldenhame died in their dozens. He longed to join the battle, to drown out Vlad's needling voice in blood and thunder, but he had to be patient. He could not risk himself, not now. He was too close to victory.

He could feel the Black Armour calling to him as the other artefacts had. It longed to rejoin them, and he could hear its whispers in his mind, imploring him to come and find it. Luckily, he didn't have to. That was what the ghosts and vargheists were for. They would locate the armour, and when they had, he would strike.

You see it, don't you? Or are you so blinded by ambition that you cannot temper it with common sense? Vlad hissed. *What did I tell you? Answer me!*

Mannfred closed his eyes and ground his fangs together. 'You said that Nagash was not a man, but a disease that afflicted any who dared use his works. A pestilence of the mind and soul, infecting those who sought to use his power.' His eyes opened. 'And maybe he is. But just as he used a plague to wipe the Great Land from the ledger of history, I will use him to clean off the world and remake it in my image. His Great Work shall be superseded by mine, and I shall do what you never could – what Ushoran and Neferata never could. I will seat myself on the throne of the world and rule unto eternity. My people will worship me as a god and I shall serve them as a king ought,' he said. 'I have waited so long for this moment. I shall wait no more.'

Then you will be broken on his altar, as Kemmler was. As Arkhan is, so shall you be, my son, Vlad said, softly.

'I am not your son,' Mannfred shrieked, bending forward in his saddle, his eyes glaring at the clouds about him.

But you might have been. Now you are... what you are, and I am dead. Yet still, you conjure me to beseech me for my advice, as a son would. I am you, boy. I am your wisdom, your wariness given voice. In this moment, you know that you can still escape the trap that yawns before you. You can still be free of the shadow of Nagashizzar and its legacy, Vlad said intently. Only now, it wasn't Vlad's voice he heard, but his own. His own thoughts, his own worries and suspicions given shape and voice.

'I am free,' he said.

The words sounded hollow.

In his head, something laughed. Not him, not Vlad, but something else. Something that had shadowed him since he'd returned from the muck and mire of Hel Fenn. He closed his eyes, glad that he had left the Drakenhof Templars to safeguard Arkhan.

Freedom is an illusion, his voice murmured. *Power carries its own chains. But you can slip this one now... Run. Retreat... Go anywhere else. Fly to the farthest corner of the world until its reckoning. Live out what remains of these final days as your own master. Leave Nagash to rot in whatever hell holds him. Just... leave.*

'I will not die,' Mannfred said. 'I shall not die. I shall not perish a beggar. I was born for greatness...'

Your mother was a concubine. You would never have ruled your city of jewelled towers and tidy streets, and you know it, his voice said. *You were born and you died and you returned. You have ever meddled and sought to control the uncontrollable, and what has that brought you, save strife and madness?*

'I am not mad. Konrad was the mad one, not me!' he shouted.

Then why are you talking to yourself? Why pretend it was Vlad's ghost haunting you when it was your own fear? Run, fool. Fly from here. Leave everything behind. Do not die again for a fool's dream!

Down below, there was a flash of light. Aged blades, blessed long ago, blazed like torches as the castellans of the castle rallied. The blessed weapons drove back the confused spirits, cutting their ethereal flesh. It was time for Mannfred to take a hand, if he still wished for victory.

Did he still wish it? That was the question. Some part of him, wiser perhaps than that to which he'd given voice, screamed that it was already too late, that he was being pulled in the wake of a black comet that could not be stopped from reaching its destination. An undercurrent of laughter greeted this and he looked up, trying to read the future in the skeins of the sorcerous storm clouds he had summoned.

He saw the moments of his life, spread across the tapestry of the wind-wracked sky. Every scheme and hope and mistake. A life lived in pursuit of one overriding goal.

If he gave it up now, what was he? What could he ever be?

The voices fell silent. The laughter faded. Determination replaced hesitation.

'It is not the dream of a fool. It is not a dream at all, but destiny. I was born to rule, and I shall, one way or another,' he said as he raised his hand. At his gesture, two massive shapes cut through the swirling storm clouds and dropped down into the castle courtyard below with twin shrieks so piercing that every window, goblet and mirror in the structure shattered all at once. The two terrorgheists had no fear of the blessed weapons that some of the defenders wielded. Driven by a ravenous hunger that could never be sated, the two beasts knuckled and lurched their way across the courtyard, snagging swordsmen and handgunners, and dragging the screaming men into their decaying gullets.

Mannfred's mount touched down on the blood-washed stones a moment later. He could feel the song of the Black Armour trilling through his mind, washing aside his suspicions and fears. He would not die again. He would triumph and stride the world like a colossus. Still in his saddle, he turned as one of the terrorgheists squalled.

He saw a limping knight duck under a flailing wing and bring his sword around in a brutal two-handed blow, which shattered the beast's malformed skull. As the creature collapsed in a shuddering heap, the knight extended his blade towards Mannfred in challenge. 'You shall defile this place not one second more, vampire. So swears Rudolph Weskar.'

'I'd be inclined to worry, if I had any idea who you were,' Mannfred said, leaning back in his saddle. He laughed. 'Well... come on. Some of us have a schedule.'

Weskar charged. And men followed him, knights and swordsmen. A desperate rabble, making their last stand. Mannfred was only too happy to oblige them. He kicked his steed into motion and rode to meet them, drawing his sword as he did so. He gave a mocking salute with the blade as he met them. Then, with barely a flicker of effort, he took Weskar's head. His next blow cleaved through two of the knights, his sword ripping through armour and flesh with ease. For a moment, he crested a wave of violence as he took out his frustration and worry on the men who sought to bring him down.

He slid from the saddle as the last of them fell. The castle echoed with the sounds of horror and butchery as those defenders who yet lived fought on against his servants. He ignored them all, his eyes fixed on the great iron-banded doors that marked the entrance to the castle's vaults, where his prize sat waiting for him to come and fetch it.

Nagash would rise, and the world would kneel at last to its rightful ruler.

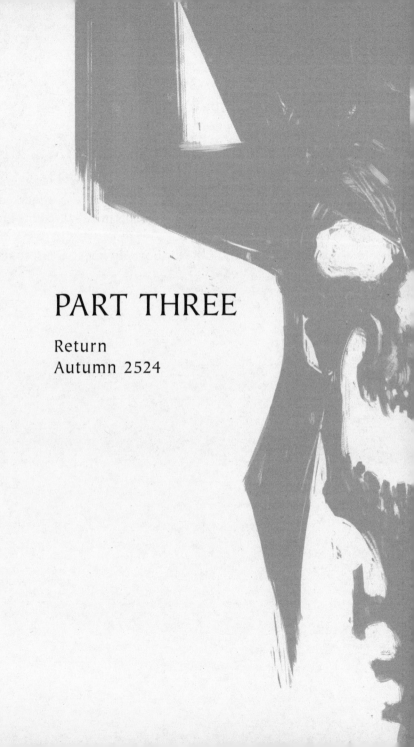

PART THREE

Return
Autumn 2524

TWENTY-TWO

 Castle Sternieste, Sylvania

'*It is almost time,*' Arkhan said as he joined Mannfred in the garden. Mannfred didn't turn around. Instead he continued to examine the worm-pale tree, whose blossoms had sprouted, flowered, and now drifted across the garden like snowflakes. He was reminded slightly of the cherry orchards of far Nippon, and the colours of their blossoms as they swirled in a breeze. There had been a beauty there that even he recognised.

'This tree has somehow blossomed, despite being quite dead,' Mannfred said. He plucked a fallen blossom from his pauldron and held it up. 'They smell of rot, and of grave mould. Is that a sign, do you think?'

'*Perhaps the land is telling you that it is ready for the coming of the king,*' Arkhan said. He held Alakanash, Nagash's staff, in one bony hand. He leaned on it, as if tired. '*Or perhaps it is merely a sign of things to come.*'

Mannfred popped the blossom into his mouth and smiled. 'A parody of life. A good omen, I should say.' He turned to Arkhan. 'I can feel it as well as you, liche. The winds of death are blowing strong. Geheimnisnacht will soon be upon us.' He cocked his head. 'Where is it to be, then? I suppose it's too much to hope that here will do, eh?'

'*I have located the site. A stone circle.*'

'This is Sylvania,' Mannfred said. He gestured airily. 'We have many stone circles.'

'*East of the Glen of Sorrows,*' Arkhan said.

Mannfred smiled. 'Ah, the Nine Daemons. Legend says that those aren't stones at all, you know, but the calcified bodies of daemons, imprisoned for eternity by the whim of the Dark Gods.' He plucked another blossom from the tree and sniffed it. 'Are you developing a sense of humour in your old age?'

'*Legends do not concern me. Those stones sit upon a confluence of the geomantic web. The winds of magic blow strongly about them.*'

'Legends might not concern you, but our enemies should,' Mannfred said. 'My spies–'

'*Your spies are your concern, as are our enemies,*' Arkhan said. He tapped the ground with the staff. '*My concern is with our master.*'

'Your master,' Mannfred spat. He calmed. 'But you are correct. They are my concern. This is my realm, after all, and I will deal with them as I see fit. And you, my friend, will see to the preparations for our eventual triumph.' He smiled unctuously. 'Do not hesitate to ask, should you need any help in your preparations. My servants, as ever, are yours.'

'*Of course,*' Arkhan said. The witch-fires of his eyes flickered slightly and he inclined his head. Then, without a word, he turned and departed. Mannfred watched him go. His smile thinned, turning cruel. He turned back to the tree.

'Well?' he asked.

Elize stepped out from behind the tree, her hand on the pommel of the basket-hilted blade sheathed on the swell of one hip. She'd been there the entire time he'd been speaking with Arkhan, listening. 'He's planning something,' she said.

Mannfred laughed. 'Of course he is, gentle cousin. We have come to the end of our journey together, after all. Our paths diverge, come Geheimnisnacht and what was begun at the Valsborg Bridge will at last be finished.' He looked at her. 'What else?'

'He's already begun transporting the artefacts. Three wagons of bone and tattered skin left by the main gate not an hour ago, accompanied by those desert-born dead things he summoned from those blasted canopic jars of his.'

'And the sacrifices?'

'They are still in their chamber,' she said, leaving the obvious question unspoken.

Mannfred shrugged. 'Let him take them, if he wishes. The ritual protections I wove about our fair land have grown so thin and weak that they are no longer necessary in that capacity. It is past time we disposed of them.' He gestured flippantly. 'Now, what of our visitors, sweet cousin?'

Almost every eye and ear in Sylvania was his to command. He knew the size and composition of each of the forces that had, in the past few weeks, begun to encroach on his realm, but he thought it best for Elize to consider herself useful, and so had left the particulars of scouting out the invaders to her.

Other than Nictus, she was one of the last of Vlad's get remaining in Sylvania. One last link to the old order. He had considered dispatching her soon after his return from the Border Princes for what he suspected was her part in exacerbating Markos's regicidal tendencies. He had reconsidered after seeing how she had defended Sternieste in his absence. Such loyalty was to be rewarded, and such commitment to his cause was to be husbanded against future treacheries. She made a fine castellan, and a fine Grand Mistress of the Drakenhof Order.

Elize cleared her throat. 'A force of men and elves approaches from the east,' she said. 'They crossed through the wall of bone a few hours ago, and are marching towards Templehof.'

'Our old friend Leitdorf and the hounds of Ulthuan, come to punish me for my many transgressions against their respective empires,' Mannfred said. He clasped his hands behind his back and examined the tree, watching the blossoms flutter in the cold breeze that coursed through the garden. He had known that the war in the north would only occupy the men of the Empire for so long. And after Nagashizzar, he had expected another rescue attempt on behalf of the Everchild from the High Elves. But given the way their island nation was currently beset by daemons and dark kin alike, he was surprised that they had sent the forces they had.

'There are beastmen in the Hunger Wood,' Elize went on. 'The herd is undisciplined, but it's enormous – it eclipses all of the other invaders combined. It's as if something – or someone – has browbeaten every filthy pack of the brutes within several leagues into joining together.'

'Yes, and I'll bet Arkhan knows who,' Mannfred said. He rubbed his palms over his skull, considering. The identity of Arkhan's bewinged nemesis was obvious in retrospect. He had long heard the stories of the enigmatic creature known as the Dark Omen; the beast was a lightning rod of sorts for its primitive kin, drawing them together to do the will of the Chaos gods. In this case, their desire was plain. Arkhan was right – the Dark Gods were intent on stopping Nagash's resurrection. He lowered his hands. 'Still, it's of little matter who's behind it. They're here and we must see them off. Who else comes uninvited to my bower?'

'More elves, from the south-west,' Elize said.

Mannfred's eyes narrowed. 'Athel Loren,' he murmured. 'Arkhan was nearly taken by them, as he crossed the Grey Mountains. Krell moved to lead them away, costing us his strength in this, our hour of need.'

'We do not need a mere wight to defend our ancestral lands, cousin,' Elize hissed.

'Krell is no more a mere wight than I am a mere vampire,'

Mannfred said, scratching his chin. 'He is a weapon of Nagash, as Arkhan is. One of his oldest and best. How large is their host?'

'Infinitesimal,' Elize said dismissively. 'It is barely a raiding party.'

'Nonetheless, we must take care. Elves are always dangerous, no matter how few they are,' Mannfred said. He raised his fingers and ticked them off one by one as he spoke. 'Men, elves, beasts, yet more elves and... Who am I forgetting?'

'Dwarfs,' Elize said. 'A throng, I think it's called. Coming from Karak Kadrin.'

Mannfred closed his eyes and hissed in consternation. The dwarfs were the only invaders who truly worried him. The warriors of Athel Loren were too few, the beasts too undisciplined, but the dwarfs were neither. For a century he had stepped lightly around Ungrim Ironfist, and taken care not to antagonise either him or his folk. Now, it seemed as if all of that was for naught. 'The Slayer King is at our gate,' he murmured. 'Tch, where is he stumping, then?'

'Templehof,' Elize said tersely. 'I think that they are attempting to join forces with Leitdorf and the Ulthuani.'

'That... would be unfortunate,' Mannfred said. He stared at the tree, thinking. None of this was surprising, though the timing was problematic. Still, he had prepared for this from the beginning. Everything had led up to this point. He had known the moment that he had kidnapped the Everchild, the moment he had seceded Sylvania from the shambolic Empire, that he would eventually face an invasion from one quarter or another. Now, at last, on the eve of his certain triumph, his enemies were making their final stab at stopping him.

He took it as a compliment, of sorts. All great men could be judged by the quality of their enemies, and after all, wasn't it the sad duty of every new empire to eradicate those older, stagnant empires that occupied its rightful place before it could take the stage?

He plucked another blossom from the tree. 'When I was but a headstrong youth, with more bloodlust than sense, a warrior came to my city. He was a terror such as no longer walks this world, thankfully. We called him "the dragon". He taught me much about war, and the waging of it, and despite our... falling out some years later, I am grateful to him.' He smiled slightly. 'His folk often waged wars on multiple fronts, so fractious was their land. Division and conquest, he said, were as good as the same thing. When your enemies converge, you take them apart one... by... one.' As he spoke, he began to shuck the petals from the blossom. 'Men are like water. They can be redirected, contained and drained away with the proper application of tactics and strategy.' He held what was left of the blossom out to her.

She stared at it for a moment, and then looked at him. 'You have a strategy, cousin?'

'Oh many more than are entirely necessary for the conflict to come, I assure you.' He dropped the denuded blossom. 'Our task is simplified by our goal – we are buying time for the inevitable.' He pointed at Elize. 'We must peel them away, one by one. And here is how we shall do it...'

The Broken Spine, Stirland-Sylvania border

Hans Leitdorf stared morosely over his shoulder at the distant and now crumbling edifice of bone and sorcery that had, until a few hours ago, barred his path into Sylvania. It had begun to collapse, even as had the walls of Heldenhame so many months ago, but it had still required sorcery to clear a path for his army. Luckily, his new allies had provided a certain amount of aid in that regard.

He surreptitiously examined the silvery figures as they studied the territory ahead from a nearby rocky knoll. Three of them – two in the ornate and delicate-looking armour characteristic of Ulthuani nobility, and the third in flowing robes of blue. All three carried themselves with the haughty surety of their folk, an arrogant confidence that no human could hope to match.

That it had come to this was a sign of the times, in Leitdorf's opinion. Dark times made for strange allies, as Thyrus was wont to say. Thinking of Gormann brought back memories of those terrible, final days at Heldenhame, after the undead assault had melted away.

He remembered finding Weskar's head, mounted on the butt of a spear that had been stabbed point first into the centre of the castle courtyard. He remembered the blood that slopped thickly down from the battlements, and the gory remains of the castle's defenders, heaped carelessly where they had fallen. He and Gormann had personally cleansed the bestial filth from the upper barracks and towers, burning and killing those shrieking vargheists that had not fled with Mannfred.

During the cleansing of the castle, they'd discovered that the vaults of Heldenhame had been torn asunder and scoured by sorcery. Ancient treasures, gathered from Araby in the time of the Crusades, had been melted to glittering slag as a sign of Mann-fred von Carstein's disdain. There was no way to tell if anything had been taken, though Gormann had had his suspicions. Leit-dorf had found them hard to credit at the time, but as the year wore on, and he had seen the current state of the Empire for himself, he had begun to believe.

Worse even than the desecration of his order's citadel had been what happened afterwards – as he had readied his sur-viving forces to pursue von Carstein back into his stinking lair to accomplish what the Grand Theogonist, Sigmar bless and keep his soul, could not, a massive herd of foul beastmen had blundered through the line of trees only just recently vacated by the undead. The children of Chaos had thrown themselves at the newly breached western wall with no thought for the consequences.

The battle that followed had done little to assuage the fury

Leitdorf had felt at the time, or indeed still felt. It had, however, gone much better than the first. A single charge by Leitdorf and his vengeful knights had sufficed to set the howling rabble to rout. When the beastmen had been thrown back, he had seen that the defences were repaired. Then, leaving Captain Volker in command of the forces of Heldenhame, Leitdorf, Gormann and a handful of knights had ridden for Altdorf, looking to procure reinforcements.

The journey had been nightmarish. Beastmen ran wild across Talabecland and Reikland, despite the efforts of the knightly orders who hunted them relentlessly. Every noble, innkeeper and merchant with whom Leitdorf spoke whispered of darker monstrosities than just beasts lurking beneath the trees, and of villages and towns obliterated by fire from the sky. Doomsayers and flagellants were abroad in ever-swelling numbers, agitating the grimy, plague-ridden crowds that clustered about every temple however large or small, begging for respite from gods who seemed deaf to even the loudest entreaty.

Things had been little better in Altdorf. Karl Franz had played his usual games, stalling and refusing to commit himself openly, and Leitdorf had waited for an audience for three days before being informed that the tide had turned for the worse in the north. It seemed as if Balthasar Gelt's magics had proven as useless there as they had in Sylvania, and the Emperor had ridden north to inspect the war effort personally, along with the Reikmarshal. Gormann had ridden out after them, to see what aid he might provide, leaving Leitdorf to scrape up what additional troops he could for the long march back to Heldenhame.

That was when he had met the elves.

Leitdorf felt a begrudging respect for Karl Franz's politesse even now – he had arranged events so that two annoyances satisfied one another, at no cost to himself or the war effort in the north. It even placed both him and the elves in the Emperor's debt, for having done so. Each had what they sought, more or less. Awkward compromise was the soul of diplomacy, or so Leitdorf had been assured by men who knew more of such things.

Leitdorf and his new allies had ridden out that night. As they reached the eastern border of Sylvania, the silvery host of Ulthuan had been joined by the full might of the Knights of Sigmar's Blood. A mightier host Leitdorf could not conceive of. Nonetheless, such a joint effort came with its own particular difficulties.

The elves were cautious to the point of hesitation, or so it seemed to him. For a race that moved so swiftly and gracefully, they seemed inclined to tarry overmuch for Leitdorf's liking. Irritated, he spurred his horse forward to join the elves on the knoll. His horse whinnied at the smell of the griffon, which crouched nearby, tail lashing. The great brute hissed at him as he drew close, and his hand fell to his blade instinctively. All three elves turned to face him as his fingers scraped the hilt.

'Stormwing will not harm you,' the woman, Eldyra, said, her voice high and musical. She spoke in an archly precise and archaic form of Reikspiel, and the harsh, jagged words sounded odd coming from her mouth. She was a princess of Tiranoc, he recalled, though he knew little of the distant island home of the elves, and so could not say what the human equivalent might be. A countess, perhaps, he thought.

'If he tried, it would be the last thing he did, I assure you,' Leitdorf growled, eyeing the beast warily. The elf woman smiled, as if amused.

'I have no doubt,' she said. 'Are your men rested?'

'Rested?' he repeated, feeling as if he had missed some vital part of the conversation.

'We stopped to allow them to rest. Humans are fragile, and lacking in endurance,' the older elf, Belannaer, said, as though he were lecturing a particularly dense child.

'Are we?' Leitdorf asked, through gritted teeth. 'My thanks. I was not aware of our limitations, or your consideration for such.'

'I could make a list, for you, if you like. For future reference,'

Belannaer went on, seemingly oblivious to Leitdorf's growing anger. Then, maybe he was. Sigmar knew that Leitdorf was having trouble reading anything on the marble-like faces of the Ulthuani... Maybe they had a similar difficulty with human expressions. The thought didn't allay his anger, but it calmed him slightly.

'That won't be necessary. We are ready to continue on, when you are,' Leitdorf said, addressing the third of them, the grim-faced elf prince called Eltharion. The Prince of Yvresse was plainly the leader of the expedition, yet he had not spoken one word to Leitdorf in their travels to date. Nevertheless, Leitdorf suspected that the prince could speak and understand Reikspiel well enough. He was beginning to get the impression that Eltharion resented the indignity of having to ally with men. It was all the same to Leitdorf, in the end. As long as Sylvania was a smoking ruin by Geheimnisnacht, he could indulge the elf's pettiness.

'Excellent,' Eldyra said. Her eyes sparked with humour. 'We were just discussing whether we should slow our pace so that the dawi have time to reach– What was it called again?'

'Templehof,' Leitdorf said. He tugged off his glove with his teeth and reached into his cuirass to retrieve a map. He tossed it to Eldyra, who caught it gingerly, as if it were something unpleasant. 'A foul little town, located on a tributary of the Stir. It's not far from Castle Sternieste, which is where the vampire is currently skulking, if the survivors of the Grand Theogonist's ill-fated crusade can be believed.' He cocked his head, considering. 'It might be wise. Ungrim is going to be fighting his way west, through the heart of this midden heap of a province. Von Carstein will be throwing every corpse between Vanhaldenschlosse and Wolf Crag at the dwarfs, if he's smart.'

'And is he?' Eldyra asked.

Leitdorf laughed bitterly. 'Oh he's a cunning beast, that one. But he's still a beast. And we have him trapped in his lair.' Which was true enough. Despite all evidence to the contrary, Gelt's wall of faith seemed to still be intact. Objects of veneration still hung in the air like a chain of holiness about the borders, shining a clean light into the murk of Sylvania. Still, he hoped Gormann was giving the weedy little alchemist an earful of it, wherever they were.

'Yes, very inspired that,' Belannaer said idly, looking at the horizon. 'I would not have expected a human mind to grasp the complexities of such an enchantment. It was crude, of course, but that cannot be helped.'

'No, it cannot,' Leitdorf said, biting off the rest of his reply. The worst of it was that he didn't think that the elves meant to be insulting. They simply assumed he was too thick to tell when they were being so. Well, all save Eldyra. The elf woman shook her head slightly and rolled her eyes. Leitdorf grunted. Unnatural as her beauty was, she nonetheless made him wish he were a few decades younger, and less cautious. 'And no, we should not. Templehof lies in the shadow of Castle Templehof, which has long been claimed by Mannfred. It is a centre of power for him, which is why I chose it for our meeting place.'

'You wish to make our intent clear to him,' Eldyra said, after a moment. She nodded and her odd eyes flashed with understanding. 'We will take it, and show him what awaits him.'

'It is a waste of time,' Eltharion said.

Leitdorf was surprised. The elf's voice was no less musical than Eldyra's, but it was filled with contempt. 'What do you mean?' he asked.

'We care nothing for centres of power, or clarity of intent. All that matters is rescuing the one we came for. Let the stunted ones catch up with us, if they can.' He looked at Leitdorf. 'We are not here to subjugate your lands for you, human.'

'No, of that I am quite aware, thank you,' Leitdorf snapped. The griffon hissed again, but he ignored it. 'What are you here for then? You still haven't even mentioned the name of the one you are supposedly here to rescue.'

'Such is of no concern to you,' Eltharion said bluntly. He looked away.

'You are right. It is of little concern to me. But we are allies, and such things should be shared between allies,' Leitdorf said. He longed to swing down out of his saddle and drive his fist into the elf's scowling face. 'I have fought these devils for longer than any other. We must take their places from them. We must burn their boltholes and dens. Otherwise they will vanish again and again, and the object of your mission with them.' He looked hard at Eltharion. 'I appreciate your desire for haste – I share it myself – but we need the dwarfs. Sylvania must be put down, once and for all, for the good of all of our peoples.'

Eltharion didn't respond. Leitdorf felt himself flush, but before he could speak, Eldyra handed the map to Belannaer and spoke to Eltharion in their own tongue. It sounded strange and off-putting to Leitdorf's ear. He hoped she was speaking on his behalf. Eltharion ignored her, but she persisted, fairly spitting words at him. Belannaer held up the map and unrolled it. He looked at the land ahead and then back at the map. He looked up at Leitdorf. 'This is Templehof here?' he asked, tapping a place on the map.

Leitdorf nodded. 'Yes. As I said, it's close to our destination. It will make an adequate staging area for the assault to come,' he said. 'We're only a few days away.'

Belannaer nodded and handed him the map. The mage said something to the others. He spoke sharply and hurriedly. Eltharion made a face and shook his head. Leitdorf looked around in frustration. 'What is it?' he barked.

Eldyra looked at him. 'Belannaer says that the route you've chosen is dangerous. There are many...' She trailed off and made a helpless gesture, as if trying to pluck a word from the air.

'Sepulchres,' Belannaer supplied.

'There are many sepulchres and places where the dead rest uneasy on this route,' Eldyra said. Leitdorf laughed.

'This is Sylvania,' he said. 'The whole province is an affront to Morr. Dig anywhere and you'll find a layer of skulls beneath the soil. The trees are nourished by mass graves, and every town is built on a burying ground.' He leaned over and spat, trying to clean the foul taste of the air out of his mouth. 'If we get to Templehof, we can more readily defend ourselves for when Mannfred inevitably rouses the dead to stop us.'

'It is better to delay or stem the tide, than merely weather it,' Belannaer said. 'I can seal or cleanse these places as we march.' He looked at Eltharion. 'We are but a small force, Warden of Tor Yvresse, and in enemy lands. Think of the fate you inflicted on Grom, Eltharion. Haste did not save the greenskin from the death of a thousand cuts.'

'Grom?' Leitdorf muttered. The only creature he knew of by that name was a historical footnote. He peered at the elves, suddenly all-too aware of the vast gulf of time that sat between them. How old were they? He pushed the thought aside. He didn't want to know. 'Most of what you're talking about is near Templehof, if not actually within its boundaries. As I said, it is a centre of power for our enemy. Taking it from him will weaken him considerably.'

Eltharion looked at him for long moments. Then, with a terse nod, he said, 'Templehof. But we will not wait long. If we have finished cleansing the place before the stunted ones arrive, they shall have to catch up.'

'I wouldn't have it any other way,' Leitdorf said.

TWENTY-THREE

The Hunger Wood, northern Sylvania

Count Alphonse Epidimus Octavius Scaramanga Nyktolos of Vargravia, Portmaster of Ghulport and its waters, hunched low in his saddle as he urged his terrorgheist to greater speed. Around him, several more of the great, bat-like corpse-beasts flew, the sound of their wings echoing like thunder. Fellbats and rotting swarms of their normal-sized cousins kept pace. Every so often, Nyktolos would catch sight of a screeching vargheist amidst the swarms and even a single bellowing varghulf, as the latter lurched awkwardly through the air. It had taken him nearly a day to rouse the denizens of the deep caves, but he thought he had managed to drag forth every flapping thing and night-flyer that made its home there.

It was an odd sort of army, this, but he had commanded worse in his peculiar career. There had been the time he had led a force of brine-soaked zombie sea turtles against the harbour guard of Tor Elasor. Or that incident with the mimes. Nyktolos shuddered and looked down. The vast expanse of Hunger Wood spread out below him like a shroud of green, and he could hear the crude drums and horns of the army marching through those woods.

Lord Mannfred had tasked him with the eradication of two of the invading forces currently assailing the heartland. It was a job that Nyktolos was more than capable of accomplishing, but he nonetheless felt a certain concern.

He had learned early on that the best way to survive the continuous cycle of incessant purges and inevitable betrayals that marked one's entry into the inner circles of the von Carsteins was to become part of the background. Show no ambition, and rarely offer more than an amusing *bon mot,* as the Bretonnians put it. If that failed, stand around looking stupid, busy or stupidly busy. In truth, it wasn't much different than being a mortal aristocrat. The von Carsteins were vicious but the von Draks had been monsters.

Below, the trees cleared momentarily, and he saw the galumphing, hairy shapes of beastmen. They were still following him, as they had been since his first attack several days ago. It had taken no great effort to antagonise the creatures. His forces had struck again and again at the flanks of the great herd before retreating ever eastwards, and drawing the beasts away from the Glen of Sorrows and the Nine Daemons.

Nyktolos hawked and spat. He could feel the world grinding to a halt, deep in the marrow of his bones. The sky boiled like an untended cauldron and the earth shuddered like a victim of ague. He wasn't a learned man, but he knew what it meant well enough. Still, the lessons of his wild youth held – stay in the background and stay alive, or as close to it as a vampire could get. Markos and Tomas and Anark had all made that mistake. They'd thought of themselves as main characters, when really they were only bit players in the story of another. Well, he wouldn't make that mistake.

No, he would play his part to perfection. And at the moment, that part was as a distraction. The beastmen composed the largest group of invaders, and were thus the most dangerous. They could be beaten in open battle easily enough, but it would take time and effort better spent elsewhere. If, however, the brawling mass could be redirected at another of the invading armies – say, for instance, the disciplined throng of Karak Kadrin – then they could leave them to it, and get on with more important matters.

A day before he had encountered the buzzing mechanical contraptions the dwarfs called gyrocopters, and swatted them from the sky with little difficulty. He'd lost a terrorgheist and more than a few fellbats in the process, but the dwarfs had been too few and too slow. He still recalled how one of the doughty little creatures had made a terrific leap from the cockpit of his machine, axe in hand, even as a terrorgheist crushed it. The dwarf had gone right down its gullet, hacking away in a most amusing fashion. Well, amusing right up until the terrorgheist had exploded.

Nyktolos shook his head, banishing the memory. He wanted no part of the dwarfs and their explosives and cannons, thank you all the same. Better to let them vent their petty grudges on more deserving targets.

Down below, horns wailed and the beastmen slowed in their tramping. That wouldn't do. The dwarfs were still several leagues away, and marching towards Templehof. Nyktolos clucked his tongue and set his spurs to his mount. 'Come, my dear. It is feeding time, I expect,' he said as the terrorgheist shrieked and dived down towards the trees. The rest of the swarm followed him, screeching and chittering. Nyktolos drew his sword as the terrorgheist crashed through the canopy and landed atop a squalling centigor. Several more of the snorting quadrupedal beastmen charged towards Nyktolos, who flung himself from his seat with a yowl. He chopped through a hairy midsection as he landed, separating the centigor's top half from its lower body.

Quicker than thought, Nyktolos spun and blocked a club that would have dashed his brains across the forest floor. The centigor reared, and Nyktolos slashed open its belly as he ducked aside. The beast fell with a squeal. Beastmen rushed headlong out of the trees, covered in bats, and the terrorgheist lunged forwards, making a meal of two of the closer ones.

Nyktolos killed another, opening its throat to the bone with a casual flick of his blade. More creatures poured out of the trees. He surged amongst them for a moment, like a tiger amongst goats, killing them with wide sweeps of his sword and his own talons. Then, satisfied that he had regained their attentions, he leapt back onto the terrorgheist and swatted it between the ears with the flat of his blade. 'Up, you great, greedy beast! Up!'

The giant bat-thing heaved itself up into the air with an explosive shriek, tearing apart the forest canopy as it clambered into the sky. Nyktolos guided the creature in a low swoop across the tops of the trees. 'Follow me, little beasts. Your playmates await you!'

Malagor roared in fury as his herd rampaged out of control through the forest. They were going the wrong way and there was little even he could do about it. The horde was driven by its primal appetites. The cloven-hoofed warriors had left a trail of devastation in their wake, burning and pillaging a path right into the heart of Sylvania, and Malagor felt little impetus to control their baser urges, so long as they kept moving in the right direction.

What lay at the end of their trail was a mystery even to him. He knew only that though he was the truest of servants, he had failed to fulfil the desires of the Dark Gods three times. Three times Arkhan the Black had slipped away from him, and three times Malagor had given chase. He had pursued the bone-man across the world, from mountain to forest to plain and back again, and always, always the dead-thing escaped. With each failure, the whispers of his gods had grown in volume, until he thought his brain would be pounded to mush inside his vibrating skull. But they had not punished him, as he'd feared they might.

The Dark Gods knew that even though he was their truest child, his kin were less so. They were too wild to ignore their primitive urges and too feral to be organised for long. His failures had been no fault of his, but a weakness in the tools he'd been gifted. The gods knew this, and they whispered their endearments to him, urging him towards Sylvania. As he'd driven what was left of his horde after the debacle at Heldenhame into the lands of his enemy, more and more beastmen emerged from the forests and submitted to his will. By the time he'd reached Sylvania's northern border, and the crumbling wall of bone that protected it, the tumult of his horde could be heard for many leagues in all directions.

It had been a simple enough matter to gain entry after that, between his magics and the brute strength of his followers. They'd poured into Sylvania like a flood, following the pull of the Dark Gods. Now, however, that pull was being disrupted yet again by his followers' bestial instincts. No matter how many he killed, order could not be restored and they still pursued the flapping abomination that had harried them for some days.

It attacked and retreated, drawing his followers ever further away from their true goal, playing on their bloodlust and stupidity. He'd come close to killing the vampire more than once, but the creature was almost as slippery as Arkhan. It avoided open battle, and seemed content to bloody his flanks and slip away, just out of view.

Malagor flew over his loping warriors, easily dodging through the twisted woodland, his frustration bubbling away inside him. If he could get ahead of them, he might be able to head them off. That hope died a quick death, however, as he exploded out of the trees and saw what awaited him in the open ground beyond.

Arrayed about an irregular circle of standing stones the colour of freshly spilled blood, was a force Malagor recognised easily, though he'd never seen them before. Gold-topped standards rose above a wall of shields, and the air was cut by the stink of gunpowder. Malagor rose into the air, his black wings flapping, and tried to understand what he was seeing.

There were dwarfs ahead, thousands of them. Their numbers were nothing compared to those of his followers, but they should not have been there, and certainly not arrayed for battle. It made no sense – why were the stunted ones here? Was this part of the Dark Gods' plan? Or was it something else?

As he tried to come to grips with it, he heard the first of his followers burst through the tree line. The big gor, a chieftain called Split-Nose, snorted in incredulity as his watery, yellow eyes fixed on the distant shieldwall. Then he brayed and raised the axe he held over his head. Malagor growled in realisation. He had to stop them. If he failed again, there would no next chance.

'No,' he roared, and fell out of the sky like a rock. He crashed down onto Split-Nose and crushed the gor's broad skull with the end of his staff. He swung the staff like a club, battering another beastman off his hooves as they began to straggle through the trees in small groups. 'No! Go back – Dark Gods say *go back!*'

A bellow greeted his cry and the ground trembled beneath his feet. A moment later an enormous doombull smashed a tree into splinters with its gargantuan axe as it charged out of the forest. Its piggy eyes were bulging redly with blood-greed, and slobber dripped from its bull-like jaws as it charged forward. Malagor bleated in anger as he thrust himself skywards, narrowly avoiding the doombull. Minotaurs, centigors and beastmen followed it. It was as if some great dam had been cracked, and a tide of hair and muscle flowed out, seeking to roll over everything in its path.

Malagor could only watch as his lesser kin charged towards the dwarf shieldwall, heedless of anything save their own desire to kill, defile and devour that which was in front of them. He could feel the displeasure of the Dark Gods beating down on him, and with a strangled snarl, he flung himself after his followers, eager to drown out the voices of the gods in the noise of slaughter.

▌ *Red Cairn, northern Sylvania*

'Come on then, scum! Come kiss my axe,' Ungrim Ironfist roared hoarsely. His voice was almost gone, and his limbs felt like lead.

Nevertheless, he and his bodyguard of Slayers bounded out from amidst the dwarf shieldwall as the pack of bellowing minotaurs and bestigors charged towards the dwarf lines stationed around the blood-red standing stones. From behind him, volley after volley of cannon fire tore great, bloody furrows in the ever-shifting ranks of the children of Chaos, but the hundreds who died only served to make room for those who thundered in their wake. The air shuddered with the roar of the guns and the maddened braying of the horde, as it had for days.

'I'll crack your skulls and gift my wife a necklace of your teeth,' Ungrim shouted, as he ploughed into a mob of bestigors like a cannonball wrapped in dragonscale. He lashed out with blade, boot and the brass knuckles on his gloves. 'Hurry up and die so your bigger friends can have a turn,' he snarled, grabbing a bestigor by the throat. The beast bleated in fury and struck at him with a cut-down glaive, but Ungrim crushed its throat before the blow could fall.

Momentarily free of opponents, Ungrim clawed blood out of his face and looked around. The beastmen had flowed around the Slayers and smashed into the shieldwall, where many were thrown back in bloody sprays. Thunderers loosed destructive volleys at point-blank range over the shoulders of clansmen as minotaurs hacked at their diminutive opponents, stopping only to gorge upon the fallen. Skulls were cracked, and blood ran in thick streams across the lumpy ground.

Ungrim hesitated. All around him, Slayers were fulfilling their oaths as they savaged the belly of the enemy horde, and part of him longed to hurl himself even deeper into the fray alongside them, axe singing. But he was a king as well as a Slayer, and a king had responsibilities. He spat a curse and lifted his axe as he started back towards the dwarf lines. He picked up speed as he ran, and he smashed aside any beastman who got in his way without slowing down.

When the Imperial herald had come to Karak Kadrin so many

weeks ago, Ungrim hadn't been surprised. It was just like the Ulthuani to go running to the humans when the dawi weren't feeling charitable. Given what he'd learned at the Kingsmeet the year before, and what tales his own folk brought east, from the border country, it wasn't difficult to see that something foul was brewing in Sylvania. Despite the fact that the thought of helping the feckless elgi sat ill with him, Ungrim had decided to set an example, to show Sylvania and the world, including his fellow kings, that the dwarfs were still a force to be reckoned with. Over the numerous and vociferous complaints of his thanes, he had gathered his throng and marched west. He had made arrangements to meet Leitdorf, the Imperial commander, at Templehof. His siege engines and cannons had easily shattered the petty defences the Sylvanians had erected – walls of sorcerous bone were no match for dwarf ingenuity and engineering – but his progress had slowed considerably as they reached the lowlands.

Dead things of all shapes and sizes had come calling, and the throng had been forced to shatter one obscene army after the next. A necklace of vampire fangs rattled on the haft of his axe, taken from the masters of each of those forces. But it wasn't just the living dead that attacked his warriors. Even the land itself seemed determined to taste dwarf blood – bent and maggoty trees clawed at them as yellowed grasses clung to their boots and sucking mud tried to pull them down. But the dwarfs had trudged onwards, until they'd reached the standing stones where they now made their stand.

They'd heard the cacophony of the horde from leagues away, and Ungrim, knowing what the noise foretold, had ordered cannons unlimbered and the oath stones placed, as the Slayers sang their death songs and his clansmen gave voice to prayers to Grimnir. Three times they'd driven the beasts back, and three times the creatures regrouped and charged again, as if the scent of their own savage blood on the air only served to drive them to greater ferocity.

Again and again and again the beasts had thrown themselves at the shieldwall of Karak Kadrin. Though it was almost impossible to tell, thanks to the sunless skies overhead, Ungrim thought that the battle was entering its second day. The dead were piled in heaps and drifts, and the dwarf lines had contracted more than once, shrinking with their losses.

Ungrim bounded over a fallen centigor and launched himself at a towering bull-headed monstrosity that was hacking at the shieldwall. It was larger than any of the others, and it stank of blood and musk. He gave a triumphant yell as his axe sank into the thick muscles of the minotaur's back. The monster bellowed in agony and twisted away from its former opponents. Ungrim was yanked off his feet and swung about as the minotaur thrashed, but he clung to his axe grimly. He reached out with his free hand, grabbed a hank of matted hair and hauled himself up towards the creature's head. 'You'll do, you oversized lump of beef,' he roared. 'Come on, let's see if you can kill a king before he boots you in the brains.'

Ungrim tore his axe free in a spray of blood and chopped it down, hooking the screaming minotaur's shoulder. He snagged one of its horns and drove his boot into the back of its skull. The minotaur reared and clawed for him, trying to drag him off. Ungrim hung on, anchored by his axe, and continued to kick the beast in the head. It wasn't particularly glorious, as tactics went, but they were good, tough boots, and the creature's skull was bound to give before his foot did. It caught hold of his cloak and began to yank at him, and Ungrim lost his grip on his axe. Flailing wildly, he caught hold of the brute's horn with both hands and, with a crack, he snapped it off.

The minotaur wailed and tore him from his perch. It smashed him down and so powerful was the blow that he sank into the soil as all of the air was expelled from his lungs. Drool dripped into his face as the minotaur crouched over him, its hands squeezing his barrel torso. Unable to breathe, Ungrim rammed the broken horn into one of the beast's eyes. It reared back with a scream. Ungrim tried to rise, but it smashed him from his feet with a wild blow. Dazed, he glared up at the monster as it loomed over him. Then, there was a roar and the minotaur's head vanished in an explosion of red. It toppled over.

'Och, are you dead then, yer kingship?' a voice shouted.

'Damn you, Makaisson,' Ungrim spluttered as a burly Slayer dragged him to his feet. 'What's the meaning of cheating me out of a perfectly good death?'

'Was that yers, then? I hae noo idea, yer kingship,' Malakai Makaisson said. A pair of thick goggles, liberally spattered with blood, covered his eyes, and he wore a peculiar cap, with ear flaps and a hole cut in the top for his crest of crimson-dyed hair. A bandolier of ammunition for the handgun he carried in one gloved hand crossed his barrel chest, and a satchel full of bombs dangled across it. As Ungrim watched in consternation, the engineer-Slayer grabbed one of the bombs, popped the striker-fuse and slung it overhand into a mass of confused beastmen.

'Stop blowing all of them up!' Ungrim roared. He kicked and shoved at the minotaur's body as he tried to retrieve his axe. If he didn't get his hands on it quickly, there was every likelihood that Makaisson would blow up the lot of them.

'What? I cannae hear you, what wi' the bombs,' Makaisson shouted as he lit and hurled another explosive. 'They're loud, ya ken.'

'I know,' Ungrim snarled. He tore his axe free in a welter of brackish blood and shook it in Makaisson's face. 'Why aren't you with the artillery?'

'Beasties are falling back, ain't they?' Makaisson said. 'They've had enough, ya ken?'

'What?' Ungrim turned and saw that the engineer-Slayer was correct. The beastmen had broken and were fleeing into the trees, as if the death of the giant minotaur had been a signal. Behind them, they left a battlefield choked with the mangled and half-devoured bodies of the dead. The throng of Karak Kadrin had control of the field.

But, as he looked at the battered remnants of his once-mighty army, Ungrim was forced to come to the conclusion that though they had won the battle, they had lost this particular war. As he moved through the weary ranks of his warriors, his mental abacus tallied the losses – with a sinking heart, he saw that almost eight in ten of them had fallen in the battle. Though they'd won a great victory – perhaps the greatest victory in the annals of Karak Kadrin against the foul children of Chaos – they had failed their allies.

He looked west. Part of him longed to push on, but there would only be death for his remaining warriors if the march continued. Perhaps Kazador had been right after all. What purpose had his march served, save to cast his warriors into the teeth of death? He had a feeling, deep in his bones, that he was going to need every warrior who remained in the coming days. And that meant he had to save those he could. He had to return to Karak Kadrin, and ready himself for whatever came next.

He closed his eyes, and felt the old familiar heaviness settle on him. Then he opened them and pointed his axe at Makaisson, who was filling his pipe nearby. He shouted, startling the Slayer into dropping his tobacco. 'On your feet, Makaisson! You just volunteered to go west and see if you can find the manlings and the elgi before they move on. They need to know that we're not going to make our appointment.'

'Me?' Makaisson said.

'You,' Ungrim said. He smiled thinly. 'Consider it your reward for saving my life.'

 Ghoul Wood, southern Sylvania

'Oh, my sweet Kalledria, you do this old beast the greatest of honours,' Alberacht Nictus said as the rag of filthy silk drifted towards him through the dusty air of the crumbling tower. He extended a talon, snatched it out of the air and brought it to his nose. 'See how she teases me, lad? She was ever a woman of passion, our Queen of Sorrows,' he said, glancing at Erikan. 'Much like our Elize, eh?'

Erikan stood back warily, his gaze darting between the hunched, bulky shape of Nictus and the hovering, ghostly shade of the banshee that faced him, her hellish features contorted in a ghastly parody of affection. 'I wouldn't know,' he said.

'Ha! Do you hear him, love? He denies what is obvious even to the blind and the dead,' Nictus chortled as he threaded the silk rag through his hair. 'Hark at me, whelp, you are her Vlad and she your Isabella, or I am a Strigoi. She will have you before the century is out, my lad, see if she does not.'

'Elize has no more interest in me, old monster,' Erikan said, sidling around the banshee. 'She never did. Only in her schemes and games.'

'Ha, and what do you think you are, boy, but the culmination of both?' Nictus asked slyly. He watched the other vampire's face assume stone-like impassivity and grinned. He had been there the day Elize had brought the scrawny little ghoul-pup into the fold, and he had seen then what both of them now insisted on denying.

Shaking his shaggy head, he looked up at Kalledria. She had been a beautiful woman once, during the reign of Sigismund. Now she was nothing more or less than malevolence given form. Her skull-like features were surrounded by a halo of writhing hair, and she wore the gauzy tatters of archaic finery. Innumerable spirits floated around or above her, all dead by her hand. There were hundreds of them, and they crowded against the cracked dome of the tower roof, their ghostly shapes obscuring the ancient, faded mural that had been painted on the underside of the dome oh so many centuries ago.

Nictus laughed. He remembered that mural well, for he'd

stared up at it often enough, in his youth. He'd visited the tower often, on behalf of Vlad. Kalledria had always been welcoming. Some stories said that she had been sealed away in the tower that her shade still inhabited, but he couldn't remember if those were the true ones or not. His mind was like a storm-tossed sea, and his memories were like helpless vessels caught away from safe harbour. Whatever her origin, he'd always thought her loveliness personified. He extended his other claw, the edges of his wings dragging on the floor. 'Oh, my sweet, you have done so well. You have collected so many new souls for your harem,' he gurgled as she drifted towards him, her ghostly fingers wrapping about his claw.

The hovering souls above were not merely men, but wood elves now, as well. She had taken them in the dark and the quiet of the forest, while her honour-guard of blood-hungry spectres had shadowed the others, snatching those who strayed too far from the host that even now impinged on the sovereign soil of Sylvania. She had drawn the invaders off course, and deep into the Ghoul Wood, just as Lord Mannfred had planned.

'Oh, my lovely lass, how you do chill these crooked bones of mine,' he said, trying to brush her fingers with his lips unsuccessfully. Some days, she was more solid than others. Her other hand passed through his face, and her mouth opened in a soft sound, like the cry of a dying hare. 'And your voice is as lovely as ever. Music to my ears, oh my beauteous one...'

'Master Nictus,' Erikan said softly. Nictus turned, annoyed.

'What is it, boy?'

'They are here,' the other vampire said, one hand on the hilt of his blade. He stood near the tower's lone window, staring down into the trees below.

Nictus sighed. He could hear the sounds of battle, now that he was paying attention. Elven-forged blades clashed with poisonous claws beneath the dark canopy that spread out around the tower. The elves had corralled one of Kalledria's servitors and traced the ancient tethers of dark power that bound the spirit to its mistress. He looked up into her hollow eyes. She had been banished before, his dark lady, and had always returned. But this time...

He was not as observant as he had once been. The weight of his centuries of unlife rested heavily upon him, and there were days where he wanted nothing more than to slip into the red haze of a varghulf and drift from kill to kill. No more plots and schemes, no more betrayals or fallen comrades. Only sweet blood and the screams of his prey. But he could feel the long night stirring deep in the hollow places of him now. Lord Mannfred, impetuous and haughty, was dredging something up out of its sleep of ages, and the world would crack at its rebirth. The Drakenhof Templars would be at the forefront of the war that was sure to follow, and so would Alberacht Nictus, broken-down old beast that he was. He had sworn an oath to the order, and his word was his bond, for as long as he remembered it.

'We must go, my love,' Nictus said, reaching up to not-quite touch Kalledria's writhing locks. 'You will do as you must, as will we.' Her mouth moved, as if in reply, and her ethereal fingers stroked his jowls briefly, before she turned and floated upwards, trailing her harem of spirits. Nictus watched her go, and then moved to join Erikan at the window.

Beneath the trees, elves and ghouls fought. There was nothing orderly about the battle. The participants fought as individuals, and the combat swirled about the sour glen below. One of the wood elves drew Nictus's attention. He was a lordly sort, clad in strange armour and a cloak the colour of the autumn leaves, wearing a high helm surmounted by a stag's antlers. He wielded his blade with a grace and skill that Nictus knew even a vampire would be hard-pressed to emulate. That one was more trouble than he was worth, Nictus suspected. He stank of strange gods and even stranger magics.

'Should we take him?' Erikan hissed. His eyes were red as he watched a ghoul lose its head to the elven lord's blade.

'That is not our task, boy,' Nictus said. He peered up at the sky. 'Come, the Vargravian will be here soon, to take us to the Glen of Sorrows. Let Kalledria deal with the elves in her own fashion, eh? A woman's fancy, and all that.'

Araloth, Lord of Talsyn, spun about, his sword trailing ribbons of red as he sent ghouls tumbling into death. He danced among the cannibals, avoiding their claws and striking them down in turn. It was a mercy, of sorts. Grubbing in graves was no sort of life for a thinking creature. He sank down into a crouch, his cloak settling about him, and spitted a charging ghoul. The beast grasped his blade and gasped out its life, its eyes wide in incomprehension. Araloth rose to his feet, jerking the blade free as he did so.

From somewhere far above him, he heard the shriek of his hunting hawk, Skaryn. Then he heard the chanting of the spellweavers, as they sought to bind the monstrous spirit that had plagued them so much in recent days.

He felt a pressure on his chest and grasped the locket the Everqueen had given him. It hummed urgently, pulling them ever towards the captive Everchild. But there were matters that needed dealing with before they could continue. Dead grass crunched behind him and he pivoted, his blade sliding upwards. The ghoul split apart like rotten fruit as his sword tore through its body. More of the grey-fleshed cannibals loped out of the trees, swarming like flies to a corpse.

'Protect Keyberos and the others,' he shouted, as his warriors retreated before the onrushing ghouls. 'They must be given time to seal the beast in her lair.' He glanced back at the small group of spellweavers who yet remained. Clad in dark robes, their flesh marked by savage tattoos, the mages flung every iota of the power that was theirs to command at the spectral creature that had emerged from the crumbling tower at the centre of the glen. Surrounded by a host of wailing spirits, the banshee drifted towards the spellweavers, her mouth open in a scream, which only Keyberos's magics kept the other wood elves from hearing and succumbing to.

Of the ten spellweavers who'd volunteered to accompany him on his mission, only four remained now, including Keyberos. Three had died in the attempt to discover the lair of the creature their fellows now confronted, and three more had gone mad. Now those who remained pitted their magics against the fell power of the thing that had stalked Araloth's warband since they'd crossed the border into Sylvania.

Blood-hungry spirits had shadowed the wood elves' every step since they'd crossed the Corpse Run. Scouts had vanished into the dark woods never to return, or else were found strewn across the trail ahead, their bodies drained of blood. Terrible dreams of long-dead kin and courts of dancing corpses had haunted the survivors, and an unlucky few had been lost to those night-terrors, never to awaken again.

Those who remained were as tense as drawn bowstrings, their faces pale with something Araloth was unused to seeing on the faces of the warriors of Athel Loren – fear. He could not feel it himself, for fear had no purchase on his heart, thanks to his connection with his goddess and the gift she had shared with him the day that she had crossed paths with a callow lordling and made him into a hero. Since that day, he had shared a portion of her prophetic gift, and was blessed with the ability to see hope in even the most perilous of days.

But now, he saw nothing ahead save darkness. It did not frighten him, for all things ended, even his folk and their works, but it did make him more determined than ever to complete his mission. If the darkness awaited them, then it would not be said that the Lord of Talsyn had gone into it a failure. He would wring one last victory from the world or die in the attempt. Hope cost nothing, and it could be purchased on the edge of a blade.

His warriors arrayed about him, Araloth met the undisci-plined charge of the ghouls. His blade licked out, glowing like a firebrand. Blood soaked the thirsty ground, and bodies tumbled upon one another in heaps as the warriors of Athel Loren reaped a toll from the inhabitants of Ghoul Wood. The ghouls were driven back again and again, but they always returned with slavering eagerness as their monstrous hunger overcame their natural cowardice.

A shrill sound rose up behind him. Araloth glanced back and saw a spellweaver topple over, black smoke rising from his eyes, nose and mouth. The banshee thrust herself forwards, as if she were trying to fly through a strong wind. Keyberos gestured, and the soil at his feet began to shift and shuffle. Vines and strong green shoots burst out of the seemingly dead ground. The nearby trees shed their withered bark and bent pale, strong branches down. Wailing spirits were brushed aside as branches and vines began to encircle the banshee. Some blackened and disinte-grated as she tore at them, but others caught her insubstantial form somehow.

A second spellweaver stumbled, her hands pressed to her ears. She screamed and pitched forwards, her body turning black and crumbling to ash as she fell. The air reverberated with a faint hum, as the magics that contained the banshee's wail began to crumble. Any moment now, he suspected that the creature would break free of Keyberos's magics and launch itself at the hard-pressed wood elves. 'Any time now, Keyberos,' he shouted.

'Keep your eyes on your own prey, Araloth,' the spellweaver snarled, his fingers curling and gesturing. More vines and branches shot towards the struggling banshee.

A wash of foetid breath alerted Araloth to the wisdom of Key-beros's words, and he turned. His sword separated a lunging ghoul's jaw from its head. He used the crook of his arm to hook its throat as it stumbled past, and broke its neck before flinging the body aside. As it fell, the remainder broke and fled, scampering away with simian-like cries of dismay. A moment later, he felt a rush of noisome air and a clap of thunder. He spun, his sword raised to fend off an attack from the banshee.

His eyes widened as he took in the large cocoon of vines, bark and leaves that hung suspended above the ground. Steam rose from the mass, wafting up into the sunless sky. Keyberos sat on his haunches, his hands dangling between his knees and his head bowed. The other spellweaver sat nearby, her face covered in sweat and her eyes hollow with grief. Keyberos reached out and gripped her shoulder for a moment. Then he pushed himself to his feet and looked at Araloth. 'It's done.'

'Will it hold?'

'For as long as this forest lives,' Keyberos said, his thin face twisting into an expression of grief. 'Which will not be long, I think. Sylvania is dying, Araloth. I can feel its death rattle echoing through me.'

'All the more reason for us to hurry,' Araloth said. Keyberos gave him a look of dismay, and Araloth caught the back of his head. He brought his brow against the spellweaver's in a gesture of brotherly affection. 'We must press on, my friend. If for no other reason than I would not have the lives we have already spent in pursuit of this goal wasted.'

He caught the locket and held it up, so that all of his warriors could see it. 'This is a promise, my brothers. A promise we made to our cousin, the Everqueen of Ulthuan. She has sworn to aid our queen in her hour of need and we must do all that we can to earn that oath. Even unto death...' He trailed off, as he realised that no one was looking at him. Even Keyberos was looking away, at something that even now approached them through the trees.

Somehow, the moon had broken through the darkness above, and its silvery radiance illuminated the form of a slender elf woman, who moved towards the weary warband through the dark trees. The Ghoul Wood seemed to sigh and draw away from her, as if her presence pained it. She was paler than death, but beautiful beyond measure, and clad in robes that gleamed with starlight.

Araloth gave a great cry of joy. He knew her face, and her name – Lileath – echoed through him like the voice of a lover. He raced towards his goddess, all weariness forgotten, ignoring the cries of his fellows. She caught him, and began to speak before he could even begin to compose a greeting.

Her words were not things of sound, but rather fragments of memory, thought and image, which coalesced across the surface of his mind, showing him what had been, what was, and what must be.

Araloth could not say for how long they stood, minds and souls intertwined, but the moment passed and he knew then what she had come for, and what he had to do. He stared at her in disbelief, his every warrior's instinct rebelling. 'Is there no other way?' he asked.

Lileath shook her head and held out her hand. Reluctantly, he placed the locket into it. With no sign of effort, the goddess crushed it and flung the shimmering dust into the air, to create a portal of purest starlight before him.

Araloth turned. Keyberos took a step towards him. 'What does it mean? What is she here for?'

Araloth glanced back at Lileath, squared his shoulders and said, 'The Everchild's fate is written, my kinsmen. And we have no power to change it.' As the elves raised their voices in protest, he held up his hand. 'But there is a task for us elsewhere. On a distant shore, a great battle will be waged and the warriors of Athel Loren must go and wage it. Lileath intends to take me there. Any who wish to follow may. There is no shame to those who do not.'

Keyberos looked around at the gathered warriors, and then smiled sadly. 'I think you know our answer, Araloth. We followed you this far. And one battle is as good as the next.'

Araloth smiled, turned and took Lileath's outstretched hand. There was a flash of light, and the host of Athel Loren passed from Sylvania and mortal sight.

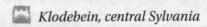 *Klodebein, central Sylvania*

'Five leagues,' Mannfred murmured, as he watched the dead fall upon the Knights of Sigmar's Blood. He stood on the edge of the vast garden of Morr, which occupied the southern edge of the village of Klodebein, and leaned on the hilt of his sword. 'Five leagues between him and his allies.' He glanced at Elize, his eyes wide in mock surprise. 'Not even my doing. His own impatience brought him here. I merely seized the moment,' he said with some bemusement. 'Would that all our enemies were so foolish, eh, cousin?'

'One could argue that any who choose to invade Sylvania on the edge of winter are prone to foolishness,' Elize said. She sat atop her horse, and looked past the tombs that crowded the garden, to where the ramshackle houses of Klodebein sat. Mannfred followed her gaze. He could hear the terrified communal thudding of the hearts of the inhabitants as they waited out the massacre occurring just past their walls. Barely a quarter of the living population of Sylvania yet remained, most in villages like this, close to the Stir. He'd wondered for a moment if the folk of Klodebein might try and warn the knights of the danger they were riding into, but instead they hid in their homes, waiting for it all to end and the never-ending night to become silent once more. He smiled and turned his attention back to the battle.

He'd have thought a seasoned campaigner like Leitdorf would know better than to lead his column through what amounted to a very large graveyard in Sylvania, but then maybe wearing all of that armour gave some men an inflated sense of invincibility. Or maybe it was Leitdorf's infamous impatience in action.

It was that same impatience that had seen him leave Helden-hame Keep undefended, and it had finally got him killed. Or so Mannfred intended to ensure.

When his scouts had reported that the joint force of knights and elves had left Templehof, he'd thought perhaps that they were planning on attacking Sternieste. Or worse, they'd some-how discovered his plan for keeping their allies at bay, and were rushing to the aid of the dwarfs at Red Cairn. Instead, they'd begun to march slowly through Sylvania's heartlands, making for the Glen of Sorrows. That alone would have been enough to prompt Mannfred into taking action; Arkhan had not yet com-pleted his preparations for the Geheimnisnacht ceremony, and if their enemies reached the glen before then, everything they had accomplished until now would be for naught.

Luckily, Leitdorf and his ironmongers had ever so obligingly ridden right into the jaws of a trap. As the knights rode through the closely packed tombs of the garden of Morr, the vargheists Mannfred had roused from a nearby well had struck. The Klode-bein Brothers had betrayed Vlad at the Battle of Fool's Rest, and they and their equally treacherous sister had been sealed in their coffins at the bottom of the village's well since Konrad and Mannfred had run them to ground in the days following their disastrous ambush. The centuries had not been kind, but it had built in them a ferocious hunger, which they duly vented on the hapless knights.

As the newly freed vargheists revelled in a maelstrom of blood and death, Mannfred gestured and incited the death-magics that had long since seeped into the tombs and graves of the garden. As the first blindly clutching hands thrust upwards through the damp soil, Mannfred turned to Elize. 'How long do you think it'll take them to realise there's no escape?'

'A few minutes, if ever,' Elize said. 'Men like these do not admit defeat easily. The original Drakenhof Templars went to the grave assured of eventual victory, if you'll recall.'

'Would you care to place a wager, dear cousin?'

'What would we wager?' Elize asked carefully.

'I'm sure we can think of something,' Mannfred said, and laughed. His mind stretched out, awakening the dead in the sparse forest that surrounded Klodebein. Soon there were hundreds of shambling cadavers filling the garden, attacking the already embattled knights with worm-eaten fingers, brown, broken teeth and rusted blades. Soon there were ten corpses for every knight, and Leitdorf's warriors began to die.

A vargheist shrieked, drawing Mannfred's attention. He recognised Hans Leitdorf as the latter smashed his shield into the monster's face, rocking it back. The vargheist reared, wings flapping, and Leitdorf rammed his sword through its throat.

'Von Carstein!' Leitdorf roared, twisting in his saddle to face Mannfred. He spurred his horse into a gallop, and several knights followed him, smashing aside any of the dead that got in their way.

'Oh dear, he's seen me. Whatever shall I do, cousin?' Mannfred asked.

'You demean yourself with such flippancy,' Elize said softly.

Mannfred looked up at her. 'Do I? How kind of you to let me know, cousin. Wherever would I be without your words of wisdom?'

Elize continued as if he hadn't spoken. 'Leitdorf has killed many of our kind, cousin. Do you recall Morliac? Or the Baron Dechstein? What of the Black Sisters of Bluthof? They were von Carsteins, cousin, and Leitdorf slew them all. You would do well not to underestimate him.'

Mannfred laughed. 'You sound like someone I used to know.'

'Did you listen to her?'

Mannfred didn't answer. His amusement faded as he watched Leitdorf gallop towards him. Elize was correct, whether he wished to admit it or not. After Volkmar, Leitdorf was his greatest foe in the region, and he had expected to feel a certain sense of satisfaction at his destruction. Instead, he felt... nothing. Annoyance, at best. He should have been at the Nine Daemons, overseeing Arkhan's preparations. Instead, he was wasting valuable time dispatching a fool. He was so close to ultimate victory that he could taste it, and he was as impatient for Geheimnisnacht as Leitdorf was to get to grips with him.

The ground shook as Leitdorf drew closer. Mannfred watched him come, impressed despite himself by the mixture of bravado and stupidity that seemed to drive men like Leitdorf. Had he ever been so foolish? He glanced at Elize, and knew that she would say 'yes'. She had seen him at his worst, skulking in Vlad's shadow and scheming away against his kith and kin. Neferata too would have agreed with that assessment, he suspected. Then, the Queen of the Silver Pinnacle had never been shy about sharing her opinion on things that did not concern her.

Mannfred shook the thoughts aside. What Elize or even Neferata thought of him mattered little enough, and would matter not at all come Geheimnisnacht. He stretched out a hand and drew up the skeletons that slumbered beneath the ground at his feet. They rose in shuddering formation, and at a twist of his hand, they formed a tight phalanx immediately before him, directly in Leitdorf's path. Timeworn spears of bronze were levelled at the approaching knights.

Leitdorf raised his sword and bellowed in defiance as he and his order struck the phalanx. The air rippled with the screams of men and horses as the impetus of the charge carried them onto the spears and in some cases, beyond. Leitdorf was thrown from his saddle as his steed collapsed, a spear in its chest. The Grand Master of the Knights of Sigmar's Blood was thrown deep into the ranks of skeletons. He crashed through them, but was on his feet with remarkable speed for one who ought to have been dead from a broken neck at the very least.

Mannfred watched as Leitdorf waded through the ranks of bleached bone, his sword flashing as he fought to reach his prey.

Spears sought and found him, but he refused to fall. Mannfred found himself enraptured by the spectacle. Leitdorf's face was not that of a berserker, or a man driven insane by fear. Rather, it was the face of one determined to see his desires fulfilled, regardless of the cost. Mannfred could almost admire that sort of determination. For a moment, he considered swaying Leitdorf to his way of thinking. Vlad had always been fond of that – turning foes into, if not friends, then allies. A brave man was a brave man, he'd always said.

Then, Leitdorf broke free of the phalanx, and his blade chopped down, narrowly missing Mannfred's face. Mannfred sprang back, a snarl on his lips. From behind him, Elize said, 'I told you.'

'Yes, thank you, cousin,' he spat. He brought his blade up as Leitdorf, wheezing like a dying bull, staggered towards him. 'Anything else you'd like to add? No? Good. Shut up and let me have this moment, at least.' He extended his sword towards Leitdorf in a mocking salute. 'Well, old man, is this it then? Come to die at last?'

'The only one who'll die tonight, vampire, is you,' Leitdorf said hoarsely.

Mannfred brought his blade up. 'Well, we'll see, won't we?' He crooked his fingers in a beckoning gesture. 'Come, Herr Leitdorf... One last dance before the world ends, eh?'

TWENTY-FOUR

 Glen of Sorrows, Sylvania

Eldyra looked up at the dark sky. Morrslieb and Mannslieb waxed full and bathed the world in an unpleasant radiance. She leaned back in her saddle and fingered the pommel of the runeblade sheathed on her hip. She said a silent prayer of thanks to Tyrion for all that he'd taught her. She'd used every ounce of skill and every swordsman's trick she'd learned in the days since they'd found what was left of Leitdorf, hanging from a tree south of the gutted and stinking ruin that had been the village of Klodebein.

She felt a pang of sadness as she thought of her mannish ally. She hadn't known him long, or well, but Leitdorf had seemed a good sort as far as humans went. But he had been as impatient and reckless as men invariably proved to be.

They'd lost the dwarfs as well – Ungrim's throng had not made the rendezvous. Belannaer had cast a spell of far-seeing and discovered that the throng had come into conflict with the largest beast-horde Eldyra had seen this far from the Wastes. She couldn't tell whether Eltharion was pleased or disappointed. He was no dwarf-friend, but even the Warden of Tor Yvresse could see that that their nigh-hopeless quest had become a suicidal one.

Nonetheless, they had not turned back. The Stormraker Host had fought its way through every obstacle Mannfred von Carstein had placed in its path – snarling packs of dead wolves, swarms of ghouls, shrieking spectres, and vampire champions clad in armour reeking of the butcher's block. Eldyra had taken the heads of more than a few of the latter, including a particularly stupid creature who had dared to challenge her to single combat.

Belannaer, guided by Aliathra's silent song, had guided them at last to this place, where the final fate of the Everchild, and possibly the world, would be decided. 'To think that it all comes down to such an uninspiring place,' Belannaer murmured from beside her. The mage stood on the edge of the slope looking down into the immense crater, at the centre of which lay their destination: nine great standing stones, arrayed on a bubo of rock and soil. And spread out around it, in all directions, was the vast and unmoving army of the dead. Eldyra doubted that they could have defeated that army even with the aid of the men and the dwarfs.

'You would prefer Finuval Plain?' Eldyra asked.

'As a matter of fact – yes,' Belannaer said. 'The air here is thick with the stuff of death. It is their place, not ours, and they have the advantage in more than just numbers.'

'Then we shall have to fight all the harder,' Eltharion said. They were the first words he'd spoken in days. He sat atop his griffon, his fingers buried in the thick feathers of the creature's neck. He leaned forward and murmured soothingly to the restive beast as it clawed at the hard ground impatiently. Eltharion's face might as well have been a mask, for all the expression it showed.

Eldyra thought that somewhere beneath that impassive mask, the Grim One blamed himself for Leitdorf's death. The man had tried several times to convince Eltharion to move faster, but he had been rebuffed every time. Eltharion had thought speed secondary to ensuring that their path was clear of potential enemies.

He had dispatched Eldyra to cleanse dozens of ruined mansions, abandoned villages and ancient tombs. And with every day, Leitdorf had grown more and more impatient, until at last he had simply given up trying to nudge his allies along and marched on ahead, to his death. Eltharion had said nothing either way. He'd shown no emotion when they found Leitdorf's body, and he hadn't mentioned the man's name since.

If Eltharion had a fault, it was that he was arrogant enough to think that the world was balanced on his shoulders. Eldyra had always wondered if that strange arrogance was the common bond he shared with Tyrion and Teclis. Heroes always thought that the world would shudder to a halt if they made a mistake.

Then, given what they'd seen recently, maybe they were right.

'Then perhaps it is time to tell them what we are fighting for,' Eldyra said softly. Belannaer's eyes widened. Eltharion didn't look at her. None had known the identity of the one whom they sought to rescue, save she, Eltharion and Belannaer. They had hidden that information from their own folk, as well as the men and the dwarfs, for fear of what might happen were it to be known. For long moments, Eldyra thought Eltharion might refuse.

Then, as if some great weight had settled on him, he sagged. 'Yes,' he said.

And he did. Once a decision was made, Eltharion would not hesitate. Eldyra watched from her horse as the warriors of Tiranoc and Yvresse mustered on the edge of the crater, and Eltharion, standing high in his saddle, addressed them. He spoke long and low, with deliberate plainness. Rhetoric had no place here, only the plain, unvarnished truth.

Eldyra watched silently, wondering what the result would be. She wasn't afraid to admit, to herself at least, that the Ulthuani had no more love of truth than their dark kin. The world coasted on a sea of quiet lies, and the truth was an unpleasant shoal best avoided.

Eltharion finished.

For a time, the assembled host might as well have been stat-ues. Then, one warrior, a noble of Seledin by the cut of the robes beneath his armour, swept his curved blade flat against his cui-rass in the ancient Yvressi salute. '*Iselendra yevithri anthri,*' he said. 'By our deaths, we do serve.'

As Eldyra watched, the salute was echoed by every warrior in turn. Eltharion stared, as if uncertain how to respond. She nudged her horse forwards to join him and drew her blade. She laid the flat of it over her heart as she gazed at him. 'You heard them, Grim One,' she said.

The briefest hint of something that might have been a smile rippled across his face. 'Yes. I did.' He drew his own blade and laid it against his cuirass as he hauled back on Stormwing's reins. The griffon, never one to miss a moment to spread its wings, clawed at the air with a rumbling screech. '*Iselendra yevithri anthri,*' Eltharion shouted. 'For Yvresse! For Tiranoc! And for Aliathra! Let us bring light into this dark place!' He pulled Storm-wing about and the great beast leapt into the air with shrill roar.

And with an equally thunderous noise, the Stormraker Host marched to war.

'By Usirian's teeth, look at them,' Mannfred hissed. He laughed and spread his arms. 'Look at them, my Templars! Look upon the pride of Ulthuan, and know that we have come to the end of this great game of ours. Our enemies lie scattered and broken, and only this last, great gasp yet remains.' Despite his bravado, Mannfred recognised the warrior leading the elves – Eltharion the Grim, whom he had faced in the battle beneath Nagashiz-zar two years before. Of all the warriors of Ulthuan, only Tyrion worried him more.

He and the Drakenhof Templars stood or sat astride their

mounts in the lee of the Nine Daemons. The ancient standing stones sat atop a bare knoll, overlooking the Glen of Sorrows. Nothing grew on the knoll, and even the raw, dark soil looked as if it had been drained of every erg of life. At the foot of each of the standing stones, one of the nine Books of Nagash had been placed, and Arkhan the Black moved amongst them, awakening the power of each eldritch tome with the merest tap from Alakanash, the staff of the Undying King.

The prisoners had been gathered amongst the stones, broken and unawares. All save Volkmar were unconscious, for Arkhan had been insistent that the old man be awake for what was coming. Mannfred was only too happy to acquiesce to that demand. He turned from the new arrivals and stalked to where Volkmar was held by a pair of wights. The old man cursed weakly and made a half-hearted lunge for the vampire. Mannfred caught his chin and leaned close. 'They are too late to save you, old man. The heat of a black sun beats down on you, and the end of all things stirs in your blood. Do you feel it?'

'I feel only contempt, vampire,' Volkmar croaked.

'That particular feeling is mutual, I assure you.' Mannfred looked past Volkmar. A scarlet light had begun to pulse deep within the standing stones, and he hesitated, momentarily uncertain. Now that the moment was here, was he brave enough to seize it? He shook himself and looked at Arkhan. The liche stood before an immense cauldron, which had been set at the heart of the stone circle. More wights stood nearby, holding the other artefacts: the Crown of Sorcery, the Claw of Nagash, the Fellblade, and the Black Armour. 'Well, liche? Are you ready to begin?' Mannfred asked.

'*I am,*' Arkhan said. He set the staff aside and hauled the first of the sacrifices up by his hairy throat. The Ulrican stirred, but he was too weak to do anything more. Arkhan drew his knife as he dragged the priest towards the cauldron. '*Do not disturb me, vampire. I must have complete concentration.*'

Mannfred was about to reply, when the winding of horns made him turn. The elves struck like a thunderbolt from the dark sky, singing a strange, sad song as they came. They drove deep into the ranks of the mouldered dead, fine-wrought steel flashing in the ill light emanating from the Nine Daemons. The elven mages, led by one in startlingly blue robes, who surmounted the battlefield atop a floating column of rocks, wrought deadly changes upon the withered vegetation of the glen, urging it to vicious vibrancy, and roots, briars and branches grasped and tore at the dead.

Mannfred lashed his army with his will, driving them forwards against the invaders. The reeking ranks closed about the elves, trapping them in a cage of the seething dead. Rotting claws burst from the sour soil, clutching at boot and greave, holding elves in place as rusty swords and broken spears reaped a bloody harvest. Mannfred flung out a hand. 'Crowfiend! Summon your folk to war!'

Erikan threw back his head and let loose a monstrous shriek, which bounced from standing stone to standing stone and shuddered through the air. As his cry was swallowed by the clangour of war, monstrous ghoul-kin, larger than their packmates scurrying about their legs and broader than ogres, hurled themselves into battle, trampling the dead in their eagerness to get to grips with the living. Bowstrings hummed and spears thrust forward, catching many of the beasts, but not all of them, and elves screamed and died as poisoned claws tore through silver mail and the flesh beneath.

Mannfred turned as scale-armoured steeds and swift chariots punched through the leftmost ranks of his army. Elven riders gave voice to rousing battle cries as they swept over the dead in a crash of splintering bone. Skeletons were ground to dust and ancient wights were burst asunder and freed from their undying servitude by the force of the thunderous charge. Mannfred cursed.

'Nothing for it now,' Count Nyktolos said. The Vargravian drew his blade. He looked at Mannfred. 'Do we charge?'

'Not all of us,' Mannfred said. He looked at Elize. 'Guard the liche,' he said softly, so that only she could hear. 'Arkhan's treachery will come at the eleventh hour. If he should try anything, confound him.'

'Do not worry, cousin,' Elize said. She blew an errant lock of crimson hair out of her face. 'The day shall be ours, one way or another.'

'Good,' Mannfred said. He climbed into the saddle of his skeletal steed and looked about him, at the assembled might of the Drakenhof Templars. A surge of something filled him. A lesser man might have called it pride. These were the greatest warriors in Sylvania, the backbone of all that he had built. It was fitting that they would be the blade that earned him his final victory. 'Know, my warriors, that this day is the first day of the rest of eternity. This day is the day we drag a new world, screaming and bloody, from the womb of the old. Your loyalty will not be forgotten. Your heroism will be remembered unto the end of all things. Now ride,' he shouted. 'Ride for the ruin of the living and the glory of the dead!' He drew his blade and extended it. 'Ride!'

And they did. Hell-eyed nightmares snorted and shrieked as night-black hooves tore the sod, and a wall of black-armoured death descended into the glen with Mannfred at its head. As he rode, he tried to gather the skeins of magic about him for an incantation, but found that the currents of sorcery shifted in his grasp, as if to thwart him. He knew at once that it wasn't merely the fickle nature of the winds of magic that prevented him from weaving his spells. His eyes were drawn to the distant figure of the elven mage on his dais of floating rock, and he snarled. He was too far away to deal with the creature himself, but was he not the master of every dead thing?

Mannfred reared back in his saddle and let slip a guttural howl, and the air above him was suddenly thick with the ragged shapes of spectres and ghosts. The spectral host shot towards the distant column of floating rocks. They flowed over the mage's bodyguard of Sword Masters like a tide of filthy water, chill fingers stretching towards the mage. The mage flung out his hands, and cleansing fires roared to life, surging in all directions. It left the living untouched, but the dead were consumed utterly. Spirits burst into clouds of ash, and zombies blazed like torches. Soon, the elves were surrounded by a ring of fallen, blackened corpses.

Mannfred laughed, despite the failure of his minions to kill the elf. They had served their purpose regardless. The elf mage had been outmanoeuvred, and his obstruction of Mannfred's sorcerous undertakings faltered as he was forced to see to his own defence. Mannfred seized the moment, and swept out his sword, carving an abominable glyph on the quivering air even as he urged his mount to greater speed. All across the battlefield, the newly dead began to twitch to life. Whatever losses his army had suffered would be replaced within moments.

Yet he could feel the elf-mage attempting to undo what he had just wrought. He gnashed his teeth and jerked his steed about. He raised his blade and the strident shriek of a horn sounded from behind him as the Drakenhof Templars wheeled about and formed up around him with supernatural discipline. It was time to deal with the sorcerer personally. Mannfred chopped the air with his blade.

As one, the Drakenhof Templars charged.

Arkhan did not bother to bid Mannfred a fond farewell. The battle did not concern him. He drained the blood of another of the sacrifices into the cauldron, and reflected on the days to come. He did not know what awaited him come Nagash's return, but he did not fear it, whatever it was. He hurled the body aside and chose the next.

Behind him, the vampire made little sound as she drew her basket-hilted blade from its sheath. Arkhan heard it regardless but did not turn around. '*Do you think that he will thank you, woman?*' There was a grim sort of humour to it – Mannfred, ever alert to treachery, had placed as Arkhan's guard the least trustworthy member of his entourage.

'At this point, what Mannfred does or does not do is of little concern to me, liche,' Elize said. The spurs on her boots jangled softly as she strode towards him, the blade held low by her side. She stepped over the bodies of the previous sacrifices, where Arkhan had flung them – the Shallyan, the Ulrican, the Ranaldite. He held the last of the preparatory sacrifices over the bubbling cauldron, his knife to the dead-eyed young man's throat.

'*I was not speaking of Mannfred,*' Arkhan said, as he drew the knife across the waiting flesh of his captive. The young priest of Morr gave a gurgling moan as his life's blood ran out to join that of the others bubbling in the belly of the cauldron. When he was satisfied that it had been drained to the last drop, Arkhan let the body fall, careful that no blood should splatter on him. The consequences of even a small drop touching him would be disastrous.

Elize stopped. 'Erikan will thank me, when he comes to his senses. Ennui is but a passing madness – a flaw in his blood. I will draw it from him, when this madness is past, and I will make him know his proper place.'

'*How like a woman, to think that only she knows what is best for a man,*' Arkhan rasped.

'How like a man, to think that a woman does not know what is best for him,' Elize said. 'Are you going to try to stop me, old bag-of-bones, or are you content to watch as I bring your plan to an untimely end?' She raised her sword to Morgiana's neck. The Fay Enchantress's eyes flickered and she tilted her head back.

'Do it,' she hissed. 'Kill me, before it's too late.'

'Quiet,' Elize snarled. She met Arkhan's gaze without flinching.

'Well, liche... Try your hand, if you would. You will get no second chance.'

'*Do it, and damn the world to madness and ruin,*' Arkhan said, his knife dangling loosely in his grip. '*If Nagash does not rise, the world burns. And you will burn with it, whatever your schemes and plans.*'

'And if he does rise, what then? Servitude and eventual oblivion? No, I'll not accept that,' Elize said. 'Better to be consumed by the fire, than to suffer a puppet's fate.'

'*Fate is a mocker,*' Arkhan said. '*A woman once told me that. Like you, she refused to surrender to Nagash. She told me that there are no certainties, save those you make for yourself. I still do not know if she was right or wrong.*' He looked down at the cauldron. '*Nagash will rise. The world will shudder. But the sun will still come up tomorrow. Sylvania will still be here, and Bretonnia as well. But if he does not rise, the sun will go dark and Sylvania will be consumed in fire, blood and Chaos. These are my certainties.*' He raised his hand and pointed to the battle raging outside of the Nine Daemons. '*That is yours.*'

Elize glared at him suspiciously for a moment, and then glanced back in the direction he'd indicated. The battle was a maelstrom of carnage; elves and vampires both lost their hold on eternity as two lines of knights crashed into one another. 'I don't see what–' she began.

'*There,*' Arkhan said. '*The Crowfiend fights alone against a hero of Ulthuan. A woman who has fought daemons and worse things than any suicidal blood-drinker.*'

Elize turned back to face him, her eyes narrowed to crimson slashes. 'You lie,' she hissed. 'No elf can kill him. I trained him myself. He is better with a blade than any among the order.'

'*Will he win, you think? Or will she take his head, as she has already taken the heads of those who fought beside him? Will your cannibal prince stand alone... or will you go to his aid one last time?*' Arkhan continued, as if she hadn't spoken.

'If he dies, he dies,' Elize snarled.

'*Then why do you hesitate?*'

He knew what she would do before she did. He had seen such looks before, in other places at other times. Some people possessed a pragmatic ruthlessness of spirit that outstripped even Nagash's histrionic malevolence. Vampires were often blessed with this quality, if they survived long enough. The drive to see their goals through at any cost. They would lie to themselves, rationalising that obsession into entitlement.

But some could only go so far.

Some went to the edge of that night-dark sea and then turned back.

Elize lowered her sword, turned and sprinted away, towards the battle.

'*Run fast, little vampire,*' Arkhan said, as he turned to the Fay Enchantress. '*We come to it at last, Morgiana.*'

'She was right, you know... Better the fire than the dust,' Morgiana whispered, her eyes closed. 'Better death than what is coming.'

'*And you shall have it, I swear to you. Your spirit will not rise at his command or mine,*' Arkhan said, drawing her to her feet. '*You shall be dead, and will suffer no more.*'

'Do you promise?'

Arkhan hesitated. Then, he nodded. '*I do.*'

'Why?'

'*It seems some small touch of mercy yet remains to me,*' he said. Morgiana smiled as Arkhan cut her throat.

Overhead, the dark sky turned ominous as strange clouds began to gather. Screeching spirits swarmed about the stone circle. The wind began to howl, like a dying beast. Turning from Morgiana's body, Arkhan gestured, and his wights dragged Volkmar to his feet.

'Do what you will, corpse, but Sigmar will have you, in the end,' the old man spat. 'Your bones will be splintered by his hammer, and the dust he makes of you scattered on the wind.'

'*I am certain he shall, and it will,*' Arkhan said. '*You were born *for this, you know. All of your years and deeds are the foundation of this moment. The blood that flows in your veins is the same as that of your god. It is the blood of the man who destroyed Nagash, and set the world on its current course.'*

Volkmar's eyes widened. Arkhan gestured, and the wights began to place the Black Armour upon the old man. Volkmar struggled and screamed and cursed, but he was too weak to break the grip of his captors. He called down the curses of his god on Arkhan's head. Arkhan looked up, waiting. Now would be the time for Mannfred's enchantment to fail at last. If this were a children's story, that is how it would go. When nothing happened, he looked down at Volkmar. *'Nothing. Proof enough that destiny holds us all in its clutches, I'd say. This was always meant to be. This moment is an echo of a promise of a thought cast forward through a thousand-thousand years. And we must all play our part.'*

The last clasp was tightened and the armour was attached. Volkmar sagged beneath its awful weight as the wights stepped back. Arkhan gestured, and a pile of iron chains, discarded when the prisoners were killed, rose at his command, clinking and rattling. The chains rushed forward and ensnared Volkmar, binding him and dragging him to his feet again. Arkhan motioned towards the cauldron, and the chains rose into the air, carrying Volkmar with them. As they deposited him feet-first into the cauldron, Arkhan reverentially lifted the Crown of Sorcery up and placed it upon the old man's bloodstained brow.

Volkmar moaned, and his eyes rolled up in his head. Arkhan could hear the crown's whispers start up as the voice of Nagash murmured in the old man's mind. Arkhan retrieved Alakanash and began to chant the ritual of invocation and awakening.

Elize sprinted across the battlefield, moving quicker than any black steed from the stables of Drakenhof. She swept her blade out, cutting down anything, living or dead that sought to bar her path. Erikan had been with the Templars. She had seen them charge before she made her move to stop the ritual, and she saw that the elves had met the assault at full gallop. Now the centre of the glen was a whirling melee of screaming horses, splintered shields and falling bodies.

She charged into the melee, her blade sweeping the life from an elven knight as the warrior rose up in front of her. She saw the Drakenhof banner, flapping in an unnatural breeze, and knew that that was where Mannfred was; and where he was, Erikan and the other members of the inner circle would be as well.

She caught sight of Nyktolos a moment later, duelling with an elven knight, his too-wide jaws agape in laughter. Nictus hurtled through the air on leather wings, plucking enemies from the saddle and dashing them to the ground, mangled and broken. And there, beneath the banner, Mannfred and Erikan, fighting back to back. But even as she caught sight of them, she saw a flash of painful light as the Drakenhof Templar bearing the battle standard fell. The source of the light was a sword, held in the hands of an elf woman, who leapt into the air while the standard fell, her blade clutched in both hands.

Mannfred turned, but too slowly. The blazing sword swept down, searing the air white in its wake. And then Erikan was there, parrying the blow. He and the elf swayed back and forth, their blades ringing as they connected. Elize fought her way towards them through the press of battle, Arkhan's words ringing in her head.

In that moment, nothing else mattered. All of her hopes and dreams and schemes turned to ash and char, consumed by the fire that drove her forward towards the man that she loved. And it was love, for all that it was built on hate and blood and deception. Perhaps that was the only kind of love available to creatures like them. Love was the reason she had schemed to bring him back in the only way she knew how, to show him that he still needed her, that he belonged with her. And she had failed. All of her lies and deceptions had done nothing save drive him even further away from her, down a dangerous path.

She bashed an elf to his knees and chopped down on him. As she jerked her blade free, she saw Erikan lose his blade and snatch up the Drakenhof banner to fend off his opponent. The elf hacked down through the standard pole as he tried to block her blow. Her sword scraped against his cuirass, and he fell.

'No!' Elize howled. She flung herself towards the elf, her lean frame moving like quicksilver. The elf woman pinned Erikan to the ground and raised her blade. Elize intercepted the blow and rocked the woman back with a wild slash. 'He's mine,' she snarled, extending her blade. She glanced down at Erikan. His eyes were closed, and his cuirass had been split open by the blow that had felled him. Dark blood welled up from within it, and he lay limp and unmoving. Elize turned her attentions back to her opponent as the elf woman spat something in her native tongue.

Elize studied her, sizing up her opponent. Her armour was battered and her robes torn and stained. But her face was composed, with no sign of weariness or fear. Her sword was steady. She lunged smoothly, and Elize was hard-pressed to parry the blow. They circled one another, feeling each other out.

They crashed together a moment later, like lionesses fighting over a kill. The elf woman was strong, surprisingly so, and more vicious than Elize expected. Even Cicatrix hadn't been as ferocious. She was forced to give ground, step by step.

Something caught her foot and she slid backwards. Her legs were tangled in the tatters of the Drakenhof banner and she almost laughed at the foolishness of it. She fell, and her sword was jolted from her hand. The elf lunged, blade raised.

Then, something dark rose up behind her and smashed into her, bearing her to the ground with a roar. Elize scrambled to her feet, snatching up her sword. Erikan had his fangs sunk into the elf woman's neck, and he tore her sword from her grip and flung it aside. She screamed and tore a dagger from her belt. The blade caught him in the chest and he staggered, clawing at its hilt. The elf woman sank down to one knee, a hand clasped to her throat. Her eyes were dull with pain as she scrabbled for her sword. Elize stepped on it and pressed the tip of hers to the elf's throat. She tensed, ready to thrust it home.

Somewhere behind them, Elize heard a monstrous roar and the earth trembled. She felt a wave of excess magic wash over her. Then something was dropped to the ground beside her. She looked down and saw a blackened corpse, clad in the burned remnant of blue robes. 'My thanks, sweet cousin. You gave me the respite I needed to deal with that pestiferous mage,' Mann-fred said from behind her.

'One moment more, and I'll add another to your tally,' she snarled. She made to ram her blade home, when she felt Mann-fred's hand on her shoulder.

'No, I think not. This one has spirit. Most elves are nothing more than trembling knots of vanity and fragile ego, but this one is something... wilder, I think,' Mannfred purred. 'She killed sev-eral of your fellow Templars, and nearly killed you both as well.' He stepped forward and crushed the charred skull of the dead mage. As the elf woman tried to get to her feet, Mannfred slapped her to the ground. She did not get up. He looked at Elize. 'I leave her in your tender care, sweet cousin. You and the Crowfiend can finish what you started with her. Be gentle, I beseech thee.'

A moment later, his smile faded. His face twisted in an expres-sion of panic and he clutched at his head. Elize felt something like a wasp's hum in her head, but as soon as it had sounded, it faded. 'What was that?' she spat.

'Nagash,' Mannfred snarled. He sprang past them, running flat out back towards the Nine Daemons. As he ran, his skeletal steed seemed to appear from nowhere, galloping beside him. With-out pausing, Mannfred reached up and swung himself into the saddle. Elize watched him go, and then turned back to Erikan.

Count Nyktolos had joined them, and Nictus as well. Both vampires looked as if they had waded through a sea of blood, and the former had plucked the blade from Erikan's chest. He held it up. 'Barely missed his heart. He has the luck of a von Carstein, if not the name,' he said, grinning.

'He'll live, child,' Nictus gurgled comfortingly. 'He is tough, your ghoul-prince.'

Elize sank down beside Erikan and caressed his cheek. He looked at her. 'W-why did you come for me?' he croaked.

'Fool,' she said gently. 'No one leaves me. Especially not you.' She leaned forward and kissed him. She could taste his blood and that of the elf woman. She sat back on her heels and tucked a stray strand of hair behind her ear as she looked back towards the Nine Daemons. The winds about the stones had reached a howling crescendo, and the stones themselves glowed with an eye-searing light. Whatever was happening there, it was too late for her to do anything about it. It was up to Mannfred now. She looked back down at Erikan and smiled sadly.

'Freedom is overrated, my love,' she said, and kissed him again.

Mannfred rode madly towards the Nine Daemons, his fangs bared in a snarl. Elize had failed him. He would punish her later, her and her pet. But for now, he had to reach the stone circle before Arkhan completed the ritual. Nagash could not be allowed to return unfettered.

So intent was he on his destination that he barely noticed the shadow that swept over him. A moment later, pain tore through him as large talons pierced his armour. Mannfred flung himself forwards, over his mount's neck, and hit the ground hard. He rolled across the hard-packed earth as his mount came apart around him, showering him with bones and bits of flesh. As the dust cleared, he saw Eltharion's damnable griffon swooping towards him like an immense, spotted bird of prey. Its shriek cut through his skull and he jerked his sword from its sheath as the elf's lance dipped for his heart.

Mannfred snarled and ducked. The lance point skidded over his pauldron and tore through his cloak as he lunged upwards to meet the griffon's descent. His blade smashed through its furry ribcage and the great beast shrieked in agony. It tore away from him, knocking him from his feet with a flailing talon, and crashed into the ground right at the foot of the slope upon which the Nine Daemons stood.

Mannfred, bloody-faced, sprang to his feet and loped towards the fallen beast. As he reached the creature, Eltharion rose, battered but unbowed. He spared a single, inscrutable glance for his fallen mount, and then he extended his blade towards Mannfred. 'You're in my way,' he said.

Mannfred grinned. 'So I am, elf.'

Eltharion strode forward. 'I haven't got the time for you today, beast. It would be best if you walked away, and lived to fight another day.'

'Make time,' Mannfred spat. Here was a creature whose arrogance rivalled his own, and he found himself stung by the sheer gall of the elf. How dare they invade his lands and presume to treat him as anything less than what he was! He interposed himself as the elf charged towards the Nine Daemons.

Two blades, one forged by the greatest artisans of an empire long since fallen, the other by the mightiest civilisation to ever walk the world's white rim, came together with a sound like the roar of tigers. Mannfred stamped forward and shrieked, a war-cry not heard in the world for ages undreamt of slipping instinctively from his lips. Eltharion made no sound, and his face betrayed no effort as he met the vampire's blow and blocked it.

Mannfred moved quicker than he ever had before in the entirety of his accumulated centuries. He moved faster than the human eye could follow, so fast that his flesh was rubbed raw by his speed. Nonetheless, Eltharion parried every blow with a grace that stung Mannfred's eyes. Every blow save one. Mannfred gave a hiss of satisfaction as the tip of his blade slid across the elf's arm, slicing easily through armour and cloth to bite the flesh beneath. Eltharion staggered, and a second blow sawed at his side, tearing at his cuirass. Mannfred laughed as the sweet smell of elf blood filled his nostrils. 'Death, warrior – death is all that you'll find here. Death and an eternity of servitude after.' He circled Eltharion and continued to spew taunts. 'You'll be my bodyguard, I think. I'm running short on those, thanks to you. Would you like that, elf? I'll let your mutilated husk lead my legions when I burn the pretty white towers of your people and make them my chattel.'

He'd hoped to provoke the elf. To spur him into attacking wildly, and without concern for his own wellbeing. Instead, the elf came at him with a chilly meticulousness. He parried Mannfred's next blow and the edge of his blade came close to opening the vampire's throat. Eltharion fought with machine-like precision, every blow calculated for maximum effect and minimum effort. If he hadn't suddenly found himself on the defensive, Mannfred would have been impressed.

He realised, as they traded blows, that for the first time in a long time he was the less-masterful combatant in a duel. For too many years, he had relied upon old skills and sheer brute strength, but here, at last, was an opponent whom he could not simply overmatch.

A blow from Eltharion's sword tore open his cuirass and sliced through the flesh beneath. A second blow smashed into Mannfred's forearm with hammer-like precision, shattering bone and shearing muscle to leave the limb hanging from a single agonised strand of muscle. Mannfred howled and staggered back, clutching at his wounded limb, his sword lying forgotten in the dust. The world spun around him, and he could see all of his hopes and dreams turning to ash before him.

'No,' he hissed. 'No! I've fought too long, too hard to be beaten now, by you!' he roared as he flung out his good hand. Deathly magics coalesced in the air before the grimly advancing elf, forming into a sextet of black swords. Eltharion weaved through the blades, parrying their every blow.

Mannfred, crouched on the slope, watched the elf fight his way through the blades. The sable swords had only been a distraction. They would fade in moments, leaving Eltharion free to attack again. He had only moments in which to act. Ignoring the pain of his mangled arm, he summoned the energy to unleash a bolt of raw, writhing magic. He rose on unsteady legs, the scope of his world narrowed to Eltharion's graceful form. If he could kill the elf, it would be done. He extended his hand, black lightning crackling along his forearm and between his curled fingers.

But before he could unleash the spell, he heard a guttural snarl. A heavy body lunged across the slope, trailing blood and feathers. The griffon's beak snapped shut on his extended arm, its talons smashing into his chest and thigh. Mannfred screamed as he was borne to the ground by the monster's weight. It was no consolation that his spell had killed the creature as it struck it.

'No! Damn you, no!' Mannfred screamed, pleading with fate as he tried to extricate himself from the dead animal's claws and beak. 'No! Not now! Eltharion – face me, damn you!' he shrieked as Eltharion started up the slope with only a single backwards glance. 'Eltharion,' Mannfred wailed, squirming beneath the corpse of the griffon.

Eltharion strode towards the standing stones, seemingly gaining strength with every step. As he reached them, light crackled between them. Mannfred cackled weakly. Of course Arkhan had cast some defensive enchantment, of course!

His cackles died away as Eltharion raised his sword in a two-handed grip and thrust the sword into the mystical barrier. The magic crackled and spat, writhing around the blade like a thing in pain. The runes upon the elvish blade glowed as red as coals, and then Eltharion pushed his way into the ring of the Nine Daemons.

With an agonised snarl, Mannfred freed himself from the dead griffon, leaving behind more flesh and blood than he liked to think about. Bleeding heavily, he staggered up after the elf and, with a last surge of strength, he pounced at the gap the elf had made.

He was too slow. He struck the mystic barrier and staggered back. Wailing spirits whirled about him as he pounded his now-healed fists against the barrier. He saw Eltharion toss away his smoking and melted blade.

Arkhan had his back to the elf, standing before the cauldron, one hand wrapped in the golden tresses of the Everchild, forcing her head and torso over the cauldron's rim. In his other hand, he held his knife in preparation for slashing her throat, as he had with all of the other sacrifices. In the centre of the cauldron, Volkmar hung limp in a mystical web of chains.

Eltharion lunged with a roar worthy of his slain mount. Arkhan released his captive and spun. Eltharion slammed into him, his hands closing about the liche's bony neck. Arkhan glared at the elf. *'Release me, warrior.'* Eltharion slammed him back against the cauldron as if to snap the liche in two. *'Very well. I have no more time for mercy.'*

Arkhan's hands snapped up and caught the elf's wrists. Instantly, a cloud of rust billowed up from Eltharion's vambraces. As Mannfred watched, the entropic curse consumed him. It rippled across metal and flesh with equal aplomb, warping and cracking armour as it withered flesh. The elf's hair turned white and brittle, and his flesh took on the consistency of parchment, but he did not release his hold on Arkhan. To the last, his gaze held the liche's.

Then, with barely a sigh, Eltharion the Grim, Warden of Tor Yvresse, burst apart in a cloud of dust.

Arkhan staggered back, the witch-lights of his eyes flashing with something that might have been regret. Mannfred began to pound on the barrier anew as Arkhan turned back and jerked Aliathra to her feet. He reclaimed his dagger. 'My father will destroy you, liche,' she said. Mannfred was impressed. There was no fear in her voice, only resignation.

'*Your father is already dead, child. My allies have seen to that.*'

'Allies? What allies?' Mannfred shouted. 'Arkhan – let me in!'

Arkhan ignored him. He looked at Aliathra as she said, 'For all of your power, you know nothing.'

'*We shall see,*' Arkhan said. He glanced at Mannfred. '*Stop striking my barrier, vampire. It's becoming annoying.*'

'Let me in, you fool,' Mannfred snarled. His mind probed at the sorcery that protected the stones, trying to find a weak point. He had to get in there.

'*Why? So that you can try and subvert this moment for your own ends? No – no, I think not. You have played your part, and admirably so, vampire. Do not ruin it now with petty antics.*' Arkhan stepped forward and dragged Aliathra towards the cauldron. She struggled for a moment, then pressed her hands against the liche's chest. Arkhan threw up a hand as a white, painful light flared suddenly. He recoiled as if burned, and then swung the elf maiden towards the cauldron. '*What have you done, witch?*' he rasped.

'You'll find out,' she said.

Arkhan hesitated, staring at her. Then, with a dry rasp of anger, he cut her throat.

As her blood spilled into the already bubbling cauldron, Arkhan began to speak. The words had a black resonance that caused the air to shudder and squirm, as if in fear. Mannfred began to pound on the shield again, howling curses at the heedless liche as he continued to chant.

As Mannfred watched in mounting frustration, Arkhan placed his knife against one of Volkmar's wrists and, with a single, efficient motion, severed the hand. Volkmar screamed and writhed in his chains. Arkhan, still chanting, lifted the Claw of Nagash and pressed it forcefully against the Grand Theogonist's pulsing stump.

Volkmar's screams grew in pitch and volume, spiralling up into the tormented air to mingle with the unpleasant echoes of Arkhan's chanting. Arkhan stepped back and snatched up Alakanash. He lifted the staff high and tendrils of dark magic burst from the stump of the Claw. The tendrils writhed about Volkmar's arm and burrowed into the old man's abused flesh. Volkmar screamed and shook in his chains, convulsing with a suffering that even Mannfred had trouble imagining.

He took no pleasure in the old man's pain, though he might have, under different circumstances. He slid down, suddenly weary, as the tendrils began to expand. As they grew, they lashed and flailed and spread across Volkmar's frame, winnowing into him and leaving only a cancerous mass of dark magic in their wake. Soon, the only thing of Volkmar that Mannfred could see were his eyes, bulging in agony.

Then, there was nothing save the mass, which swelled like an abominable leech as it feasted greedily on the blood in the cauldron. Chains snapped as the mass thrashed about, drawing sparks from the stones around it. It continued to swell as Arkhan held the Fellblade extended, point-first towards the cauldron.

Arkhan spat words like arrows, piercing the air with the hateful sound of them. The Fellblade rose from his hand as if plucked by invisible fingers. It hung in midair for a moment and then, with a loud crack, it shivered into a thousand steaming fragments, which swirled about the mass like tiny comets before striking it and burrowing into its surface.

Outside the circle, Mannfred hunched closer to the stones as the wind picked up, and the howling of the spirits grew deafening. The stones trembled and glowed with daemonic fire. Thunder rolled across the sky above, and he screamed in pain as the enchantment he had laid across the land – *his* land – was torn asunder. Something vast and terrible descended into the stone circle with a volcanic sigh.

His head was filled with fiery wasps, and his bones felt as if they would tear from his flesh to join the maelstrom swirling about inside the circle. His heart swelled and wrenched in his chest, and he crawled forward as the spell that had barred him entry shattered like glass. Something spoke in a voice that echoed through his mind.

'*YOU HAVE DONE WELL, MY SERVANT.*'

Nagash.

It was the voice of Nagash and it tore through him like a blade, cutting through his arrogance, his ambitions, his hopes and his vanities. Mannfred shuddered in his skin as he crept towards the cauldron. He felt sick, as though a great pressure had settled on him. He knew then that his dreams had only ever been that – dreams. Arkhan had been right, in the end. There was no controlling what had come back into the world. What now spoke in a voice like sour thunder. '*THE GREAT WORK CAN BEGIN.*'

He saw that Arkhan had prostrated himself and he could not stop himself from doing the same. He bent low, hoping that the thing that now gazed at him with eyes as deep and as empty as a hole in the world could not sense the bitterness in his heart.

'*DO YOU SERVE ME?*' Nagash asked, looking down at him.

Mannfred von Carstein closed his eyes. 'Yes,' he croaked, 'I serve you... master.'

EPILOGUE

Geheimnisnacht

Mannfred von Carstein screamed.

For the first time in a long time, he truly screamed. Not a howl of frustration, or the cry of a wounded warrior, but the shriek of a frightened beast, caught in a trap. Nagash's servants had stripped his cuirass and cloak from him, leaving him bare-chested. They held his wrists pinned, and skeletal hands sprouted from the ground like hellish mushrooms to grasp his feet and ankles.

'No, I refuse – I will not let you do this – I forbid it!' Mannfred screamed, struggling vainly against the withered grip of the ancient, long-dead warriors who held him.

'*YOU... FORBID?*' The sickly green witch-lights of Nagash's eyes flickered. The fleshless jaw sagged in what might have been laughter. Nagash loomed over the vampire. '*YOU FORBID NOTHING, LITTLE FLEA. YOU SIMPLY SERVE.*'

'Then you don't need him! You have me,' Mannfred howled, jerking in his captors' grip. 'I have always been loyal to you! I brought you back – me, not him!'

Nagash took Mannfred's chin in one black claw. 'LOYAL. YOUR KIND DOES NOT KNOW LOYALTY. DO THEY, ARKHAN?' The witch-lights flickered towards Arkhan, where the liche stood watching.

'*Loyal or not, he has served you,*' Arkhan said, one hand still pressed to his chest where the Everchild had struck him. He could feel something there, as if she had passed something to him, but he could not say what. '*As have I.*'

'YES. AS YOU WILL CONTINUE TO DO, UNTIL THE GREAT WORK IS COMPLETED. AS THIS ONE WILL DO. AS ALL HIS KIND WILL DO.' Nagash leaned towards Mannfred. 'YOU WERE CREATED TO SERVE ME. YOU ARE AN EXTENSION OF MY WILL, NOTHING MORE. AND I WILL DASH YOU DOWN OR CALL YOU UP AS IT PLEASES ME.'

With that, Nagash sank his fingers into Mannfred's chest and wrenched a gobbet of flesh free. Mannfred screamed and thrashed as Nagash turned and squeezed the bloody hank of meat onto the pile of dust and soil his servants had created earlier. When the last drop of blood had been wrung from it, he tossed it aside without a second glance.

'RISE,' Nagash said. It was not a request. The air, murky and foul, twitched like an inattentive cat. 'RISE,' he said again.

The air twitched again. Dust billowed, mixing with Sylvanian grave soil and Nehekharan sand. Something vague was beginning to take shape. Mannfred's howls of denial grew louder as the pool of his blood began to bubble and froth.

Arkhan watched, curious. The blood of all vampires was, at its base, the blood of Nagash, albeit diluted by poison and sorcery. The black brew devoured and replaced all that was human in them, making them over into something else. It made a dreadful sort of sense that Nagash would know how to manipulate it.

For as long as he could recall, the vampires had thought themselves separate and superior to beings such as himself. They had thought themselves the inheritors of Nagash's legacy, rather than merely another sort of servant.

Today, Nagash proved them wrong.

The blood began to spread, increasing in volume, and rising upwards like a geyser to encompass the dust. The vague shape became less so. To Arkhan, it was as if someone were swimming towards him across a great distance. A sound drew his attention.

Mannfred was weeping. Great red tears rolled down his cheeks, and his mouth was open in a soundless howl of fury and fear. He'd been forced to his knees by Nagash's servants, and he'd ceased his struggles. He stared at the pulsing column of blood as if it were the end of the world.

Then, maybe it was.

Arkhan turned back as Nagash stepped close to the blood and, without hesitation, plunged his arm in. There was a sound like the ocean's roar and the crash of thunder, and then Nagash jerked something out of the blood and tossed it aside. As it struck the ground, Arkhan saw that it was a human figure, flesh stained red.

The blood splashed down and lost all cohesion. The figure lay on the ground, curled into a ball. Nagash reached for it, as if to shake it to wakefulness. A bloodstained hand snapped out, seizing his wrist. Nagash paused.

A voice, hoarse with disuse, said, 'I... live.' The figure uncoiled and rose awkwardly, as Nagash jerked his wrist free and stepped back. Beneath a mask of dried blood, feral, handsome features twisted in confusion as dark eyes gazed down at clawed hands in incomprehension. 'I live? I-I... Isabella?'

The eyes flickered up as Mannfred at last tore himself free of his captors and lunged towards Arkhan. Unprepared, Arkhan could only stumble back as Mannfred tore his tomb-blade from its sheath and shoved him back.

'No,' Mannfred wailed, 'No, not again, never again!' He hurtled towards the newcomer, his stolen sword licking out to remove the latter's head.

The newcomer sprang aside, stumbled and dived for one of Nagash's warriors. He ripped the archaic blade from the wight's belt and whirled about, bringing his newly procured weapon up just in time to block Mannfred's next blow.

'You,' he said, eyes narrowing as they fixed on Mannfred's contorted features. Thin lips peeled back, revealing an impressive mouthful of fangs.

'I killed you once, old man. *I can do it again,*' Mannfred shrieked.

Arkhan moved to break up the duel, but stopped at an imperious gesture from Nagash. The Undying King wanted to see what happened next. The two vampires lunged towards each other, their blades connecting in a screech of metal. They spun in a tight circle, their swords locked together. For a moment, Arkhan thought Mannfred had the advantage. The other vampire seemed weak, uncertain... But then, slowly, steadily, he began to gain the upper hand. Arkhan realised that he'd been feigning weakness, in order to draw Mannfred in.

Mannfred was too blinded by rage to see what his opponent was up to. He lunged, and the other vampire performed a complicated manoeuvre that Arkhan had last seen on the proving grounds of Rasetra more than a thousand years before, blocking the blow and disarming Mannfred all in one smooth motion. Mannfred, unable to halt his lunge, stumbled forward. His opponent's blade was suddenly there to meet him, and it slid into his belly with a wet sound. Mannfred coughed and his eyes bulged in shock as he clawed at his opponent's blade.

He forced Mannfred down to his knees, the sword still in his gut. With his free hand, he grabbed the back of Mannfred's scalp and dragged his head up. 'Where is Isabella, boy? Where is my ring?' he hissed, glaring down at Mannfred.

'Dead, and gone,' Mannfred spat weakly. 'Just as you were.'

'You should know better than that, boy,' the other vampire growled. He kicked Mannfred off the blade, and raised it over his head, as if to split Mannfred's skull. But before the blow could fall, Nagash raised his hand.

'*HOLD, VAMPIRE. YOUR STUDENT STILL HAS HIS USES, AS DO YOU.*'

The vampire turned, his eyes widening in shock. 'Usirian's teeth,' he hissed. 'Nagash...'

'*YES. AND IT IS NAGASH TO WHOM YOU OWE YOUR FEALTY, VLAD VON CARSTEIN.*' Nagash loomed over the two vampires, his eyes burning like twin infernos, the air turning sour around him. '*KNEEL, VAMPIRE. KNEEL AND RECEIVE MY BLESSING. KNEEL, AND JOIN ME.*' Nagash raised his claws as Vlad sank slowly down to one knee, his sword planted blade-first into the ground. There was a great roar, as of a thousand-thousand voices raised in agonised protest, and the world contracted like a beast in pain. The earth trembled, and the sky wept oily rain. And Nagash found it good.

'*THE GREAT WORK CAN NOW COMMENCE.*'

ABOUT THE AUTHOR

Josh Reynolds is the author of the Warhammer 40,000 novellas *Hunter's Snare* and *Dante's Canyon*, along with the audio drama *Master of the Hunt*, all three featuring the White Scars, and the Blood Angels novel *Deathstorm*. In the Warhammer World, he has written The End Times: *The Return of Nagash*, the Gotrek & Felix tales *Charnel Congress*, *Road of Skulls* and *The Serpent Queen*, and the novels *Neferata*, *Master of Death* and *Knight of the Blazing Sun*. He lives and works in Sheffield.